Look Long

into the

Abyss

A novel of war and love

◆ ◆ ◆ ◆ ◆

A. R. Homer

Llumina
Press

This book is a work of fiction. Any resemblance to actual events, locales, or persons, living or dead, is entirely coincidental.

Cover picture of Nuremberg, 1945, courtesy of The National Archives, photo 208-AA-207L-1. Photo reproduction by Photo Response.

Requests for permission to make copies of any part of this work should be mailed to Permissions Department, Llumina Press, 7915 W. McNab Rd., Tamarac, FL 33321

ISBN: 978-1-60594-531-6 (PB)

Printed in the United States of America by Llumina Press

Library of Congress Control Number: 2010905563

To Carol

My editor, typist, critic, mentor, muse, wife, and love.

Other works in A.R. Homer's *Novels of War and Love* series:

The Mirror of Diana

The Sobs of Autumn's Violins

The Devil's Alchemists

"When you look long into an abyss,
the abyss looks back into you."

—*Friedrich Nietzsche*

PART ONE

Bavaria, Germany. Near the old border with Austria. Two a.m.

As he huddled in the shadow of a coal bunker, the man shivered and pulled his jacket tight. Through the bitter-cold darkness he saw the engine standing on the tracks beyond the station, hissing steam like the breath of a wild beast.

The train had only two cars and a caboose; what little light there was came from the coaches. He focused on the second car. Soldiers. A dozen or so. Some had stepped off for a cigarette, thumping their arms around themselves against the cold.

He withdrew into the shadows. The job was dangerous but paid well. A wooden box in the caboose. To be identified by a label stenciled on the box. Take it and hide it in the crypt of Errenbach Monastery. One hundred thousand Reichsmarks, his paymaster had said. Enough to set him up for life.

A stout middle-aged man in uniform climbed down the steps of the first carriage. From the shadows, he recognized the officer from the photographs in the *Völkischer Beobachter*, the Nazi newspaper. Hans Frank, the Hitler-appointed Governor-General of occupied Poland. On the run from the Russians. Whoever wanted his property must be important.

The Nazi shouted orders to the soldiers, who quickly crushed out their cigarettes and stood rigidly at attention before turning on their heels to follow him onto the train. A long wail from the engine split the air; the pistons heaved and the train began to move.

The man pulled down his balaclava and began to run after the train. As the engine's whistle rang in his ears, he grasped the railing on the steps of the caboose and pulled himself aboard. Another ten minutes and the hundred thousand Reichsmarks would be as good as in his pocket.

The caboose lurched as the train gathered speed. Steadying himself, he fished out a small flashlight and aimed the beam at the padlock while his free hand unclipped the jimmy attached to his belt. His plan was simple. In ten minutes the train would have to slow as it passed a village and approached a sharp curve. Nearby was his brother's farm. As the train slowed, he would jump down from the train with the box.

The flashlight beam caught the face of his watch: six minutes before the bend. He pushed the jimmy into the padlock and heaved. The lock resisted. He shoved the flashlight back into his pocket and pulled on the jimmy with both hands. The wood splintered and the door flew open.

The beam flitted around the deserted caboose. To his left was a pile of suitcases, beyond them a stack of soldiers' duffel bags. On the other side was a heap of file drawers. No box.

The train began to slow and he stumbled. He looked at his watch. Two minutes. The light ran frantically around the caboose, at last falling on a box hidden behind the file drawers. He craned his neck and saw that the box's side bore the stenciled label he had committed to memory. The box was made of rough wooden panels and was the size he had been told to expect: about two by three feet and four inches deep.

The wheels began screeching on the tracks. His hands felt clammy as he pulled the box from behind the drawers. He hurried to the rear of the caboose. Within a minute, the train would pick up speed. He tucked the box under his arm, clambered down the steps, and jumped.

Germany. A farm in Bavaria. Five p.m.

Stanislaus Konec sat in the barn milking a cow, the knees of his long legs rising high in the air above the low stool.

Soon the time would come. Outside, the afternoon was drawing to a close, leaving only the tips of the snow-covered Bavarian Alps bathed in a golden glow. Soon. Soon he would escape his slavery. The Americans were coming. The Nazi regime was collapsing.

Stanislaus had already heard of other slave laborers who had managed to escape. His long, slender fingers yanked at the teats as he tried to contain the hope that struggled to overcome five years of despair. He would escape and return to Poland, even if he had to walk the entire way.

As he bent over, he caught a reflection of his face in the bucket of warm water he used to wash the animal's teats. A clean-shaven face made more angular by a bare subsistence diet. Eyes, ringed with shadows, that had seen better days. A closely-cropped head of hair liberally flecked with gray. He wondered if his patients in Warsaw would recognize him. He wondered if any of them were still there. Hands that had once performed delicate surgery grasped the bucket and poured the milk into a churn.

He placed the stool beside another cow and washed her udder with warm water. The faces of his wife and son still haunted him. They had been killed by a German bomb while he was working at the Children's Hospital in Warsaw; a few days later, the Nazis shoved him into a railroad boxcar with hundreds of other Poles, all heading for a life of slavery, working in German factories and farms. Five long years ago.

The cow lowed and stamped her feet, sensing the anger in his hands.

"Konec!" The shout made him jump. He turned his eyes to the doorway of the barn. Herr Beck, the farmer Stanislaus worked for, stood there with another man. "Finish up with the milking, Konec, and get the horse and trap ready for my brother."

So, the other man was Beck's brother. He'd arrived soon after dawn, disheveled, clutching a wooden box under his arm while Stanislaus had been preparing to drive the cows out to pasture. He had overheard the man say to the farmer that he wanted to leave for some monastery just before nightfall. 'Errenbach Monastery' Stanislaus thought he had heard. The man had begun to say something about a crypt, but the farmer had hushed him and tilted his head toward Stanislaus; his brother seemed not to have considered that a Polish slave laborer might understand German.

The farmer snapped his fingers. "I told you to get the horse and trap ready! Now!" Beck's lips curled over his yellowed teeth.

"*Ja, mein Herr.*" Stanislaus emptied the last of the milk into the churn and rose. As he walked past the two men, he stole a glance at the words stenciled on the wooden box leaning against the wall.

He kept his face expressionless even as he realized what the box contained. He had seen it once, many years before the war. In a Krakow museum.

Errenbach Monastery, Lake Hallstatt, Bavaria. Two a.m.

B eck dragged the rowboat onto the shore. He pulled the brim of his workman's cap low over his forehead and turned up his coat collar against the drizzle filtering down from the cloud-laden night sky. He reached into the back of the boat, carefully lifted out the box, and set it on the ground.

From the boat, the church had looked like a ship moored at the far side of the lake. Now it was just an immense black shape silhouetted against the mists that rose from the foot of the mountains. He realized why his paymaster had chosen this remote spot for the hiding place. Accessible only by boat, the monastery was isolated from the world. For centuries the monks had worshipped in solitude.

Beck silently cursed the rain. Only the feeble beams of the cloud-covered moon, reflecting in the puddles between the cobbles of the church's courtyard, gave any light. He glanced at his watch. Just after two. Four hours before the brothers would file into the choir of the church for Matins.

The rain became stronger. He pulled the brim of his cap down farther, picked up the box, and strode up to the church. A final look. Nobody. He winced at the noise as he turned the latch and stepped inside, easing the door shut behind him. Pausing at the end of the aisle, he allowed his eyes to adjust to the cavernous darkness. The place smelled of dank wood and ancient stone, the only illumination coming from two huge candles on the altar.

His wet rubber-soled shoes squished on the stone floor as he made his way down the aisle toward the apse. At the bottom of a short flight of steps that descended in front of the altar an iron grille barred his entry to the crypt, but the latch quickly yielded to his touch.

His flashlight picked out a brace of tombs lining the side of the crypt. Relics locked in the sleep of death for centuries. He edged his way forward to the far wall. The beam suddenly lit up scores of skulls grinning sinisterly at him. The shaking beam cast shadows into the sightless eye sockets and on the cracked, rotten teeth in jaws locked in timeless, gruesome smiles.

The ossuary filled the eastern wall of the crypt. Skulls resting on intertwining femurs extended from the floor almost to the arched ceiling. Monks who had trodden the cloisters above centuries ago, now locked together in a final, eternal devotion.

His flashlight sought the hiding place he had been told to expect. At the left of the ossuary he found a gap between the mound of bones and the wall, a recess about ten inches wide that ran the full depth of the ossuary, about twelve feet. He pushed the wooden box into the recess as far as his arm could reach. The vacant eye sockets of a skull, inches from his head, stared at him. Quickly, he drew back and began to retrace his steps.

He tried to exercise caution but his feet, almost with a mind of their own, carried him swiftly from the fearsome place. The stolen box was now hidden from the eyes of the living world, guarded by the eternal sentinels of the dead.

Schwan Hotel overlooking Lake Hallstatt. Late morning.

"I followed your instructions. It's been hidden where you asked." Beck spoke softly as he eased himself into an armchair that faced a window in the lobby looking out on the yellow walls of the Baroque monastery across the lake. "It'll be safe there," he gave a half smile, "provided the monks don't decide to begin rearranging the bones of their dead."

His voice dropped to a whisper. "I've carried out my part of the deal." He held up his hand and ran his thumb over the tips of his middle fingers. "Now I'll just take my money and be on my way."

Gestapo Kriminal-Direktor Emil Gruber nodded. "You've done well, Herr Beck." He spoke evenly, in a matter-of-fact way. "Now, why don't we celebrate your success with a drink? It's not quite noon, but it's never too early for a glass of schnapps." Gruber caught the waiter's attention, held up two fingers, and pointed to the table between their chairs.

"Cut out the soft soap," Beck hissed. "I've done my job. Where's my money?"

"But of course, Herr Beck." Gruber's eyes darted around the lobby before he reached into his inside pocket. He leaned forward and pressed an envelope into the thief's palm.

The man looked down at the thick package, then raised his eyes to the officer, who gave him a benevolent smile. He didn't look like a Gestapo man. His figure was well-rounded, his red face plump with overindulgence, his mustache luxuriant, his bald head smooth and shiny. Still, he couldn't trust him; trusting the Gestapo was never a good policy. He thrust the envelope into his pocket and stood up. "I'll be back in a minute."

"But our drinks are arriving—"

"In a moment, I said." Beck headed for the men's room.

The Gestapo man's smile quickly vanished as he watched the retreating figure. As the waiter placed the drink on the table, Gruber's hand reached into his pocket.

Beck was relieved to find the men's room empty. Ripping open the envelope, his hands shook as he counted the notes. He counted again. One hundred thousand Reichsmarks. The agreed amount. He raised his head in surprise – Herr Direktor Gruber was a man of his word, after all. He carefully placed the envelope in the pocket of his jacket and pushed open the door. Now he could relax and enjoy his drink. And then go home, to enjoy the rewards of his work.

"Ah, there you are, Herr Beck." Gruber stood as the thief returned to his seat in the lobby. "Everything in order, I hope?" He smiled and sat back down.

"Everything's fine." Beck reached for his glass. "Sorry if I offended you, but in my line of work, you can't be too careful."

"I understand completely. Now, let's drink to your success." He raised his glass. *"Prost."*

Beck downed his schnapps in a single swallow. "And now, mein Herr, I really must go." He stood up and put on his hat. "For me, it's been a long day and I've got to get home."

"Yes, of course. Take care, and get home safely."

As the door of the hotel closed behind Beck, Kriminal-Direktor Gruber sipped his drink, his face impassive. Beck, his work done, would get home safely in his horse and trap, he was sure. But there would be little pleasure after his homecoming. At first, he would feel a chill, some influenza symptoms. A few hours would pass before the blinding headaches would begin. Then would come the searing pain as the poison worked its final deadly course. As a last outrage, his hair would fall out before his nervous system collapsed and death released him from his agony.

The Gestapo man finished his drink. Thallium sulfate was the ideal poison. Odorless, colorless, the compound did not begin its deadly work until twelve hours after ingestion. Gruber put on his hat. The fool wouldn't even have time to find out that the notes were counterfeit.

He stepped outside and gazed over the lake to the monastery. He would leave the box in the crypt for the moment. The treasure would be safer there than in the vaults of the Reichsbank. He could barely suppress a chuckle. In a crumbling Germany, anywhere was safer than the Reichsbank.

He pulled up his collar. The sun promised spring, but the cold wind reminded him that only yesterday winter had held sway. He headed back toward his office. He needed to contact the count immediately; the aristocrat would be pleased to know that everything had gone according to plan.

He pulled out his notebook to check the description of the painting that now lay in the crypt of the Errenbach Monastery. *Raphael of Urbino. Portrait of a Young Man. 1514. From the Czartoryski collection in Krakow.*

West of Stuttgart, Germany.

S ergeant Bill Terrill stopped the jeep in the middle of the road, about ten yards from a dense grove of trees. He no longer pulled over to the side. Lafferty had done just that a week before, and had been blown to hell. The Krauts put their mines along the edge of the road as they retreated.

"What the hell's going on here?" Captain Henderson jumped down from Terrill's jeep to address a group of men standing at the edge of the grove. Terrill didn't like Henderson. The captain treated him as his private chauffeur. He wasn't a bad guy, but he was a bit of a cold fish. And as company commander he always had to be driven to trouble spots. Where the Germans were. Where the lead was flying. That had been Terrill's job for the previous three months. Why couldn't he have landed an easy number, someplace well in the rear driving generals from chateau to chateau?

"We ran into some trouble, sir," a corporal spoke from the middle of the group, "with these Hitler-loving motherfuckers." He jerked his thumb over his shoulders at what Terrill thought was a dozen or so boys with their hands tied behind their backs.

"Trouble?" the captain shouted. "From that lot?"

Terrill looked at the captured enemy. At first glance, they seemed like a bunch of kids. Not one of their smooth faces could have been more than sixteen years old; most looked like high school freshmen. They were even wearing short pants. But Terrill's attention was locked on the look in their eyes. Hatred. Glowering hatred directed at their captors. Hitler was some evil genius if he could turn boys into mad, fanatical murderers.

"Don't be fooled by their baby faces, sir." The corporal waved his rifle at the sullen group. "They were waiting for us up ahead. Two of them were hidden as snipers. They got Lambert."

Terrill scanned the unshaven faces of B Platoon. There was a look in their eyes, too. They had lost Lambert. A buddy. Everyone knew

9

that death lurked around the next corner. But all held snipers in contempt. Unfair. Sneaky. Sniping was the occupation of murderous lowlife. Terrill understood the resentment on his comrades' faces. He watched them, smoking, shuffling their feet, all eyes on the German boys.

"That's bad." The captain looked uneasy. "But we gotta get this show back on the road." Terrill wondered what they taught at officer school. Henderson was a machine, not a man.

"There's more, sir." The corporal tossed his cigarette to the ground and stamped it under his boot. "After the firefight, one of the Krauts was injured – a bullet clipped his arm."

Terrill saw every man in the platoon stiffen as the corporal went on.

"They'd all surrendered. Or so we thought. Mancini, our medic, went to help the wounded Kraut. As Mancini knelt by his side, the bastard pulled out a grenade, looked Mancini in the eye, and yanked the pin. Both of them blown to pieces."

Terrill saw that even the captain was dumbstruck.

"Permission to escort the prisoners to the rear, sir?" Terrill heard Blake's voice, soft, but cold. Blake had been Mancini's close buddy. After his friend Kolevsky bought the farm, Terrill tried to avoid friendships; the war could end them in a moment.

The captain looked at Blake briefly and then averted his eyes. "Permission granted."

Terrill watched as Blake unslung his submachine gun from his shoulder and began to prod the German youths in the gut. He directed them toward the grove.

"Okay, Terrill, back to the command post." The captain jumped into the jeep. Terrill punched the stick shift into gear. As he pulled away, he saw Blake disappear into the trees with the prisoners.

"With respect, sir," Terrill looked across at the captain, "you know what's going to happen."

"Do I?" Henderson's eyes were fixed on the road ahead. The rattle of machine gun fire chattered in their ears.

"That's murder, sir."

"It's war, Terrill. I'd have thought you'd have learned by now."

Merkers, Central Germany.

Five straight hours of sorting through documents had given Lieutenant Gina Cortazzo an appetite even for C-rations. She pushed aside a pile of papers and set down her mess kit plate.

"Mmm, just like Cook used to make." Her boss, Major Alan Donovan, wriggled his nose in distaste at the mound of pork and beans on his own plate. "With the right Cabernet and some crusty French bread, the cuisine would be perfect."

Everything was chaos. They had arrived at Merkers only hours after Patton's Third Army had secured the town. A patrol had found a huge Nazi treasure trove, and Gina and Donovan had been rushed in. As part of the Monuments, Fine Arts and Archives task force, their job was to identify and classify all the plundered art that was found.

"So, Gina, did you hear who they nabbed yesterday?"

"No, who?" Gina tried to blow away a stray lock of dark hair dangling over her brown eyes as she plunged her fork with gusto into her hash.

"Frank."

"Frank who?"

"Not Frank Who. Hans Frank. Hitler's erstwhile Governor-General of Poland."

Gina's plate clanged as she dropped her fork. "Wow! That's one big fish to catch! Where'd they find him?"

"At his home in Bavaria. He'd decided to move back there last month. Apparently, his neighborhood in Poland had begun to go downhill – the Russians were moving in."

"Say, wasn't he the one," Gina drew her eyebrows together, "who stole that prize piece from the Czartoryski collection in Krakow?"

"The very same. Raphael's sublime *Portrait of a Young Man.*"

She sipped at her mug of reheated coffee, conjuring up a memory of a monochrome print she had seen of the masterpiece. "That's really big news. Have they found the painting yet?"

"Well, it's rather curious, actually. Frank insists that he left Krakow on his private train with the painting."

"And—?"

"When he got off, the Raphael was missing. And I always thought the Nazis were such efficient record keepers."

"Oh, dear." Gina sighed forlornly. "How very sad. It'll be hard enough trying to find the masterpieces the Nazis have hidden. How do we even begin to try to find the ones they've lost?"

Germany. On the road to Berlin.

T he pre-dawn sky to the south was red with the flames of buildings burning with the fires of war. The town of Gemunden was dying. Brigadeführer Reinhard Hofmann turned from the rear window of his staff car and looked at the road ahead.

As an SS leader, he had learned to stifle his emotions. Pity and compassion had long been snuffed out, but images of his men fighting and falling against the enemy in battle tumbled like macabre lifeless dolls in his mind.

"Faster! Faster!" he yelled at the driver, who peered through the windshield at the road ahead, lit only by the fiery sky. Hofmann's men had fought valiantly, but the Americans had superior forces. Endless air attacks had sprayed death from the skies. He punched the door of the car in anger. There had been no defense. Where was the Luftwaffe? Goering had promised that the air force would defend the Reich, but sat on his fat ass in Karinhall enjoying his art collection while Hofmann's men were being slaughtered.

Hofmann leaned back in his seat and closed his eyes, but the relief of sleep was denied him by the order in his pocket. He sat back up and pulled the order out; the signature was unmistakable. He had wanted to remain with his men, but he had been summoned to report to the Führer in Berlin. But why did the Führer wish to see him?

"We shall have to stop soon, mein Herr." The driver's voice interrupted his thoughts. He looked up and saw the first glimmer of dawn in the east. Hofmann understood. Driving on an open road during daylight was a clear invitation to the American fighter planes to fire down upon them and anything else that moved. And he knew the forward enemy patrols could not be far behind them.

The car drew into a small town. Hofmann looked up at the rooftops, and was stunned by what he saw.

"Mein Gott! Stop at once!" He leapt from the car, anger mounting within him. From the upper windows of the houses around the town square were draped white bed sheets. His soldiers were dying in battle and this town was showing flags of surrender!

A man scurried across the square, clutching a battered suitcase. Hofmann grabbed him by the arm and pushed him against a wall. "Where do you think you're going?"

"The Americans are coming." The man's voice was a self-pitying whine.

"And you are running away, you wretch?" Hofmann's fist hit the man in the face. "Well, let me give you something better to do." The man crumpled as another blow brought blood from his nose. "You will collect all those sheets and bring them to me!"

"But, mein Herr—" His protest died on his lips as Hofmann pulled his pistol from its holster.

"Every single rotten sheet!" He grabbed the man as he began to turn away. "Before you obey my order, you will tell me where the Bürgermeister of this cowardly town is."

A trembling finger pointed to a house at the corner of the square. Hofmann pushed the man aside. "Not one sheet is to be left!"

His hammering on the door was answered by a small, fat man with terror in his eyes.

"What is the meaning of this?" Hofmann bellowed, pointing to the sheets. "Are you, as Bürgermeister, responsible for this outrage?" The brigadeführer's tall body loomed over the cringing man.

"It's the women of the town," the Bürgermeister whimpered. "They refuse to help build the anti-tank ditches. They insist we surrender to save their homes from being destroyed by American shells."

Hofmann's face reddened with rage, the vein at his temple bulging. "So Germany has come to this!" He slapped the man across the face. "While brave soldiers are dying at the front, we have a cowardly Bürgermeister who lets old women tell him to surrender!"

He half-dragged the man to the center of the square. A few people, curious at the disturbance, had gathered at the far corner.

"But mein Herr," the Bürgermeister shrugged his shoulders, "what can I do? The war is lost."

Hofmann's eyes flashed in fury. "I'll tell you what you can do." The SS man spat out the words. "You can die like the cowardly dog you are!"

He turned the Bürgermeister around roughly, slammed him against a war memorial, and shot him in the back of the head.

"This is the fate that befalls traitors!" Hofmann shouted at the cowering bystanders as he got into his car. "Let's go!" he ordered his driver. "I would rather risk the American fighter planes than stay in this nest of treachery."

Germany. A cottage in the Bavarian Alps.

Frieda Engelsing knelt at the small flower patch in her vegetable garden, her long fingers deftly plucking a bouquet of daffodils. In days of scarcity and gnawing hunger, some had questioned the indulgence of a flower patch, but part of her hunger was for the beauty of nature in a bleak and battered world.

She lifted a bloom to her nose, savoring the gentle aroma. The war seemed so far away. The wan April sun struggled through the clouds that scudded over the mountaintops dominating the southern sky. She looked over the wall, down the hill to the tidy red rooftops and the tall church steeple. The village of Vordergern seemed unchanged, nestling among the hills as it had for centuries. As if the war that had savaged Europe had taken place on another planet. She placed the flowers in her basket, got up and sighed. She knew that the war would soon come home to her part of the world.

As she walked up the rocky path to her cottage, the breeze ruffled her gray-wisped blond hair. Stepping inside her small hallway, she brushed the lock back into place as she confronted herself in the mirror. The years were beginning to tell, she thought as her image gazed back at her. The bloom of her youth had long since passed, and now even the memory of it was beginning to fade. Shadows lay beneath the sharp, blue eyes, eyes that had seen too much, eyes that knew the deep pain she had borne.

She tried to affect a smile, but the image displeased her and she quickly turned away and walked into the kitchen. From a cupboard, she took down a chipped blue vase and filled it with water. She shook her head; she didn't know what to do. Tales she'd heard that slave workers were escaping from local farms terrified her.

Her sister had urged her to return to Sulzbach, her home town that had been spared the brunt of the bombing. But she knew the Soviet Army was approaching from the east, and she'd heard rumors of the Russian soldiers raping German women.

Perhaps she should sit tight; perhaps the war would pass by the sleepy village of Vordergern. Or maybe she should take her daughter and go to Munich. The Americans were approaching the city; surely their soldiers would not defile German women.

Munich. She sighed heavily. She had spent four years as a student in Munich. The buzzing Marienplatz, old Frauenkirche, the beer halls, the lovely Hofgarten – all came flooding back into her mind. She placed the flowers in the vase and made her way into the living room. Someone in the village had told her that Munich was already in ruins. A bombed-out shell. Munich.

Other memories came back. Had twenty-five years really passed since she had met Hans in Munich? She had been a student at Ludwig Maximilian University and he was the assistant curator of the Flemish collection at the Alte Pinakothek. She'd been peering at a picture in the art gallery, taking notes for a paper, when she had sensed a presence at her side.

"Do you like Rogier van der Weyden's portraits?" he had asked.

Startled, she turned away from the painting and looked into his brown eyes. Flustered, she mouthed words she'd been mentally preparing for her paper. "I think the artist had the ability to penetrate the sitter's very soul."

Hans had tilted his head as he considered her words. "You're right – van der Weyden was interested in more than just making literal maps of faces." When he explained how the painting's elements conveyed the artist's conception of the subject, she was transfixed. "Come," he'd said, "since you appreciate van der Weyden's work, let me show you a recent acquisition." He smiled and led her off to a gallery that was not open to the public.

Afterwards, they had met often, and there were times when Frieda wished they hadn't. She tried to force the memories from her mind as she set the vase down on the table next to Hans's photograph. His smile – that wistful smile – beamed up at her. She tried to check the sob that came to her throat, but failed.

SHAEF Headquarters, Rheims, France.

"So, I gather Churchill wasn't exactly thrilled with the communiqué you sent to Stalin." Lieutenant General Bradley looked at the figure framed in the window of his office at the *Collège Moderne et Technique* in Rheims.

"Brad, let's say he exploded like a German '88 shell." A boyish grin creased the supreme commander's face. "He wasn't at all happy that I'd decided to let the Russians capture Berlin." Eisenhower looked down from the window and scowled at the noise of the trucks on the major convoy route below.

"It was the right decision, Brad," he lit a cigarette as he walked from the window and faced the large situation map on the wall behind his oak desk, "whatever the prime minister thinks." His hands gestured in front of the map. "Right now, the Russians are about forty miles from Berlin. Soon they'll be knocking on the door."

He motioned to Bradley to take a chair as he sat at his desk. "Have you seen the G2 Intelligence report from the eastern front?" He opened the file before him.

"Yeah." Bradley leaned forward in his chair. "The Nazis are defending the approaches to Berlin like cornered rats. SS fanatics, crazed Hitler Youth, even old men – everything. The casualties on both sides are enormous."

"That's exactly what I'm trying to keep our own troops out of, Brad." Eisenhower crushed out his cigarette into an already overflowing ashtray and immediately lit another. "The war's nearly over." He drew deeply on the cigarette, leaned back in his chair and exhaled the smoke, watching it drift to the ceiling. "If Churchill and Montgomery had their way, we'd be caught up in one hell of a bloodbath." He pointed at the report from the eastern front.

"But if we advance gradually on a broad front," he got up and went to the map, "and if we meet the Russians here on the River Elbe," his finger aimed at a spot in central Germany, "then we'd cut the Nazis in two, and the war would soon be over."

"Sounds like the best strategy to me," Bradley nodded his endorsement, "and I'm sure thousands of American GIs and their wives and mothers would agree with you, Ike. No one wants to get killed when the war's about to end."

Eisenhower looked reassured as he resumed his seat, but anxiety soon returned to his face. "I've still got one big worry, Brad."

Bradley could barely suppress a sardonic smile; he couldn't recall any time when Ike wasn't worried. "You mean the possibility of the Nazis making a last stand in the Bavarian Alps?"

"Yes, it could be a huge problem." Eisenhower opened another file and put on his horn-rimmed glasses. "This intelligence report says the Nazis could set up a fortress there. Think about it, Brad," his fingers tapped on the report, "the whole mountainous terrain is a natural defensive position. If Hitler could move substantial SS forces in there, it'd be a tough nut to crack."

"Especially," Bradley grimaced, "especially if they were strengthened by divisions pulled out of Italy."

"It's an even worse nightmare than that." Eisenhower turned the papers in the file. "The report suggests that Hitler has ordered the stockpiling of his rocket weapons. Just imagine what SS troops armed with rockets could do. Jesus Christ, how many American lives would it cost?" The supreme commander's fist thumped the desk. "It would take us months to defeat them, to clear the area where they were making a last desperate stand – what do the Nazis call it?" He peered over the report. "An Alpenfestung."

"An Alpine Fortress." Bradley gave a rough translation. "A last-stand redoubt. And intelligence is also reporting that the Nazi High Command has plans to move American POW's into the area. If we hit the fortress with saturation bombing…." His voice fell away.

"Bastards!" Eisenhower spat out the oath with venom, his face suffused with rage. "Bastards!" He breathed deeply for several moments, regaining his composure a little as he picked up a sheet of paper. "I've already drafted this order, Brad." He pushed his glasses onto the bridge of his nose and began to read.

To the Combined Chiefs of Staff,

Present evidence indicates that the Germans intend with every means in their power to prolong their resistance to the bitter end in the most inaccessible areas which their troops still occupy.

To reduce the length of time for which the enemy may prolong hostilities, it is necessary to capture those areas where they might effectively form a last stand. The capability of enemy forces in the south to resist will be greatly reduced by a thrust to join the Russians. However, the Nazi fortress could even then remain in being, and it must be our aim to break into it rapidly before the enemy has an opportunity to man it and organize its defense fully.

Eisenhower placed the paper on his desk and picked up his pen. "I've tried to stress the importance of the fortress without causing too much alarm. I'll get copies off to Devers and Patton immediately." He signed the order. "We've got to strike first. There must be no Alpine Fortress, no last-stand redoubt."

Frieda's cottage. Bavaria.

Frieda picked up the photograph and softly ran her finger over the smiling lips that smiled no more. Hans had been dead for over nine months. No soldier's death, his. He had been caught up in the plot to assassinate Hitler the previous July.

Hans had been making frequent trips to Switzerland under the guise of attending international conferences with other museum directors. One day, Frieda learned that he had been serving as a courier, using the conferences to pass on messages to make the Allies aware of the intent to kill Hitler. Frieda had begged him not to have anything to do with the scheme, but he'd been resolute. If Germany was to be saved, he had said, Hitler had to be eliminated.

She remembered the day the grim-faced men had come to their Munich apartment. Hans had been resigned, accepting his fate after the plot had failed so disastrously.

She never saw him again. A week later, a man had come to the door of the apartment and handed her a small box that contained Hans's few personal possessions. He bluntly told her that her husband had committed suicide – how, she never learned. She'd heard later that Hans had been given a choice: if he didn't take his own life, then the rest of his family would be punished.

She felt intensely the pain that would not go away. She'd decided immediately to leave Munich. An old friend had let her stay at the cottage. Now she was far from Munich and the war, but she knew her safe haven could not survive. She thought the Nazis might still be watching her – they had spies everywhere – and now the war was closing in on her. The escaped slave workers roaming the countryside would soon force her to move. But where? And when?

"I have to go, mother." She turned to the voice and felt another type of pain seize her. In the doorway stood her sixteen-year-old son, Wolfgang. His brown shirt was emblazoned with insignia and merit patches, and a black neckerchief was tied beneath his collar. A bandolier crossed his chest on the diagonal, and the belt on his black corduroy shorts bore a Hitler Youth knife, its Bakelite handle decorated with a swastika. White knee-high socks and a black cap on his blond head completed the sorry picture of the indoctrinated youth who used to be her son.

"I have to report to the barracks in Munich. I may be needed at the front."

"And don't you think that I need you?" Her voice crackled with anger. She knew her words were wasted.

"Auf Wiedersehen, mother." The boy clicked his heels and rigidly extended his right arm. "Heil Hitler." His arm shot back to his side and he left, spinning around on his heel like a wind-up toy soldier.

Still clutching her husband's photograph, Frieda dropped into a chair and sobbed in futile anger and sorrow. She and Hans had tried to prevent it, but years of Nazi brainwashing had stolen her son's soul and turned him into a monster.

"Mutti, are you alright?"

Frieda looked up to see her daughter, Trudi, standing in the doorway, a frown of concern weighing down her blue eyes. Frieda brushed away the tears and forced a smile as Trudi, her blond pigtails flying, rushed into her open arms.

Berlin. The Führerbunker.

S S Brigadeführer Reinhard Hofmann sat anxiously on a bench in the small ante-chamber in the bunker complex deep beneath the Reich Chancellery. He had no idea why the Führer had demanded his presence. He tried to straighten his gray Waffen SS uniform, disheveled by the hazardous journey from the front, but there was nothing he could do about the three-day stubble that added to his haggard look. He ran a hand over his tired face, his fingers combing through his black hair. With its closely-cropped back and sides, at least his hair would not appear too unkempt.

Hofmann was disgusted by the memory of the cowardice he had encountered on his way to Berlin. His men, remnants of a once-proud division, were being cut to ribbons while German citizens waved white flags at the first sound of gunfire. He reached for his pack of cigarettes, but stayed his hand as the adjutant gave him a reproving look: the Führer did not approve of smoking.

The room was quiet, save for the whirring fans vainly trying to clear the fetid air from the bunker deep in the bowels of Berlin. To Hofmann it was almost surreal – a world strangely buried below the mayhem of war. An orderly walked by, a piece of paper in his hand, as if part of some peacetime exercise. Everywhere was stifling silence. Weren't they aware that the Russians were swarming like a plague of locusts towards Berlin?

Almost without moving, his fingers began to trace the opening bars of a Beethoven sonata on his pant legs. Besides the Führer and Germany, only two things mattered to Hofmann. Music was one, and the other was dead. His son, his beautiful boy, Kurt, dead now for almost a year, his plane shot down while he was defending his homeland from the sadistic attacks on civilians by the Americans and the British. His fingers dug deeply into his thighs as he played a chord progression. He saw Kurt's face the last time they were together; Kurt was returning to his base after his final leave, waving goodbye to him, his hair catching the glint of the sun. He saw Kurt's smile...

Hofmann forced his mind back to the matter at hand. Why would Hitler send for him? Wasn't he, too, aware that the war was lost? There were rumors that the Führer had become unbalanced. Perhaps he ought not to speak of the realities of the war; he'd heard tales of officers being executed for 'defeatism.' But then surely that couldn't apply to him – he himself had shot cowards. Exactly what did Hitler want of him?

The telephone on the adjutant's desk rang shrilly. The officer spoke quietly, then replaced the receiver. "The Führer will see you now."

Hofmann ran his fingers through the top of his hair one last time, then tucked his cap under his arm and made for the door to Hitler's sanctum.

Merkers.

Lieutenant Gina Cortazzo searched frantically through the pile of papers on the desk. "Alan, have you seen that card file I was working on?"

"I'd like to help, Gina," Donovan's voice was hurried, "but we have the biggest big shots of all time arriving in half an hour and you and I have landed the job of showing them around the site."

He tugged on his uniform and squinted at his image in the reflection in the window. "I rather imagine that their interest in art is in inverse proportion to their aptitude for the military." He sighed. "Sometimes I wish I were back teaching the Quattrocento masters at Harvard."

"Damn! I need the file to start cataloging all the stuff we've found here." They had only begun to scratch the surface of the huge site and were amazed at the treasures they had already uncovered. Dürer drawings, Holbein paintings, and priceless books lay haphazardly with the thirty-five-hundred-year-old bust of Queen Nefertiti.

"Got it!" Gina exhaled audibly as she unearthed the file.

Everywhere Nazi treasure was found, a team of art historians, each a respected expert in his field, was rushed in to make an inventory of the booty. Once the works were catalogued, they were carefully packed and sent to collecting points for photographing and, if needed, restoration. If possible, they would then be returned to their rightful owners.

Had it been only three months – it seemed to Gina like years – since she had been recruited as one of the 'Monuments Men,' as the art experts who were selected to be Monuments, Fine Arts and Archives officers were called? As a woman and as a graduate of a mere state university in an organization dominated by men holding sway at national museums and Ivy League schools, she sometimes felt out of her depth. But she, too, was well-respected; a paper she had published on her post-graduate research had caught the attention of art restoration experts, and here she was.

The work was exciting. Only a month before, at Siegen, they'd found hundreds of paintings and sculptures as well as the original manuscript of Beethoven's Sixth Symphony. But that find was dwarfed by what had been unearthed at Merkers. The vast salt mine had already yielded not only art, but rooms full of gold bullion.

Gina returned to her work of compiling the catalogue. As ever, they were under pressure. Barely had the dust of war settled on the town than they were rushed in to begin work. She paused to look out at the shattered town. Nearly every building was a battered, burnt-out shell. Already US Army bulldozers were clearing mountains of debris and fallen masonry from barely-identifiable streets, along which wandered broken people, unable to comprehend what had befallen them. She wondered what would happen to the people in her home town of Wilkes-Barre, Pennsylvania, if it were reduced to such a ruin; and what if the Wadsworth Athenaeum, the museum in Hartford where she once worked, had been smashed to debris?

"My tailor in Cambridge would have been able to do something around the shoulders to make this jacket fit better." Donovan's voice cut across her thoughts, bringing her back to the present.

Gina giggled as she watched Donovan turn one side, then the other toward the window, still trying to evaluate the appearance of his uniform in the reflection. With his slight frame and wire-rimmed glasses, he hardly seemed ready to charge the enemy.

"Alan, we're about to catalogue one of the most valuable art collections in history and you're worrying about your uniform?"

"Do you know who's about to arrive, Gina?" Donovan took off his cap, breathed on the badge and polished it with his sleeve. "Eisenhower, Bradley and Patton!" He placed his cap on his head. "And maybe a few colonels and other mortals. And we're to be their ciceroni – we've got to give them a conducted tour of the site." He lifted each foot and rubbed it against the back of his pants' legs. "Why they don't just stick to waging war and leave the art to us, I know not."

"Perhaps the war has turned them into art-loving highbrows." Gina gave a half-smile.

"Art-loving highbrows? Those latter-day versions of Genghis Khan?" Donovan laughed scornfully. "There's more chance of our finding the Raphael that Hans Frank seems to have misplaced. More likely, they can't resist taking a peek at that mountain of gold."

Gina looked through the window and saw the convoy of cars flying high-ranking pennants. "Well, Alan, our moment has arrived. The warlords are here."

The Führerbunker.

"Mein Führer!" Hofmann snapped to attention, his arm rigidly outstretched.

Hitler limply waved the salute away. Hofmann was forced to suppress his alarm at his leader's appearance. The last time he had seen the Führer was in his vast Chancellery Office in the happy days, when almost the whole of Europe had been within his grasp. Then he had seemed like a colossus astride the globe. Now, in this small, spartan office, deep in the bunker, he appeared a broken man. He sat hunched over his desk, his shoulders stooped. Hofmann thought he saw a tremor in the left hand, but Hitler quickly placed it in his lap.

"Hofmann! How good to see you!" He fixed the SS officer with a mesmeric stare. There was still fire in the eyes; Hofmann felt relief. The Führer he remembered had returned, still in control.

"It is always a pleasure to see a loyal soldier." As Hitler rose and walked around his desk he seemed to drag his left foot; his right hand reached out and lightly clutched Hofmann's shoulder. "Loyalty has become a rare commodity these days."

Hitler looked away, his thoughts elsewhere as he pondered his words, before turning sharply back to the SS officer.

"Hofmann, I have a task for you." His eyes burned fiercely. "A task that can yet win the war!" He punched his fist into an open palm. "Come, look at the map."

As he followed Hitler to the map table, Hofmann wondered if the rumors about the Führer's mental imbalance were true. From his own experience on the western front, a final victory would need a miracle.

"As you can see, Hofmann," Hitler's fingers ran over the map, "while the Jewish-Bolsheviks are here in the east," he then pointed to the other edge of the map, "the Americans and British have crossed the Rhine." He raised his head from the map and looked directly at Hofmann, "where you have recently been fighting so valiantly. Never say die – that's your motto, isn't it?"

"Mein Führer, it is my duty to serve you!" Hofmann pulled himself to attention. "To the end, if necessary."

"Spoken like a true National Socialist." He gazed into Hofmann's eyes for a few moments before returning his attention to the map. "Of course, there are some who say that the war is lost." There was growing anger in his voice. "Some are already trimming their sails."

Hofmann understood what he meant. The Führer was saying there was treachery at the heart of the Third Reich.

"Which is why I have need of men such as you, Hofmann, for a vital mission."

"Mission, mein Führer?"

"All that Germany needs now is time. You know, of course, about our Wunderwaffen?"

"The wonder weapons – yes, I've heard of our rockets that have bombed London, mein Führer."

"Pah!" Hitler gave a brash laugh. "They are merely fireworks compared to what is to come!" His eyes bulged in their sockets and his face lit up at the prospects running through his mind. "Think, Hofmann – a huge cannon capable of hurling thirty-kilogram shells up to a hundred miles at the rate of six hundred shells an hour. A jet-powered fighter plane flying at almost the speed of sound." The Führer punched the air as excitement seized him. "And a new rocket with ten times the power of the V2. London will be destroyed!" His fist smashed down on the table.

Hofmann was agog with the prospects Hitler had outlined. "It is truly amazing, mein Führer." He could not avoid the question. "But may I ask when—"

"That is the critical question!" Hitler cut him short. "If I leave matters as they are, it will never happen. But if my plan succeeds, the weapons will be ready in a month, two at most."

"But what is my role, mein Führer?" Hofmann was anxious. "I have no specific scientific knowledge."

"None is needed. Here's my plan." He turned his attention back to the map. "I have already ordered the production of the wonder weapons to be moved to this area." His right hand swept over a large part of Bavaria. "Here, in caves and tunnels in the Bavarian Alps, the manufacture of rockets can proceed, free from the enemy's bombing raids."

Hofmann leaned forward, his hands resting on the map, his eyes following the Führer's fingers. "But what of the invading armies, sir? Patton and his American Third Army are already pressing into south Germany."

"Yes, but if this area," Hitler picked up a crayon and circled the position, "if this area is defended properly, it will be practically impregnable. Bordered by the Italian Alps in the south and the Bavarian mountains to the north, it will be an unassailable fortress, a Festung – my Alpenfestung."

Hitler's face flushed as he warmed to his plan. "Orders to commence works in this area were given last winter. In the heights around Koenigsee, in the old salt mines in the area, massive depots of munitions, repair and maintenance shops are being built, industrial facilities to produce the Vengeance weapons are under way."

He paused for breath. "Just think, Hofmann. Impregnable fortifications, vast underground storehouses loaded with supplies, subterranean factories, and – this is where your expertise is needed – all defended by elite troops willing to fight faithfully to the last man." He tossed the crayon down onto the map in a gesture of finality. "What's more, I have ordered that thirty-five thousand American and British prisoners of war be moved into the area as hostages." He smiled smugly. "The enemy could not – dare not – bomb or attack. Their casualties would be politically unacceptable."

Hofmann was overwhelmed by the audacity of the plan. "It's wonderful, mein Führer – a stroke of genius. Are you giving me the honor of defending the Alpenfestung?"

"With complete command." Hitler moved away to his desk. "You are to take the 29th Waffen SS Division immediately. More troops will be made available later. Kesselring, as southern commander, will provide you with troops from Italy." He reached for an official paper from his desk. "Wherever you go, whatever you want, just show them this Führer Order." He signed his name with a flourish. "And you must brook no opposition, Hofmann." Hitler fixed him with a cruel stare. "You must be brutal, if necessary – even with your own people. On you depends the success of the mission and the survival of the Third Reich!"

Hofmann clicked his heels and began to raise his arm in salute, but the Führer stayed his hand.

"There's one thing more, Hofmann," Hitler added in a soft voice as he sat at his desk, his gaze never leaving the SS man's eyes. "Something very close to my heart."

Merkers.

"It's amazing what the Germans have hidden in this salt mine, General." Donovan was nervous; it wasn't every day that a major got to speak with the Supreme Commander of the Allied Armies. He glanced at Gina and wondered how she could be so calm, as if she were entertaining members of a Rotary Club.

"I can't wait to see it." Eisenhower held tightly to the rail of the small elevator cage as it rattled during its rapid descent into the pit.

"You realize, Ike," Patton's voice was high-pitched, nervous as the cage lurched against the shaft, "that there's only a single clothesline separating us from the Great Hereafter?"

"Yeah, perhaps we should have come down separately." General Bradley looked uneasy, his four-star helmet bobbing on his head as the cage continued its plunge.

"If that cable snaps," Patton clutched the support rail, "promotions in the United States Army will be considerably stimulated."

"That's enough, George," Eisenhower snapped nervously.

"It won't be long now, gentleman." Gina found it difficult to reconcile the cowering trio in the elevator cage with the fearless leaders of invading armies.

A thud and a bounce announced their arrival at the bottom of the shaft, twenty-one hundred feet below the surface. "Amen to that!" Patton heaved a sigh of relief and looked around at what had formerly been the Kaiserode Salt Works.

"As I was saying, General," Donovan addressed Eisenhower as they stepped from the cage, "we have found treasures beyond compare – things that even as a professor at Harvard I little dreamed of ever seeing." He sensed the officers bridle, realized they had little liking for academia, but persisted. "There are works of art that are priceless – such as *The Greenhouse* by Manet, and the centuries-old head of Nefertiti."

Bradley snorted, and Donovan detected a marked lack of enthusiasm for fine art as they walked down a long tunnel.

"What's in here?" Eisenhower stopped in front of an alley leading off to the right.

"Works by the French masters." Gina stepped into the small dimly-lit chamber. The three men followed and watched as she pulled paintings one-by-one from a stack leaning against the wall. "This is Daumier's *Don Quixote.*"

"Very interesting." Eisenhower looked up. "What do you think, Brad?"

The general gave a brief glance. "Very interesting."

Gina replaced the painting; the generals' scant interest in art had been easily sated.

"What do you plan to do with all this stuff?" Eisenhower asked.

"After we catalogue it, we'll send it to a collecting point in Munich," the major answered. "After that, it's up to the powers-that-be to decide." His face flushed as he realized he was in the presence of the powers-that-be.

"What about the gold?" Patton asked the question Donovan had long been expecting.

"Yes, can we see the gold?" Eisenhower echoed as they resumed walking along the tunnel.

Gina sensed that their interest had been renewed. "It's another fifty yards along here." She chuckled inwardly as the generals' footsteps quickened.

The Führerbunker.

"For many years, Hofmann, I have labored to build the world's finest art collection." Hitler spoke softly, but could not disguise the passion in his voice. "Some of my treasures, like the Ghent Altarpiece, were already Germany's property, so I repatriated them. Other works I purchased. Some of the owners were not eager to sell, it's true, but I gave them a fair price. A marble sculpture by Michelangelo I took out of Belgium to save it from American bombs."

The Führer rose and walked around his desk to face Hofmann. "But most of my artworks had no real owners – I rescued them from the hands of Jews. My favorite painting, *The Astronomer,* by Vermeer, was one of those." He lifted his chin and studied an invisible point in the distance as he thought about his treasures. "One day, I intend to bequeath my collection to the German people."

"But mein Führer—"

Hilter waved away Hofmann's protestation. "The collection will be housed in a Führermuseum specially designed for the purpose. Come, see." He led Hofmann into a side room.

Hofmann's eyes widened as he looked over the model of a huge, open complex of buildings nestled between wide tree-lined avenues and vast squares. He couldn't suppress a low whistle of appreciation.

"Impressive, isn't it, Hofmann?" Hitler braced himself by his palms on the edge of the model, barely able to conceal his pride. "You've been to Linz?"

"Yes, mein Führer."

"You won't recognize the city once my work is complete." He beamed down at the model with the affection of a father admiring a new-born son in a crib. "Here will be the Adolf Hitler Hotel, over there a conference hall," his fingers danced over the model, "and here, next to the opera house, will be the largest library in Europe." Hitler breathed deeply, carried away by his vision. "And here," he pointed to the center of the model, "will be the glory of the entire art world. The Führermuseum." He turned to Hofmann. "What do you think?"

"A fitting cultural center for the Reich, mein Führer." Hofmann felt uncomfortable, out of his depth in rendering an appraisal. "Indeed, for the world."

"Hofmann, you have an important role to play in the achievement of my dream."

"How so, mein Führer?"

Hitler moved to a map pinned to the wall. "Most of my collection, destined for the Führermuseum, is stored in a mine – here." His finger stabbed at a location in the Bavarian Alps. "At Alt Aussee. In the heart of the Alpenfestung you will command." He beckoned Hofmann, who followed him back into his office.

For a few moments the dreamy look remained in Hitler's eyes as he envisioned his future museum. In an instant, his eyes hardened as he turned to Hofmann. "So, Brigadeführer, I'm entrusting my life's work – and a great deal of priceless art – to your care. As commander of the Alpenfestung, one of your most important duties will be to protect my collection."

"Mein Führer, I shall defend it while there is breath in my body."

Hitler's chair scraped on the floor as he drew it to his desk and sat down. "I don't doubt your allegiance, Hofmann." Hitler forced a brief smile. "You've proved yourself many times."

Hofmann came to attention, preparing to salute.

"There's one final part to my orders, Brigadeführer." Hitler's chest began to heave and the tremor in his hand became more pronounced. "I have not striven all my life to build my art collection to have it fall into the hands of philistines." Hitler's body stiffened and his eyes flashed as anger seized him. "Did you know that the American swine are already at Merkers, Hofmann?"

"Merkers, mein Führer?" Hofmann furrowed his brow.

"Yes, Merkers, the mine to which we have entrusted the Reichsbank's gold reserves along with art treasures from German museums. *From German Museums, Hofmann!*" His hand cut the air with jagged blows as he spoke.

He seethed silently, contemplating this abomination. "The thought of my personal art collection being pillaged by the Jewish-Bolsheviks or the American mongrels cannot be contemplated!" His fist pounded the desk with each of the last three words. "Should that possibility ever arise, Hofmann, you are to destroy the entire collection!"

Hofmann struggled to suppress his shock.

"Yes, every last painting, sculpture, altarpiece!" Hitler shouted. "Dynamite them all! Blow them all to smithereens! Reduce them to rubble! The enemy must not be allowed to steal them from the German nation!"

Hofmann stood uncomfortably before Hitler's desk and heard a clock tick as he waited for the Führer's rage to subside.

After a long moment, Hitler regained his composure and rose from his desk. "My orders are clear, Brigadeführer?"

"Perfectly clear, mein Führer."

Hitler came from behind the desk and grasped Hofmann's hand in both of his. "There will be happier times, I assure you, Hofmann."

For a moment, the Brigadeführer saw again the glint of zeal in his Führer's eyes, the zeal that had propelled Germany to be the greatest power in Europe.

"Now you must go. You have no time to lose. Act swiftly and, if you must, ruthlessly." His eyes fixed Hofmann. "The fate of Germany is in your hands."

Hofmann took a pace backward, raised his arm in salute, and turned on his heel, his anxieties about the task ahead overcome by a newfound enthusiasm.

Merkers.

The tunnel led into an immense cavern two hundred yards square. From the twenty-foot high ceiling hung bare light bulbs that bathed the white walls of the cave in a fiercely bright light; the air was heavy, musty and stale. Tram railway tracks ran down the center of the cave. On both sides of the tracks were piled thousands of sacks filled with gold bullion.

Patton's eyes widened. "Well, look at what we got here! The Führer's Fort Knox!"

"Exactly what have we got here?" Bradley's pointed question was directed to Donovan.

"We're not sure." Donovan averted his eyes. "We've been concentrating on the art."

Patton threw his head back and laughed. "Didn't they teach you the value of money at college, son?"

31

Patton's laughter died away as the supreme commander fixed him with a stare.

"I've had our G-5 guys do a preliminary evaluation." Eisenhower fished a piece of paper from his pocket. "Gold bullion, German gold reichmarks, British gold sovereigns, everything," he looked up from the paper, "even twenty-dollar gold pieces from the United States."

"Jesus Christ!" Patton spat out the profanity. "How in hell did Hitler get his hands on Uncle Sam's money?"

"Who knows?" Eisenhower shrugged his shoulders. "It says here," he tapped the inventory, "that there's more than a hundred tons of gold bullion in this cave. Millions of dollars worth. My people estimate it's most of the total gold reserve of the German Reichsbank."

Patton's eyes glazed over. "Makes me kind of wish we were waging war in ancient times. Like Scipio at Carthage. All the spoils of war to the conquering generals."

"I'd have thought you'd be more interested in taking the art, George," Bradley chuckled, "what with all that classical education you had." He playfully nudged Patton's ribs with his elbow. "Ike and I don't have your lofty pedigree. We'd be too dumb to grab the art – we'd settle for the gold instead."

Eisenhower threw back his head and guffawed, a rare occurrence; the supreme commander found little occasion to laugh.

"There may be some treasure you would not want, General." Gina saw Donovan's sharp look and wished she could call back the words; perhaps she had overstepped the mark.

"What's that?" Patton growled.

Donovan led the generals into an adjoining chamber. From floor to ceiling against the walls were piled hundreds of sacks. The major pulled out a sack, opened it and tipped the contents onto the floor. Silver and gold jewelry, cigarette cases, diamond-encrusted timepieces fell to the earthen floor with a dull clatter.

"These were once the cherished possessions of people," Gina spoke softly, "perhaps people like those you saw at the concentration camp a few days ago."

"Goddamn those Nazi—"

"Enough, George." Eisenhower turned to Donovan and Gina. "Major, Lieutenant, thank you for the tour. I wish you every success with your catalogue of the art." He pulled out a cigarette and accepted the light offered by Bradley. "But the gold will be removed tomorrow." He turned to the general. "See to it, Brad. Don't skimp on the escort. The whole lot back to Frankfurt. Before we have to hand over this town to the Russians."

"Yeah, you're right – we're now on Russkie real estate." The concept of handing over the zone to the Russians stuck in Patton's craw. "Good thing the Yalta agreement didn't say anything about doing a little house-cleaning before the Commies move in."

The Führerbunker.

Brigadeführer Reinhard Hofmann was excited, his mouth dry. He was overwhelmed with emotion as he emerged from the Führer's office into the pallid electric light of the bunker. He had entered to tell Hitler that the war was lost, yet he had come out charged with saving the Reich by forming a National Socialist fortress, an Alpenfestung, in Bavaria. Could the wonder weapons save them all?

"You look bemused, Hofmann." The voice cut across his thoughts. Framed in the doorway was the short, solid uniformed figure of General Krebs.

"General!" Hofmann recognized the Führer's Chief of Staff and sprang to attention, his heels clicking in salute.

"There's no need for such formality, Reinhard," Krebs came forward and grasped his upper arm, "in these troubled times."

"Sir, I have urgent orders from the Führer—" Hofmann realized he was speaking loudly; the adjutant had raised his head from his paperwork and had turned his eyes to him.

"Come with me." Krebs grasped the situation, his squat figure turning to the door, beckoning Hofmann to follow. "Let us discuss your orders in my office."

Hofmann had expected a larger office for the Army Chief of Staff. The room was small, almost claustrophobic. Taking up much of the space was a large oak desk, incongruous, like a relic of a bygone age. The air was stale, laden with tobacco smoke that the whirring fans struggled to expel. On the wall behind the desk was a map of

Germany. The pins showing the enemy armies' positions were not encouraging.

"Now, what is this order given to you by the Führer?" Krebs planted himself in the chair behind the desk. Hofmann pulled the paper from his pocket and handed it to the general.

"I am to form an Alpenfestung, a National Socialist fortress in Bavaria." He accepted Krebs's waved invitation to sit on the opposite side of the desk. "And I am given command of the 29th Waffen SS Army to achieve this task."

Hofmann felt awkward at Krebs's prolonged hesitation following his announcement. Only the insistent hum of the air-conditioning plant cut through the silence. Eventually, Krebs placed the paper on the desk and looked up at the SS officer.

"Did you think the Führer looked well?" Krebs's question caught Hofmann off guard. Was the general setting a trap?

"Yes." Hofmann could see that Krebs knew he was lying. "Of course," he added quickly, "he looked tired and care-worn." He stiffened. "But his eyes were ablaze when he explained how we could still win the war."

"It never ceases to amaze me," Krebs leant back in his chair, lit a cigarette and blew a stream of smoke up toward the overburdened fan, "the effect the Führer has on visitors." A long pause followed as Krebs considered his next words. "Reinhard, you are a man of the world." Krebs barely suppressed a sigh. "You have just come from the western front – your own eyes have seen the position there." He got up and stood before the situation map. "Let me tell you that the eastern front is worse, much worse." He ran his hand over the map, then returned to his chair, his thin lips pressed into a laconic smile. "And yet the Führer has convinced you that the war can still be won. Remarkable!" He stubbed out his cigarette. "A truly remarkable man."

"But, Herr General," Hofmann was flustered, confused, "the Wunderwaffen—"

"Ah, yes, the wonder weapons." Krebs's voice was not encouraging. "They could win the war. Fearsome armaments." The light from the bare bulb reflected on his glasses as he fixed Hofmann with a stare. "But I fear it's too late."

Merkers.

"Let's get this over with." Patton followed Ike and Bradley into the cage to take them back above ground. Major Donovan checked that everything was ready and Gina gave the signal to the operator to start the ascent.

The initial jolt caught Patton unawares and he swore as he struggled to maintain his balance. "Hell, I'll be glad to get back to the war – it's safer."

Eisenhower allowed himself a smile. As his eyes caught those of Gina, his smile broadened; in the last few weeks he had witnessed sights more hideous than any he had seen before in war. He found her pretty face refreshing.

Gina returned his smile. "There's still a lot of art missing, General. We've heard reports—" She hesitated, anxious not to appear insubordinate, but Eisenhower gave her his attention. "The German art curators we captured when we found this hoard told us there are several other caches," the cage slowed as it reached the end of its long climb, "probably, they say, in Bavaria and the Austrian Alps."

Eisenhower's eyes flashed. "The Bavarian Alps?" His lips tightened as he looked across at Bradley, who answered the unasked question. "The Alpine Fortress!"

The cage ground to a halt, the gates clattered open and the party stepped out into the cool morning air.

"All this talk of a damned last-ditch fortress," Patton's tone was dismissive, "I tell you our intelligence guys have gone mad. The Nazis have lost the game – they've got no more dice to roll."

"That's what everyone said last December, George," Eisenhower raised a reproving finger, "and then the Krauts hit us hard in the Ardennes."

"But we dealt with that situation." Patton waved away the argument as they made their way to the mine office.

"At a cost of too many American lives." There was anger in Eisenhower's voice as he stopped and turned to confront Patton. "I can't afford to take any chances, George." His index finger stabbed into Patton's chest. "If the Germans get a chance to form that fortress, who knows what they can do?" His face reddened with rage. "Then, as you put it, George, how are we going to deal with that situation?" He didn't wait for an answer. "And if they've got the rocket weapons in that fortress, it'll cost us a river of blood to flush them out."

Eisenhower's voice fell away. Donovan saw that he was breathing deeply, trying to regain his composure. Somehow, the art historian had naively believed that the leader of the Allied armies didn't have emotions.

"George, you are to push your Third Army hard." His voice was more controlled. "I want Munich in two weeks and then occupy Lower Bavaria. No messing. No delays. And make sure there's no damned fortress. Do you understand?"

Patton, chastened, nodded in assent.

"Here comes your car, sir." Donovan came to attention.

Eisenhower turned to him sharply. "What's your name, Major?"

"Donovan, sir." There was trepidation in his voice. He had just heard a three-star general bawled out.

"Major Donovan," the blue eyes were piercing, "you and your lieutenant's outfit – what's it called?"

"Monuments, Fine Arts and Archives, sir."

"Whatever – you and your outfit are to follow on General Patton's heels. Follow up on all those German contacts – find out where in the Alps the bastards have their hidey-holes. And when you find out," he climbed into the staff car, "let General Patton know." The other generals joined him in the car. "Now, let's go."

Donovan belatedly saluted as the car departed.

Gina turned to go. Recovery of stolen art had suddenly acquired a new meaning.

The Führerbunker.

"Too late? Is it your opinion the war is lost?" Hofmann felt his body go rigid. "But the Führer said—"

"Unfortunately, the Führer is sometimes given to exaggeration nowadays." Krebs opened a file on his desk. "Speer, as Minister for Armaments," he quickly scanned the contents of the file, "did move some facilities to caves in Bavaria – some workshops and production lines, together with a number of foreign slave laborers, but—"

"Then perhaps the Alpine Fortress can preserve the Reich," Hofmann was surprised at his own enthusiasm, "by buying time."

"Perhaps." Krebs became pensive, like a poker player pondering a major play.

"Herr General," Hofmann pressed his case, "if I can fulfill the Führer's order, if I can establish the Alpenfestung, it could provide a haven for the Führer – and the army leadership – until the wonder weapons—"

"Ah, the Führer's order." Krebs picked up the paper from his desk and read it again. After a few moments, he let the order fall from his fingers. "I see he allocated you the 29th Waffen SS Division." He shrugged his shoulders. "I'm afraid the Führer has failed to grasp the reality of the military situation."

Hofmann started; he had never heard Hitler's judgment questioned before. "But the 29th Division—"

"It no longer exists." Krebs's voice was cold. "Perhaps a battered regiment somewhere, trying to stem the Russian tide."

Hofmann could not hide his dismay. "But the mission the Führer just gave me—"

"That mission is still of paramount importance." Krebs lit another cigarette. "To establish an Alpenfestung – a place where National Socialism can regain its strength, even if the rest of Germany falls."

Krebs sat quietly, looking at his cigarette as he pondered his next statement.

"However, I must be honest with you. All I can offer you are two battalions of Waffen-SS troops." He spoke quickly to prevent the astonished Hofmann from responding. "With these troops, you will take a convoy of trucks containing a portion of the Führer's art collection to the place he told you about." His pencil circled a dot on the map. "The salt mine at Alt Aussee. Just over the old border, in Austria. The rest of the Führer's collection is already there. The mine will ensure the collection survives any aerial bombardment, and I'm told conditions are—"

"Two battalions? Two thousand men?" Hofmann exploded. "You expect me to form an Alpenfestung with just two battalions and a convoy of trucks full of art?"

Krebs leaned back in his chair and looked at the brigadeführer. "Hofmann, it is not for us to question the will of the Führer. When you spoke with him just now, did he fail to impress upon you the importance

37

of his art collection?" Krebs's words, spoken softly, carried a force that made Hofmann sit up stiffly in his chair. "As for the SS troops, I assure you they are the finest in the Reich."

Krebs softened his tone and gave Hofmann a mollifying smile. "You must try to buy us time, Hofmann." He returned his attention to the map. "I shall detach two divisions from Kesselring's command in Italy to you. As soon as the situation there allows."

"But how long before these divisions—"

Krebs waved aside Hofmann's question. "As soon as is humanly possible. Also, there's an addendum to your orders." He cleared his throat. "You are to collect additional artworks from Count von Schellendorf's castle at Lumberg in Bavaria. These, too, are to be taken and stored in the mine at Alt Aussee."

"Hauling art across Germany would hardly seem to be an effective way to save the Reich." Hofmann could not disguise his sarcasm. "Wouldn't it be better if I were to take the men to fight at the front?"

"I know it seems unorthodox, Hofmann, but it's an important part of your mission." Krebs picked up his cap. "Let me repeat what I'm sure the Führer has already told you. None of the art treasures – both the ones you will be transporting as well as the immense collection already stored in the salt mine – must fall into enemy hands." He thrust his cap onto his head. "In the unlikely event that you can no longer protect the works of art, you are to ensure that all are destroyed. Do you understand the orders?"

"Jawohl, mein Herr!" Hofmann sprang to attention and saluted.

"Hofmann, despite the difficulties I've outlined, the future of the Führer and National Socialism depends upon you. Prepare to leave after nightfall." He turned as he reached for the door handle, his eyes fixing the SS officer. "The Alpenfestung, Hofmann. A place where National Socialism will be able to regroup and revitalize. Should it become necessary in the difficult days ahead."

Army camp north of Erfurt.

B ill Terrill jumped down from his jeep and tried to work out why Captain Henderson had called them together. Most of Fox Company had been pulled out of the line after forty days of point duty. Point duty. The head of the line, marching first towards the Krauts' welcoming committee and every instrument of death they had available.

"At ease, men." Bill shifted his feet. He hoped to Christ this wasn't going to be some morale-boosting talk. His morale was low, and it would stay low until he was out of the godforsaken hole that was Germany, away from the daily threat of death. He was twenty-seven, and his ambition was to be twenty-eight and back in Mulligan's Bar, a frosty mug of beer in his hand.

The captain clambered up onto a trestle table. Bill was tired of driving the captain to forward positions to assess the battle, putting his life on the line. But the man was cold. He treated his men like pawns on his personal chessboard. He had become accustomed to ordering men to their deaths, then shrugging his shoulders, sweeping the chessboard clean and setting up new pieces again.

"Men!" The captain held up his hand to command silence. Terrill suppressed a smile. Why didn't he say 'Pawns!'?

"I'm afraid I have some bad news for you."

Terrill felt panic seize him. They were going back into the line. He scratched his crotch, pulling at the underwear he'd worn for over a week. The company was entitled to a shower, clean underwear when on relief. His hatred for Henderson grew. No shower. No clean underpants. Back into the valley of the shadow of death.

"Yesterday," the captain's voice rang out, "our President, Franklin Roosevelt, passed away."

Terrill heard the gasps from the men around him but did not share their shock. So the president was dead. So was his good buddy, Joe

Kolevsky. Joe had been with them, probing the approach to Munich, when the German Artillery 88's had opened fire. You always knew when an 88 was coming in. The shell screamed, louder and louder, announcing someone's imminent death.

The platoon had been advancing down the road. Kolevsky had been at the head of the troop. One moment he had been there, the next he was gone, his guts splattered, hanging on the trees at the side of the road.

"I'm sure you all share our sorrow." The captain's voice interrupted his thoughts for a moment.

No, I don't, Terrill thought. President Roosevelt died in his bed at the age of sixty-three. Kolevsky was sprayed all over the German countryside. He was twenty-two. Nobody called a special meeting for him. Nobody would write history books about him.

Frieda's cottage.

F rieda turned the sock inside out and slid in the wooden darning egg. The socks were Wolfgang's, but he had outgrown them and she was mending them for Trudi. They would not look pretty on her daughter, who, even at seven, was conscious of her appearance, but they would keep her warm.

Had she been able to give her children more, perhaps Wolfgang would have turned out differently. After Hans's death, the Gestapo had seized the money in his bank account, so Frieda had little in the way of resources; she managed to feed and clothe her children by bartering with the town's merchants. Last week, she made baby clothes for the grand-children of the butcher in the village at the bottom of the valley, who gave her blood sausages and a bit of ham in exchange. A week before, she had altered a dress for the wife of the owner of the dry goods store, who gave her two yards of cotton printed with violets and daisies; from the cloth, she had made Trudi a new dress.

Things were better in this part of Germany; the war had not yet reached them, and the shortages were less severe. But she knew that was soon about to change. She finished her darning and went to check on Trudi, who had felt unwell.

She smiled with joy as she opened the bedroom door and saw her little girl, one hand propping up a book she was reading with wide eyes, the other arm around the little rag doll she had loved since she was five. Clothilde had blue sewn-on button eyes; her ochre-colored yarn hair was done up in braids, and she wore a tiny red-checked pinafore. The doll was Trudi's special friend and confidante, and she wouldn't go to sleep at night unless Clothilde was at her side.

"Are you feeling better, Liebchen?"

Trudi nodded. Frieda sat down on the edge of the bed and felt Trudi's forehead.

"Mutti, what does 'rape' mean?"

41

Frieda struggled to suppress a gasp. "Trudi, that's a bad word, and I don't want you to use it ever again. Where did you hear that nasty word?"

"Marta overheard her mother tell Frau Winkler that some of the Polish workers raped a farmer's wife—"

"That's enough, Trudi!" Frieda's tone was sharp because she knew there was more truth in Trudi's gossip than her daughter knew. "You mustn't believe everything you hear." She moved the book to Trudi's bed table and pulled the blanket up, gently folding it over at the top and tucking in the sides. "Get some rest, Liebchen. You'll always be safe with me." She leant forward and kissed her little girl on the forehead.

Frieda had heard the same rumors and wondered if she could keep her child safe. And herself. Again she thought of the packs of escaped slave workers roaming the countryside and looting. The war was closing in on her and Trudi. She had heard towns that did not surrender had been bombed by the Americans and towns that tried to surrender were punished by the Nazis.

Frieda looked wistfully at Trudi in her snug bed, her school art on the walls, her favorite things arranged neatly on her dresser. They had been content for the past year in the little cottage and she did not want to leave.

But she was becoming even more afraid to stay.

Army camp west of Weimar.

"Hey, Sarge, the captain wants to see you," the corporal shouted from the doorway of the washroom.

Terrill rolled his eyes. Now what did Henderson want? He was off duty, his first break in two weeks. But he felt better. He looked in the mirror as he wiped his razor clean. He ran his hand over his smooth jaw; without the stubble he no longer resembled a Bowery bum.

And still in the land of the living. He combed his wet brown hair, making a ruler-straight part on the left side with the edge of the comb, then smiled at himself in the mirror and blew a raspberry at his image. Kolevsky, Lambert, and a score of others were all dead. He regretted their loss, but that was the luck of the draw in war. He was still here. And in clean underwear for the first time in a couple of weeks. Luxury.

Perhaps Henderson was going to issue him a four-poster bed with silk sheets. He chuckled as he stole a last glance in the mirror, buttoning his uniform. Surely the war would be over soon. One month? Two? And then he'd be home, scot-free, seeing a Bogart movie at the Roxy, wolfing down juicy hotdogs at Yankee Stadium.

He turned from the mirror. Don't push your luck, Terrill. Maybe there's an 88 shell out there waiting for you. Or some fanatic Hitler Youth.

His hand adjusted his cap. In the meantime, better go see what Henderson had in store for him.

"I'll be straight with you, Terrill." Henderson didn't bother to look up from the papers on his makeshift desk. "You're going to be transferred."

Terrill didn't know what to think. He'd driven the son of a bitch through hell and high water for three months, and now he was passing him on.

"It seems your ability has been noted in high places."

What was he saying? Was there a hint of a smile on the bastard's face?

"The transfer order," the captain picked up a piece of paper, "comes from General Patton's chief of staff."

Terrill said nothing. A vision of driving Patton around his chateau headquarters far from German shells and bullets briefly crossed his mind but he dismissed the thought. The smile on the captain's face tipped him off. Something wasn't kosher.

"You're to be transferred to a Monuments, Fine Arts and Archives unit."

Terrill felt he was losing touch with reality. "What the hell's that, sir?"

The captain looked down at the order. "Apparently they're looking for paintings that the Nazis have stolen from all over Europe." Henderson sniggered. Terrill hated him. He hadn't seen the captain smile in three months.

"Well, sir, at least it's an easy number." Terrill had visions of driving some big shots far away from the action.

"Hardly, Sergeant." Henderson smiled. "Apparently this group operates right behind the front line. As soon as our point men find a stash of art, these people move right in."

Terrill felt uneasy. But at least the guys in the motor pool wouldn't look down their noses at him.

"You're to report tomorrow, Terrill," the rare smile was still stuck on the captain's face, "to Major Alan Donovan—" he paused, "and Lieutenant Gina Cortazzo."

Terrill saluted and turned to go before the name registered. "Gina?"

"Gina." The captain nodded.

Terrill stopped in the doorway. He was reporting to a broad. He could already hear the smartass remarks of the other drivers. Shit, piss, and corruption.

On the road to Lumberg Castle, five miles north of Nuremberg.

"Sir, it'll soon be time to get off the road." The voice of Brigadeführer Reinhard Hofmann's staff car driver stirred him from his somnolent state, brought on by the endless hum of the tires on the road. "It's nearly dawn."

Hofmann stifled a yawn and stretched himself in the passenger seat, rubbing his eyes in an attempt to focus them. He peered to the left at the glimmer of pinkish yellow in the eastern sky and sighed. All progress stopped at first light.

He reached forward for his map case on top of the dashboard. The driver was right. The day before, the convoy had been forced to seek refuge in a road tunnel, hiding through the daylight hours from the American fighter bombers that dominated the skies. He'd even been told by farmers that the enemy planes dived and shot at them when gathering their cows for milking.

He pulled a map from the case. Where was the damned Luftwaffe? Not a German plane in the sky. Not one. That braggart Goering had a lot to answer for. He grabbed a flashlight from the glove compartment, held it over the map, and tried to fathom the convoy's position.

In the growing light his driver scanned the skies for the dreaded American Jabos. "Perhaps, sir, we should take refuge by going off the road into the forest." The driver's voice betrayed his anxiety.

Hofmann was inclined to accept his advice, but remembered his orders. He had to collect another consignment. How art would sustain the Alpenfestung he wasn't sure. But orders were orders.

He stuffed the map back into the case and snapped it shut. "No. We've lost too much time already." He lit a cigarette and drew heavily on it. "We have to take a chance. The turn to Lumburg is only twenty kilometers away. Drive on." He opened the window and watched as the cool day sucked out the smoke.

He had to buy time. His eyes scoured the overcast sky. At least the clouds would keep the American planes at bay. But he felt time was not on his side.

Brettheim.

Wolfgang saw the clouds gathering and knew rain was on the way. He shivered in the crisp early morning air, but held his body ramrod straight like the others in the troop, just as they had been taught at Hitler-Jugend camps. He looked along the line of the troop. All, like him, stood erect, proud, waiting for the officer who was to command them.

He checked his swastika armband. Everything must be perfect. The Senior Squad leader had made it clear – rigorous discipline was the hallmark of the Hitler Youth, together with implacable hatred of the foe. He felt anxious, but proud. Soon would come the time to prove to the Führer – and to Germany – that he was willing to fight, to the end if necessary, to defend the Fatherland against the Americans and their allies, the Jewish-Bolshevik swine.

He could not suppress a sneeze, and quickly sneaked the back of his hand under his runny nose. Why was everything taking so long? Where was the officer? He stole another glance along the line, his eyes catching the smirk on Ulrich's face. He did not like Ulrich, the troop leader. Always puffing himself up like a peacock, boasting about how he had been in action. The back of Wolfgang's hand ran under his nose again.

Willi, his friend since they had joined the Hitler-Jugend in Munich together, had told him that Ulrich had been part of a troop that had helped deliver shells to an artillery unit. That wasn't action. Real action was when you could see the enemy, when bullets were flying all around you. That was what Wolfgang wanted – to prove himself a man – and a soldier. He sneezed again and cursed the delay.

There wasn't much opportunity for action for a troop cooling its heels in a small town several miles behind the front. Where were the officers? Wasn't it their job to provide leadership? Leadership. The most important factor. Every instructor at camp had stressed the principle. The Führer provided leadership. The supreme leader.

A fine rain began to fall, dampening his spirits. He continued to hold himself erect, but wished he were in front of a warm fire, like the many times at camp. And he wanted a piss. He sneaked another look at Ulrich. Was the great hero shivering?

At least Ulrich didn't know about Wolfgang's father. He'd told no one about it, keeping the damning secret hidden. To think that his own father had been involved in the cowardly plot to kill the Führer. He would never be able to live down the shame. Ulrich would mock him and he'd be forced to leave the service.

Sleet began to mix with the rain. Wolfgang was miserable, chilled to the bone. He wanted to go to war. And he needed a piss.

Lumberg Castle, north of Nuremberg.

Count von Schellendorf pulled his watch from the pocket of his brocade vest as he paced the Great Hall of Lumberg Castle. He looked through the huge arched window at the end of the hall. Nothing, except for the early morning mists that had gathered around the castle every morning for centuries. Nine-fifteen, and still no sight of the SS troops promised by General Krebs to collect his art treasures.

The count eased his corpulent frame into a leather armchair and let his rheumy eyes wander around the high walls, adorned with his acquisitions of art. Lumberg had been in the von Schellendorf family since the sixteenth century, and the Great Hall spoke eloquently of the count's wealth. Medieval suits of armor worn by knights of the Hohenstaufen dynasty guarded the base of the grand staircase; magnificent sixteenth century tapestries adorned the wall, along with paintings of the masters: a Rubens looked down at the count from the west wall and a van Dyck hung on the north wall, beneath the raftered ceiling.

He peered over his pince-nez and sighed. He had just taken a last look at his special collection, acquisitions he had made since the start of the war. He kept his special collection in a room off his bedchamber, and now he was waiting for the SS troops to package the works and remove them to a safe haven far from the grasp of the American cultural philistines who were fast approaching. He looked at his watch again. Where was this Brigadeführer Hofmann that Krebs had promised?

His thoughts were disturbed by the chink of Dresden china as his butler, Florian, poured his breakfast tea. He took the delicate teacup from the old family retainer and sipped. Even in this dreadful situation, with Germany collapsing, surely Krebs would not let him down.

For, not only was the count a man of immense wealth, he was also a man of considerable power and influence. Indeed, his wealth had brought him power. After Hitler's failed putsch in '23, the count had supported and contributed handsomely to the National Socialist Party's finances.

Not that he liked the Nazis – in fact, he thought them coarse and crass petty bourgeois. His true allegiance had belonged to the old empire, but that golden age had collapsed in '18 with the loss of the war and the abdication of the Kaiser, never to rise again. The count absentmindedly studied the family crest on the side of his cup. Where Hitler and his cronies had been useful was in destroying the communists and social-ists that threatened the count's wealth, together with the hated Weimar regime that had nurtured the Bolshevik criminals.

And Hitler had delivered. Even better, the war he had launched had offered the art treasures of Europe for plunder. Of course, Hitler and the top Nazis had always sought the best, but the count had placed his own agents in many conquered nations, and his haul had been substantial. He was particularly fond of a Franz Hals portrait formerly in the collec-tion of a Dutch Jew, but two fourteenth-century illuminated manuscripts from the library of a Belgian monastery were also quite charming. Often he had snatched priceless works from under the Nazis' very noses.

The count finished his tea and dabbed the napkin at his lips. Besides, Hitler's mob had poor taste, understandable given their humble origins. He recalled a visit to Goering's ghastly Karinhalle. So pretentious, so lacking in class. The man was worse than a morphine addict – he was a boor. The count had never been invited to Berchtesgaden. Like the lowly corporal he had been, Hitler didn't like the aristocracy, although he had been happy to accept the count's money. The feeling was mutual; although he had used the Nazis, the count despised them, and had no compunction stealing from them. Especially, he chuckled inwardly, a final coup that was now a fait accompli.

A smile came to the count's lips. His money had brought him power and influence. He had made inroads into the Nazi hierarchy. He could ask for favors.

And now he needed favors. With the collapse of Germany, the Nazis would soon be gone. But he – and his art – would survive. And, after the war, when the dust had settled, he would reclaim his collection. His plan had one flaw: if the SS unit didn't arrive to take away and hide the acquisitions he had stolen since the start of the war, they would fall into the uncouth hands of the Americans.

Nervously, he looked at his watch again. He thought about phoning Krebs, but discarded the idea. Krebs, like him, was of the old school. Krebs would keep his word.

The roar of engines drew him back to the windows and brought a smile to his face. Krebs had honored his promise.

Twenty miles from Nuremberg: temporary headquarters of a Monuments, Fine Arts and Archives unit.

"You must be Sergeant Terrill."

"Yes, ma'am." Terrill looked at the woman standing by the side of his jeep. She was tall, maybe five or six inches shorter than his own six-foot-one, and she looked smart in her uniform. Very easy on the eyes – trim figure, cheeky smile, deep brown eyes, dark hair done up in a bun. He wouldn't mind seeing her take the bobby pins out of her hair; in other circumstances.... He pushed the thought from his mind and looked over the hood of his jeep; the corporal by the fuel pump was trying hard to suppress a guffaw.

Times were changing; Roosevelt had a woman in his cabinet. But she was in Washington – women didn't belong so near the front line. He saw the corporal lose the struggle and begin to snigger. Probably couldn't wait to get back to the mess tent to tell all the other NCO's that Terrill was personal chauffeur for a woman. Big laughs all around.

"I'm Lieutenant Cortazzo," her smile was friendly, "but please call me Gina. Welcome to our temporary headquarters. Please, come this way." She turned, leaving a faint scent of flowers mixed with citrus in her wake, and Terrill followed her toward the house that had been commandeered for their use.

He saw the sign, 'Monuments, Fine Arts and Archives.' What the hell did that mean? Why did art and archives matter in a war? Men dying for paintings and bits of paper? What a waste.

As he followed her into the house, he couldn't stop his eyes from dwelling on her swaying hips. Nice tush. And she was friendly enough. Not la-di-dah, not snooty in her voice. Maybe the duty wouldn't be so bad after all. No driving Henderson up to the point where the bullets were flying. Better than a poke in the eye with a sharp stick.

Terrill's raised feelings of hope fell when he heard the officer behind the desk.

"I'm Major Donovan." His Boston Brahmin accent grated on Terrill's ears. "Let me explain your duties." Not so much as a how d'you do. An upper-class snob, born with a silver spoon in his mouth. Probably never had to work for a living. Worst of all, probably a Red Sox fan.

After ten minutes of listening to the prick, Terrill was confused. "So, sir, I'm to drive you and the lady—"

"Lieutenant Cortazzo." The major was so formal he'd probably want him to shine his shoes in the morning.

"So, Major, I'm to drive you and, uh, Lieutenant Cortazzo around Germany as you search for stolen art treasures?"

"Yes, that's correct."

"Sir, are you the guys they call the Monuments Men?"

Donovan closed his eyes, as though enduring an insult. "Some may use that appellation, but for my part I prefer not to be confused with a dealer in headstones."

"But, sir, why are you so close to the front line? Isn't it a mopping-up operation?"

Donovan rolled his eyes.

"Perhaps I can explain." The lieutenant's warm smile gave Terrill a welcome break from the major's stuffiness. "We have to move quickly once a trove is found."

He liked the way she said 'trove,' pursing her full lips as though she were about to be kissed. Terrill wondered if he was going to be a party to discovering high-toned art worth a lot of moolah. Maybe he'd be on a commission basis; he laughed at his ridiculous thought. He'd be last in the line, behind the generals, colonels, and all the other jerks who ran this shithole of a war.

"You find our mission amusing, Sergeant?"

Sour-Face cut Terrill's amusement short. He wasn't sure he could get along with this asshole. He was as cold as a seat in the latrine on a February morning.

"Your role is extremely important to our task." Her voice made him feel good, and she was as easy on the eyes as the Varga Girl pin-up in last month's Esquire. "Indeed, we're very privileged to have you. Some of the Monuments Men have to fend for themselves to get from place to place." Her smile warmed him. "In any event, we need your help right now."

Terrill was taken aback. He thought there'd be a leisurely introduction, driving around the back lanes of Bavaria.

"That's correct." The major peered over his papers. "We've had news that advance American elements are approaching Lumberg Castle."

Advance American elements. That's how the stuffed shirt described the soldiers Terrill knew. Flesh and blood putting their lives on the line. For pretty paintings.

"We believe there may be important art there." Important art. The broad's voice no longer gave Terrill comfort. "We need to move soon. Do you know where Lumberg Castle is?"

Sure, Terrill thought ironically. Perhaps the babe thought he knew every back road in Germany. Sometimes he even got lost in lower Manhattan.

"No, ma'am, but I have a map."

"Good. The castle should be in our troops' hands by this evening. " The major gathered up his papers and looked at his watch. "Shall we say six o'clock?" He stood up.

Terrill saluted and turned to leave. It sounded like an invitation to cocktails.

Frieda's cottage.

It had begun as a normal day, but now Frieda was afraid.

She had walked Trudi down to the village school, stopping along the way to pick up her daughter's friend, Marta. It was no longer safe for the girls to walk there by themselves, and Marta's parents were out tending their farm animals at break of day. Later that afternoon, Marta's father would collect the girls from school in a wagon and would drop off Trudi at the end of the path leading up to the front door of the cottage.

She had just finished eating the day-old potato soup she had reheated for her lunch when she saw the men. Her hands clutched at her apron as she peered through the window. There were two of them. They stood on the road at the bottom of the hill, looking up at the cottage. One was bearded and dressed in rags, with hair that was long, unwashed, matted; the other was clean-shaven and neater in appearance, tall, lanky, gaunt, with closely-cropped hair.

Her chest heaved, her breathing becoming shallow and rapid as the fear began to seize her. Her eyes remained riveted on the sinister figures. She'd never seen them before, but she knew what they were. Escaped foreign farm workers. She knew the German farmers treated them as cheap labor, little better than slaves.

She held her breath. Perhaps they'd move on. Like many others, she'd turned a blind eye when they'd arrived on the farms. It was part and parcel of Nazi Germany – what could she have done? Hans had tried to do something, and had paid with his life.

The bearded man raised an arm, pointing up the hill to the cottage. She knew they'd escaped. As the war came closer, law and order were breaking down. She'd heard stories of how groups were roaming the countryside, foraging for food, in some cases exacting revenge for the slavery they had endured. The bearded man with matted hair was gesticulating to the clean-shaven man, who shook his head and walked away.

She stiffened, the color running from her face. The bearded man was coming up the path.

Brettheim.

Wolfgang could sense the relief among the troop as an army truck, gears grinding, lurched into the town square. The rain had abated, but he still felt cold and miserable, and his bladder was becoming insistent. He was disappointed when he saw a feldwebel jump down from the cab and walk across to them. He had expected an SS officer, not a sergeant, a non-commissioned army man.

Ulrich, as scharführer – the troop leader, called them to attention, their heels clacking on the cobbles as arms snapped out in salute. Wolfgang was not impressed when the sergeant waved away the salute, a dismissive smirk on his unshaven face. The man didn't look like a leader; his uniform was ruffled, unkempt, and there was mud on his boots.

"Sir," Ulrich's reedy voice grated on Wolfgang's ears, "the Fifth Troop of the Munich Hitler-Jugend is ready to go to the front!" Wolfgang thought Ulrich sounded pompous, but was horrified when the sergeant guffawed with laughter. Such behavior was insubordination; he would report the man at the first opportunity.

The sergeant struggled to contain his amusement. "Son," he put his face close to Ulrich's, a wry smile upon his face, "hold your horses. You're not going to the front!"

Wolfgang shared the barely-disguised consternation within the troop. Not going to the front? What was the man thinking?

The soldier stood back and looked dismissively up and down the line, shaking his head. "But don't worry, my young comrades." There was sarcasm in his voice. "The front is coming to you!" He threw back his head and laughed again, baring his nicotine-stained teeth. "And faster than you think." He raised his left hand, pointing to the west. "Just twenty kilometers over there is General Patton's Third Army." He dropped his arm to his side. "And the whole shooting match is heading for me." He paused to look along the line, a thin smile on his lips. "And for you!"

Despite the sergeant's condescension, Wolfgang felt a rush of exhilaration: they would soon be in action.

"Sergeant, sir," Ulrich's voice echoed the eagerness of the troop, "when are we to receive our weapons? We have been trained to use the Panzerfäust – we know how to attack tanks!"

"All in good time, my lad." The sergeant grimaced. "There'll be plenty of time to die like heroes. There'll be so many American tanks you can take your pick!" His laughter was brief; his jaw was set as he addressed the troop.

"But first, there's another patriotic job for you." He turned to Ulrich. "Scharführer, get your troop to unload the equipment from the truck. Those men," he pointed to two SS soldiers in the cab, "they'll show your people how to assemble it." He saluted, turned on his heel and strode out of the square.

53

"All right, troop, let's get on with it!" Ulrich led them as they ran to the truck and began unloading the equipment, the SS soldiers giving instructions.

"Say, Willi," Wolfgang whispered in his friend's ear, "can you cover me for a minute? I need to take a leak."

"Sure – but you'd better get back quickly." Willi lowered his voice. "Can't you see what we're about to assemble?"

Wolfgang looked at the wooden sections already unloaded. "I can't make it out – what is it?"

"It's a scaffold, Wolfgang." There was a hint of fear in his friend's voice.

"A scaffold?"

"Yes. A scaffold. For hanging people."

Frieda's cottage.

Frieda hurried to the door and turned the key. A futile gesture but, in her desperation, she could think of little else. Perhaps she should escape, make a run for it, but she couldn't leave Trudi: what would happen when her little girl came home from school?

She hastened back to the window and saw the man with the long hair coming up the hill, his breath laboring as he struggled against the steep incline. If only Wolfgang were still with her, instead of being away on a foolish mission to save a Germany she now despised.

The man paused to recover his breath. Her eyes cast about the cottage in desperation, seeking something to help her fend off the intruder. The rifle! The thought leapt into her mind. When she moved into the cottage, she had found an old rifle standing in one of the closets.

She saw the man resume his climb and scurried to the small bedroom at the back of the cottage. Where was it? She pulled open a closet door, and then another, her fingers nervously fumbling with the latches. Her body stiffened as she heard the man struggling with the knob on the locked door at the back of the cottage. She pulled aside some brooms and saw the rifle, propped against the corner.

The man was hammering on the back door, shouting in a language she didn't understand. Her hands pulled out the weapon from the closet.

She heard repeated thuds as the man threw his weight against the door. Her breath quickened as she reached for the small box of ammunition on the shelf. The box slipped from her fingers, the bullets scattering over the floor. The man's voice was angry; she heard him kick at the lock.

Her fingers trembled, fumbling as she grasped a handful of bullets from the floor. She sat on the bed, placing the cartridges beside her. The man's boot was repeatedly banging against the lock. She pulled on the rifle bolt, but her efforts were futile. The bolt was jammed. A cracking sound came from the back of the cottage. The wood around the kitchen door lock was splintering.

Brettheim.

The town square echoed with hammering and the shouts of the troop as they toiled at erecting the wooden structure. Each piece taken from the truck was identified and positioned by the two SS soldiers, who directed everyone to the task.

"Sir," Willi paused at his labors and addressed one of the SS men, "why have we been given this job?"

Wolfgang winced. Willi sometimes asked the most stupid questions.

The man pushed his cap back from his forehead and laughed. "Naturally, we'd do this job ourselves," he turned to Willi, a sardonic smile crossing his face, "but we decided to give the Hitler-Jugend the chance to do its duty for Führer and Fatherland."

His colleague guffawed before yelling at the troop to get back to work. The structure began to take form. The platform, the ten-foot-high support pieces at the sides. Wolfgang, the armpits of his brown shirt stained with sweat, climbed one of the four ladders along with Willi and two more of the troop to fix the crosspiece into place. As he hammered at the wood, Wolfgang tried to remember its technical name – he had read about it somewhere. The word came to him. Gibbet. That was it. The gibbet. The piece of wood from which the condemned man would hang. The sweat bothered Wolfgang; he felt uncomfortable.

"Excuse me, sir," Wolfgang cringed as he heard Willi's hesitant voice again, "but do you use this equipment often?"

"It's getting to be a full-time job, son." The SS man laughed before shouting up instructions to Wolfgang. "Another two nails – make sure the crosspiece is secure – we don't want any accidents, do we?"

No more stupid questions, Willi. Wolfgang checked the sturdiness of the gibbet as he climbed down the ladder.

"It's good to know we're capturing so many spies, sir."

"Spies?" The SS man looked incredulously at Willi. "Nothing as interesting as spies. We're executing traitors to the Reich."

"Wouldn't it be easier to just shoot the traitors, sir?"

"Ah, yes, but, you see, it wouldn't have the same effect on the others."

"Effect, sir?"

"The gallows always draw a crowd, and when they see it, they're reminded of their own strong loyalty to the Fatherland."

"It's our duty to hang traitors." Ulrich clicked his heels and saluted. All eyes turned to him. Wolfgang sighed. He agreed with the troop leader. Traitors should be executed on the gallows. But why did Ulrich always have to be the center of attention?

"Quite so, Scharführer," the SS man agreed. "You've done a good job, lads." He turned to look up at the scaffold. "Take a break."

He glanced at his watch. "Our customer isn't due to arrive for twenty minutes."

Frieda's cottage.

Frieda ran for the bedroom door, her heart pounding, the rifle in the crook of her arm. The man stood in the doorway, his hands clutching at the jambs; the door, shattered at the lock, hung skewed at an angle. His face was raw, weather-beaten, the skin drawn drum-tight over his cheekbones.

He had not seen her. Frieda hung back, peering through the crack of the slightly ajar bedroom door. She saw his eyes, set deep in blackened sockets, flit from side to side as if searching for something. Frieda held her breath; perhaps he would think the cottage empty and go away.

But the smell of the potato soup she had had for lunch still hung heavy in the air, an aroma that seemed to seduce him. He would know that someone was home in the cottage. Frieda gripped the rifle tightly with whitened knuckles, although without bullets it did little to stay her shaking hands.

She had to lean forward to see as the man approached the kitchen table. He peered at her empty soup bowl before his eyes alighted upon the half-eaten loaf by the side of the plate. With a barely suppressed roar, his hands fell upon the bread, his fingers tearing the loaf to pieces, cramming it into his mouth, his stained and decaying teeth devouring every crumb.

Frieda eased away from the bedroom door, the back of her hand sweeping beads of sweat from her brow. Perhaps the man would eat his fill and move on.

She should lie low. She cast her eyes around the bedroom. Perhaps the closet. She would be safe in there until the man left. As she turned to cross the room, the butt of the rifle caught on a cabinet, sending some of the curios inside clattering to the floor.

Brettheim.

The waiting was boring. Willi sat on the edge of the scaffold's platform playing his harmonica. A martial tune, Wolfgang noted. *Wir fahren gegen Engeland.* He recalled when he had seen German soldiers sing the song as they marched along the streets of Munich. *We are marching against England.* It was at the start of the war, the year he had joined the Hitler Youth, just after his tenth birthday.

The afternoon sun was warm, a marked contrast to the bitter morning chill that had lingered late. The soldiers he had seen heading off to war had done their duty. Now came his turn. He looked up at the stark frame of the scaffold. He'd prefer to be facing an American tank with his Panzerfäust. His instructor had congratulated him on his skill with the tank-destroying rocket gun, and he couldn't wait to use it.

Willi turned to another tune. The Horst Wessel Song. The martyr of the National Socialist movement. Next to *Deutschland über alles* the Führer's favorite. The troop began to sing.

> *With flag held aloft and with ranks closed*
> *The SA marches with a silent steady pace*

Comrades murdered by Reds and reactionaries
March with us in spirit in our ranks

The street is free for the Brownshirts
The street is free for the Storm Troopers
Full of hope, millions gaze up at the swastika
For freedom and for bread the new day dawns

A sneeze interrupted Wolfgang's singing; he pulled out a handkerchief and blew his nose. He saw Ulrich's disapproving look and stuffed the rag back in his pocket.

Frieda's cottage.

Frieda's first thought as she looked at the shattered pieces was to blame herself for having kept the curios. She dismissed the thought as she heard the intruder's footsteps running from the kitchen. The weapon was useless, she knew, but perhaps she could frighten him, bluff her way to an escape. Her hands shook as she gripped the stock of the gun and pulled herself unsteadily to her feet.

The bedroom door crashed against the wall as the intruder threw it open. Fear overwhelmed her as she looked at him, an apparition from hell framed in the doorway. His long, lank hair clung to the sides of his skeletal face. Spittle drooled from his lips onto a bedraggled beard that was flecked with crumbs from the bread he had just devoured. Frieda glimpsed into his eyes, dark, menacing, set deep in their sockets, burning with a hatred born of years of slave labor.

She pointed the rifle at his chest. If there had been a bullet in the chamber, she would have shot him. She had no option but to confront the demon. Her breast heaved as she struggled to overcome her fear. She kept prodding the gun toward him and was relieved when he began to back away. Fear replaced the anger in his eyes. The demon was human.

He waved his arms in front of his body. *"Nicht verletzt! Nicht verletzt!"* She saw that he struggled with the German words. "Not hurt! Not hurt!"

Frieda again pushed the rifle and he slowly retreated. *"Nicht verletzt!"* He raised a finger and pointed to his mouth. "Food. Need food."

If she gave him food, she reasoned, perhaps he would go away. She motioned with the gun, forcing him back into the kitchen. *"Setzen Sie sich."* She pointed to a chair. He sat, but she saw that his eyes never left her.

She went to the far end of the kitchen, tucked the gun under her arm, and reached up into the larder for a small slab of cured ham. She heard the chair rattle as he got up, driven wild by the sight of meat. Frieda put the meat down on the table and leveled the gun at him. "Sit down." He retreated into his chair. She smelled the salty tang of the ham as she put it on a plate. The man squirmed impatiently on his chair, his eyes now fixed on the meat, like an animal watching its prey. With the rifle in one hand, she pushed the plate across the table with the other.

He looked up at her briefly. There was no gratitude in his eyes, no human feeling, only the look of a hungry and cunning beast. He made a sawing gesture with his hand.

"No. No knife!" Frieda shouted. "Do you think I'm a fool?"

He muttered a few words in a language she didn't understand and seized the ham. His long dirty fingernails tore at it, like a wolf with fresh kill. Driven by intense hunger, he raised it to his mouth, his rotting teeth gnawing at the meat.

Frieda struggled to contain her fear. Not only the fear of the monster seated at her table, but also fear of her own emotions. She knew that, had the rifle been loaded, she would shoot him without a moment's hesitation, shoot him like a mad dog.

Perhaps he would eat his fill and go. Frieda watched as he savaged the meat and realized the futility of her thought. There would be more demands. Soon he would demand drink, and then—

Her mind would not accept the obvious outcome. She would fight back. Perhaps she could—

Her hands shifted on the rifle, her fingers gripping the barrel. She could use the gun as a club, bringing the stock down on his head, crushing his skull.

He did not notice her as she moved around the table behind him, his attention fixed on devouring the meat. She held the weapon behind her back as she focused on a spot on the back of his skull; soon she'd be free of this monster. As her arms began to swing the stock over her head, the man leapt from his seat and sent the rifle clattering to the floor. His fist crashed into her jaw.

Brettheim.

A few townspeople had gathered around the scaffold; Wolfgang saw the awe and fear in their eyes. A woman burst into tears and scurried away. Weakness, Wolfgang thought. Just like his mother. She hadn't understood the need for duty. Duty was the responsibility of every National Socialist. That's what the officer at camp had told them. Duty. Sacrifice. Everything for the Führer and the Reich.

> For the last time will the roll be called
> Now we all stand ready for the struggle
> Soon Hitler's flag will fly over every street
> Servitude will soon be vanquished

The troop sang the last lines of the Horst Wessel Song with the full power of their lungs. His father had been a traitor. All traitors deserved to die.

The crowd had grown, and began to move aside as a truck, engine racing, drove into the square. Wolfgang struggled to suppress another sneeze. Duty, he thought. Duty.

Frieda's cottage.

The late afternoon sunlight streaming through the shattered doorway returned Frieda to the living world. She opened her eyes, then closed them, her mind rebelling at the images she saw. The searing pain that burst from her jaw brought her back to the inescapable reality. Her eyelids lifted again, slowly, reluctantly. She was lying on the tiled kitchen floor. Her hands lifted to her face in a vain attempt to ease the pain as her eyes struggled to focus.

Perhaps he had eaten the food and left. The brief hope lasted no more than a moment. The intruder was there, an ominous hulk sitting above her at the end of the kitchen table. He had found the schnapps and the bottle was thrust into his bearded face. She saw his Adam's apple bob up and down as the liquor went down his throat. In his other hand he held the long, sharp knife she used for slicing roasts.

"Look, I have money—" The pain in her jaw stopped her words.

He slammed the bottle on the table and waved the knife at her menacingly. She struggled again to rise, but he leapt up from the chair, took one step toward her, and kicked her in the thigh.

Frieda yelped in pain and fell back again prone on the floor. Her hand rubbed futilely at the pain in her thigh, her eyes casting around in vain for any form of escape. There was none. He stood astride her, his feet planted by her ankles.

She tried to avert her eyes, but they somehow could not escape his. Her fear grew as she saw his look. His hunger and thirst had been sated. Now another need fired his eyes.

He lowered himself, his knees on the floor bestride her hips. His face hovered above hers. She turned her head as his lips sought her mouth; his coarse beard grated against her cheek.

Her fists began to pummel him until she felt the cold steel of the knife against her throat; his other hand began to lift her skirt, tugging at her stockings, anything that resisted the path of his fingers. No, dear God, she pleaded. Please help me.

His hand retreated, but the other hand still held the knife against her neck. He grunted as he undid his trousers. She felt him against her thigh, thrusting. She closed her eyes, trying to blot out the image. But still she could smell him, the reek of his unwashed body, the odor of ham and liquor on his breath, the smell of stale urine on his clothes.

Please, dear Lord, don't let Trudi come home now, she prayed.

Brettheim.

Wolfgang saw the truck coming across the square, bringing the traitor to justice.

"Squad, to your positions!" Ulrich's order echoed around the town square. The tune from Willi's harmonica stopped, and the troop's singing died quickly in the warm afternoon air. Their boots clattered on the cobbles as they raced to line up. Wolfgang blew his nose and hurriedly stuffed his handkerchief back into his pocket as he took his position in the line facing the scaffold.

"Squad, attention!" Their boots stamped to the ground as one. Wolfgang stole a glance at Ulrich. At seventeen, the troop leader was only a year older, yet Ulrich was acting like a puffed-up general. He had told Wolfgang how proud his parents were. Wolfgang had shrugged off the remark. He did not have parents who were proud of him, but it didn't matter to him. He hated them. His father had been a traitor. To the people. To the Fatherland. Above all to the Führer. His eyes looked up from under his cap at the scaffold: the SS man stood on a chair adjusting the noose. And now he was to be witness to the death of another traitor. One people. One Reich. One Führer. The words rang in his mind again and again. He heard the brakes of the truck screech as it stopped by the side of the scaffold. One people. One Reich. One Führer. His hand sneaked under his nose.

"Squad, at ease!" Again, the sound of all boots in unison crashing to the ground. For some reason the sound gave comfort to Wolfgang. He recalled the instructor's lecture at camp. "The individual is nothing unless he works with others for the National Socialist state. One people! One Reich! One Führer!"

Frieda's cottage.

Suddenly, Frieda heard a noise. The man pinning her down cried out and fell from her body to the floor. She opened her eyes and saw the other man who had been on the road below, the one who had walked away. His foot stamped sharply on her attacker's hand; the knife clattered to the tiles. He grabbed the brute's collar, hauled him to his feet, and struck his face twice.

The wretch saw the newcomer pick up the knife and fled through the doorway. Frieda sat on the floor unable to move, her hands covering her face as the agonizing sobs wracked her body.

The stranger knelt beside her. "I'm sorry," he said in German, "I'm so very sorry this happened."

She pulled her hands away from her face; his grey eyes seemed heavy with compassion. He ran his hand over her reddened jaw. She winced, although his touch was gentle.

"I don't think your jaw is broken," he said, "although your face will be badly bruised for a while." He stood up, wet a cloth, and brought it to her. "Here, hold this against your jaw; it will relieve the pain."

She held it to her face and continued to whimper.

"Stay there until you're ready to get up," the stranger said, still speaking in German.

After a few moments, Frieda managed to rise, with his help, and moved to the kitchen sink. Her whole body still shook as she rubbed the wet cloth over her face to wash off the stench of her assailant, her knuckles white as she wrung the liquid from the cloth. Her mind was a confusion of horror, relief, and fear.

"I'm sorry," he said again. She turned to look at him as he placed the knife on the table.

"Please believe that not all of us are like him." His hand gestured in the direction the man had fled and his voice was soft. "Many, perhaps. But not all." She saw his tall figure framed in the shattered doorway, silhouetted against the sky.

Fear still consumed Frieda. She looked at the knife on the table. She began to reach her arm out toward the handle of the steel blade.

"You have no need of that." He spoke calmly. "I mean you no harm."

Her trembling fingers drew back from the knife. He spoke German almost perfectly, but she detected a slight accent and she could see from the pale eyes that sat above his high cheek bones that he was a Slav. He was clean but his jacket and trousers were shabby; without doubt, an escaped slave laborer.

"Who are—" Her tongue struggled with her fear and the pain from the blow. "Who are you? What do you want?"

"From you, I want nothing."

"Please sit down." She motioned to a chair at the kitchen table and took a seat on the other side. Her hands still trembled, but she no longer felt in danger. Perhaps it was his manner: he was no savage. Perhaps it was because he spoke her language.

"You speak German fluently, but you're not German, are you?"

"No, I'm Polish. But I studied medicine for five years in Heidelberg. And I've been in Germany since early nineteen-forty."

Frieda shifted uncomfortably on her seat. He didn't have to tell her the rest of his story. She remembered when Germany had invaded Poland in September of '39. The huge, cheering crowds in Munich celebrating the German army's conquest. And Hans, her husband, shaking his head at the news. She and Hans had followed events with disgust as the Nazis bombed Polish towns and cities, destroying everything. But somehow this man had survived.

"You say you're from Poland. How did you manage to escape?"

His emaciated face offered an ironic smile. "As you can see, I didn't escape." He ran his finger over his cracked lips. "Of course, I escaped death. Unfortunately, my wife and son did not." He tightened his jaw and stared abstractedly at something behind her. "They were killed by a German bomb." Although his voice was controlled and his memories were not new, she could see in his eyes that the emotions they evoked were still raw. "When the Nazis came, they were bent on eradicating Polish professionals, so I went to my father's farm in the country and pretended to be a laborer there." He ran his fingers over his short hair. "So they shipped me here. To Bavaria. To milk cows."

Frieda wanted to concentrate on the man's story but she had a more pressing concern. She stood up and went to the window.

He sensed her anxiety. "Is something wrong?"

"It's my daughter, Trudi." Even though Marta's father was bringing her home, she worried about her child abroad in a world swarming with brutes who had lost all sense of humanity.

"There she is!" Like a child, Frieda clapped her hands in relief, laughing at the clatter of the front door closing and the sound of her daughter's footsteps running in the hall.

"Mutti! Mutti! I got good marks on the—"

Breathless, Trudi stopped short when she entered the kitchen and saw the stranger. Her pigtails tossed as her eyes flitted between her mother, the man, and the shattered doorway.

"Mutti, your face is all red – and the door is broken—"

Frieda ran to Trudi, took the schoolbooks she was cradling in her arm, and helped her off with her coat. "It's all right, Trudi. There was an accident, but now everything's fine. This gentleman helped me."

Trudi stared open-mouthed at the strange man.

Frieda knew she had to spare her child any knowledge of what had happened, knew she had to shield her as much as possible from the hideous dangers that surrounded them in a broken world. "Trudi, this gentleman is Herr—"

"Konec. Stanislaus Konec," the man supplied.

Trudi's eyes grew larger.

"Trudi, please say hello to Herr Konec."

The child continued to stare at Stanislaus Konec, then abruptly turned and ran into her bedroom. Frieda's hands flew up to her mouth in embarrassment.

Stanislaus looked down at his ragged work clothes and worn-out shoes. That his appearance was able to frighten a child was a sad reminder of the depths to which he had fallen in life. "Before the war came to my country, I wore a suit and tie every day." He stood up. "Perhaps I'd better—" His eyes turned to see Trudi come back into the kitchen; she had a rag doll in her arms.

"Herr Konec," Trudi said, "would you like to meet Clothilde?"

Stanislaus smiled. "Yes, Trudi, I'd very much like to meet Clothilde."

"Clothilde, this is Herr Konec. Herr Konec is Mutti's friend. Herr Konec, this is Clothilde."

"I'm very pleased to meet you, Clothilde." For the first time in many years Stanislaus felt tears begin to well up in his eyes as he reached out to shake the rag doll's hand.

Brettheim.

The man was old. Wolfgang was shocked when the traitor was dragged from the truck. He reminded Wolfgang of the old man in the Englischer Garten in Munich, the one who shuffled around Kleinhesseloher Lake, throwing crumbs to the ducks. But this man was dressed in a shabby Volkssturm uniform.

"Squad! Attention!" Ulrich snapped his order. The boots snapped on the cobbles. It mattered not, Wolfgang thought. All traitors must be punished. Young or old.

The man looked up at the scaffold and Wolfgang could see the pathetic tears in his red-rimmed eyes. He opened his mouth and let out a wail, like a mortally wounded beast. Wolfgang remembered a deer the troop had hunted down in the forest, how the animal had bayed its death throes.

He heard Willi's whisper. "Why don't they hurry up so we can get out of here?"

The old man fell to his knees, screaming, shouting. Wolfgang heard the words 'wife' and 'grandchildren,' then closed his ears to the rest. "He's a disgrace to the uniform," Wolfgang hissed through his teeth.

He saw that a small crowd had gathered around the square, watching sullenly. A woman with a baby carriage walked quickly away, fear on her face as she glanced over her shoulder.

The two SS men manhandled the wretch to his feet. One quickly tied his hands behind his back. He began to wail again, and the private smashed his knuckles into his face.

Get on with it, Wolfgang screamed inwardly, silently. The SS men raised the old man by his armpits and dragged him to the scaffold, lifting him to stand on the chair. The noose was placed around his neck.

The crowd became silent as the SS scharführer pulled a sheet of paper from his pocket. "Gustav Müller," his voice rang out, "you have been found guilty of desertion. The sentence is death!"

The silence gripping the square was broken by a slow whine that came from the sky. Wolfgang looked up, searching for the source of the noise. The whine deepened to a roar.

The shell burst at the far end of the square. Wolfgang saw the church steeple collapse, saw the clouds of dust as the bricks crumbled to the ground.

"Everyone to the truck!" He heard Ulrich's voice as another shell came crashing from the sky.

Wolfgang's arms and legs pumped hard as he ran to the truck. He hadn't realized that the Americans were so close. The second shell crashed into the Ratthaus behind the scaffold.

The truck was already moving, but Wolfgang leapt at the tailgate and pulled himself up. As the truck left the square, he looked back at the scaffold and saw the SS man kick the chair from under the condemned man before running to the truck.

Temporary headquarters of a Monuments, Fine Arts and Archives unit.

"Ouch!" Gina pricked her thumb with the needle again. Even though she'd be thirty come September, sewing a button back on a blouse still seemed an arcane skill.

As she put down her sewing and sucked her bleeding finger, the framed snapshot of her father on the tiny table next to her cot caught her eye. Her dad was her whole family. Her mother had died when she was three; perhaps that's why home economics had never been her best subject. But while she had burned the cake in sixth grade and a year later made an apron that became a dust rag, she aced all her other classes and had gone on to win a scholarship to college. And all because of her dad. Gianfranco Luigi Cortazzo. She tried to take another stitch but the thread tangled and broke; she tossed the sewing into her lap and took a deep breath.

Things had been tough for her father. Her grandparents had left everything behind in Sicily to follow their dream to live in the United States, and after the fourth grade her dad had been pulled out of school to help the family stay afloat. But while her father was short on formal education, he had an unquenchable thirst for learning. She cut off the offending thread, unrolled another length, and squinted as she tried to guide it through the needle's eye.

When she was six, her father bought a set of encyclopedias from a door-to-door salesman. Every couple of months, the salesman would knock at their fourth-floor walkup, collect seventy-five cents, and hand over a volume with the next few letters of the alphabet. Her father would rub his hands together in anticipation, sink into his battered easy chair, and begin reading it cover-to-cover. She plunged the needle into the buttonhole a few more times, ran it through the unsightly bundle of stitches on the back to complete the knot, and cut the thread.

Her father had never taught her how to sew on a button or hem a skirt, but he had opened new worlds to her. "Never forget, Gina," he used to say, "wealth is not here," and he'd pull a few coins from his pocket and hold them out on his calloused palm. "Wealth is here," he'd say, tapping his forehead. He liked to quote his own father on the subject. *"L'oro ha meno valore della sapienza."* Gold has less value than knowledge.

At bedtime, instead of reading her fairy tales, he'd treat her to selections from the encyclopedia. By the time she was seven she knew something about Aristotle, Alexander the Great, and the Altamira cave paintings. A little later, when he was reading through the C's, she became spellbound by the story of Charlemagne. While her young mind was drawn to the more bizarre aspects, such as Charlemagne's saving the pope from having his eyes and tongue ripped out, the story led to an abiding interest she would build upon in her later studies.

The set of encyclopedias was her father's last real luxury – after that, every extra dime he earned went into Gina's college education fund. Which was why she was here and why she took her work so seriously.

She put on her blouse. Thirty come September. And still not married. A bone fide old maid, but she had no regrets. Meat loaf recipes, PTA meetings, and children's skinned knees would have to wait; all of her passion and energy were now funneled into her field.

There had been men in her life, particularly during her university years, but they always became lost in a calendar of lectures and a mountain of research papers. If ever she did find a special man to love, he'd be someone in her field, someone as intensely devoted to art as she was. She buttoned her jacket and grabbed her cap.

As Gina began to walk toward the motor pool, she felt a jolt of exhilaration that she could participate in such important work. Of course, she had no illusions. Her role in the MFAA would always be minor – analyzing, cataloging the discoveries made by Donovan and his ilk. Still, it beat changing diapers by a wide margin.

Who had time for men when there was such exciting work to be done? She looked around the motor pool wondering where she could find Sergeant Terrill.

Frieda's cottage.

"I think Trudi was asleep even before her head hit the pillow." Frieda sighed. "Oh, to be young again and free of the fears which keep us awake." She lit the oil lamp and drew the curtains. The sun was about to set and the light would soon fade.

"So now you know who I am." Stanislaus was still sitting at the kitchen table. "You also asked if I wanted something. May I ask if you have any food?" His voice was soft, almost shy.

"I'm sorry. I hadn't realized. You see, he—" A vestige of fear ran through her body.

"I understand." He waved away her apology.

She opened the larder door. "I have some bratwurst, fresh this morning. The rations are very bad now, but I make a deal with the local butcher. He gives me some cuts of meat and I make dresses for his wife and daughters."

"Bratwurst would be wonderful." He spoke calmly, despite his gnawing hunger. There was no hint of savagery. Not like—Frieda turned her attention to the larder.

"I also have part of a loaf of rye bread. And some sauerkraut." Somehow, talking about normal things eased her fear. "It'll only take a few minutes." She reached for a kettle hanging from a hook.

"It sounds truly delicious. While you're doing that, I'll try to fix this mess." He walked over and picked up the broken door.

She glanced at him as she pricked the skin of the sausages with a fork. He was about her age, perhaps in his mid-forties. She filled the kettle with water from the hand pump, hung it from a hook over the fire and tossed in the sauerkraut. She looked again and saw him heaving the heavy door into place between the jambs, a look of intense concentration on his drawn face. She added the bratwurst to the kettle.

"The food will be ready in a few minutes," she called to him.

He glanced up at her and smiled, but she saw no happiness in his eyes. Only the hard sadness of his past.

"When you're finished eating," her voice dropped close to a whisper, "I think you should leave." She picked up a large spoon and filled the dishes.

Lumberg Castle.

"Mein Herr, the dinner was excellent," Hofmann pushed away his empty plate, "and the dessert wine is superb."

"A Château d'Yquem. My favorite." Watercolor blue eyes twinkled within a rubicund face as the count took a sip. "My great thanks to you, Brigadeführer, for the wonderful rendition of Chopin. It's been a long time since anyone played on the old Blüthner." The count raised his glass.

The brigadeführer responded to the toast. "It was my great pleasure, Count von Schellendorf. The nocturne is one of my favorites. It was one of my son's favorites, as well."

"Was?"

"Kurt was a night fighter in defense of the Reich. He had five kills before he was shot down a year ago."

"I'm sorry. But he died a hero."

"And the reason why I would stop at nothing to see Germany win the war."

The count's rheumy eyes ran up and down the officer, appraising him. Not much past forty. One of the new breed. He would know little of the glory of the old empire. But he would remember the treachery of the socialist politicians at the end of the Great War. Treachery. November, 1918. The stab in the back that had betrayed the German army, leading to the humiliation of the Versailles Treaty. The treaty that had robbed Germany of land and pride.

"You're aware of the value of my acquisitions, Brigadeführer Hofmann?" The count tamped down the tobacco in his Meerschaum pipe.

"Mein Herr, I am informed they are priceless. You may rest assured that my men will take the greatest care – they've spent the day packing them securely for transport. But we must hurry. There have been reports of American patrols in this area."

The count could see the officer was impatient, as if more important things were on his mind. "The monetary value of the collection is unimportant, Brigadeführer Hofmann." He reached for his gold lighter. "You have responsibility for a legacy of Germany." He drew deeply on the pipe. "And you are taking away my children."

"Your children?" Hofmann looked at the count incredulously.

"Yes. My children." The smoke rose above him, swirling to the high ceiling. "Everything you take is a child of mine. And of Germany." He laughed and fixed his eye on Hofmann. "Although the ones you are taking are all illegitimate."

"Mein Herr, all will be well." Hofmann needed to cut the conversation short. "But we must move on quickly." He rose from the table. "It will soon be dark, and my convoy must cover a great distance."

The count stood and grabbed the SS man's lapel to whisper in his ear. "Krebs told you where to take these treasures?"

"Yes, mein Herr." Hofmann responded with a whisper. "To Alt Aussee. There's a salt mine there where the conditions are perfect for their protection. The Führer's own collection will be housed in the salt mine along with yours until the Führermuseum is built in Linz."

"And if my acquisitions ever come into danger of falling into enemy hands?"

"I am to ensure their destruction. Along with the Führer's collection."

"I hope to God it will not come to that."

"It is the Führer's express wish." Hofmann freed himself from the count's grip and stepped backward. "And now you must excuse me, mein Herr. I have far to go." Hofmann inclined his head in salute.

"But of course, Brigadeführer."

The count drew on his pipe as he watched the SS officer leave the room. He felt confident in the man. Hofmann's battle group would take only those works of art that he had acquired by the plunder of his agents. Everything that must be prevented from falling into the hands of the Americans, everything that could incriminate him. Those works of art that had come down to him from previous von Schellendorf generations would remain in the castle. Surely the Americans could not confiscate what was rightfully his property?

The count went to the sideboard and poured himself a glass of port, despite his doctor's orders. It had been a long, trying day. He deserved it.

Frieda's cottage.

"A scrumptious meal," Stanislaus put down his fork. "I haven't eaten so well since—", he smiled as bittersweet memories flooded back.

"What are you going to do, Herr Konec?" Frieda watched the oil lamp's flickering light play across his face.

"Get back to Poland." There was a quiet determination in his voice, as if his aim were nothing more than catching a bus. "To find what is left of my family."

"But the Russians—" Frieda held back her words. He would surely know the Red Army had swept across his country.

"I'll take my chances." He broke off a crust from the loaf and mopped up the last drops of juice. "And what are you going to do?" His question caught her off balance.

"I'm not sure. It's clear Trudi and I are no longer safe here." Her hands nervously twisted her handkerchief. "I probably should go to Sulzbach, to my sister, but the thought of leaving – of being on the road with a child – it scares me." Frieda was distraught; never had she felt so paralyzed with indecision.

"The war has taken everything from us." He got up from the table and went over to the bookcase. "There's no longer a place we can call home. Where we feel safe." His eyes wandered over the books. "What about your husband? Is he still fighting for the Führer?"

She thought she heard resentment in his voice. "He's dead." She wanted to tell him more, but she still found it difficult to talk about his death.

"I'm sorry." His commiseration was brief. "So the war has taken from both of us the persons we love."

She looked for any emotion on his face but there was none, only a grim determination to escape.

"But you must realize that wherever you go," his thumb pointed to the door, "there are hundreds like him roaming the countryside."

The memory and fear returned to Frieda. The clawing hands, the smell of the man's breath.

"Anyway, you asked me to go, and I will." He picked up the small bundle he had brought with him and began to tug at the rickety door. "But when you do work up the courage to go, make sure to take that with you." His head nodded at the rifle propped against the bookshelf.

"It doesn't work." She looked at him, cursing her inadequacy. "Please, please don't go."

North of Nuremberg.

The light was fading fast as Terrill ran through the gears of the jeep. The sergeant's new job of being chauffeur to two art treasure seekers was supposed to be an easy number, but these guys were crazy.

"Can't we go any faster?" Major Donovan's voice came from the passenger seat.

Faster? Was the son-of-a-bitch in his right mind? The dusk was closing in, and he wasn't sure of their position. Perhaps the road ahead hadn't yet been fully cleared of Krauts; maybe there were some Hitler lovers beyond the bend in the road. His first mission with his new bosses was making him long for the good old days with Captain Henderson.

"I'm sorry, sir, but I think we're lost." Terrill fought to keep disrespect from his voice. He brought the jeep to a halt.

"Lost?" The lieutenant's voice came from the back of the jeep. She was beginning to get on Terrill's nerves. What the hell was a broad doing so close to the combat zone anyway? He reached for a map and shaded his flashlight with his hand.

"But we've got to get to the castle before nightfall." Her voice was strident. "There are reports of artworks there."

"Yes, ma'am." Terrill pored over his map, trying to suppress his anger. There was a war out there. Men were dying. And she wanted to look at paintings.

"We received a report that our troops will occupy the castle this evening." The major added his two-cent's worth. "It's important that we make our presence known there as soon as possible so we can begin our inventory of the castle's important art objects. GIs have been known to have sticky fingers."

Terrill wondered how many GIs had died capturing a castle full of fancy paintings. So what if the ones who made it helped themselves to a silver fork or two for their troubles?

"Sir," Terrill folded his map, "the castle is about eight miles away." He turned to the major. "But the sun is setting, and I can't be sure that the road ahead is clear of the enemy."

The major peered at his watch. "Let's press on – I'll take my chances."

Terrill thought of defying the major's order. Probably a month in the stockade. His hand reached for the gear shift.

"What's that noise?" The question came from the dame.

Terrill tensed. The rumble came from up ahead, beyond the brow of the hill. He listened to the growing noise. He had heard such a noise before.

"A lot of trucks." He looked through the gathering gloom. "Maybe some half-tracks." He moved the shift stick into gear.

"Maybe they're ours." The woman shouted.

Terrill backed up and did a U-turn.

"I don't think we should hang around to find out." He pressed his foot on the gas pedal.

Frieda's cottage.

For a long moment Stanislaus did not speak. The half smile on his lips gave Frieda cause for anxiety.

"Please don't go, Herr Konec," she repeated, hoping he would not misunderstand her.

"As you wish, mein Frau."

"My name is Frieda Engelsing."

"Frau Engelsing," he said, dipping his head. He put down his bundle; his smile broadened. "I must say I wasn't looking forward to roaming the mountain roads of Bavaria in the dead of night." He returned to the bookcase, his eyes scanning the shelves. "And now I get to read for the first time in months." His hand ran along the books. "I'm overwhelmed with the choice. Goethe. Schiller." She saw him pluck a volume of Heine's lyric poetry off the shelf. "And not a copy of *Mein Kampf* in sight." He turned and looked at her. "This is not the library of a Hausfrau."

She got up from the table and tossed another log onto the fire; the wood crackled and sparks shot up. "I studied at the Ludwig Maximilian University in Munich. My husband was—"

He raised his palm to stop her. "Let's not talk about the past. Only tomorrow is important."

"Yes, tomorrow." She sighed; she didn't want to think about the following day. She didn't know what to do. "Do you have a specific plan?"

"My plan is to read a little," he smiled, "and then sleep on a comfortable bed for the first time in years."

He saw her body tense as he sat down on the settee. "Right here, if I may."

"But what are you going to do—", she lingered over her next word, "tomorrow?"

"I'm going to head eastward." He seemed annoyed by her question; he put down the book, got up from the settee, and picked up the hunting rifle.

"But you'll be heading towards the Russians. From what I've heard, they've not been any kinder to your people than the Nazis."

He shrugged. "What can I do? I'll just have to risk it." He tried without success to move the jammed bolt of the gun. "Do you have any oil?"

"I have a bit of lard." She went to the cupboard next to the sink and pulled out a jar.

He brought the rifle over to the table and sat down; his hands ran over the weapon and then set it aside. "Look, if you're serious about leaving this place, maybe you and your daughter should come with me tomorrow."

His proposal stunned her. "Go with you? Why would I go with you? I don't want to head east. Dear God, I've heard talk about the Russian soldiers—I've heard they have no respect even for young girls." She squeezed her eyes shut and sat down at the table opposite him. "Besides, where would I be heading?"

He shrugged. "If you don't want to head east, I guess you'll need to go west, towards the Americans." He looked at her and then averted his eyes. "And if you do that, you'll probably meet hundreds of…." He picked up the rifle and began to work on it.

Frieda recoiled at his words, fear shooting up from the pit of her stomach to her scalp. Perhaps she could just stay put, go neither east nor west, just stay in the cottage. She clung to the option briefly, but knew it was a false choice. Although the cottage was isolated, she and Trudi could soon become prey to the marauding bands of slaves. No, they had to go. But where? And how?

Through the doorway she could see the blue vase with the flowers she had picked that morning. Picking daffodils, planting her vegetable garden, sewing dresses for the butcher's daughters, darning socks – suddenly she ached for all the commonplace comforts she had taken for granted and now knew she would have to abandon. The day had brought events that had destroyed her normal life forever. Worse, it had brought decisions that needed to be made but offered little choice.

Whatever her decision, the Pole would be heading east. If she headed west she might find the Americans less brutal than the Russians, but she and Trudi would be alone on the road facing the laborers who were now looting Germany, seeking revenge.

She looked at the Pole, who was absorbed in repairing the rifle, and realized that the war that had thrown them together had cast her down into his position. Like him, she and Trudi no longer had a home. Worse, none of them had a country. His Poland had been destroyed; her Germany had been broken beyond recall.

Her mind desperately sought a shred of hope. She had no close friends nearby to whom she could turn. But in her last letter Erika, her sister, had urged her to bring Trudi and stay in her home in Sulzbach. The town was farther from the fighting; perhaps she and Trudi could find some respite there, a haven the war would pass by. But how would they get there? Train connections were complicated; God only knew if any trains were even running. Frieda was alone, confused, defenseless. She closed her eyes tightly and fought to hold back tears.

"I think you and your daughter should come with me, Frau Engelsing." The Pole spoke softly without looking up from the rifle that he turned in his hands. It was as though he had read her thoughts.

She hesitated. She wasn't sure she trusted him. She wasn't even sure she liked him. But what options did she and Trudi have? "Why should you want to help us, Herr Konec?"

"Perhaps it's an exchange for the bratwurst and sauerkraut." He looked up at her and smiled. "Or perhaps it's because I think we can help each other. How's your jaw?"

Her fingers ran over the bruise. "I'm fine. I'll survive."

"Let's hope we all do. Now I suggest you get some sleep." He tried to stifle a yawn. "I'm rather tired, myself. Perhaps I'll skip the reading tonight."

As he settled himself on the small sofa, she picked up the oil lamp and forced her weary body toward her bedroom. She had made her decision.

She turned as she heard his voice.

"Sleep well, Frau Engelsing. We'll need all our strength. For tomorrow."

North of Nuremberg.

The jeep slewed from side to side as it careered along the road. Terrill cursed under his breath. He wanted to floor the gas pedal, but the hooded headlights barely picked out the road ahead. And the noise of the motors behind persisted, a throbbing that filled the night air.

"I can see lights behind." The woman's voice came from the rear seat.

"Thank you, ma'am." He peered through the windshield, trying to pick out the road. "Please let me know if they get any closer." He wondered why he was speaking politely. He was scared shitless.

He knew the convoy was German – they moved at night to avoid getting shot up by American fighter planes. The Americans didn't move after nightfall. Unless they were crazy treasure seekers, like the major and the broad.

His eyes scanned the road ahead. Any turn-off would do.

"They're getting closer."

Almost too late, Terrill saw a track leading off to the right. The sliver of a moon picked out a farmhouse a quarter of a mile back from the road. There were no lights.

"Hold tight!" He turned sharply onto the track, hoping the jeep wouldn't turn over in the mud. The vehicle slithered to a halt. He switched off the lights and killed the engine.

"Is there anything we can do, Corporal?" The dumb question came from the major.

"Yes, sir." He heard the roar of the approaching convoy. "Be quiet. And pray."

Lumberg Castle.

Although darkness had long since fallen, the magic of the Sauternes still lingered and the count reminisced about the first time he had tasted Château d'Yquem. He had made a visit to Poland to see his agent in Warsaw in '37 and had been thrilled to receive a kind invitation from Prince and Princess Czartoryski to visit their estate near Krakow. The count puffed contentedly on his pipe as he recalled his stay in the Czartoryski chateau. Such refinement, such elegance. The prince had recently inherited the chateau from his father and had great plans for his castle, his museums, and his art collection. Understandably, he was anxious about the threat of Hitler.

The princess was fragrance personified. Had he been a younger man…. the count dismissed the thought – his tastes had long since become more ethereal. For many years, his desire had been fired by fine art, by the lines of classical sculpture, by portraits from the hands of the masters.

And there was one portrait in the Czartoryski collection with which he had fallen in love. On the last day of his visit, the prince and princess had taken him to see some of their collection. He had marveled at the many excellent paintings, but had been stunned by one in particular: Raphael's *Portrait of a Young Man.*

The Raphael was a three-quarter portrait of a handsome youth, a fur draped rakishly over one shoulder, an elegant hand resting nonchalantly on a ledge. The young man's enigmatic half smile and scornful gaze spoke to him. 'I know all about your indiscretions, but still I love you.' From the moment he saw the Raphael, he knew that he had to own it, to possess it, that it had to be his alone, to be denied the eyes of the Czartoryskis, Hitler, and the rest of the world. His alone.

The count put down his pipe and smiled. The Raphael was indeed his. Almost. The painting was not in Hofmann's consignment. His prize, stolen from Hans Frank, Hitler and the Nazis, was hidden well away from human eyes.

The count went to the sideboard and poured himself a port. He deserved it. After the war, when Hitler, the Nazis, and the Americans had all gone, he would retrieve the portrait from its hiding place. The rich taste of the port rolled over his tongue. And Raphael's Young Man would be his. And his alone.

North of Nuremberg.

The three Americans crouched in the jeep in the barnyard off the edge of the road, their breath ghostly clouds in the cold night. The roar of engines from the other side of the hill grew louder, rolling around the night sky like an unending rumble of thunder.

"How do you know they aren't our troops?" Gina whispered.

"I don't." Terrill grabbed his submachine gun from the rear seat. There was a click as he released the safety catch from the weapon. "But let's play safe and keep quiet."

The hooded headlights of the first truck appeared at the brow of the hill leading down towards the farm, followed by another and yet another. Terrill saw half-tracked troop carriers and cursed under his breath as he saw the German cross painted on the door. The ground began to shake as the convoy neared the farm. Gina pressed her hands to her ears to ward off the all-enveloping noise.

Terrill watched the half-shapes in the glimmer of light given by the moon and grimaced as he saw the SS insignia. He'd long since lost any belief in the power of prayer, but he hoped his luck would hold. A submachine gun against a battalion of SS thugs was not a good hand to hold. The choking diesel fumes rasped in his throat, but he could also smell his fear and that of the major beside him. Fear knew no rank.

He glanced behind at a barn, and then the farmhouse, some two hundred yards back from the road. Surely they could hear the noise. But there were no lights. Perhaps the farmer was keeping his head down, hoping the war would pass him by.

Just one minute. One more minute and the Germans would be gone. Suddenly, there was a loud crack, followed by the screeching of brakes. The convoy, tires screaming, ground to a halt.

"Hurry," Terrill whispered, "head for the barn."

"Why have they stopped?" Major Donovan whispered anxiously as he peered through a crack in the barn door. "Did they see the jeep?"

"I don't know." Terrill watched as a score of SS men jumped down from one of the trucks. He saw flashlights penetrate the dark. Please don't see the jeep. Please don't see the jeep. Terrill's mind repeated his silent prayer.

In the beams of the flashlights, he saw an officer approach the men, barking orders. He was surprised at the lieutenant's voice in his ear. "The truck has a flat tire." She whispered.

"How do you know?" Terrill asked without taking his eyes from the throng of SS soldiers.

"Because I understand German."

There was more shouting from the road.

"What are they saying now?"

Gina listened. "The officer's mad. He wants the convoy to get moving."

"They haven't seen the jeep?"

"No, he's cursing his men, telling them to change the tire on the double."

Terrill saw two soldiers roll a spare tire from the back of the truck. The officer shouted and gesticulated. Suddenly, Terrill tensed. In the pale light, he saw that an SS soldier had walked across to the entrance road to the farm. Surely he could see the jeep, even in the weak moonlight. The soldier took one step, then another.

"Vorwärts!" The shout came from the officer.

"They're going." Gina said.

The air filled again with the roar of engines. The SS man turned and ran with the others, scampering to board the trucks. Terrill, his body shaking, watched with relief as the last truck disappeared from sight.

South of Nuremberg.

A t last they were going to see action. Wolfgang was nervous but excited. After they'd escaped the shelling of the town, a truck had taken them to a depot where they each were issued a Panzerfäust. Wolfgang drew comfort from the feel of the cold steel of the tank-destroying weapon in his hands.

The squad had been posted to join a regular infantry unit. Wolfgang had felt insulted by the army regulars. They sneered at him and his Hitler-Jugend comrades. Wolfgang clutched the weapon tightly. He would show them.

Ulrich was leading the squad, marching behind the regular troops along a tree-lined road. Wolfgang looked up at the shoots burgeoning from their buds. Spring. The lonely warble of a solitary bird. He heard other noises up ahead. Explosions. The rattle of machine gun fire. The crump of shells.

Aim for the tracks, the drill sergeant had said. Disable the tank.

"Wolfgang," Ulrich, turned to him and called out. "I can't go on. My boots are killing me."

Wolfgang ignored him. Ulrich had always played the big shot at camp, and, now, as they were about to go into action, he was moaning about his boots. He was a disgrace to the Hitler-Jugend. He was—

The noise came from beyond the hill ahead. The roar was unlike anything he had ever heard, like a thousand wild beasts searching for prey.

"Hit the dirt." The shout came from the sergeant at the head of the convoy. Wolfgang scrambled for the ditch at the side of the road. The mud clutched at his knees and elbows as he struggled to prop his weapon on the edge of the ditch. The noise grew, swelling, filling the air, pounding pain into his ears. The ground began to shake. He looked up and saw the American tank loom at the top of the hill.

On the road to Lumberg Castle.

Terrill maneuvered the jeep carefully through the debris of a bombed-out village. Rubble littered the streets; the smell of cordite hung in the air; smoke wafted from the smoldering ruins.

"Are we on the right road for the castle today? Or are we lost again?" Donovan's voice came from the back seat.

"I think this is the road, Major," he brought the jeep to a halt, "but we'll have to wait a bit while our guys clear a path." He pointed to a team of engineers working on the road ahead with a bulldozer. "Mind if I have a cigarette while we're waiting?"

Terrill took the impatient grunt to indicate agreement, cut the engine, and leapt out of the jeep.

"I think I'll join you." The lieutenant jumped out, pulling her jacket down over her hips.

They both moved to the front of the jeep. He offered his pack of Lucky Strikes and she took one.

"It was a bit of a wild ride yesterday." Terrill felt nervous in her presence.

"Our thanks go to you, Sergeant, for getting us back to camp safe and sound."

He was charmed by her smile. "But it was you knowing the lingo that really saved the day." He raised the lighter to the cigarette in her pursed lips and wondered if she felt his sudden tremble as her long fingers grasped his hand to steady it. "Are your folks from Germany?"

"With a name like Gina Cortazzo? Hardly. I learned German in grad school. I wanted to write my dissertation on Matthias Grünewald, and all the good source material was in German." Smoke drifted from the half smile on her lips.

Terrill looked at her blankly. "Matt—*who?*"

"Grünewald. He was a painter of the German Renaissance. I really worked myself silly in school. Had to do it for my dad – he was working his own rear-end off to pay for my education."

"What does he do?"

"Janitor. For a school in Wilkes-Barre, Pennslyvania." She wondered why she was revealing her past to him. "What does your father do?"

"I think the road is clear now." The shout came from the major in the back of the jeep. "Let's get going."

Terrill looked down the road at the group of engineers beckoning them forward. He ground out his cigarette with his heel and watched as she swung her long legs into the passenger seat.

"My dad works hard, too. Runs a candy store on West 45th and Tenth Avenue." He climbed into the driver's seat. "But I never made it to college, so I guess he didn't work hard enough." Their eyes met for a moment before he slammed the jeep into gear.

On the road in Bavaria.

Frieda was tired. They had been walking for hours. Trudi clung to her hand, her steps weary, reluctant. They stopped for a few moments and Frieda put down the suitcase that contained some changes of clothing for herself and Trudi. With her free hand, she tugged her beret down over her blond hair and pulled her overcoat tight around her body. Never had she known so cold an April. Was there no end to the winter? Would there be no spring, no hope, ever again?

She picked up the suitcase and hurried after Stanislaus walking before her, his eyes fixed on the road ahead. He had slowed his pace, she knew, to allow her to keep up with him. The knapsack, crammed with his few clothes and with every morsel of food from the house, swayed on his back with every step he took.

Before long, he would desert her, she knew. He had the food, and he clutched the rifle he had repaired in his hand. She had come with him only because of her fear and the need to protect Trudi, the hope of reaching her sister's house. The shudder of her body owed little to the cold, more to her memories of that leering face, the dirty grasping fingers—

She forced herself to concentrate, to make a plan. She would get away from him, too. At the first opportunity she would take a bus, a train to the east. To Sulzbach. To her sister. But what if there were no buses, no trains? What if the bombs had destroyed the roads and the railroad tracks?

Stanislaus had stopped. On the road stood a group of men, gaunt of face, their clothing scruffy. In their eyes, she saw the look of the slave laborer who had smashed down her door.

"Mutti, I'm frightened." Frieda felt her daughter's body press anxiously against her own.

"Don't worry, Liebchen." She squeezed Trudi's fingers reassuringly, trying to hide her own fear. The men came closer. She could see hatred in their sunken eyes. About a dozen. Several were carrying cudgels; one held a spade and waved it menacingly. She felt her daughter's hand tighten in her own and turned her eyes to Stanislaus.

His face was tense, his jaw clenched. He stood between the men and Frieda, holding the rifle against his chest. The men stopped; some edged backwards, fearful of the weapon.

She heard Stanislaus's voice, speaking in a language she didn't understand. The men suddenly relaxed. Like Stanislaus, they were Polish slave laborers.

"What do they want?" she asked.

"Nothing." He spoke over his shoulder. "They want to go west, into American hands."

She saw their anger return at the sound of spoken German.

"Stop talking." His voice was curt, anxious. "They think I'm defending Germans."

The crowd began to encroach on Stanislaus angrily; the man with the spade raised it in the air.

Frieda heard the noise come from nowhere. At first a drone, then an angry screeching of airplane engines. The men began to scatter, diving for the ditch at the side of the road. Stanislaus turned, pushed Frieda toward the ditch, then grabbed Trudi. The bullets of the fighter planes began to rip into the road. One man was hit. His body jerked and his knees buckled as he fell to the road.

Stanislaus tossed the child into the ditch alongside her mother and threw himself atop both, trying to cover them with his outstretched arms and sparse frame. He heard the spatter of bullets and the raging roar of the plane's engine. But above the roar he heard another plaintive sound. The wail of fear from the child beneath him. He felt the shaking of her body.

"Mutti, Clothilde's frightened."

South of Nuremberg.

Wolfgang peered through the long grass at the edge of the ditch. The behemoth lurched forward, engine growling, tracks clacking on the road. He had seen tanks in the newsreels at the cinema, but nothing compared with the huge beast lumbering towards him.

His hands began to align the sights of his Panzerfäust. There was a tug at his ankles. He turned his head. Ulrich's face was white; his eyes bulged and his body shook with fear.

Wolfgang kicked the hand away. He, too, was afraid, but knew he must not show his fear. The words of the SS leader at the Hitler-Jugend camp returned to him. Duty to the Führer and to the Fatherland comes before self. He struggled to aim his weapon. The tank was almost upon them. One shot. One shot to expunge the guilt of his father. He swung the weapon around. A father who betrayed the Führer. Aim for the tracks.

The explosion surprised him. Someone else had fired a shot. He watched the shell bounce harmlessly off the tank's armor. The tank paused, then came on again, bullets spitting from the machine gun port, kicking up dirt on the road.

Shouts came from the ditch ahead of him as the bullets found their mark. He felt a movement behind him and turned. Ulrich had leapt up from the ditch and was running down the road, away from the tank. Wolfgang glanced back as he ran through a gate and across a ploughed field. Ulrich's flight stopped as the bullets hit him. His hands flailed in the air before his body crashed to the road.

Ulrich's boots would hurt him no more. Wolfgang ran for his life.

On the road to Lumberg Castle.

"Sir, there's something I'd like to ask, if I may." Terrill glanced in the rear-view mirror at Donovan and cleared his throat as he shifted down.

"Yes," Donovan replied distractedly, his finger continuing to move along the map he was studying, "what is it, Terrill?"

"I hope you won't think this question is out of line, but why is all this art we're trying to find so darned important? A buddy of mine got killed, and no one made as much of a fuss over him being dead as this art that's gone missing." A vision of Kolevsky passing around the goodies his mom sent him darted through Terrill's mind; one Kolevsky was worth a dozen of the horse's ass in the back seat.

Donovan looked up. "Hmm…why does art matter? Interesting question; we used to have this conversation over drinks when I was an undergraduate at Harvard."

Terrill could see the stuffed shirt holding a fancy scotch glass with his pinkie stretched out. Oh, how too, too divine.

Donovan furrowed his brow, trying to think of a way to explain concepts he and his classmates had debated at Harvard to a man with only a high school education whose father owned a candy store in Hell's Kitchen.

"Art matters because, well, it's an expression of beauty that has the power to move us." He looked up at the sky as he savored his next words. "I'd say that art has the power to speak to our souls through the language of our eyes. We have to save the art because it's the purest expression of our collective spirit – all of our pain, love, and fear, all of mankind's truth – it's all embodied in art. Art outlives man."

"I see, sir. Thank you, sir." Pompous bastard. His bullshit plus a nickel would pay for a ride on the New York City subway.

Gina rolled her eyes. She could tell that Donovan's academic gibberish hadn't even begun to get through to Terrill. Probably Donovan had made things worse; while Terrill's friend lay dying, the privileged scions of rich men with expensive art collections debated aesthetics over cocktails. She craned her neck toward Donovan in the back seat. "May I add something?"

Donovan, once again absorbed in the map, flourished his hand in the air by way of reply.

"Sergeant Terrill, look out the window and tell me what you see," Gina said.

They were driving through the outskirts of the bombed-out village. A woman was sifting through the rubble, searching for something. A small scowling child with dark shadows under her eyes clung to the woman's skirt and sullenly watched the jeep go by. A dead, bloated horse lay by the side of the road.

Terrill was about to say that it looked as though the world was up shit creek without a paddle, but decided to tone it down. "As my old man would say, it looks like the world's gone to hell in a handbasket."

"Exactly." Gina nodded and looked out at a tree, split down the middle, stabbing the sky with barren boughs. "Outside is the face of war. And war is us at our worst."

Terrill frowned. "Us?"

"Human beings. All of us."

"Oh, right."

Gina brightened. "But art is us at our very best. If we don't save the art, we'll forget who we can be and lose the better part of ourselves. We might as well go back to living in caves."

Terrill narrowed his eyes. "Yeah, I think I get it. We messed up the world pretty bad. The Krauts may have started it, but what good did it do for us to go and bomb these poor folks to kingdom come?" He slowed the jeep as they passed an old man hobbling on unfamiliar crutches, a bandaged stump for a leg.

"I guess we can't undo all the bad stuff that's already been done." With a flicker of a smile, Terrill glanced at Gina. "But saving the art – hey, maybe that's something."

On the road in Bavaria.

The hum of the aircraft engine faded as the plane receded into the western sky, leaving a momentary silence of fear and death.

"Quick, we need to get away from here." Stanislaus leapt from the ditch, lifting the sobbing child gently, then pulling Frieda to her feet.

The escaped laborers also scrambled to get up. Some gathered around the body lying in a pool of blood by the side of the road; others stared sullenly at Stanislaus. Frieda stooped to comfort her daughter.

"Pick up your suitcase and start walking." There was a harsh urgency in Stanislaus's voice. Frieda recovered the suitcase from where she had dropped it in the middle of the road, her hands still shaking with fear. She saw the men move slowly towards Stanislaus, menace in their eyes.

He leveled the rifle at them and they stopped.

"Walk, Frieda!" His voice was insistent. "For God's sake, walk!"

She grasped Trudi's hand and they made their way behind Stanislaus toward the men in the middle of the road. Stanislaus thrust the rifle forward and the men stepped aside. The child looked up fearfully as they passed through.

"So you're now a protector of a German whore."

Frieda turned to Stanislaus. "What are they saying?"

"It doesn't matter. Keep walking."

Stanislaus prodded the rifle into the belly of one of the men. The rest stood aside, allowing them through.

She followed Stanislaus, pulling Trudi behind her.

"Mutti, I'm afraid." The child's other hand clutched her rag doll tightly.

Frieda shared her daughter's emotions. Would they ever be free from fear?

Lumberg Castle.

"That's some swank joint." Terrill eased the jeep to a halt in the castle courtyard and whistled. "Outside of Penn Station, I never saw anything like that before."

"The 'joint,' as you call it, Bill," Gina smiled as she jumped down, "is known as Lumberg Castle."

"The ancestral home of the von Schellendorf family for centuries." Major Donovan's voice was almost reverent. "History is embedded in its walls."

"History in its walls." Terrill thought for a moment. "The most history we ever had on our walls was a picture of Lincoln on a calendar from the coal company."

Terrill looked at the dogfaces guarding the building, smiling, chewing gum, glad they had landed a cushy post. He bet they didn't care about the history, embedded or not. Terrill edged toward Gina. "Lieutenant—"

"Bill, I've told you to call me Gina." Her smile disarmed him.

"Gina, refresh my memory – why are we here?" He leant forward and whispered in her ear. "Why have we risked life and limb to get to this place?"

"As Major Donovan explained, we received reports that there is stolen art in the castle."

Stolen art. Terrill looked again at the GIs standing listlessly around the courtyard and wondered if they knew they had risked their lives for old paintings. Perhaps the lieutenant should speak to them about art. Better yet, let the major explain.

They made their way to the castle's entrance.

"Guten Morgen, my lady and gentlemen." Terrill could not believe his eyes. The guy who opened the door was dressed like a penguin. Eleven thirty in the morning and the guy was dressed in tails, like Fred Astaire about to do a routine with Ginger Rogers. The penguin said something else in broken English.

"What'd he say?" Terrill asked Gina. "I couldn't understand him. And who is he?"

"He's the count's butler," Gina said. "And he's inviting Major Donovan and me to lunch with the count."

"Terrill, wait here with the jeep," ordered the stuffed shirt's snooty voice.

Gina turned to Terrill and shrugged her shoulders. "I'm sorry, Bill; I'm afraid you're not invited."

South of Nuremberg.

Wolfgang's lungs heaved as he ran across the ploughed field. The Panzerfäust weighed heavily on his shoulders, the oozing mud clung to his boots. Ahead, he saw several Wehrmacht soldiers, like him running for their lives. The bullets zipped around him like angry insects. There was a gap in the hedge at the far end of the field.

A soldier in front of him suddenly stopped and fell to the ground, his hands clawing at the earth for a few frantic moments until his body shook and fell still. The gap. The gap. Wolfgang called upon his legs to overcome his fear, his exhaustion. He had to make it to the gap. He cursed as he tripped over a furrow. The Panzerfäust flew from his hands as he fell to the ground.

He struggled to his knees and looked behind him. The American tank had smashed through a gate to the field. The tracks struggled with the mud, but the beast came on. Wolfgang reached for the Panzerfäust. Maybe one shot would delay the tank, giving him time to make the gap.

He swung the weapon to his shoulder. Despite the noise he heard only the voice of the camp instructors. Check projection. Aim for the tracks. Keep the hands steady. Squeeze the trigger gently.

The recoil hit his shoulder, knocking him backwards. He dragged himself up from the soft earth. Flames came from the side of the tank. Elation overcame his fear. He had struck a blow for Germany! For the Führer! He punched the air.

And then he saw the American solder. He was standing away from the tank. Wolfgang turned to run, but he slipped on the mud of the field. His fingers clawed at the mud as he tried to scramble on hands and knees. He heard the crack of the rifle; a bullet zinged past his head.

Fear pulled him to his feet. He looked over his shoulder; the American was again taking aim with his carbine. There was no escape.

The explosions made him jump. The American was tossed into the air by the shells bursting around the tank.

Mortars. German mortars.

Lumberg Castle.

"My dear Major, I'm so delighted to meet you." The count inclined his head as he shook Donovan's hand. "And I find it a great pleasure to welcome a lady to Lumberg Castle." His fingers gently lifted Gina's as he bent forward to place a formal kiss on the back of her hand.

Gina felt embarrassed. "Thank you, Count von Schellendorf, but our visit is official. We're from—"

"Of course, your visit is official," the count smiled, "but we can still make it pleasant." He motioned to his butler, who began to walk across the room. "And Florian has prepared an excellent lunch of roast lamb. Please join me in the dining room." The butler stood aside as the corpulent count, rocking from side to side, made his way down the hall.

Gina felt uneasy. She looked across at Donovan and saw an obsequious smile on his face as he followed the count.

"My compliments to your chef, Count von Schellendorf." Donovan placed his knife and fork, tines down, in the center of his plate. "I haven't tasted lamb like that since I left Boston. And while I regret to say that I speak no German, I must say that your English, too, is excellent."

"The result of a privileged education. I spent three years at Oxford. Some more Margaux, Major?"

"May I ask, Count," Gina dabbed her lips with a crisp, monogrammed napkin, "where you get such fine meat? Everywhere we go in Germany we find such great privation." She ignored Donovan's reproving look. "Many of your people are very hungry."

"Yes, I know; it is most unfortunate." The count looked down into his glass of wine. "I must admit, dear lady, that the situation is bad in Germany, and that I receive the benefits of aristocracy." He took another sip of wine and set his glass down; the butler carefully poured him some more. "Perhaps I should feel guilty, but these things are not easy for an individual to correct."

Gina was flushed, angry. "Maybe—"

Donovan cut her off with a sharp look accompanied by a barely-noticeable shake of his head.

The count ignored Gina and addressed Donovan. "I believe you came to discuss an official matter."

"Well, sir, we have reports that important works of art are being stored in Lumberg Castle."

The count threw his head back and gave a polite laugh. "But of course there are important works of art here, Major." He leaned forward and smiled. "The von Schellendorf family has been collecting art for centuries." He motioned to a portrait over the fireplace. "That man, Count Alois Ludwig Friedrich von Schellendorf, began the collection," his hand turned to point toward a large oil painting over the sideboard, "when he traveled to Venice in 1562 and purchased that masterpiece."

Gina's eyes widened as she beheld Titian's *Susanna and the Elders.*

"Magnificent, isn't it?" The count signaled to his butler. "But I am neglecting my duty as host. Port, Major? I'm sorry," he laughed, "but the British stopped shipping the Stilton five years ago."

Donovan smiled his acceptance, but Gina held up her hand in refusal.

Donovan sipped at his glass. "A truly magnificent vintage, Count."

"I'm sorry to be blunt, Count," Gina saw Donovan's smile disappear, "but we're not here on a social visit. We're looking for stolen art."

"Stolen?" The count quickly put his glass down and frowned; his body stiffened. "I can assure you, young lady, that every work of art in the castle is the legitimate property of the von Schellendorf family."

He turned to address Donovan. "Major, the provenance of the von Schellendorf collection has never been called into question; you need only consult the appropriate *catalogues raisonnés* for any works you see here to authenticate ownership." There was anger in his voice. "Surely, you're not going to impound the art that has taken generations for the von Schellendorfs to collect?" He threw his napkin on the table. "If you will follow me to the library, I can show you records of—"

"There will be no need for that, Count." There was embarrassment in Donovan's voice as he got up from the table. "Our people will come in the next few days and make a catalogue of your art, but it will be a mere formality."

The count turned and nodded, then reverted to his native language as he spoke to his butler.

Gina stiffened, then got up from her chair. "Thank you for an excellent lunch, Count, but now we must leave." Hiding her anger, she gave the German her best smile. "I'm sure you realize we have much work to do."

"Of course, of course." The count pressed his lips to the back of her hand, then shook hands with Donovan. "Major, you can be assured of my every cooperation."

As they walked out into the courtyard, Donovan released his anger. "Why did you have to give the count such a hard time, after he received us so cordially? Clearly, he's completely aboveboard."

"Aboveboard?" Gina spoke sharply. "When he spoke to his butler, he said he was expecting a phone call from General Krebs."

"What does that matter? Who the hell is Krebs?"

"Krebs, if you read last week's report, Alan, is Hitler's Chief of Staff."

On the road in Bavaria.

Stanislaus felt spots of rain on his face and knew he had to find them shelter before nightfall. The small rail worker's hut by the side of the track looked deserted; he motioned for Frieda and the child to stay back as he approached warily.

He had decided that they should stay off the roads and follow the railroad tracks. Although the tracks were sometimes bombed by the Americans, he judged it a better risk than another encounter with a vicious band of feral human beings. Besides, they needed to get to a train and there would be a station somewhere down the track.

But stations meant other people, and other people meant trouble, so they'd have to time their arrival at the station carefully – just in time to catch a train, if possible. Maybe eventually they'd find a train to Sulzbach for Frieda and Trudi and then, with luck, he'd find a way back to Poland.

Stanislaus held the rifle tightly as he approached the railroad worker's hut, praying to a God he knew no longer existed. He was surprised to find his prayers answered as he discovered the door to the hut locked – there was no one inside. He smashed at the lock with the stock of the rifle until the door flew open.

"Mutti, it's not a very nice house." Trudi hesitated in the doorway of the hut. Stanislaus tried to smile reassuringly at the girl and ruffled her hair. He turned to her mother. "Wait here while I check it out."

He could see little in the darkness of the hut. He struck a match and was relieved to find an oil lamp hanging just inside the door. He had trouble prying the glass off and he needed two matches to prompt the stubborn wick, but the lamp's pale light eventually flickered into life.

He looked around and shared Trudi's opinion. There were few creature comforts. There were no windows and the low roof forced him to bow his head. A small canvas cot occupied the full length of one wall. In an opposite corner sat a squat stove, covered in dust, and a box with kindling wood. A wooden stool and a chair stood in front of the stove.

"Well, it's hardly the Grand Hotel," Stanislaus beckoned Frieda and Trudi inside, "but at least it's a roof over our head."

The girl made her way to the cot, propped her rag doll at one end and sat down. "Mutti, I don't like it here. Neither does Clothilde. Please, Mutti, let's go home."

Frieda stooped and held her daughter's face in her hands. "We can't, Liebchen. There are nasty men there."

"You mean like the men we met on the road? Men who—" She saw the reproving look in her mother's eyes and fell silent.

"Perhaps we can get a fire going in here." Stanislaus stood the rifle in a corner, eased the knapsack from his back and opened the door of the stove.

"Mutti, I'm hungry."

"Doesn't the child ever stop—" He bit his lip as he saw the pained look on Frieda's face. "I'm sorry." He busied himself with the stove. "I'm tired."

"Let's see what we've got left in the knapsack." Frieda pulled out the wrapped packages of food. "Look, we have some ham and sausage." She gingerly removed the thermos. "Maybe the soup's still warm."

"Mutti, I got to go pee-pee."

Stanislaus sighed heavily.

Grounds of Lumberg Castle.

Terrill could see that all was not well between the lieutenant and the major as they approached the jeep. Gina looked as though she'd got a run in her last pair of nylons and Stuffed Shirt looked as if he'd just seen his beloved Red Sox lose a five-run lead to the Yankees in the bottom of the ninth.

"There was no need to be so rude to the count, Gina." The major shot her a withering look. "He's a man of refinement and taste – and excellent lineage – trying to protect his art collection."

Terrill could smell the booze on his breath. No wonder he hadn't been invited to the party – a low-class guy like him wouldn't have appreciated the vintage.

"But what about the phone call from Krebs?" Gina's eyes flashed angrily. Terrill made a mental note not to get on the wrong side of the lieutenant.

"You're being paranoid, Gina." He climbed into the rear seat of the jeep.

Terrill thought the lieutenant was about to explode but she caught his eyes and bit her tongue. She flounced into the passenger seat. "Let's get back to headquarters, Sergeant."

She must be really angry. Lately she'd been calling him Bill.

Terrill's hand turned the ignition and hovered over the gear shift. "Say, does your count own a fleet of trucks?"

"What are you talking about, Terrill?" the major asked angrily, leaning forward.

"Well, I haven't seen so many tire tracks since I was in base depot." He pointed to the paving of the courtyard.

"What are you trying to say, Sergeant?"

"Look at all the oil stains. There's been a lot of trucks here. Recently."

"Really, Terrill." Donovan crossed his arms over his chest and looked away. "You have such a vivid imagination."

Terrill slammed the stick into gear and let out the clutch quickly, deliberately throwing the major back hard against the seat.

"Do you really believe there were trucks at the castle recently, Bill?" Gina asked.

"Yep. As sure as the pope's Catholic."

"There's no need to bring religion into it, Sergeant."

It hadn't occurred to Terrill that the Boston Brahmin would be a religious man. A man from Boston. With a name like Donovan. Terrill ran through the gears. He should've known better.

A railway worker's hut.

The smell of wood smoke filled the hut. "Pity about the leak in the stovepipe." Stanislaus sat on the floor in front of the stove. "But at least it's warm. And she's comfortable." He nodded towards the cot where Trudi lay asleep, her rag doll enfolded in her arms.

Frieda got up from the stool and smiled as she put her coat over the child. "Why are you doing this, Stanislaus?"

"Doing what, Frau Engelsing?" The question caught the Pole unaware.

"Protecting us." She squatted back on the stool. "And please call me Frieda. We've been through too much together to continue to address each other formally. But tell me – why are you helping us?"

"I don't know." Stanislaus looked at her eyes, made brighter by the light from the flickering oil lamp which cast rippling shadows on her face. "You helped me back at the cottage." He gave a sheepish grin. "Maybe I just want to get you and the child to safety."

Frieda looked at her sleeping daughter and then stared into the light of the lamp. "Where can we ever be safe again, Stanislaus?" Her body began to shake; the light picked out the tears on her cheek.

Stanislaus got up and put an arm about her. "I don't know, Frieda." He tried to ignore the warmth of her body. "But we mustn't give up hope. Maybe tomorrow we'll get a train to Sulzbach."

"Maybe the Nazis will just go away." She could not hide the sarcasm in her voice. "Maybe the Americans will suddenly stop bombing. Maybe it will be nineteen twenty-six again."

He ran his hand over her hair. "Maybe we'll find a train tomorrow. And soon the war will be over."

A square in a town south of Nuremberg.

Clump! Clump! Clump! Clump!

Wolfgang was mesmerized by the measured beat of the boots of the Waffen SS battalions on the cobbles of the town square. The sun was about to set and the light was beginning to fade. The soldiers quickly formed three sides of a square; at the open end of the assembled storm-troopers was a hastily-erected dais. Wolfgang saw the tall, erect figure of the brigadeführer enter the square and felt a surge of hope. At last they had leadership.

Wolfgang stood with the Hitler-Jugend troop just to the right of the dais. Two members had been lost in the action. He tried to push the memory of Ulrich's boots from his mind as he watched the brigadeführer mount the platform. Wolfgang had escaped death only by luck. If the SS battalion hadn't arrived…The shape of the American tank leapt into his mind, the angry whine of the bullets rang again in his ears. Wolfgang shivered, despite the warmth of the evening sun.

"Soldiers of the Third Reich." Hofmann's powerful voice brought Wolfgang back from his nightmare. His eyes glistened with pride as he looked at the SS officer; he was a true leader, a man in the mold of the Führer.

"Today, we gave the Yanqui swine a bloody nose."

Wolfgang heard a murmur of agreement from the thousand men gathered in the square, all standing erect and proud. Surely with such men the Reich was safe.

"We have won a battle." The brigadeführer's triumphant cry rang around the square. "Now we will win the war!"

Wolfgang joined in the cheer that rose from the troops.

"Soon," the bridageführer lifted his hand for quiet, "soon, we will go to form a fortress against the barbarian hordes to protect our beloved Führer, Adolf Hitler."

A greater roar rang around the square. The brigadeführer raised his arm in salute and a thousand arms lifted in unison. *"Heil Hitler! Heil Hitler! Heil Hitler!"* Wolfgang's heart beat fast and his lungs pumped hard as he joined in the tumultuous shout.

The brigadeführer lowered his arm and the troops were suddenly silent, as if he had given an order.

"We will win the war through bravery. Courage will be the corner-stone of our success." Although his voice was quieter, in the stillness of the square every word was clear.

"I have seen many acts of valor from you men. But today I saw one defender of the Reich whose act of selfless heroism must not go unrewarded. Alone and unaided, one of our young soldiers destroyed an American tank. Step forward, Hitlerjunge Wolfgang Engelsing."

Wolfgang felt shock at hearing his name and did not move.

"Our young soldier is modest." The brigadeführer laughed. "Hitlerjunge Wolfgang Engelsing, come forward."

Wolfgang marched toward the dais, his heart swelling with pride as he heard the cheers of the troops. He stamped his feet as he came to attention in front of the brigadeführer.

"Hitlerjunge Engelsing, effective immediately, I promote you to scharführer. And this," the brigadeführer turned toward a box on a table behind him, removed something, and held it out to Wolfgang, "is a token of my appreciation of your bravery."

Wolfgang looked down at the knife with its SS insignia, like twin lightning bolts, on the pommel; a fine leather-encased steel scabbard with an embossed swastika enclosed the blade. His pride consumed him as the troops cheered.

97

"And as a scharführer, you will also need one of these." The brigadeführer turned again to the box and pulled out a Luger. As he held it out in
the palms of his hands, Wolfgang thought that in all his life he had never
beheld an object so splendid. He was breathless; at last he had begun to
expunge his father's treachery. Another cheer went up as he reached out
and took the pistol.

The brigadeführer shook Wolfgang's hand. "Scharführer Engelsing,"
he spoke in a conversational tone, "in further recognition of your contribution to the Fatherland, I invite you to ride with me in my staff car on
the next leg of our journey."

Hofmann turned to face the troops. "And now, men, we have work to
do!" he shouted. "We march to save the Reich!"

A railway worker's hut.

F rieda's dream vanished as she awoke. She had been in a favorite Munich restaurant with Hans in the halcyon days....Her fingers brushed the sleep from her eyes. The shabby interior of the hut quickly destroyed the magic of her dream. The smell of wood smoke still hung in the air, but the stove had gone out; it was cold. She rubbed her limbs, aching and sore from sleeping on the hard wooden floor.

Bleak reality jolted her as though she had been kicked in the stomach. They were homeless, wandering around the country. Would there be any end to their misery? She looked across at the cot. At least Trudi was asleep, at peace temporarily from the nightmare. Frieda gave a rare smile as she saw Clothilde's button-eyed face locked in her daughter's arm. She remembered when she had sewn on the buttons—

He was not there. Stanislaus had gone. Her eyes cast quickly around the hut. No rifle, but he'd left the bag of food. She began to hurry to the door, but stopped and eased herself gently onto the cot, anxious not to disturb Trudi.

She heaved a sigh of weary resignation. She'd half expected it. He owed her and Trudi nothing. He'd saved her twice, and now he just wanted to pursue his dream of returning to Poland.

"Mutti," Trudi stirred slowly from her sleep, "are we going home soon?"

"Soon." Frieda felt guilt at her facile ability to lie to her daughter. Where was home? Perhaps she could reach Sulzbach to be with her sister, to be with family. But what would she find there? Russians approaching?

"Clothilde wants to go home, too, don't you Clothilde?" Trudi bobbed the doll's head up and down to show her agreement.

"Soon." Frieda forced a smile as she repeated a promise she knew she could not keep. She knew that when her daughter expressed feelings through her doll, there was a yearning deep within her heart.

Trudi looked around the hut. "Herr Konec's not here, Mutti. When is he coming back?"

"I don't think he'll be back for a long time, Trudi."

Her daughter frowned as she considered her mother's words while Frieda picked up the knapsack and rummaged through it for the remnants of their food. The loaf was hard, stale, almost finished. There was half a sausage and a half-full water bottle. She struggled to hide her despair.

"What's a long time, Mutti? Will Herr Konec be back by this evening?"

"I don't think so, Liebchen."

She could see that Trudi was disturbed, but she couldn't go on lying to the child forever. She had other problems – she hadn't washed since yesterday morning, her body was aching, and her heart was heavy. Her son had deserted her. And how was she to find food? She couldn't stay in the workman's hut, but if she stepped outside....She realized how dependent she'd become on Stanislaus. She hadn't meant to. If only—

"I think he'll be back soon, Mutti."

"Perhaps, Liebchen."

Perhaps. If only. Frieda put down the knapsack. Too many 'if onlys.' Stanislaus had gone. Now she'd have to find her own way. "Come, Trudi," her hand reached out, "we'll have breakfast later."

Frieda knew that once she left the shed she'd be alone to confront the dregs of society who were roaming the roads of Bavaria. Hungry, desperate, devoid of all reason. Like the rabble they had met on the road and the beast who had burst into her cottage. When they left the sparse comfort of the hut, there would be men seeking to defile her, and worse, her daughter.

She stepped back in fear as the door to the hut flew open. "Frieda, bring Trudi, quickly." Stanislaus stood in the doorway. "I've been down at the station – there's a train leaving for Sulzbach later today."

Trudi jumped up from the cot and ran to him. "Herr Konec! We missed you!" She turned to her mother and beamed her a smile. "You see, Mutti, I told you he'd come back soon."

Frieda could not suppress a sigh for the relief she felt. But there was also another emotion stirring within her, and it troubled her.

Workroom at US Third Army Base. After lunch.

"Good afternoon, gentlemen," Gina called out cheerily to the two GIs who had been recruited to help pack artworks for shipment to the collecting point in Munich.

She looked through the window at the pale afternoon sun, her mind dwelling on yesterday's encounter with the count. His suave, man-of-the-world façade had fooled Alan, but she wasn't taken in by him.

Halfheartedly she began to think about her tasks for the rest of the day, but no sooner had she taken off her cap than she put it back on and made for the door. Perhaps it was female intuition, but she was sure the count was lying. The phone call from Krebs was the clincher. When Donovan said he didn't understand German, the count must have assumed that she, Donovan's lowly female subordinate, didn't understand what he was saying either. But why would the count need to talk to Hitler's Chief of Staff?

Gina was surprised to find Terrill outside, leaning against the wall and twirling his cap around his finger. When he spotted her, he put on his cap and snapped to attention.

"Lieutenant," he gave her a salute, "can you spare a moment?"

"Bill, I thought we were on a first-name basis when you're off duty."

"Sure thing, Lieutenant." He returned her smile nervously. "I mean, Gina."

"What's on your mind, Bill?"

"Well, it's about those tracks and oil patches back at the castle."

"You think you were wrong about them?"

"Hell, no. I—" He stopped and put his finger to his lips. "I'm sorry; I didn't mean to swear."

Gina ignored his apology. "So you think trucks really did call at the castle?"

"Yeah, lots of them." Terrill nodded. "And I got to thinking about the other night, you know, when we almost got run down by that German convoy."

"What about it?"

"Perhaps that Kraut convoy had stopped at the castle – perhaps they were the trucks that left those tracks." Terrill shrugged. "Of course, I can't be sure. It's just a hunch." He wondered if he was getting in over his head; looking for danger at this point in the war ran counter to his personal philosophy of staying alive.

"But why would a convoy of trucks be calling at the count's castle?"

"I don't know." Terrill stooped down and picked up a few pieces of wood shavings from the ground. "Say, what is this stuff?"

"It's excelsior – wood shavings that we use to pack art objects before we ship them to the Munich Collecting Point. Why do you ask?"

"There was a lot of this stuff in the stables at the castle." He let the shavings drop from his fingers. "I was having some bad java there with the dogfaces while you and the major," he smiled, "were drinking fine wine—"

"You saw excelsior in the count's stables?" Gina ignored his jibe.

"Excelsior?"

"The wood shavings."

"Yeah, it was all over the floor of the stable—" He stopped short as he made the connection. "Say, maybe the trucks – the Krauts—"

"Were packing works of art. And then took them away." She looked at her watch. "Bill, can you take me to the castle this afternoon?"

"No problem. Now that the Krauts have been pushed out of the area, it'll be easy."

"Then let's go." She strode to the jeep and jumped into the passenger seat.

"What about the major?"

Gina knew Donovan wouldn't ask the count the kind of questions she had in mind. "We don't have time." Her hand rapped on the dashboard as Terrill turned the ignition. "Move it."

Train station in Bavaria.

The crowd filled the platform. "Stay together," Stanislaus shouted above the hubbub as he grabbed Frieda's hand. He hadn't expected so many people; he should have known better. Desperation was written on every face. Some milled around; others, resigned, sat on their suitcases. All, like them, looking for escape.

Escape from the war – a war that had seemed remote, but was now coming to their doorstep. He looked at the frightened faces strewn along the platform. Perversely, he wondered what their emotions had been in the early years of the war when Hitler's armies had conquered most of Europe. Perhaps they had raised their glasses to celebrate his victories; now their glasses were empty. All they wanted was to get away, to seek refuge in a place that had somehow escaped the war's reach. They were like victims of a tidal wave, seeking higher ground and hoping the water would come no farther.

He steered Frieda and Trudi through the crowd, most of whom peered down the track, as if willing the train to arrive. A man on a bench glanced up, looked askance at Stanislaus's gun, and yielded his seat to Frieda. She pulled Trudi onto her lap.

"Have you any money?" Stanislaus leant forward and whispered his request.

"Money?" She frowned as she looked up at him.

"We need to buy tickets."

"Oh, of course." She pulled a small purse from her pocket and opened it. "There's fifty Reichsmarks." She looked around her warily as she thrust the notes into his hand.

"Wait here," he squeezed her fingers, "and hide this." He pulled the gun from his shoulder and shoved it behind the bench. "We can't take a weapon on the train with us – too suspicious."

Trudi looked up at him with a smile. "Come back soon, Herr Konec."

On the road to Lumberg Castle.

Terrill slowed the jeep to a halt at the camp's exit.

Gina furrowed her brow. "Why are we stopping?"

"Just a sec." He traded a few wisecracks with the guard at the gate. "Radio a message to those guys guarding the castle – tell 'em we'll be arriving in about half an hour."

He slipped the jeep into gear and pulled away from the gate, then turned to Gina. "To answer your question, with the war nearly over the last thing I'd want is for us to get killed by friendly fire." He chuckled.

"I wonder what high-ranking genius thought up that claptrap. 'Friendly fire.' Since when has fire ever been friendly?"

"Oh, I hadn't thought of that."

"That's okay. You just keep taking care of the important stuff, like finding the lost portrait of Lord and Lady Throgmorton. I'll look after the minor details, like keeping you and me alive." He wore a cocksure grin. Their exchange that morning seemed to have emboldened him.

He saw her eyes flash reproach. "Look, Gina, all I'm saying is that sometimes you gotta rely on gut instinct."

"I beg your pardon?"

"Gut instinct. It's got me through a lot of this war so far. That, and a bit of luck."

She crossed her arms. "But after the war, what are you going to do then? Do you plan to rely on your so-called gut instinct then?"

"Only if the right girl comes along." He turned to her and gave her a wink. "But I'll still need luck for that to happen."

Gina sighed and gazed up at the sky; the clouds reminded her of a Constable landscape. "Seriously, Bill, what do you plan to do after it's all over?"

Terrill thought for a moment. "Seriously? Nothing serious." He grinned at what he thought was his clever play on words. "Share a serious pizza pie with my buddies at Luigi's, play some serious stickball with my kid brother—"

"But don't you want to make something of yourself, Bill?" Gina looked at him earnestly as she continued to try to elicit a reasonable response. "Just in case the right girl comes along?"

"At the moment, my only ambition is to become a civilian. A *live* civilian."

She sighed and turned in her seat as she fell silent. Why, she wondered, was it so hard to have an intelligent conversation with this man?

"Heck, I'm sorry, Gina," he saw she was annoyed and rapped his fingers on the steering wheel, "but, damn it, I find it difficult to take the future seriously anymore. I've seen so much shit—beg pardon, Lieutenant."

"Don't you want something better after all you've been through?" Gina realized she was lecturing him and softened her voice. "Have you heard of the GI Bill?"

He scratched his head. "The GI bill? Jeez, don't tell me they've figured out a way to make GIs pay for being over here."

Gina rolled her eyes but couldn't suppress a chuckle. "The GI Bill, for your information, is a move to give all GIs returning from the war a free college education."

"Wow." He gave a low whistle. "That's great, but I really don't need a college degree to drive a cab around New York." He took the jeep through the gears and waved a hello to one of the guards on the approach road to the castle. "But now that I think about it, maybe that's not such a bad idea. Say, after I become educated, do you think highbrows like Major Donovan will be able to stand the competition?"

Gina held his glance for a few moments and then looked away as he winked at her again; she was beginning to wish she had kept her relationship with Terrill more formal.

As they passed through the gates of the castle, the guards saluted. At the end of a tree-lined avenue rose the castle, the morning sunlight glinting in the windows of its tall towers.

"Well, here we are." Terrill stopped the jeep on the cobblestone courtyard, pulled on the handbrake and jumped down. "Let's go see what your count has to say for himself."

Lumberg Castle.

The portraits of his ancestors looked down from the walls of his study.

The count sat in his favorite armchair, scanning his private notebook that lay on his lap and sipping from the port glass in his right hand. He felt good, his well-being warmed by the digestif and the news he had received from Krebs. His art acquisitions of the past several years were on their way to Alt Aussee, to be stored with the Führer's own collection.

He put down his glass and read a few of the entries on the open page. Botticelli's *Bacchus and Ariadne,* Rubens's *Allegory of Wisdom,* Rembrandt's *Christ Feeding the Five Thousand.* When the war was over, he would be reunited with his precious treasures. And if he could not enjoy them after the war, then no one would. Because they would not exist – Hofmann would have destroyed them, along with the Führer's own collection. And no one would ever be the wiser.

But one masterpiece would always survive. He turned the page and checked the entry in his notebook. *Portrait of a Young Man.* The priceless Raphael. Only one other knew the hiding place. He would retrieve it when it was safe to do so, after the war.

The count closed his notebook and reached again for the glass of port his doctor told him to avoid. He took another sip. What did doctors know?

A train in Bavaria.

Stanislaus looked at the humanity crammed into the carriage. While he longed to go home to Poland, he knew that Frieda and her daughter would have a rough time alone in a world of every-man-for-himself. Now, having begun this journey with them, he had to see them to safety before striking east to his homeland.

The train was crowded but there was little noise. People sat on the benches, hugging the cases and sacks containing their meager possessions. Some looked through the window, but their eyes did not see the passing Bavarian countryside. Others looked vacantly at their feet, their thoughts remembering a better past or pondering an unknown future.

He sat uncomfortably on the floor, his arms wrapped around his knees, rocking as the train rattled along the tracks. He looked up at Frieda. Her eyes were tired, but she returned his smile. Trudi's head lay on her lap; the child was lost in the land of dreams. Stanislaus yearned for the escape of sleep, but knew he had to remain vigilant. Some had already looked at him with suspicion, the dark three-day growth on his face making him stand apart from the blond Germans.

"It's all over." An old man spoke to no one in particular. "Why doesn't Hitler surrender?"

"Shush!" His wife sitting next to him dug her elbow into his ribs. "You don't know who's listening."

Despite his perilous condition, Stanislaus found it difficult to suppress a smile. Though these people had celebrated when Hitler's army had crushed Poland, they were now dancing to a different tune.

"It's terrible, isn't it?" The woman addressed her remark to Frieda. "And you and your husband having to care for a child, as well."

Stanislaus caught Frieda's hasty glance before she looked back at the woman. "Yes, it's terrible."

The train lurched. Trudi stirred and raised her head from her mother's lap. "Mutti, when are we going home?"

Stanislaus sensed the silence in the carriage. Home. They all wanted to go home. He wanted to go home, too. But where was home?

There was a screech of metal as the brakes began to grind the train to a halt.

"Everyone off the train!"

Stanislaus heard the shout and looked out of the window. The train had stopped. SS soldiers lined the platform.

"Everyone off the train!" the gruff, disembodied voice shouted. "Papers! Show your papers!"

Lumberg Castle.

"We're here to see the count!" Gina brushed past the butler as he opened the door into the dimly-lit hall.

"Nein, dear lady," he stuttered in broken English, grabbing her arm.

"Better not do that, penguin." Terrill grabbed the man by the lapels and the German let go. "Hey, what d'ya know, he understood my German." Terrill laughed as he thrust the butler aside.

Gina spoke to the butler in his native language. "I need to see the count."

His eyes widening as he realized she was fluent in German, the servant answered her at once.

"What's going on?" Terrill asked.

"The count's in the library. Let's go!" Her shoes clipped on the parquet floor as she hurried down the hall. Terrill followed, keeping an eye on the butler, who followed them warily.

Gina clutched the polished brass handle and threw open the door to the library. She stopped in the doorway and gasped, her hand flung over her mouth.

The count was lying on the floor. Beyond his outstretched hand lay a broken glass; a red stain spread near it on the carpet. From his ashen face, his sightless eyes looked at the portraits of the ancestors he had joined.

"Christ!" Terrill's shout broke the eerie silence. "Shall I call for the medics?"

Gina stepped forward, bent down, and lifted the count's wrist. "It's too late. He's dead."

Terrill took a step backward, amazed at Gina's poker face as she let the hand drop.

"Mein Herr, mein Herr!" The butler, tears running down his face, raised his hand to his mouth in alarm and pushed his way past Terrill.

Gina saw the small leather-bound notebook half-hidden under the count's body. Her hand reached out and grabbed it as the butler fruitlessly stroked the count's face. She glanced quickly through the pages.

"Call the medics, Bill." Gina tucked the notebook into her pocket. "Get him out of here." She looked down at the body. "Fortunately, it doesn't look as though the count has taken everything to the grave." She tapped her pocket. "I may have his secrets here."

On the train.

"Papers! Have your papers ready!" The voices of the SS soldiers carried above the murmurings of the people on the train.

Stanislaus hastily looked through the carriage windows as the occupants shuffled to the front of the car. On one side stood the station. He could see the hostile expressions on the faces of the soldiers lining the platform. Through the windows on the other side, he saw a lake.

"Everyone off the train!" He heard the shout again. "Papers! Have your papers ready!"

"What are we going to do?" Frieda whispered as she stood up and grabbed Trudi's hand. Stanislaus raised his eyebrows as he looked at her. She needed to do nothing. She could just get off the train. Her papers were in order.

"Perhaps you'll think I'm crazy," she hesitated, about to answer his unasked question, "but I want to help you, as you have helped us. Besides," she lowered her eyes, "we need you." She ran her hand over her daughter's head.

"Are we going home now, Mutti?" Trudi looked up at her mother.

"Soon, sweetheart, soon." She bent down and planted a kiss on her daughter's head.

"Perhaps we could pass you off as my husband," she suggested as she followed the others to the end of the car.

"It wouldn't work." He looked again at the soldiers on the platform and could feel beads of cold perspiration breaking out on his forehead; his mouth was cotton dry. "I haven't any papers."

Lumberg Castle.

Gina sat on an armchair by the fireplace in the Great Hall, thumbing through the count's notebook, heedless of the American medics carrying out the stretcher on which lay the mortal remains of the German nobleman.

"You're a cool character, Gina." Terrill's jaws continued to move as he chewed a stick of Wrigley's Spearmint. "Shouldn't you be showing some respect for the dead? Even though he was a Kraut?"

"The man was a fraud, a rogue." Her eyes remained riveted on the notebook. "The evidence is in this book. He stole some of the finest artworks of Europe."

"Well, they're sure no good to him now," Terrill grinned, "unless there's an art gallery in hell."

Gina ignored him and continued to turn the pages of the notebook. As she reached the last page, she gave a low whistle. "Wow, jackpot!"

"Huh?"

"Listen to this." She read from the notebook.

"Holbein's *Portrait of a Saxon Prince*, Canaletto's *View of Santa Maria del Glorioso*, Bellini's *Madonna with Olive Branch*, Leonardo's *Virgin of the Cave....*"

"Big-time art, I suppose?" For Terrill, she might as well have been calling out the runners in the fifth at Belmont.

"Big? They're huge." Gina's finger ran down the list. "Hmm, there's an asterisk next to each of these works. Let me see if I can read the footnote at the bottom of the page." She tried to make out the count's handwriting. "I think it says *to be taken to Alt Aussee to be stored with the Führer's personal collection."* Her eyes widened as her head shot up. "My God, Bill – we've won the biggest jackpot of all time with this one!" She furrowed her brow. "I wonder where this Alt Aussee place is."

"Search me." The sergeant shrugged. "Damned if I know."

Gina's eyes turned back to the notebook. "Hey, here's one that doesn't have the asterisk. Raphael's *Portrait of a Young Man."* She raised her eyes, remembering a conversation about the painting she had had with Donovan a while ago. "As I recall, the Raphael was stolen recently – from a man who had stolen it from a Polish museum."

"You mean the thief stole the painting from another thief?" Terrill bit his lip but couldn't suppress a snort. "I guess there's just no honor among thieves anymore."

"This is not a laughing matter, Sergeant. That painting is one of the greatest works of one of the greatest masters of the Renaissance."

"Sorry, Lieutenant."

"Strange." Gina closed the notebook. "The fact that there's no asterisk next to it means there's no destination listed for the Raphael." She rose from the armchair. "Maybe it'll be found somewhere here at the castle when our guys come to catalogue all the count's works." She frowned. "Or at least, I hope so. But somehow I doubt it. And if the painting isn't here, then where is it?"

On the train.

Stanislaus forced himself to keep calm. He looked out of the other side of the car; the sun was beginning to set behind the mountains that framed a broad expanse of water. There were no guards on that side of the train.

Stanislaus spoke quickly. "When we get to the front of the car, go to the side opposite the station – the side where the lake is." They joined the end of the line of exiting passengers and inched their way forward.

As a large knot of people began to clamber down from the train towards the guards, Stanislaus used them as a screen and jumped out the opposite door, reaching up to lift Trudi to the ground, then helping Frieda down. He took a quick glance under the carriage and saw the legs of the passengers milling about and the shiny black boots of the guards. They had not been spotted. A hiss of steam released from the engine pierced the gathering dusk.

He turned and looked across the lake, placid, unruffled by any wind. A large building stood on the other shore, now almost invisible against its backdrop of mountains in the gathering gloom of dusk.

In front of him was a grassy bank leading down to a path by the side of the lake. "Quick!" He picked up Trudi and motioned Frieda to follow as he descended the bank. The hubbub on the platform began to die away as people began to reboard the train.

"Where are we going?" Frieda asked as they half ran along the path.

"To be honest, I'm not sure." Stanislaus tightened his grip on Trudi as his feet negotiated the unpaved path. He felt sharp stones through the thin soles of his worn shoes and Trudi seemed to become heavier with every step he took. He stopped and looked around for Frieda; she was far behind.

"Stanislaus!" she called to him in a low voice as she came nearer. He waited for her to catch up. "Stanislaus, there's a monastery across the lake." Her words were choked as she tried to catch her breath. "If we can make it over there somehow, you could ask for sanctuary."

Frieda's suggestion surprised him. "Sanctuary? Sanctuary from the Nazi thugs?"

"Can we please stop for a moment?" Frieda asked, panting as she put down her suitcase. "I'm out of breath."

Stanislaus looked behind him up the hill; the train was beginning to depart and the guards were leaving the platform. "Five minutes, no more." He gently dropped Trudi to the path and squatted next to Frieda, who lay on the grass next to her suitcase.

"The Benedictine monks at the abbey across the lake used to have a tradition of giving sanctuary." Frieda regained her breath and reached for her daughter. "Perhaps they still do."

"How do you know all this?" Stanislaus rummaged in the haversack for the water bottle he had refilled on the train.

"I used to come here with my mother and sister when I was a girl."

Stanislaus saw her eyes mist over, gazing into a long-distant past; he handed the water bottle to Trudi, who drank thirstily.

"It was so long ago," Frieda sighed. "Happy days. We used to—"

"How can we get to the monastery?" The urgency in Stanislaus's voice dispelled her reminiscences.

"We always went across the lake by boat from the station." Frieda clutched Trudi, whose head had fallen on her breast. "She's very tired."

"We can't afford to stop any longer. I'll carry her. The boat's not an option; is there any other way?"

"There's a footpath that goes around the southern end of the lake, but it's a long walk."

"We have no choice." He took the sleeping child from her arms, gently draped her over his shoulder, and began to walk along the path. He looked across the lake at the monastery, which was now caught in the light of a full moon. "What's the name of that monastery?"

"Errenbach." Frieda hurried behind him with her suitcase. "It's very old; it was founded hundreds of years—is everything all right?"

Stanislaus had stopped dead in his tracks.

"What's the matter?" Frieda asked again.

"Nothing." Stanislaus resumed walking. Errenbach. He remembered the farmer's brother and the box he had stolen. *I have to get to the monastery at Errenbach,* the man had said. *To the crypt.*

Portrait of a Young Man. Raphael. That was what Stanislaus had seen stenciled on the box. Was the painting hidden in the crypt?

US Third Army Headquarters North of Nuremberg.

"So what's this evidence of hidden art treasures you say you've found?" Colonel Philpott leaned forward over the battered table that served as his desk. His fingers tapped the table impatiently. Having two 'Monuments Men' attached to his staff was a distraction from the real war, but General Patton wanted him to be involved, and Patton was the boss.

"It's all in this book, *Catalogue of Artworks Acquired 1939-1945,"* Major Donovan pushed the count's notebook across the desk, "that Lieutenant Cortazzo found at the castle."

The colonel began thumbing through the pages.

"It's the biggest lead we've had so far." Gina spoke enthusiastically. "There're so many precious works of art listed in that book, works that have been stolen from all over Europe. And most have been moved to a salt mine in Alt Aussee."

"*The Rape of the Sabine Women, The Ecstasy of St. Francis* – sounds interesting but it's all gobbledygook to me." The colonel put the book back down. "We're supposed to be fighting a war." He sighed. Donovan and Cortazzo were self-sufficient and kept out of his hair, but they sometimes ate up his time.

"But this salt mine in Alt Aussee could be the biggest repository of masterpieces the world has ever seen." Gina ignored Donovan's scowl. "German museum curators who have been interviewed say that Hitler's personal collection of looted art may be there, as well. And there's a reference to that effect in the notebook."

"Don't get excited, Lieutenant." The colonel gave her a patronizing smile. "For some reason, General Patton is interested in this stuff." He turned to Donovan. "Is it possible that we'll find more gold with this stuff?"

"Stuff?" Gina's voice was angry.

Donovan gave her a glare that told her to shut up.

"It's possible, sir." Donovan spoke deferentially. "In a few places, we've found a mixture of art and bullion."

"Then you have General Patton's full attention." The colonel stood up from his desk and looked at a map on the wall. "But we have a little problem." His fingers searched over the map. "You say the cache is in a place called Alt Aussee?"

Donovan nodded.

The colonel put his finger on the map. "Unfortunately, Alt Aussee happens to be well behind enemy lines. Our men won't be there for at least two weeks."

"Two weeks?" Gina's voice betrayed her disappointment.

"Look, young wom—" The colonel stopped and corrected himself. "Look, Lieutenant, apart from the military objectives, we've got to consider your safety."

His hand ran over the map pinned to the wall. "We have to make sure all the German troops are captured or swept from this area." He turned from the map. "Not to mention the Werewolves."

"Werewolves?" Donovan wasn't certain that he had heard correctly.

The colonel smiled. "According to our G2 Intelligence, it's the word the Nazis used for partisans." The smile disappeared. "We're treating it seriously. These people – mainly fanatical Hitler Youth – wage guerilla war behind our lines. They engage in arson, sniping, and the like. One of their more gruesome tricks is decapitating motorcyclists by stringing wire across roads."

Donovan gave a low whistle. "But, colonel, surely they know the war's as good as over."

"For some of these people, the war will never be over." The colonel sat down at the table and tapped a cigarette from his pack of Camels. "So, you see, Lieutenant," his condescension made Gina's face redden with anger, "we have your best interests at heart."

"Okay. Thank you, sir." The words came tersely from Gina's lips as she got up. "We'll wait for further orders." She saluted and turned to go.

"But wait, Lieutenant." The colonel reached for a file. "There's something else here that you might like to take a look at." He flipped through the papers. "Apparently, our people have found something in a mine about fifty miles north of Weimar."

"A repository of art, Colonel?" Donovan's voice was respectful.

"I'm not sure." The colonel shrugged his shoulders. "Apparently, our boys have found some coffins."

"Coffins?"

The colonel thrust the file toward Donovan. "Yep, coffins. Why don't you go take a look?"

Along the shore of Lake Hallstatt.

Stanislaus was tired, bone weary tired, but he forced his feet to plod on. Trudi still slept on his shoulder and, despite her small frame, he felt as though he was carrying a lead weight.

"Please, Stanislaus, can't we stop and rest again?"

He looked back at Frieda. Her shoulders were rounded and her head hung as she shuffled along, her suitcase almost dragging on the ground. The moon was beginning its descent in the sky and there was little light.

Stanislaus set Trudi gently down on the grass. "We can rest here for ten minutes." He wiped his brow. "But then we have to press on – we've got to find shelter before dawn. We can't take the chance of being caught on the road in broad daylight."

Frieda dropped her suitcase, crumpled to the ground, and wrapped her arms around her sleeping daughter. Stanislaus sat down and fell back on the grass, straining to keep his eyes open and willing himself to stay awake.

He awoke with a start and cursed himself for having fallen asleep. The pale light in the eastern sky announcing the dawn's approach made his heart sink.

Frieda was still asleep, Trudi locked in her arms, as he stood up, rubbing his eyes. He groaned: there was little chance they'd reach the monastery before daylight; more likely, they'd be discovered by a Nazi patrol. He leaned over and shook Frieda by her shoulders.

"Wake up! It's late and we've lost time! We've got to get a move on!"

Eyes half-closed, Frieda rolled over, propped herself on her elbows, and tried to shake herself awake. Slowly, she stood, picked up Trudi, and handed the sleeping child to Stanislaus. She pulled her coat around her, lifted her suitcase, and set out behind him.

Stanislaus looked across at the monastery, its edifice frozen in the faint pre-dawn light. Perhaps there lay sanctuary. And the art treasure that belonged to his country. Although it was also possible that their reception would be anything but warm if the brothers had thrown their lot in with the Nazis.

"Look! There's a rowboat!"

His head turned quickly to see Frieda pointing to a small dock; at the edge of the water he could make out the shadow of a boat.

"Quick!" He passed Trudi to her mother, ran to the pier, and knelt down to undo the ropes.

Frieda put down the sleepy child and led her toward the boat. "What happens when the owner reports it missing?"

"That's a problem for another day." Stanislaus held the rowboat against the dock. "Get in, but take care – small boats aren't very stable."

The boat rocked awkwardly as Frieda put her foot on the side of the boat.

"No, step inside the boat," Stanislaus whispered urgently. "Sit in the center and I'll hand Trudi to you."

He picked up the girl, Clothilde still clutched tightly in her hands, and gently passed her to Frieda before carefully boarding himself. The moon gave him enough light to ease the oars into position. He began to pull, rowing clear of the dock.

Trudi woke up and, dislodging herself from her mother's lap, began to jump. "Mutti, we're on an adventure!" The boat began to rock violently.

"Tell her to sit down!" Stanislaus shouted angrily. "For pity's sake, hold the child still!"

He looked over his shoulder at the grey expanse of water that lay between the boat and the monastery. "Let's hope we can make the far shore before dawn." The oars swung in his hands and the rowboat headed slowly across the lake.

The first light of the new day began to breech the horizon behind the rowboat. Stanislaus saw Frieda's head nod, unable to ward off the insistent demand of sleep. Trudi, her head nestled in her mother's lap and a pigtail flung across her cheek, had once again succumbed.

The oars creaked in the rowlocks as he pulled on them again, his muscles aching. The water rippled as the oars sliced through it, then slapped against the hull as the boat headed for the shore. He looked over his shoulder: only fifty meters. His arms redoubled their efforts.

The sound of the boat crunching onto the pebbled shore awakened Frieda.

"Let's get out." Stanislaus jumped over the prow and offered his arms to take the sleeping Trudi. Frieda gingerly climbed out of the boat.

"We made it." Stanislaus, breathing heavily from exertion, managed a sigh of relief.

"We have been watching you." The voice came from the shore behind them. "You must come with me."

Stanislaus felt a stab of fear and turned quickly; surely all their efforts had not been for nothing. He saw a man in a dark clerical robe drawn tightly around him with a white rope for a waistband. A monk.

Hofmann's convoy.

H ofmann knew he had taken a major gamble. He tossed his cigarette out of the window of his staff car and ran his hand over the two-day stubble on his chin as he pored over the map. He had decided to run during the day, to chance the possibility of air attack by the Americans.

"So far, so good, sir." His driver leaned forward, looking upward through the windshield at the sky. "No sign of enemy fighter planes."

"Perhaps, Wolfgang," Hofmann looked at the youth sitting next to him, "our luck will hold."

"I have no doubt of it, sir," Wolfgang replied.

Hofmann's finger ran over the map. Another two hundred kilometers to the salt mines of Alt Aussee. He had diverted the convoy onto minor roads; going through large towns would delay progress. The back roads were tortuous, but at least they were unencumbered, and time was of the essence. Any delay would be fatal to his mission to deliver the art treasures to Alt Aussee and to establish the Alpenfestung.

A glance in the mirror showed the trucks containing the art with their armed guard. Behind the trucks, the armored troop carriers stretched into the distance, carrying his men and his newly-acquired Hitler-Jugend platoon.

He looked up again at the sky: still no trace of American jabos. Hofmann was not afraid to confront the Americans on the ground, but he dreaded their air superiority. Besides, the Führer had ordered him to avoid battle until he entered the area of the Alpenfestung and had hidden the art at the salt mines. There, he would have some immunity from air attacks: the Führer had said thirty-five thousand POWs were to be moved there – if there were air attacks, the Americans would be firing on their own men.

As they turned a bend, the driver applied the brakes sharply. "Gott in Himmel!" Hofmann and Wolfgang lurched forward, recovered themselves, and looked at the mass of people blocking the road ahead.

"What is this riff-raff?" Hofmann jumped down from his car, over-come with rage. The throng of wretches filled the road, gaunt, bedraggled figures clad in dirty striped clothing. A handful of SS soldiers stood at the side.

"Sergeant," Hofmann grabbed one of the SS men by the lapels, "what the hell is this rabble blocking my way?"

"Can't you see, sir?" The sergeant pointed to one of the abject creatures at the head of the throng. Hofmann saw the symbol sewn on the man's garb. The Star of David.

Jews. Hofmann knew about the camps for Jews and other *untermenschen,* but he had never seen any of the prisoners.

But what were they doing on the road?

Errenbach Monastery.

Stanislaus's mind raced as they moved along one side of the cloister following the monk, his cassock swaying, his sandals treading softly on the flagstones. Would the monastery give them sanctuary? Or would the monks report him to the local Gestapo office? His eyes caught Frieda's; she responded with a tired smile, then reached her hand out to Trudi, who was trudging wearily behind them.

"Brother Helmut," the booming voice echoed around the cloister, "bring our visitors into my office."

Stanislaus turned in the direction of the voice; through a large Baroque doorway he could see a broad-shouldered man with graying hair sitting at a desk.

"Of course, Father Hieronymus." The monk ushered Stanislaus, Frieda, and Trudi into the room. "Father, these people were found on the shore."

The abbot quickly ran his blue eyes over the three figures standing before him. Frieda gave Stanislaus an anxious look; Trudi tightened her grip on Clothilde, her frightened eyes downcast to the floor. The abbot rose from his chair, and Stanislaus was surprised to see a tall, muscular man of about fifty. There was no sign of religious meekness in his hard, unsmiling face; his calculating eyes continued to flick from him to Frieda, then to the child, probing.

"Why have you come to the monastery?" His voice was low and measured.

"We seek sanctuary." Stanislaus fought against looking away from the glacial, penetrating eyes.

"In the monastery I remember with fondness from my childhood," added Frieda.

The abbot gave a gentle sigh. "So many people seek sanctuary." His fingers toyed with the large crucifix that hung low on his chest. "If we gave sanctuary to every fugitive—" He shrugged and spread his arms wide.

"Mutti, is Clothilde a—" Trudi struggled with the word, "—a fugitive?"

The abbot looked down on the child, a trace of a smile on his lips. "And who is Clothilde?" The hard eyes looked at Frieda. "Is that the child's name?"

"No, it's her doll," there was a nervousness in Frieda's voice, "Clothilde's the name of her doll."

The abbot nodded and returned to sit at his desk. "And why should we give you sanctuary?"

"Because—" Stanislaus started to speak, but Frieda quickly interrupted him.

"My daughter and I were no longer safe in our home," her nervously-spoken words came out fast, "because of the escaped slave workers. This man, here, saved me from one of them."

"So this man," the abbot turned his head and fixed his eyes on Stanislaus, "this man is not your husband."

"No, my husband is dead." Frieda dropped her eyes. "The war."

"So many people have died in the war." The abbot gave another world-weary sigh.

Desperation for the safety of her daughter drove Frieda to take a gamble. "My husband died on July twentieth of last year." July 20, 1944. The date of the failed assassination attempt on Hitler. Frieda knew it was not the precise truth – Hans had died a few weeks later – but he was as good as dead on that day. Frieda waited for the abbot's reaction to the date, a date that had been branded into every German's mind.

For a few moments the abbot said nothing. Then there was the merest flicker in his eyes. "July twentieth?" He stood up from his desk.

Frieda looked down at her daughter and shook her head, hoping the abbot would understand they could not discuss it in front of Trudi: she hadn't told her the true circumstances of her father's death.

"I see." The abbot turned to the monk standing by the door. "Brother Helmut, take the child to the refectory and give her food and drink."

Trudi looked up at her mother anxiously.

"It's alright, Liebchen." Frieda bent down and kissed the top of her daughter's head.

"Will we be going home soon, Mutti?"

"Soon, Trudi." She lifted the child's hand and placed it in the monk's fingers, wondering how many more times she would have to lie to her daughter.

The abbot remained silent until the door clicked shut.

"Do I understand you correctly? Are you saying your husband was involved in the plot to kill Hitler?"

Stanislaus was stunned to see Frieda nodding. He had known nothing about it.

The abbot walked to the window and looked down at the lake. "What was your husband's name?"

"Hans Engelsing." Frieda was subdued as she recalled the memory. "He was a courier for the Resistance. He passed messages to the Allies." Her voice began to tremble as she remembered the day of his arrest, the hard face of the Gestapo man, her husband's mute acceptance of his fate.

"Hans Engelsing." The abbot turned from the window. "I think I remember the name. I read about it in the *Völkischer Beobachter*. A tragic affair." He returned to his desk and sat down. "We have always offered sanctuary to German patriots." He turned to Stanislaus. "But who is this man? He's not German, is he?"

"Let me answer." Stanislaus stepped forward. "I will tell the truth. My name is Stanislaus Konec, and I am a Pole." He said the word with pride. "I was a doctor until the Nazi invasion." He lifted his chin and spoke the next words with no loss of dignity. "Now I am an escaped slave laborer. I did not ask to come here. Now all I ask is repose to wait out the war until I can go home."

The abbot sat impassively as he listened to Stanislaus's story. "My son, I'm deeply sorry for your misfortune. But opening the doors of the monastery to escaped slave laborers would be like opening the flood-gates – we couldn't possibly accommodate them all." His hand toyed with his wooden rosary beads. "Why should God's sanctuary be given to you?"

"For the love of humanity." The vehemence in Frieda's voice surprised Stanislaus. "The man saved me and my daughter from attacks by," her mouth spit out the word, "savages."

"Were they German savages?" The abbot looked at Frieda, who shook her head.

"Whatever you think of me," Stanislaus struggled to control his temper, "surely you'll give sanctuary to the woman and her child. They are German."

"If they are German," the abbot's voice was cold, noncommittal, "then they won't need sanctuary."

"But it could be interpreted that she gave succor to an escaped slave." There was a hint of desperation in Stanislaus's voice. "Wouldn't the police view that as a crime punishable by prison?"

"Probably worse." The abbot got up from his desk. "You must understand that the granting of sanctuary is difficult in these days. People under our protection must be fed and clothed. The Nazi authorities often check the financial books of the abbey. I can hide nothing. And there are regular visits from the Gestapo." The abbot wandered back to the high window that looked over the lake and the approach to the abbey. "Speak of the devil." He gestured down toward the lake. "Here comes a boat with our old friend, Herr Direktor Gruber."

Stanislaus walked to the window and looked out. A stout, bald man with a bushy mustache sat in a rowboat with another man at the oars. "Who is he?"

The abbot gave Stanislaus a thin smile. "Herr Direktor Gruber is in charge of the local Gestapo." Stanislaus felt a flash of fear.

The abbot continued watching out the window. "I suppose he's come about the missing boat. No doubt he's already spotted it on our shore."

A wave of nausea engulfed Stanislaus. "What will you tell him?"

Father Hieronymus turned away from the window and looked straight into Stanislaus's eyes. "I shall tell him the truth, of course. A man of God always tells the truth."

US Third Army Headquarters, north of Nuremberg.

"Catching up on your Dick Tracy, Bill?" Gina entered the canteen and smiled a 'good morning' to Terrill, who was reading the *Stars and Stripes,* a cup of coffee and a half-eaten breakfast roll before him.

Terrill looked up with a sheepish grin. "Nah. I'm strictly a Terry and the Pirates sort of guy. How's the art world making out?"

Gina poured herself a cup and added some powdered milk. "You don't like art very much, do you Bill?"

He shrugged noncommittally.

"Have you ever actually been in an art gallery?" She sat down across from him at the table. "Mind if I join you?"

"Please do." He folded up the paper and put it aside. "Yeah, I was in an art gallery once. On a class trip in sixth grade. I remember we went to see some portraits at the Metropolitan over on East 83rd and Fifth. All the people in the paintings were wearing doilies around their necks and frowning. Like they were auditioning for the 'before' picture in a laxative ad."

Gina laughed, but sighed inwardly. She liked Bill, but they just didn't seem to have much in common.

He leaned forward. "Say, what makes old art better than new art? For ten cents you could buy a Saturday Evening Post and get a free Norman Rockwell on the cover that would look better on your wall than anything I saw at the Met that day."

She wondered if he was intentionally trying to tease her. "Old art isn't necessarily better – it's just rarer. The world will never again see a masterpiece from the hand of Leonardo, so what we have from his studio is priceless."

Terrill pondered what she said. "How do you know there isn't one of his paintings out there that you just don't know about?"

"We don't. As a matter of fact, we know Leonardo painted a number of works that have been lost." She blew on her coffee to cool it.

Terrill tried not to be distracted by her freshly-rouged lips. "Couldn't someone practice painting like he did and pass it off as his?"

"Oh, it's been done many times, but usually it doesn't work. For example, the materials – the wood panels Leonardo painted on right down to the nails in the frames – would have to be of his period." Gina took a sip and put the cup down.

Terrill thought for a while as he popped a piece of bun into his mouth. "What if someone found an old painting on a piece of wood like the painter used and just painted over it?" He leaned back in his chair. The conversation interested him. He liked to learn about ways you could beat the system, even if he personally would never try them.

"Wouldn't work. X-ray analysis would reveal that there was an older under-painting that was not by Leonardo."

He scowled and thought some more. "How about if you took all the paint off first?"

"Still wouldn't work. Chemical analysis of the pigments would indicate the paints were modern. So you'd have to grind your own pigments, as Leonardo did." A shaft of sunlight caught the sheen in Gina's dark brown hair. "Then you'd have to find a way to make the paint dry fast – oils actually take decades to dry completely." She finished her coffee and blotted her lips. "And finally you'd have to find a way to achieve the network of fine cracks that develop over the ages. And your imitation of Leonardo's style would have to be flawless, right down to his strokes and the type of bristles he used in his brushes."

Terrill looked at her, open-mouthed. "Say, that's really interesting."

He caught her off guard; she had expected another wise-guy remark. "It is?"

"Yeah, it is." Terrill slouched back in his chair and propped his hands behind his head. "So if someone figured out how to do all that—"

"If he could fool all the experts, he could make thousands of dollars."

Terrill whistled. "Wow!"

She looked at her watch and put down her cup. "I'd better go. Big day today."

As she rose, he stood up as well. "Thanks, Gina. I really enjoyed talking to you about art."

She looked into his eyes and saw that, for once, he wasn't kidding. "So did I."

While he was finishing his coffee, Terrill watched Gina walk away. The world was going to hell, and here he was talking about art. What was this woman doing to him?

Hofmann's convoy.

From his seat in Hofmann's staff car, Wolfgang could see the muscles in the brigadeführer's jaw clench and unclench with anger.

The wretched crowd of Jews shuffled anxiously. Some looked at the SS men with fear; most averted their eyes, looking disconsolately at their feet.

"Sergeant," Hofmann screamed into the soldier's face, "where are your officers?"

"They've—" the soldier struggled for his words, "sir, they've disappeared."

"Disappeared? *Disappeared?*"

"Yes, sir," the soldier stamped to attention, "the officers gave us orders back at the camp and then left. There are only four of us to guard five hundred prisoners."

"Orders? What orders?"

"These vermin," he tossed his head to indicate the prisoners, "are to be taken to the Flossenbürg Concentration Camp."

"Flossenbürg is now in American hands, you dummkopf," Hofmann ignored the soldier's startled look, "and you now have new orders."

"But, sir—"

"Clear this scum off the road!" Hofmann pulled his Luger from his holster and began firing over the heads of the Jews. Panic seized the mass of people and they scattered in all directions, further infuriating the brigadeführer; he aimed at a Jew and fired a bullet into the man's skull. Gore from the creature's head splattered the surrounding Jews, who sent up an otherworldly wail; the man sank to the ground, his clothes bloody rags.

"If you don't get this filthy lot out of here, I'll kill every one of them." Hofmann's Luger kicked as he fired into the air again. "And I'll shoot you, too!" he shouted at the soldier.

Wolfgang was filled with admiration for the brigadeführer. He was a true leader. The Hitler Youth's eyes turned to look at the pathetic rabble. Some shuffled to the side of the road on bloodstained bare feet, others fell to their knees and were trampled in panic. A few hit their fellow prisoners with their fists as they sought to flee from the guards, who were herding them with their rifle butts.

Above all the mayhem, Wolfgang heard a plaintive moan rise from the throng, a subhuman wail of injured beasts. He felt nothing but revulsion for the creatures before him.

One of the Jews did not move. He stood in front of the car, his staring, vacant eyes fixed on Wolfgang. Rage seized the youth. How dare this Jew be defiant? He jumped down from the car, pulled out his prized Luger and brought the butt down hard onto the Jew's face.

The man continued to stare ahead as he rocked before the blow. As Wolfgang raised the pistol above his head again, a woman's voice cried out from the roadside.

"Can't you see he's blind?"

Errenbach Monastery.

Gestapo!

Frieda gasped and felt faint; she held onto the back of a chair for support.

Stanislaus was seized with panic. He turned to rush to the door, to get away, but the abbot's hands locked around his arms and body. The Pole looked up into the cleric's hard blue eyes, surprised at the strength of his grip.

"Don't be foolish. Do you think you'd get far?" The abbot's question was delivered with an ironic smile. "Gruber's Gestapo bloodhounds would sniff you out in hours."

Stanislaus struggled, but could not free himself from the powerful man's bear hug.

"Brother Helmut, come quickly!" the abbot shouted over Stanislaus's shoulder through the closed door. There was a rapid shuffle of slippered feet on the flagstones in the hall and the door flew open.

"Father!" There was a look of astonishment on the monk's face. "Is everything all right?"

"No, it's not," the abbot said gruffly. "Our old friend Gruber's boat is nearing the shore." He released Stanislaus, his breathing deep with tension. "Brother Helmut, take our Polish guest and give him a robe, a tonsure haircut, and a shave. Even Herr Direktor Gruber wouldn't be fooled by a monk with stubble on his cheeks." The abbot waved away Brother

Helmut, who led a bemused Stanislaus to the door. "And then bring the child back!" he shouted after them.

Stanislaus looked briefly at Frieda and shrugged his shoulders as the monk led him through the door.

Frieda struggled to fathom the abbot's actions. "Father, I don't understand – why are you hiding him?" Her brow furrowed. "You said you were going to tell the Gestapo the truth."

"I always tell the truth." The abbot smiled benignly. "I have found it to be the best policy."

"But if you do that, Stanislaus will be in a Gestapo cell within hours!"

"Truth is a difficult concept to grasp, my child." He looked distractedly at the carved architrave above the window. "I remember reading about an ecumenical council in which the concept of truth was debated for several days—" He broke away from his theological musings and turned toward her. "In any event, what I tell Herr Direktor Gruber will be the truth." He grinned. "However, with Herr Direktor Gruber, I sometimes forget to tell the whole truth."

He walked over to the window and looked out. "But this isn't the time for a discussion of ethics. Gruber will soon be here."

With a swirl of his robe, Father Hieronymus swung away from the window and returned to his desk.

"So, Frau Engelsing, you are a German war widow, are you not?"

Frieda nodded.

"And your papers are in good order?"

"Yes." She reached into her handbag for her passbook.

He took it from her and examined it. "Excellent. I didn't imagine there would be a 'J' on the cover." He looked up at her. "So, to save yourself and your beautiful Aryan daughter from defilement by the rampaging hordes of escaped slave laborers, you came a great distance and borrowed a small boat to seek sanctuary in the monastery you remember with great affection from your childhood. Is not this all true?"

"Yes, but—"

The abbot lifted his palm to silence her. "Herr Direktor Gruber need not know the *buts.*" His eyes sparkled as he savored his conspiracy. "Do you have any other children?"

"I have a son, Wolfgang." Frieda sighed deeply and shook her head. "I'm ashamed to say that he's on active duty with the Hitler-Jugend."

"Ashamed?" Father Hieronymus tapped his fingers on his desk. "Herr Direktor Gruber would not recognize that as the truth, so you'd better leave that part out. He knows you would be proud!"

He stood up. "Your story will warm Gruber's heart. Hitler, himself, might be inclined to pin a medal on you."

A half smile came to Frieda's lips as she grasped the abbot's intentions.

"So, your story is simple. And truthful." The abbot chuckled. "There are a few details that need not concern you. We shall return the rowboat with our apologies to the rightful owner. And we shall make sure that Herr Direktor Gruber will have several bottles of our excellent monastery beer that he enjoys so much."

"But what about Stanislaus?"

The abbot smiled and put his arm around her shoulder. "Ah, yes, Stanislaus. It's really for him you seek sanctuary, isn't it?"

Frieda reddened and looked at the floor.

"Say nothing about your friend." He removed his arm from her shoulder and pressed his index finger to his lips. "And let our beer point Herr Direktor Gruber to the path of truth."

Inside the Bernterode Mine, near Weimar, Germany.

The mine gallery, eighteen hundred feet underground, was large and well lit, but the air was oppressive, heavy, and stale.

"Why did you have to invite Terrill along, Gina?" Donovan hissed his angry whisper into her ear. "He's just a driver – he knows nothing about art and he'll get in the way."

Gina didn't answer at once. She and Donovan were following the captain of the unit that had discovered the hidden coffins. Terrill was walking behind them, swapping stories with one of the engineers.

"I thought Sergeant Terrill might appreciate finding out what he and his buddies are risking their lives for." Gina kept her voice low.

"Tantamount to casting pearls before swine," Donovan harrumphed.

Gina ignored him. "Captain," she called out, "how did you learn about this hiding place?"

"Interesting story. First, some of our guys were lucky enough to find the ammunition cache." His voice echoed around the chamber. "You see, the Germans were storing hundreds of thousands of tons of explosives in this mine. Then we found a wall with fresh plaster, so we knew it had to have been built recently. And here it is." He stopped in front of a demolished wall that had stood across the mine gallery. Bricks littered the floor. "My men needed an hour to break it down – the wall was five feet thick. Behind the wall was a chamber."

"I hope your men didn't disturb the contents," Donovan said curtly.

There he goes again, thought Terrill. The GIs break through a hole in a five-foot wall in a mine filled with dynamite and all Stuffed Shirt can worry about is whether they moved any of his fancy thingamajigs.

"Hardly. In fact, when they got into the chamber, they hightailed out like chickens with a fox on their tails. Seems they'd rather build pontoon bridges under heavy fire than hang around coffins."

Gina shivered, as much with anticipation as with the chill from the musty air that whispered through the chamber. "And that's where you found the coffins?"

"Much more than that. Step in and take a look." The captain pushed on the door that had been behind the wall. Gina caught an amused look on Terrill's face, as though he were about to enter the House of Horrors at an amusement park. She pulled out her notebook as they all followed the captain into the chamber.

"Dear God!" she gasped as she entered.

"I don't believe it!" Even Donovan was slack-jawed.

In the partitioned room lay several immense caskets, dimly-lit by hastily-rigged lights. Unfurled and hung high over the caskets were dozens of German regimental flags, some so old they were encased in mesh to prevent their disintegration.

"Dear God," Donovan looked up at the banners, "some of these must go back to the Franco-Prussian war."

"But who's in the boxes?" Terrill knocked on the coffin closest to him, as though he were ordering a beer at a bar.

Gina edged her way forward. "Look – there are labels taped to the caskets." She peered closely, then drew back. "My God, this one says Frederick the Great!"

"Frederick the Who?" Terrill asked.

"Frederick the Great, as most educated people know, was the most important of all Prussian monarchs," Donovan intoned haughtily.

Gina brushed some dust off the tag on another casket. "This one says Friedrich Wilhelm."

"The Soldier King," Donovan whispered with reverence. A silence hung in the fetid air of the chamber. "It's like the scene of some pagan ritual." He wandered in awe among the coffins and flags.

"How do you know that this guy – the 'Soldier King' – is actually in the box?" Terrill's question broke the magic of the moment.

"It's him, all right. We checked."

"You mean," Gina looked aghast, "you opened the coffin?"

"Had to." The captain shuffled nervously. "The Nazis could have hidden explosives in there."

"Explosives?" Donovan's jaw dropped. "In the coffin of the Soldier King?"

"The Krauts have done much worse, Major. There was the time that—"

"So, is the Soldier King's body in there?" Gina asked urgently. "In the coffin?"

"Without a doubt, miss." The captain moved toward the coffin. "His uniform bore all the medals and regalia of a royal personage." He paused. "Of course, he didn't look too good."

Terrill bit his lip to suppress a laugh, but Gina shivered at the image. She pulled out her folding ruler, extended it to full length, and took the measurements of the coffins. The whole scene seemed oppressive; she felt the weight of centuries bearing down upon her.

Gina bent over to read another tag. "Heck! Wish I'd remembered to bring my flashlight," she said, moving closer. Then she gasped. "I can't believe it!" She rose slowly, wide-eyed and pale. "The tag on this one reads—"

Suddenly, inky darkness descended upon them like a shroud.

"My, God, what's happened?" cried Gina. "I can't see a blessed thing!"

The captain switched on his flashlight. "Sorry about this, folks – the darn generator's gone off again. My guys above will soon have it up and running. Martinez, give us a little more light; switch on your flashlight."

"I can't, sir. No batteries. The supply sergeant ran out. He says he keeps ordering them, but they keep sending him boxes of screwdrivers, instead."

The captain laughed nervously. "Well, that's the US Army for you. But we'll have them back on in a jiffy."

"I certainly hope so, Captain," Donovan said sternly.

"Anyway, as you were saying, Lieutenant—God damn!" The captain's words were cut off by darkness and a rapid clicking as his own flashlight died. "Sorry for the language, miss – I think my bulb must have blown. But everything's under control; no need to worry."

But one person in the party was more than worried. In a corner, leaning against the casket of the Soldier King in the black darkness, Bill Terrill shook with fear. His monster had returned.

Hofmann's convoy.

"Ah, Scharführer Engelsing," Brigadeführer Hofmann looked up from his makeshift seat on the running board of the truck. "You did well back there, helping clear the road of the Jewish scum."

"Sir!" Wolfgang stood ramrod straight in front of his leader. He was proud to serve such a dedicated leader, a man completely devoted to the Führer and the Third Reich. And proud to wear the Luger pistol given to him by the brigadeführer.

"At ease, Scharführer." Hofmann took the cup of coffee from the corporal as Wolfgang stood easy. "I believe I have a special assignment for you."

Wolfgang's eyes opened wide in excitement. Perhaps he would have another chance to fight for the Führer. His victory over the American tank had shown him that he could be tough under fire, that he was brave.

The brigadeführer grimaced as he swallowed the brown liquid. "Pah! Ersatz! When I taste real coffee once again, I'll know we've won the war." He put the cup down on the ground and looked up at Wolfgang.

The youth bore a resemblance to his son, Kurt, when he had been the same age.

"Scharführer, how good a shot are you with a rifle?"

"Sir, I received three gold stars in marksmanship at the Hitler-Jugend camp." He remembered the day when he had been presented with the 'Best Shot in Troop' award.

"Impressive. And are any of your comrades good shots?"

Wolfgang thought for a moment. "Only one, sir. My friend Willi."

"Excellent!" The brigadeführer finished his coffee with a grimace and stood up. "The new mission for you and Willi is to become Werewolves." He chuckled.

"Werewolves, sir?" Wolfgang asked hesitantly.

"A new tactic for the struggle to win the war." Hofmann pulled on his gloves. "Small groups who go behind enemy lines to strike decisively, shatter the enemy's confidence, and then withdraw. With your marksmanship – and the courage you displayed against the American tank – you have all the qualifications to be a Werewolf."

Wolfgang swelled with pride at the brigadeführer's recollection of his exploit, but was still anxious about his mission. "As Werewolves, what are Willi and I supposed to do?"

"You will give me some time by delaying the American armored division that's hard on our heels." He threw his head back and laughed as he saw the disbelieving expression on Wolfgang's face. "Don't worry, you'll have help." He put his hand reassuringly on Wolfgang's shoulder.

Wolfgang felt relieved. Perhaps the brigadeführer would assign a mortar company to help them.

"Sergeant Stieger!" Hofmann waved forward a man standing by the truck.

Wolfgang looked at the sergeant. He was muscular, square-jawed, every inch a German soldier.

"Brigadeführer!" The sergeant snapped to attention and saluted with a smile, revealing a gold tooth.

"Sergeant Stieger will show you how it's done." Hofmann returned the soldier's salute. "Like you, he's an excellent marksman."

Wolfgang still could not hide his anxiety. The sergeant looked like a fine German soldier, but how could the three of them hold up an armored division?

"You'll leave tomorrow. Now I wish you good luck." Hofmann ran his eyes over them. "Remember – we fight for the Führer!"

For the Führer. Wolfgang sprang to attention. For the Führer, he would fight an armored division alone.

Inside the Bernterode Mine.

Terrill felt his knees begin to buckle. A clammy sweat ran down his face. *Please, somebody turn the lights back on,* he silently prayed.

Bill was scared to death of the enveloping black void, the inability to see anything with his eyes wide open. Even on a moonless night in a dark alley, he could see shapes and make out images, however vague and indistinct – ambient light was always around somewhere. But eliminate that light, however dim, and it was like being blind. Or dead.

"Really, Captain, I'm shocked you don't carry backup lighting equipment with you."

"Sorry, Major, but I checked my flashlight before you arrived."

"Gina," Donovan said, "just before the lights went off, you were about to say what you read on that tag. What was it?"

"Oh, my goodness, yes, the tag on the coffin with the wreath and red ribbons. Alan, I think it would be better if you took a look at it yourself when the lights come back on. I'm not sure I'm ready to believe my own eyes."

Their words were a blur to Terrill, like sounds heard underwater. He felt lightheaded, sick to his stomach; he struggled to contain his terror. He returned to a time when he was a seven-year-old boy – a memory that was lodged forever in some deep recess of his mind. The moment when his monster had been born.

He had wanted to hang out with the older boys, wanted to be one of them, but they always managed to give him the slip or shoo him away. Except on that day, the day he saw them snickering and whispering as they watched him approach.

"Hey, Billy, wanna see where old man Shapiro hides his dough?"

He had nodded, happy that at last they were including him in something.

"Come on." They led him down into a coal cellar. One of the boys turned on the cellar lights and pointed to a small room full of coal. "Shapiro keeps his dough in there."

Bill had held back and frowned. "No, he doesn't; that's only coal in there."

"Yeah, that's the beauty of it. Old man Shapiro's hid his moolah in the last place he thought anyone would look. He keeps it underneath the coal. Take a look, Billy, why don'tcha?"

He took a tentative step inside, but before he could pick up a piece of coal he heard the door slam shut and the outside bolt driven home. There was a little light from the cellar coming in under the door, but when they turned it off the room was as black as the coal inside. He called to them but heard only receding laughter and footsteps trailing off.

For hours he had cowered in the coal room, fear and terror consuming him until old man Shapiro came down to get coal.

There was a chorus of relief as the main lights came back on.

"Thank heaven!" sighed Gina. "Okay, Alan, now come take a—" She frowned as she glanced over at Bill and saw the beads of perspiration on his ashen forehead. "Bill, are you all right?"

"My God!" The cry came from Donovan, who was squatting down next to the ribbon-draped coffin; he pushed his glasses down on his nose to read the tag. "Dear God! This is not possible!"

Errenbach Monastery.

"Good afternoon, Herr Direktor Gruber." Father Hieronymus, smiling broadly, extended his hand. "So good to see you."

To Frieda, who sat in a heavy carved oaken chair, Gruber did not look like a Gestapo officer. He was short and squat, with cheerful eyes in a round, well-fed jovial face. There was no leather topcoat, the hated, familiar hallmark of the Gestapo that Frieda had grown to fear. Instead, he wore baggy pants and a tweed jacket with leather patches at the elbows.

He shuffled into the room with an ungainly gait, giving Frieda a smile as he leaned over and chucked Trudi under the chin. "Such a beautiful girl!" Trudi recoiled and withdrew to her mother's lap.

"I presume you've come about the boat, Herr Direktor Gruber."
Father Hieronymus spoke with a gentle voice.

"Oh, the boat." Gruber spun on his heel to face the abbot. "Yes, the
boat." He placed his hands behind his back and struck a formal pose.
"Father, as you know I turn a blind eye to many things, but even in these
trying times the theft of private property is a serious offense."

"Of course, Herr Direktor Gruber." The abbot took his seat behind
the desk. "Please take a seat while I explain. Perhaps a beer?" He gestured to Brother Helmut, who nodded and left the room.

Gruber listened intently while Father Hieronymus described
Frieda's plight, how she had fled to escape rampaging slave laborers, how she had borrowed the boat to find safety for herself and
her daughter.

"I'm sure you'll agree it's a sad tale, Herr Direktor. Although not
unusual nowadays." The abbot smiled as the monk returned and handed
a stein to the Gestapo officer. "Particularly when you realize that she's a
war widow. And how her only son is now fighting for the Reich with the
Hitler-Jugend."

"But of course, Father." Gruber accepted the blue and cream ceramic
stein that Brother Helmut held out to him and took a draught. "We can
all be proud of the German women who, like this lady, have sacrificed
so much for the Fatherland." He wiped the beer froth from his mustache
with the back of his hand and smiled at Frieda and Trudi. "However, I
will have to check her papers." The smile vanished from his lips as he
assumed his formal role. "You will please let me see your passbook." He
looked coldly at Frieda.

Frieda lifted Trudi from her lap and searched in her handbag, desperately trying to control the trembling of her hand.

Gruber took the passbook from her hand and opened it. "Frau
Engelsing," he read. "Engelsing. What a beautiful, if somewhat unusual,
name." He took another swig from his stein. *Angel singing* – somehow
befits a monastery, doesn't it?" He chuckled at his little joke. "Brings
to mind Father Hieronymus's monks singing Gregorian chants at the
Christmas services." He handed the passbook back to Frieda. "My late
wife and I always attended the Christmas service. Nothing lovelier." He
drained his stein, rose, and made for the door. "Everything's in order,
Father. My men will return the boat to its owner."

"You are welcome at all times, Herr Direktor Gruber." Father Hieronymus bowed his head graciously toward the Gestapo man. "Brother Helmut will make sure you have a crate of our beer, as well as a ham smoked by our butcher."

Gruber followed Brother Helmut from the room. Father Hieronymus was always helpful and generous with the excellent monastery beer. Still, he felt something was wrong. The woman looked too nervous. Engelsing. An unusual name, but he felt sure he'd heard it before. Engelsing. He'd check the name back at the office.

Inside the Bernterode Mine.

"I don't believe it!" Donovan read the tag attached to the coffin bedecked with ribbons. "This tag says Adolf Hitler's inside!"

The captain of the engineers chuckled. "Don't get your hopes up, Major. I'm afraid that's the only casket here that's empty."

"Of course, Captain, I realize that!" Donovan snapped.

Terrill, in the corner, pulled out a handkerchief to mop his brow. He was glad for the distraction; maybe no one would notice his hands shaking.

"But why place an empty coffin with Hitler's name on it down here?" Gina stole an anxious glance at Bill, who looked pale and sick.

"Think about it." Donovan spoke as if lecturing. "The war for Germany is all but lost, and with it will come the downfall of the Führer. But Nazis in positions of power may be vowing to carry on. So they place a coffin with Hitler's name on it, among the coffins of German national heroes, as a symbol that National Socialism will prevail beyond the end of the war. Even beyond the inevitable death of their leader. It's very disturbing."

"It is, indeed, sir," the captain agreed. "But we didn't find just coffins here. There's lots more – boxes and boxes of art we've already moved out of the mine. If you'll follow me, I'll be happy to show you." Ducking under the regimental flags, the captain led Gina and Donovan to the door and back into the tunnel.

Terrill shook himself and followed them on rubbery legs to the elevator for the ride up to the top. It was the first recurrence of his phobia since the time the lights went out in a subway car in between stops. The long elevator ride ended and Bill stepped out into the welcome sunshine. He filled his lungs with fresh air and let the sun's rays beat down on his face.

Hofmann's convoy. A makeshift German military hospital.

Wolfgang was thrilled that he had been invited to attend the ceremony. He hurried after Brigadeführer Hofmann's officers for the commemoration as they filed into the resort hotel that had been converted into a military hospital.

The Führer's birthday. He recalled his Hitler-Jugend swearing-in ceremony, which had taken place on the Führer's birthday. The oath he and the other boys had sworn, *We are born to die for Germany,* made the hairs on the back of his neck prickle with pride.

The smell of antiseptic and stale urine dampened Wolfgang's ardor as he entered the hotel and he was taken aback by the vast array of beds in the huge dining hall; the beds were tended by busy nurses, and in them lay men swathed in stained bandages. So many brave men, he thought; surely the Führer would lead them to victory.

Wolfgang took his place with the other officers standing between the beds, his eyes riveted on the brigadeführer as he strode into the hall and leapt onto a table.

"Soldiers of Germany!" His voice echoed around the hall. "We are here to commemorate the most important day of the year, the birthday of our Führer!"

A cheer from the soldiers rang out but was cut short by a wave of the brigadeführer's arm. "It is fitting that we celebrate this day in the presence of these German heroes."

Wolfgang looked at the wounded men, taking heart from the glow of hope in many eyes. But some gazed vacantly, their eyes sullenly fixed ahead.

"Because these heroes know," Hofmann's voice recaptured Wolfgang's attention, "that today symbolizes the rebirth of Germany." The brigadeführer's fist pumped the air. "Because Adolf Hitler is Germany, and Germany is Adolf Hitler!"

Another cheer came from Wolfgang's throat and from the officers. The excitement reminded him of the time in '38 when he had been in a delegation to the annual party rally in Nuremberg.

"When the Führer calls and commands, we obey without question!" The brigadeführer continued despite a cry of pain coming from one of the beds. "Because with the Führer we are everything! Without him we are nothing!"

Another cheer echoed around the hall. Wolfgang remembered the Day of the Youth at the party rally, when a great host of boys had paraded before the Führer with drums beating, flags and banners flying in the Nuremberg stadium. As he had marched past the podium, Wolfgang felt that the Führer was looking at him directly and his heart almost burst with pride and devotion.

"Posterity will call our Führer one of the greatest men of history, a man who stamped an entire epoch with his will, a man who changed the world political order." The brigadeführer raised his right arm stiffly and cries of 'Heil Hitler!' rang out around the room; Wolfgang was proud to see that all the nurses and some of the injured men also saluted.

As the brigadeführer lowered his arm, the room fell silent, apart from the repeated insistent cries of pain coming from a bed. Wolfgang saw a nurse hurry to the bedside.

"In the hour of Germany's greatest need, the Führer gives us strength!" Hofmann shouted over the cries. "On your birthday, mein Führer, we salute you!"

Wolfgang saluted once more, but, like others, he was watching the wounded man screaming with pain as a nurse reached for a hypodermic needle. Suddenly, the man stopped screaming, shook violently for some moments, and then fell still. Wolfgang looked at the nurse, who shook her head slowly from side to side as she pulled the blanket over the dead man's face.

North of Nuremberg.

"Looks like we might actually get some spring weather this year after all." Bill Terrill pulled on the wheel of the three-quarter-ton Winch Dodge truck as he negotiated the meandering road through the forest.

"Yes, sure does look like a nice day." Gina, seated in the middle between Terrill and Donovan, leaned back, took a deep breath, and smiled. "Good to have a little outing, even if it is to pick up the fragments of some hapless sculptures that got in the way of our bombs." She frowned. "Hope they can be salvaged. Alan, what do think? Will our restoration experts be able to work their usual magic?"

Donovan looked up from the papers he was reading. "Hmm? Sorry, Gina, I missed what you said – I was engrossed in this report. Apparently, our boys have finally taken Nuremberg. It was quite a struggle, but the city fathers handed over the keys yesterday."

"On the twentieth?" Gina laughed. "You've got to be kidding!"

"Ironic, isn't it?" Donovan smiled at their private joke.

Terrill frowned. "Anybody care to let me in on what's so funny?"

"Sorry, Bill, I should have explained," Gina said. "You see, Nuremberg was Hitler's favorite city – he used to call it 'the most German of all cities.' April twentieth, the date our troops captured Hitler's favorite city, happens to be Hitler's birthday."

Terrill whistled and slapped the wheel in delight. "Hot damn! The perfect birthday present for the man who had everything. Including France and Belgium."

Donovan, unhappy with sitting three abreast, continued to pretend Bill was not present. "You'll recall, Gina, that Nuremberg was also the site of the Nazi party rallies. Before the war, that is. You may remember that the '39 rally, 'The Nazi Party Rally of Peace,' had to be cancelled at the last moment because of another commitment."

Gina thought for a moment. "Oh, right, Alan, I remember – they had to cancel their peace rally so they could invade Poland!"

Gina smiled at Donovan's dry wit and looked up at the sun filtering through the canopy of the trees. The warmth was in marked contrast to the wintry cold that had lingered so long in Germany. "You're right, Bill – perhaps spring has come at last. Although I think I see some storm clouds up ahead." She looked at Terrill and he appreciated her smile, warmer than the spring sun.

"How long will it take to get there and back?" The cold, matter-of-fact voice came from Donovan.

Terrill sighed. Didn't the guy have any feelings? Spring – maybe the end of the war – was around the corner, and he wanted to know how long before he got back to the creature comforts of base camp. "About forty minutes, sir." Terrill stole a glance at Gina, who rolled her eyes upward.

"Step on it, Sergeant." The major leaned forward and looked past Gina to address Terrill. "I'm invited to dinner with the colonel tonight."

"As you wish, sir." Terrill floored the pedal, throwing the major back against the seat.

Gina struggled to suppress a giggle.

Behind enemy lines in American Territory. North of Nuremberg.

Wolfgang struggled for breath as he climbed the wooded hills behind the sergeant. His rifle hung heavy on his shoulders and the straps of his rucksack cut into his flesh. Behind him, Willi gasped as he fought his way up the incline. Wolfgang worried about his friend: he was only fifteen and he had always needed help at the Hitler-Jugend exercises at summer camp.

"Come on, lads, we're nearly there." The sergeant's voice gave Wolfgang confidence. He looked at the soldier's powerful physique, his resolute jaw thrusting out from below his helmet. Wolfgang felt a surge of euphoria: with such men, the Third Reich would surely survive.

He couldn't suppress the excitement that eclipsed his fear; the battle with the tank had boosted his confidence. And the brigadeführer's reliance upon him. His prized Luger pistol and SS knife were tucked into his rucksack along with his rations and ammunition. Now he was on a Werewolf mission, behind enemy lines.

"Okay, let's take a break." The sergeant stopped and squatted, looking down from the brow of the hill at the road below.

Wolfgang heard Willi heave a sigh of relief as he fell on his knees. The sergeant raised his index finger to his lips, pulled his binoculars from his rucksack, and looked at the road below. Wolfgang could see little through the trees, which thinned out as the hill ran down to the road.

"It's all clear." The sergeant turned to the two Hitler Jugend. "Soon we can get to work."

"Excuse me, sir." Willi's reedy voice annoyed Wolfgang. Willi didn't even know that NCO's weren't addressed as 'sir.' Wolfgang knew that he was going to ask a stupid question.

Willi continued. "How can such a tiny group like us hold up the American army?"

Although Wolfgang knew the question was stupid because Willi had asked it, he, too, wondered about the same thing. They were three soldiers with sniper rifles. American tanks were in the area, but none of the three had a Panzerfäust.

The sergeant threw back his head and laughed; Wolfgang caught the reflection of the sun on his gold incisor tooth. "Can you shoot straight, lad?"

Willi's young face showed surprise. "At Hitler-Jugend camp," his chest swelled, "I won the sharpshooter competition."

The sergeant slipped his knapsack from his back. "And you, the brigadeführer's little hero, can you shoot?"

Wolfgang stiffened to attention and pointed to the Hitler-Jugend marksman's badge on his sleeve.

"Then together we can stop a division." The sergeant rummaged in his rucksack and pulled out an explosive charge. "All we need is a tree."

Wolfgang flinched as the sergeant tossed the explosive charge from hand to hand. "A tree?" Wolfgang shook his head; the sergeant must be mad.

"Wait here and watch the road," the sergeant called up as he began to shuffle down the hill. "Let me know if any vehicle begins to approach; what I've got to do can't be seen by the enemy."

Minutes later, the sergeant looked back at Wolfgang. The youth scanned the road, saw nothing, and gave the thumbs up.

The explosion made Wolfgang jump. As the sound died away there was another noise: the swish of leaves, the rustle of branches as the tree fell with a crash astride the road.

The sergeant scrambled back up the hill. "That's how we can stop an army." The broad, gold-toothed smile gave Wolfgang confidence. "Come on, lads, let's make some sniper covers."

Terrill felt fear grip at his stomach. The fallen tree was a roadblock, a trap. He stopped, checked for his M3 submachine gun, then swiftly pushed the gearshift into reverse.

"What the matter? What's—" Gina's voice was cut short as the windshield shattered.

"Shit! Get down, Gina!" Terrill's right hand reached out to push Gina down into the well of the cab as he tugged at the wheel with his other hand, his knuckles white. His foot slammed on the gas pedal as he heard the second bullet zing past his ear.

"I'm hit! I'm hit!" Terrill heard the cry of pain from Donovan, then felt the truck lurch as a third bullet hit one of the front tires. He lost control, and the truck skidded on the edge of the road before slipping into the ditch. For a moment, the vehicle teetered; then it rolled over on the driver's side. Gina fell from the seat, her head slamming into his jaw. Donovan fell on top of her.

Wolfgang peered through the branches and leaves covering his sniper's hole. He was almost certain that his first shot had been a hit. The truck lay on its side, the front wheels spinning slowly. There was no sign of any movement. He looked back at the sergeant's hide and saw him put his index finger in front of his lips. Silence. The lips then mouthed the word 'patience.' The sniper's creed. Wolfgang settled back in his hide, fixed his eye to the telescopic sight. The spinning wheels of the overturned truck were slowly coming to a halt.

Terrill was dazed. He shook his head, trying to force focus back into his eyes. The truck was lying on its side, the driver's window smashed, and gravel and small bits of glass were embedded in his left cheek.

He felt the weight of Gina's body upon him. He sensed her aroma as he freed his right arm from the tangle of bodies, his hand clutching for his submachine gun lying behind the seat.

He looked at Gina and gave a brief sigh of relief as her eyes fluttered opened. "What in Christ's name—" she began to scream.

Terrill clamped his hand over her mouth. "We've been ambushed. Snipers. Just get off me and don't move."

Her arms pushed against him and he felt her hips wriggle as she tried to free herself from the weight of Donovan lying on top of her. He grabbed the machine gun and checked the magazine. Full.

A groan came from Donovan as Gina brushed against him. "I'm hit, I'm hit." Donovan was clutching his shoulder, and Terrill could see blood seeping through the major's fingers.

"Don't move!" Terrill hissed the command as he freed himself and scrambled toward the back of the upturned truck. He was disoriented, but knew the back of the truck would be the best place to try to return the fire. If he had a chance. He took a brief glance through the rear window at the felled tree and the hills at the side of the road.

Zing! The bullet made him flinch, but then he realized it was not meant for him. He heard the sound of metal on metal and then smelled the pungent odor. The sniper had hit the bottom of the upturned vehicle. The gas tank.

Wolfgang looked again at the sergeant. Through the foliage he could see the gold-toothed smile. The bullet in the gas tank was a masterstroke. He glanced across at Willi. His friend was laughing, and he understood the reason. They hadn't had so much fun since hunting down a deer at Hitler-Jugend camp.

Wolfgang pressed his eye back against the telescopic sight. Soon the leaking gas would flush out the enemy.

"Gas!" Gina cried out in terror as the smell began to fill the cab of the upturned truck.

"Stay still!" Terrill shouted as he slung his machine gun toward a tear in the canvas of the truck, desperate to find some counter to the snipers.

Through the small hole, his eyes ran over the terrain beyond the fallen tree. To hit the gas tank, the sniper had to shoot from the hill to the right of the tree. His eyes scanned the foliage. The sniper could be anywhere. He needed a clue, any clue. He fired a single shot wildly, without aiming, his eyes fixed upon the trees. He saw two flashes: one bullet hit the ground by the side of the truck; the other came through the canvas of the truck, zipping close to his head.

"Jesus Christ, there are two of them!" Terrill clambered back toward the cab.

"We have to surrender." With his good hand, Donovan pulled his white handkerchief from a pocket. "I need treatment." He began to push himself up through the open window.

"You idiot!" Terrill lunged for the major's legs. "Gina, help me grab the jerk's feet."

Wolfgang was surprised by the white handkerchief and relaxed his fingers on the trigger. Surrender? The man wanted to surrender? He wasn't sure what to do and turned to look at the sergeant, seeking guidance, but was startled to hear the crack of Willi's rifle.

Wolfgang pressed his eye back to the rifle's sight. The handkerchief disappeared as the American's body jerked and fell back into the truck. Willi's shot had found its mark.

"I got him!"

Donovan fell heavily onto Terrill. Blood poured from the officer's face. The bullet had torn away a section of his left cheek; he was unconscious with shock. Gina, crouched down by the pedals, pushed her fist into her mouth to stifle a scream.

Terrill pulled himself free from the weight. He knew he should try to staunch the bleeding, but he heard the shout from beyond the fallen tree. He moved quickly back to the rear of the truck. For a moment he thought his eyes were deceiving him. Charging toward the truck was a German in uniform. A German boy.

"No, Willi, no!" Wolfgang knew he shouldn't shout, but his friend was in danger. He looked behind him, saw the sergeant shaking his head, then turned his eyes back to the road.

Willi had clambered over the felled tree and was approaching the upturned truck. He ran with an awkward gait, his rifle held before him, his oversized helmet bobbing on his head. Wolfgang switched his attention back toward the truck. Nothing, no movement. There was no sound. Perhaps Willi was right; perhaps he had scored a bull's-eye.

The silence was broken by the sound of a single shot. Birds flew up from the trees, their cries startling Wolfgang. He saw Willi thrown backward by the violence of the bullet, his arms akimbo, his rifle flying through the air. His friend fell to the earth, his body twitching for a few moments before it fell back and lay still. Dead.

Rage consumed Wolfgang. He raised his rifle and began shooting at the truck. He could see no target, but pumped several bullets at the vehicle.

"Stop!" He heard the hissed command. He lowered his rifle and watched as the sergeant crept forward and slipped into the hide that had been Willi's. Wolfgang breathed deeply to ward off the sobs that threatened to wrack his body. He wanted to be back at the Hitler-Jugend camp he had enjoyed years before. He wanted to be back there with Willi.

Terrill felt numb. He'd had no option but to shoot the German boy. The startled look on the boy's face when the single bullet struck lingered in his mind.

The bullets from the hill snapped him from his paralysis. He fired another single shot but his aim was wild. A quick, cautious glance through the opening of the torn canvas of the truck gave him a good guess at the source of the shots. Halfway up the hill, slightly to the right.

A moan came from Donovan, who was lying awkwardly against the upturned ceiling of the truck. "He needs help fast." Gina knelt over the shattered face, trying to staunch the flow of blood with her handkerchief. "And we need to escape this gas."

"For the moment, we're stuck. Damn it all to hell!" Terrill slammed his hand against the door in frustration. "I don't know how many there are out there." He stole another quick look. A bullet crashed against the truck.

"Are you all right?" Gina screamed.

"Just." Terrill shrugged to control his breathing, his heart pounding. "Gina, I need your help."

"What can I do?" Her voice was resigned as she pressed her drenched handkerchief against the major's wound.

Terrill reached down and picked up Donovan's cap. He paused as he looked at the cap; perhaps he should not ask her to take the risk. But he had no option. If they were to have any chance, he had to flush the snipers out.

Wolfgang crouched low in his hide. The day had suddenly turned cloudy and rain began to fall, the drops hitting his hand as they fell from the foliage. He looked down the hill at Willi. Pools were gathering around his body, reddened with his blood. Wolfgang felt sick.

"Leave the next shot to me." The sergeant's hissed order brought Wolfgang back to the danger of the moment. There was no longer excitement, such as he had felt facing the American tank. He felt only fear. He cleared the water from the sight of his gun and looked down at the overturned truck, watching for any movement, listening for any noise.

"Gina, listen carefully." Terrill looked into her worried eyes as he clutched the major's cap. "We need something long to prop the cap on so you can hold it out the window."

"I can't leave Alan." She looked down at the major's shattered face.

"Gina, you'll have to," there was desperation in his voice, "if we're going to have any chance of getting out of this alive."

She ducked down and rummaged through her case. "There's this." She held up the folding ruler she used on her field trips.

"It'll do the job." Terrill checked the bullets in the clip. "Now this is what you have to do."

Wolfgang saw the movement at the side of the truck. An officer's hat. The sergeant had been right. Patience. After so long, the foolish Americans believed they had left.

Just the top of the hat was showing in his sights. Wolfgang stole a quick glance at the sergeant. His eye was glued to his telescopic sight. Why hadn't he fired? Was he waiting for a better shot? Wolfgang looked down at the truck. Even he could pick off the officer wearing the hat.

Crack! The sound of the sergeant's shot echoed briefly from the hill. Wolfgang saw the hat fly as the bullet hit. Got him! But then he heard a rattle of shots, the chatter of a submachine gun.

A strangled cry came from the sergeant's hide, startling Wolfgang. He saw the officer clutch at the side of his head for a moment before he slumped lifeless into his hide.

Wolfgang felt the snake of fear return, slithering in his gut. His eyes turned back to the truck. There was no movement, only Willi's body lying still in the puddle.

He cowered down low in his hide. What could he do? Willi and the sergeant were dead. His hand brushed the rain from his eyes.

A noise broke the silence, a growing racket from the road beyond the tree. He knew the sound. Tanks. The first monster roared into view. He had no Panzerfäust; he no longer felt brave. Wolfgang slid from his hide and crawled back beyond the brow of the hill, stealing a last glance at Willi's body lying in the mud.

"Take it easy with him," Gina shouted at the medics who carried the stretcher; the major, sprawled upon it, was unconscious. "He's badly hurt."

"Okay, lady, keep your shirt on – we're doing our best!" the medic holding the IV snapped back.

Gina sighed. The man was right. The fear, the tension still gripped her body. Her fingers ran through her hair, limp with the falling rain; her other hand brushed futilely at the mud and bloodstains on her skirt. She looked around for Terrill and found him leaning against the radiator of the upturned truck, his eyes fixed on the hill behind the fallen tree, his hands clutching his submachine gun. She ran to him and grabbed his arm. "Bill, it's over! It's over!"

Terrill jumped like a scared jackrabbit at her touch. His hooded eyes turned and fixed hers. "It's never over with these people, Gina." He nodded toward the dead German youth.

"But we're alive, Bill! Thanks to you we're alive!" She threw her arms around him. He drew back, but she clutched him to her, feeling comfort in the warmth of his body.

For a moment he held her tight; then he pushed her away. He walked over to the German boy. He looked down at the body surrounded by blood seeping into a pool of rainwater.

Gina saw Terrill's frame begin to shake, his lower lip trembling. She looked away, embarrassed, as though she should not be intruding on his privacy. As she stared at the raindrops falling into the puddles, she heard his deep breaths as he struggled to control his emotions. Suddenly, he turned from the body.

"Bill?" She looked up into his reddened eyes.

He shook his head and spoke in a raspy whisper. "Gina, we've reached the bottom of the abyss."

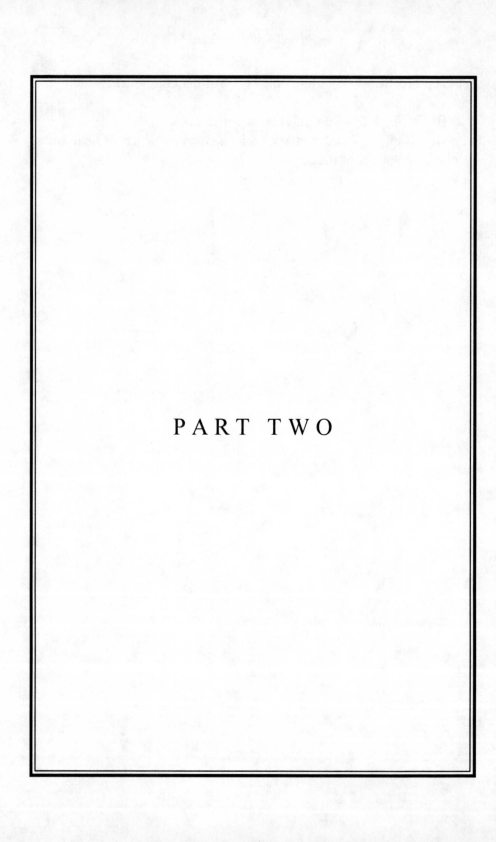

PART TWO

US Third Army Headquarters.

G ina looked in the mirror, stretched her lips into a false smile, and applied a decorous pink shade of lipstick.

Everyone had been on edge after the sniping incident. She was often anxious for no reason, and recurring nightmares had her tossing sleepless in her cot at night. Worse, she was afraid that somehow her father would hear of the sniping incident; she worried about him worrying about her. She blotted her lips on a tissue.

Alan was going to live. For almost a week it had been touch-and-go, but the army surgeons had pulled him through and had even saved his eye. As soon as he was well enough, he'd be shipped home. Gina tossed the lipstick into her makeup case and pulled out a brush.

But Bill had become silent and morose. The sharp comments had disappeared; the feisty spirit had been subdued. As much as they used to irritate her, one of Bill's wise-guy remarks would now be music to her ears. She ran the brush through her hair; what passed for shampoo in the army was making it as dry and listless as a handful of wood shavings.

When Gina had told Bill the good news about Donovan, all he could do was blame himself for not having been able to stop the major from trying to leave the truck with the white handkerchief. Donovan's injuries were troubling to Bill, but something else was gnawing at his soul. The German boy. The brush in Gina's hand paused as the unwelcome image of the boy's body lying in the bloody pool of rainwater flashed into her mind. If the memory was bad for her, it had to be worse for the man who had pulled the trigger. With a start, she remembered that Bill had killed another sniper up on the hill. Was it easier to take the life of someone whose face you never saw?

She put down the brush and picked up her powder puff. The face in the mirror staring back at her as she applied the powder to her nose made her grimace. She wanted to look good for the meeting with Colonel Philpott, the first she'd have without Donovan, but there was nothing in her makeup case that would lighten the dark shadows under her eyes. Or the stress that had put them there.

She glanced at her watch. After the meeting with Philpott, she'd try to catch up with Bill. She had to talk to him, had to help him shake off the blues; she desperately wanted the old Bill back.

A loud sigh of exasperation signaled common sense trying to assert itself. Bill was becoming an obsession; why couldn't she stop thinking about him? He was just another GI, a man with whom she had little in common. He didn't give a damn about the one thing that really mattered to her – art – and she was growing tired of his asking why art was being saved while men were still dying.

As she reached for her cap, tears of frustration pricked her eyes; damn it all, she couldn't stop thinking about him because she'd become fond of him. She liked Bill; he had a no-nonsense approach to life that cut through pretention; he was sweet and funny and cool under pressure. She missed the way his huge grin lit up his face.

Pulling her cap down firmly on her head, she checked the finished product in the mirror. Whatever she thought of Bill, one thing was undeniable. She opened the door and began to make her way to Philpott's office. He was the man who had saved her life.

Errenbach Monastery.

Perhaps he was wrong. Stanislaus moved quietly down the aisle of the abbey church, his soft sandals sliding over the stone floor. Perhaps the painting wasn't hidden at Errenbach. In a shadowy side chapel, candlelight danced hesitantly across the face of the Virgin, accentuating her look of fearful awe as she recoiled from a kneeling angel offering her a lily.

He felt ill-at-ease in the flowing robe; coarse fabric chafed his body and unfamiliar skirts threatened to trip him. He was a man of science, and religious orders were antithetical to all he cherished: reason, logic, cause and effect. But the kindness of the abbot had given sanctuary to him, Frieda, and the child, who were blessed to have been provided with a place to wait out the last agonizing days of a war that refused to die.

The flashlight in his pocket clunked against a pew. He stopped and looked around; a lone monk, deep in prayer, seemed not to have heard. Stanislaus went to an opposite pew and knelt. Prayer was hardly in his mind; his thoughts were of the painting, the Polish national treasure, as he tried to recall the conversation he had overheard when he was a forced laborer. Errenbach Abbey. The crypt. He was sure those were the words the farmer's brother had used. And he had seen the box with the writing on it. *Raphael. Portrait of a Young Man.* His fingers played with the cord tied around his waist. What if he was right? What if the painting was in the crypt?

Disturbing thoughts leapt into his mind. Perhaps the abbot knew of the theft – perhaps he was part of the plot. Perhaps he had even organized—no, surely not. Stanislaus willed the thoughts away.

And if the Raphael was hidden in the abbey, what then? What was his plan? He'd be lucky enough to get himself back to Warsaw in one piece, let alone a fabled work of art. The repatriation of a priceless masterpiece by an escaped slave laborer mired in enemy territory five hundred miles away – a lunatic concept. His eyes, nervously flitting about the apse, suddenly became ensnared by the stern, disapproving gaze of God the Father thundering down upon him from the altarpiece. Even though his religion had long since gone, he reached up and crossed himself.

A forest south of Nuremberg.

Wolfgang could not escape his shame.

The mud splashed over his boots as he trudged along the deserted road. His head hung low as he forced his legs forward. The straps of his backpack cut against his flesh through his uniform, still sodden from an early-morning rain.

Wolfgang had walked through the woods for several days, sleeping rough at night; he knew he should seek shelter, but he was lost. He cast a fearful glance over his shoulder; the advancing Americans were probably not far behind him. He hurried his pace, despite the despair that clutched at his heart.

The bodily misery would not drive out the doleful images lodged in his mind. His friend, Willi, lying dead in the mud. The shattered face of the sergeant.

Wolfgang began to run and then stopped. He squatted by the side of the road, disconsolate, the wind chilling him to the bone. But there was another coldness that troubled him more. A coldness of the spirit. He was running away. A scharführer in the Hitler-Jugend. Running away. He had betrayed the oath he had taken at the Hitler-Jugend swearing-in ceremony. *We are born to die for Germany!*

Wolfgang felt his eyes well up again. He had not kept his oath – he had failed the Führer. Willi had died. The image of his friend, lying in the mud, his lifeblood running away, was burnt deep in Wolfgang's mind. Willi had kept his oath. Died for Germany. As had the sergeant.

He opened his knapsack and reached for the last piece of sausage. His hand brushed against the SS dagger presented to him by the brigade-führer. He remembered the battle with the tank. He could be brave, he knew.

He stood up, trying to salvage the last vestige of his pride. Perhaps he could make atonement. The Führer had said that those who fear an honorable death shall die in shame. If he could have another chance, he would not fear an honorable death. If he could rejoin the brigadeführer's command, maybe he could yet have a chance to redeem himself.

Suddenly, he tensed as he heard the noise: trucks were coming down the road.

US Third Army Headquarters.

"Please take a seat, Lieutenant Cortazzo." Colonel Philpott took off his glasses and rubbed his tired eyes as he spoke. "I hear Major Donovan is expected to recover enough to be shipped back home soon."

"Yes, thank God, he'll survive." Gina eased herself into her seat. "It's been touch-and-go over the last week."

"But his absence from your section must be causing some problems for you. I imagine the loss of Major Donovan is a severe blow to your work."

"Let's hope Major Donovan has a speedy recovery, sir." Gina reflected on the colonel's attitude. The task first, people second. So like a man.

"Of course, of course." The colonel rifled through the papers on his desk. "I received this wire from your regional commissioner this morning. It says Major Donovan can't be replaced for," he put on his glasses and moved his finger down the paper, "for at least a week. Says they're hoping to line up a replacement in time for when our forces seize a place called Alt Aussee."

"Major Donovan was looking forward to playing a role in the rescue of the Alt Aussee art. He'll be very much missed, sir, but there's a lot of sorting and cataloguing I can do until his replacement arrives."

Philpott pushed his glasses down on his nose and looked over them at Gina for a long moment without speaking. "You speak the Kraut lingo, don't you?"

Gina nodded.

The colonel pushed the glasses back in place and plucked another report from the stack of papers on his desk. "Think you could put your cataloguing on one side for a couple of days?" His eyes scanned the paper in his hand.

"Why, what's the matter?" she asked, intrigued.

"Well, General Patton is very interested in this report that came from Nuremberg yesterday. Apparently, some of our guys there think they're on the track of the crown jewels of Charlemagne."

Gina's eyes widened. The regalia of the Holy Roman Empire! Even as a child she had been enraptured by Charlemagne, and in college she'd aced the course on the Carolingian Renaissance. She recalled having seen the images of the regalia in a textbook – Charlemagne's bejeweled crown, prayer book, scepter, orb, sword – wonderful relics of the larger-than-life man who united Western Europe and was the ancestor of many crowned heads.

"Do they know where the regalia are, sir?" Gina knew the Nazis had stolen them from Vienna, where they had been displayed for two hundred years.

"They're not sure." The colonel's eyes ran over the paper. "According to this, there's some indication that some SS officers took them away and dumped them into the middle of some lake."

Gina shuddered that such a fate should befall so legendary a treasure.

He pored over the report. "Seems there's lots of confusion. With your art knowledge and language skills, perhaps you could help out?"

Gina said nothing, but every fiber in her body screamed. She could do it. She knew everything there was to know about Charlemagne's regalia.

The colonel misread her silence. "Of course, it's a lot to ask, but I'd appreciate it." He put down the report. "General Patton is putting a lot of pressure on me. Seems he's interested in this stuff. I know it's a lot to ask, Lieutenant," Philpott eyed her nervously, "but if Sergeant Terrill goes with you as protection, do you think you could handle it?"

Gina suppressed the urge to leap from her chair and dance with joy. "I'll do my best, sir." She looked at her watch. Three o'clock. If Bill was willing to cooperate, they could be in Nuremburg by nightfall.

She got up, saluted, and turned to go.

"There's one more thing I should mention, Lieutenant." The colonel's voice stopped her in her tracks. "This document from your regional commissioner asks you to take over Donovan's responsibilities until his replacement arrives, but there's no mention of a promotion for you."

So it really was a man's army, she thought. Not for nothing was she called a 'Monuments Man,' and they surely didn't want any female captains in their midst.

"I understand, sir." She made her way hurriedly to the door. She didn't care. For the chance of finding Charlemagne's regalia, she'd agree to be busted to private.

Errenbach Monastery.

Stanislaus clasped his hands and bowed his head in pretended prayer. The abbot had learned that he was a doctor and had asked him to tend to the health needs of the monks. But the brothers, though old, were robust, and in Stanislaus's spare time he kept the financial records for the monastery. He was happy to be of use to the monastery in return for his keep – his work was a big improvement over cleaning out cow sheds or foraging on the road.

Another monk entered the church and genuflected before the altar. The books were easy to keep, the day-to-day entries straightforward. Income from the sale of beer and produce from the abbey's garden. Expenditures for things the monks did not grow or could not make themselves. Cash flow was negligible; the abbey was just scraping by.

As the monks prayed silently, Stanislaus waited patiently. In some ways, he envied the men who shuffled around the abbey. The world about them was falling in ruins, into the abyss of hell, but these men of God had enough faith to believe their mumblings to the Deity made a difference. They did not live in the present; they were lost in the rites of a long-gone age. At any moment the real world – the world of war and pain – could invade their silence and threaten their peaceful devotion.

He watched as the monks stood, made the sign of the cross, and pulled the hoods of their robes over their heads, as if to shield themselves from the future, to cosset them in a serene way of life that might soon be no more. He waited for the shuffle of their sandals to fade away at the back of the nave and listened as the door creaked open, then shuddered shut.

Stanislaus felt the vast emptiness of the church. He looked up at the all-seeing eyes of God the Father on the altarpiece and made his way to the entrance of the crypt.

US Third Army Headquarters.

In the light rain, Gina half-ran excitedly toward the motor pool. Charlemagne's imperial regalia. She could scarcely believe her luck: the chance of a lifetime. Her pace and spirits slowed as she recalled Bill's gloomy mood, casting a pall on the thrill of trying to return Charlemagne's crown jewels to the world.

She saw him standing by his jeep. His Ike-style jacket hugged his slim waist, accentuating his strong back and broad shoulders and making his long legs seem even longer.

He turned and, seeing her, strode over with a happy look she hadn't seen since the morning they drove out with Alan in the truck. "Hiya, Gina!"

She was surprised by the cheerful voice; she liked the way his hazel eyes smiled when he did. "Well, you're sure looking chipper."

"Haven't you heard?" He gave her a surprised look. "We met up with the Russians at Torgau yesterday!"

"And?" Military strategy was not Gina's forte.

"Don't you realize?" He looked at her incredulously. "It means the Germans are split in two! The war can't last much longer now." He grabbed her in a joyous hug. "Soon we all get to go home!"

Gina smiled and slipped from his hands. "That's great news, but you and I have a job to do first." She told him of their new assignment. "Bill, do you think you can get us to Nuremberg before nightfall?"

Terrill stood back and gave an exaggerated salute. "Your chariot awaits, Lieutenant Cortazzo." He hugged her again, a little harder than the first time. "Your every wish is my command," he murmured in her ear.

Gina, giggling, pulled away. "There's no time for horseplay – I've got to get out of this rain and pack my kit bag; you'd better get ready, too. We've got work to do!" she said as she turned and walked briskly off.

Terrill lingered in the motor pool, still smiling. *'We,'* she had said. *'We've got work to do.'* Donovan would never have said 'we'; to him, Bill was just another flunky, about as important to his mission as the swizzle stick in his martini glass. Henderson might have said 'we have work to do,' but he would have meant *'you* have work to do,' meaning 'you're the grunt, you're the cannon fodder.'

Donovan had made him feel like a benched player. Henderson made him feel like the batboy. But with Gina, he felt like a key man on a good team. He liked that feeling.

South of Nuremberg.

Wolfgang's eyes, seeking to give form to the approaching vehicles, tried desperately to penetrate the fog. His heart quickened anxiously as he heard the growing sound of engines.

He could take no chances. Perhaps the American advance units were coming towards him. The noise grew; soon they would be upon him. His eyes glanced at the ditch at the side of the road. He had no option. He pulled his knapsack from his back, tossed it into the ditch and threw himself on top. Perhaps the Americans would pass by. He pressed himself into the mud.

The screech of the tires alarmed Wolfgang; his pulse pounded in his ears.

"Ich dachte, dass ich jemand auf der Straße sah, mein Herr."

Wolfgang felt relief rush through his body. *I thought I saw someone on the road, mein Herr.* The soldiers were German.

Wolfgang stood up and moved toward the car. He felt safe as he saw the swastika pennant on the hood and the familiar SS uniform of the officer getting down from the car.

"What have we here?" The hard grey eyes of the SS standartenführer bore down on Wolfgang. "Another deserter?"

Wolfgang couldn't believe how wrong the officer was. "No, sir, I'm not a deserter."

"Then what are you doing alone in the middle of nowhere?" The officer eyed him coldly.

"I've become detached from my unit."

"A likely story." The officer sneered. "I meet so many who have become, as they say, 'detached from their units.'"

A sergeant approached from the right. "What's your unit?"

Despite his growing fear, Wolfgang stamped to attention. "Brigadeführer Hofmann's battalion."

"Another tall tale!" the sergeant snickered. "A sniveling little Hitler-Jugend attached to a high-ranking SS officer. Now I've heard it all."

"But really—" Wolfgang began to protest.

"Shut up!" The sergeant slapped Wolfgang hard across the face. He fell to his knees, trying desperately not to cry.

The sergeant pulled his Schmeisser from his shoulder. "You're nothing but a cowardly deserter." He looked across at the officer. "Shall I shoot him now, Standartenführer?"

"Don't be a fool," the officer spat out. "What use would that be?" His eyes hardened beneath his peaked cap. "We can use him to teach other would-be traitors a lesson."

He turned on his heel and returned to his car. "We'll return to Schwanstetten." He pulled a clipboard from the car and flipped through the papers. "Our reports show that the mayor and citizens are refusing to build anti-tank ditches." He turned to Wolfgang, a thin smile of menace on his lips. "Let's see their reaction when they watch this pathetic deserter dangling at the end of a rope." He climbed into the car. "Toss the little wretch into the truck."

Errenbach Monastery.

Stanislaus descended into the crypt, pulling the flashlight from his pocket to dispel the almost impenetrable gloom. Where to look? He moved forward from the bottom step, the beam of light ranging over the darkness. The dank, fetid smell assailed his nose. The two sarcophagi afforded no solution; the dust on their heavy lids had probably lain undisturbed for a hundred years. He ran the beam along the gap between the tombs and the wall of the crypt. Nothing. Only cobwebs and rat droppings.

The noise made him jump. Despite the dank coldness, a sweat of fear broke out on his brow. From the sepulcher of death came a sound of life. He swung the flashlight around to the darkness on his left. The beam fell on a large rat; for a moment the creature squatted motionless on the floor before scurrying away.

He swung the light to the far wall. The array of skulls startled him; he had heard of ossuaries but had never seen one before. But he had seen the monastery's tiny cemetery and knew it could not hold the mortal remains of centuries of monks. He paused to study the pile with the curiosity of a scientist; the bones of the dead could not threaten him, but the living form of Direktor Gruber could.

He ran the beam of the flashlight over the bones, the changing shadows of the skulls' eye sockets mocking him. The painting must be hidden here, he knew. A perfect hiding place – a place that would strike fear into the heart of anyone. But not him; Stanislaus had seen much worse in medical school and in his practice. Somewhere among the heap of bones was the painting.

He tried to imagine himself in the position of the thief. The painting clearly wasn't on the top of the bones. He ran his finger over a skull in the middle, thickly coated with dust. And it couldn't be underneath the bones – they hadn't been moved for decades. Perhaps somewhere to the side of the ossuary. He went to the right. Nothing. Maybe he had been wrong about the painting being here after all. Soon he would have to return to the monastery, before questions were asked.

The beam penetrated the gap at the left side of the ossuary. Stanislaus saw the box at the back of the gap. He had found Raphael's *Young Man.*

Schwanstetten, south of Nuremberg.

Wolfgang could not control the shaking of his body as the truck pulled into the town square. His mind tried feebly to blame the cold, but he knew he was afraid. How could the SS officer make such a mistake?

He looked out of the rear of the truck. The gallows stood in the center of the square, the noose swinging in the late afternoon breeze. His thoughts raced back – was it just a couple of weeks ago when he and Willi helped build a similar apparatus of death, happily singing Hitler-Jugend songs?

He recalled seeing the old man being dragged to the scaffold. The fear in the man's eyes had not moved him. But now…

"Down, get down from the truck!" The sergeant prodded his machine gun into Wolfgang's back.

Wolfgang picked up his knapsack and jumped onto the cobblestones, landing at the officer's feet. A small crowd milled around the sides of the square.

Wolfgang sprang to attention before the officer, driven by desperation. "Heil Hitler, mein Herr!" He extended his arm in the traditional Nazi salute. "I can prove that I am loyal to the Führer," he spoke quickly, "and that I belong to Brigadeführer Hofmann's battalion."

The officer hesitated, taken aback by Wolfgang's outburst. "And how does a pathetic creature like you plan to do that?"

"The proof of my allegiance is in there, mein Herr!" He pointed to the knapsack at his feet.

The officer looked at the knapsack with disgust, then fixed his eyes on Wolfgang's. "Hauptscharführer! Let's get this matter cleared up once and for all." He turned impatiently on his heel and began to walk away. "Bring this annoying boy and his filthy knapsack to my office."

Nuremberg.

The rain had stopped and the sun was low in the sky as Terrill edged the jeep through the outskirts of Nuremberg. They passed a troop of GIs moving up the road. Gina saw the weariness on their dusty faces, but many broke out in a smile as they spotted her in the jeep. Perhaps they were cheered, sensing the end was near, even though there was still work to do. She blushed at the wolf whistles sent in her direction, but ignored them. She, too, had work to do.

"Holy Moses, get a load of that," Terrill said, pulling the jeep over to the side of the road. "That's one helluva mess." He jumped down and clambered over rubble to survey the ruined city center that rose on the other side of a river.

Gina stayed in the jeep and said nothing as her eyes took in the devastation. Mountains of rubble lay everywhere; almost no building had been spared. Macabre fingers of chimney stacks tenuously clawed at the sky. Smoke swirled from the blackened shards of walls. And everywhere was the nauseating stench of decay and death that invaded her nostrils and would not leave.

Gina tried to pull herself from a vision of a hell she had hoped never to see. Her mind ran back to pictures she had once seen in a National Geographic magazine. Nuremberg, the beautiful medieval city, ringed with walls. High on a hill a castle, the Kaiserburg, overlooked ancient churches and half-timbered buildings with steeply-pitched roofs and stepped gables. Home, during its golden age, to the great master, Albrecht Dürer. Home, also, to the revered German National Museum. Before the Nazis arrived.

Bill jumped back into the jeep. "We sure pounded the hell out of this place." He started the engine and swung the wheel.

"Perhaps it was Hitler who provided the hell, Bill."

Terrill grunted his acceptance. "Gina, sorry to ask a simple question, but where are we supposed to be heading?"

Gina plucked a paper from her briefcase. "Hunterhalle," she read. "On Ludwigstrasse."

Terrill brought the jeep to a halt. "Perhaps we'd better ask an MP." He took off his cap and ran his fingers through his hair as he looked around. "There don't seem to be many strasses left in this town."

Schwanstetten.

Wolfgang's hand shook as he reached into his knapsack; his fingers were pulling out his Hitler-Jugend identification card when the sergeant slammed his meaty fist into his forearm, sending the knapsack thudding to the floor.

"Hands out of there!" the sergeant shouted as he picked up the knapsack. "Who the hell knows what you might have hidden in your bag?"

Wolfgang's arm hurt but his fingers held tenaciously onto the card.

The officer snatched the card and glanced at it with contempt. "You're offering your Hitler-Jugend identification card as proof you're attached to Brigadeführer Hofmann?" He leapt from his chair in rage. "You're wasting my time! Every Hitler-Jugend carries an identification card, and there are millions!"

"No, sir, no," Wolfgang stammered nervously. "Please, sir, if you would look into my bag yourself."

The officer nodded to the sergeant, who plunged his arm into Wolfgang's knapsack, his hand emerging with an SS dagger. The officer held out his hand and the sergeant placed the dagger on his palm.

The officer sat back down and turned the scabbard in his hand. "Without doubt, an SS officer's knife." His hand grasped the hilt and pulled out the knife; the blade glistened in the light of the desk lamp. "Where did you find this?"

Wolfgang's heart sank. "Please, sir, I didn't find it. Brigadeführer Hofmann presented the dagger to me. For service to the Führer and Fatherland. For destroying an American tank with my Panzerfäust."

The officer put the dagger down, sighing and shaking his head. "Maybe you're one of the Brothers Grimm." He reached down, unclasped his own dagger, and laid it alongside the other. "All SS officers carry such daggers. Perhaps you found the dagger." He fixed Wolfgang with an icy stare. "Or, more likely, stole it!"

"Sir, I don't tell fairy tales, and I don't steal. Please look at what else is in my knapsack."

The sergeant's hand returned to the knapsack and pulled out the Luger.

"Brigadeführer Hofmann," Wolfgang swallowed hard, trying to will his voice not to tremble, "the brigadeführer also presented me with this – one of his personal pistols."

"You've assembled quite a little treasure trove for yourself, haven't you?" The officer leant back in his chair. "Either you're a hero of the

Third Reich, or," he narrowed his eyes, "as I'm inclined to believe, a lying deserter who deserves to dangle at the end of a rope."

Wolfgang felt terror rip through him; there was no way left to prove his loyalty to the Führer. The silence was broken by the slamming of the door. He looked up as a messenger entered briskly.

"Standartenführer Schneider, you've received urgent new orders." The messenger placed some papers on the officer's desk and left.

"Perhaps we can save time by dealing with the deserter now, Standartenführer?" A hint of a smile on the sergeant's face suggested that such a prospect would not be entirely devoid of pleasure.

Schneider scanned the order and looked up at Wolfgang. "Perhaps not quite yet, Hauptscharführer." He folded the paper in two. "We'll be seeing Brigadeführer Hofmann shortly. A special assignment for the Führer."

He drummed his fingers as he looked at Wolfgang. "Well, we'll soon find out if you're telling the truth." He picked up Wolfgang's Hitler-Jugend identification card and read the name. "Engelsing."

Wolfgang winced at the sound of his father's name.

Hofmann's convoy.

H ofmann began to read his new orders, put down the paper, and slammed his fist on the dashboard in anger. "Stop the car, Hans!"

Had Krebs gone completely mad? Was it possible he was being ordered to surrender control of his SS troops? He picked up the order and leapt down from his staff car, barely able to contain his rage.

"You are to pass command of your troops to Standartenführer Otto Schneider." His eyes blazed as he read. "Regrettably, a difficult situation has developed, and your battalions are needed to plug a gap at the front of the American advance."

Had Krebs and the entire General Staff become unhinged? If his troops were to go to the front, why couldn't he command them? The Führer knew his battle record, knew that he had no more able an officer. And to hand his command over to Schneider, of all people. He paced up and down. Schneider. He remembered his face from SS training school. A sly opportunist who knew all the right people in all the right places in order to work his way up the greasy pole of ambition. The brigadeführer kicked out in frustration at the tires of his car. The idiot had built his career on hustling Jews into cattle cars; now he spent his time rounding up deserters and malingerers. The man had never heard a shot fired in anger, except for the bullets fired by his own firing squads. And this was the man who was to take command of his troops.

Hofmann lit a cigarette and drew deeply, trying to bring his rage under control. Tossing the match to the ground, he continued to read the order.

"The Führer orders you to continue with your mission. You are to take two companies and begin initial preparations to establish an Alpenfestung at the specified location. You will be joined shortly by SS divisions moving north from Italy, over which you will assume command.

"On your way to the specified location, you are to place the cargo you are carrying in the salt mines at Alt Aussee."

The cargo. The treasures. A good portion of the Führer's artworks. He stamped out his cigarette. All to be defended by two companies. Had the Führer himself tipped the balance into insanity, as well?

"The Führer wishes you to know that, in entrusting you with said cargo, he is conferring upon you an honor of the highest degree."

So that was it: he was losing his current command because no one else could be trusted with the art. Schneider and the troops were expendable, but his precious art collection was not. Except in certain circumstances. Hofmann had received from the Führer's own lips the order to destroy the art should it ever be in danger of falling into enemy hands. The Führer had placed his trust in Hofmann, knew he could rely upon him to deliver the coup de grace should the need arise.

Hofmann understood his orders; he would be true to his oath. He climbed back into his staff car and tapped on the dashboard. "Let's go, Hans."

Errenbach Monastery.

Stanislaus pushed aside the account books, put down his pen, and moved his chair back from the desk. He needed a break.

The previous bookkeeper had been drafted into the army. Conscripting elderly monks was a measure of how low the Master Race had fallen. Every able-bodied male from fifteen to sixty was now in the service. Among the elderly white-headed monks that were left at the abbey, Stanislaus worried that he looked like a piece of unpicked ripe fruit; he hoped Father Hieronymus was right when he assured him that he received advance warning of Gestapo visits.

He closed the books, stood up, and stretched. The task bored him, but it made the hours pass away. Hours that marked time until the end of the war. But he wasn't sure he wanted to continue waiting at the monastery until the end of the war.

Frieda had kept him back. And Trudi. They had needed his protection, and the child had a myriad of special needs and wants. Here at the abbey they were well-provided for and safe. They no longer needed him. Why should he stay?

And the Raphael enticed him, goading him to leave the abbey, to restore it to his native land. He thought of the proud, defiant look on the Young Man's face. Pride and defiance: fitting symbols for a nation he knew would survive despite being crushed by the Nazis.

He gathered up the books in his arms to return them to the storage closet. The truth, he reluctantly admitted, was that he was torn. At odds with his desire to get back to Poland was a real fondness for the woman. He could not deny his feelings.

As he placed the books on the shelf, his eyes fell upon the small steel cashbox in the corner. Father Hieronymus had told him the box contained some deeds and historical documents, but only the abbot had the key, tied among his rosary. Stanislaus closed the door to the closet. Something did not ring true. What did Father Hieronymus have to hide?

Nuremberg.

Gina felt a great sadness as she looked at the ruins of the once-magnificent city in the bright light of mid-morning. Amidst the carcasses of buildings and twisted wreckage, her eye caught a freshly-painted sign that had been put there by the GIs who had taken the city:

> *"Germans! Give me ten years and you will not recognize Germany!"*—Adolf Hitler

Gina fought back her emotion. "I always hoped that one day I'd see Nuremberg. But not like this."

"The Krauts didn't exactly make it easy on themselves." The captain helped Gina step over a pile of rubble. "Hitler ordered the city to be defended to the last man."

"Nice guy." Terrill trod gingerly over the broken glass that crunched beneath his feet. "Say, how long did it take you guys to capture the city, sir?"

"Five days of hell. Pardon my language, miss. The defenders had really dug in. We gave the Krauts a hammering, but most of the devastation that you see was caused by Bomber Harris."

"Bomber Harris?"

"Sorry. He's the big cheese in the Royal Air Force. His flyboys had already taken a pretty good whack at the place." The captain stopped and pulled out a box of Chiclets. "Care for one?" He rattled the candy-coated gum inside the box as he held it out to Gina.

"No, thank you." Gina was anxious to get going again.

The captain popped a piece into his mouth. "You won't believe this, but some of the die-hards defending the Nazi Party Rally Grounds actually broke down and cried when we took it."

Gina shook her head. "What amazes me is how long so many Germans have stayed hoodwinked by that monster. He's destroyed their families, their homes, their lives, but still they remain faithful."

Bill nodded. "Say, Captain, I hear you had quite a celebration a few days ago."

"Yeah, we did. Our victory parade around the rally grounds ended with one hell of a fireworks display – I wish I'd had a camera on me when we blew up the swastika. You've seen pictures of it, I'm sure – the huge swastika on top of the grandstand where Hitler used to speak?" They started on their way again.

Bill remembered newsreels of Hitler standing at the podium beneath the swastika punching the air with a clenched fist above a forest of upraised arms; too bad the Führer hadn't been in the grandstand when the swastika went up in a burst of flames and smoke. He grasped Gina's upper arm to steady her as she half-stumbled.

"Let's turn here." The captain directed them down a tree-lined street that had escaped the worst of the bombings and the three walked in silence as they thought about the horrors the city had endured.

"Anyway," the captain said, "let's get back to business. I want to show you something I think you'll find interesting."

Schwan Hotel, southern Germany.

Emil Gruber eased his ample frame into his favorite seat at the table by the window overlooking Lake Hallstatt. He gazed across the water; the yellow walls and red roofs of the abbey across the lake were illuminated by the sun against a dark backdrop of mountains. He picked up the menu. The fare was limited – the effects of the war were now reaching

even the countryside – but at least his favorite bockwurst with fried potatoes and onions was still offered.

"The usual, Herr Direktor?" The waiter placed a glass stein of dunkel
beer on the table.

"But of course, Dietmar." Gruber sipped from his glass, cleared away
the foam from his mustache with his napkin, and leant back in the chair.
A Gestapo officer's life in the countryside had its compensations. The war
was going very badly, he knew. But his bailiwick, the Lake Hallstatt district, had escaped the worst. The bombs that had devastated the cities had
not reached them yet.

He mulled over the events of the other day. Father Hieronymus. The
abbey. After he had interrogated the Engelsing woman, he had done the
usual check around the abbey. Everything was in order; most importantly,
the painting was still nestling in its hiding place among the monks' bones.
But something was not quite right. The abbot was a wily fox, but the cleric
didn't fool him. Always the smooth talk, always buttering him up with
gifts.

"Your bockwurst, Herr Direktor." The waiter carefully placed the
steaming food in front of Gruber. Spooning a dollop of mustard on the
side of the plate, Gruber savored the aromas wafting up from the dish. He
was in a much better place than his friend, Ulbrecht, in Regensburg. There
was a slight pop as his teeth punctured the casing and exposed the salty
flesh of the sausage inside; he allowed the juices to linger on his tongue.
In Regensburg, Ulbrecht had told him, they were chasing down traitors,
hanging people from lampposts.

He put down his fork. That was the trouble with the Lake Hallstatt
district: not enough action, too few enemies of the state to chase down.
He refreshed his palate with a swig of beer before sawing off another cyl-
inder of bockwurst and swirling it in the mustard. The previous month,
he and his men had rounded up a mob of escaped slave laborers and
shipped them off to Mauthausen concentration camp where they were
shot. And they'd broken up a ring helping American prisoners of war
to escape to Switzerland; his own men had shot them. Apart from that,
nothing. The few Jews in the area had long since been rounded up and
sent to the camps. He finished his bockwurst, mopped up the juices with
the remains of his potatoes, and tossed his knife and fork onto the plate
with an angry clatter.

Gruber took his pipe and pouch from his pocket and tamped some tobacco into the bowl. His lack of involvement in the action rankled him and the annoyance took the edge off the pleasure of his meal.

"Another beer, Herr Direktor?"

He waved the hovering waiter away and leaned back in his chair, absorbed again in thoughts about the Engelsing woman. Her papers were in order, but he was sure he'd heard that name before. Perhaps Ulbrecht in Regensburg could answer the query he had sent by Telex. Provided Ulbrecht had the time, between dodging bombs and hanging traitors from lampposts.

Gruber got up from the table. Engelsing. Somehow, the name rang a bell.

Nuremberg.

"What exactly is this place you're taking us to, Captain?" Gina was relieved that the street they had turned down was free of rubble. Spring-green leaf buds sprouting on undamaged trees were like beautiful brush-strokes on a palette of greys.

"It's the place where we thought Charlemagne's regalia might be hidden."

"But you didn't find it there."

"No. And we have no leads. The only lead, if you can call it that, came from a museum director. He says some SS officers took the regalia away last month. His curators give the same story." The captain directed them to a shop at the corner of the street. "Every damned Kraut I've spoken to, they all tell the same tale. The SS supposedly took the stuff and dumped it in some lake south of here."

"What about the mayor? Have you interrogated him?" Gina asked hopefully. "He ought to know where the regalia is – after all, he was the one who orchestrated its theft from Vienna."

"Unfortunately, no, we haven't talked to him." The captain cleared his throat. "He blew his brains out just before we got here. Apparently life without his Nazi Germany wasn't worth living."

"If all the Krauts would just follow his example," Terrill said under his breath, "it sure as hell would save us a lot of trouble."

Gina gave Bill a look of reproach and glanced over at the captain, who seemed not to have heard. "Captain, doesn't it seem a bit fishy that everybody's telling the same story?"

"Well, uh, yes, I guess so, Lieutenant. Particularly in view of what we've found."

"What exactly have you found, Captain?" Gina asked.

"Let me show you." He stopped outside a shuttered shop and pushed open the door.

Errenbach Monastery.

She was on her knees in the vegetable patch when Stanislaus went into the garden behind the refectory. "Frieda!" he called out in a half-whisper; he hadn't seen her in days. She looked up and gave him a warm smile; her eyes seemed brighter and the color had returned to her cheeks. He hadn't realized how much he had missed her.

She got to her feet, brushing the soil from her hands against her apron.

"Stanislaus! How good to see you." She held a hand across her forehead to shield her eyes from the afternoon sun. "How are you?" The question came with genuine concern.

He began to stride forward, then cursed as his foot caught in the hem of his habit, causing him to fall on his backside. Frieda started to laugh, then put the back of her hand over her mouth.

"I'm sorry I swore." Stanislaus looked shame-faced as got to his knees.

"And I'm sorry I laughed." Frieda reached out a hand to help him up.

"It's all right—I realize how ridiculous I must look." Stanislaus struggled to get up. "I have to say that I can't wait to wear pants again."

"At least you're safe here," her hand lingered in his, "even if your skirts keep trying to trip you." Her lips struggled to suppress another laugh.

"Yes, I suppose so." He slowly pulled his hand away and looked in the direction of the vegetable patch to hide his embarrassment.

"I was just preparing the beds for the spring planting." Frieda looked at the plot, proud of her handiwork.

"I see." He turned back to her. "And how is Trudi?"

"Trudi's fine." She walked alongside him as they passed a trellis that would support the newy-planted runner beans. "She's being taught by Brother Helmut, who dotes on her. Needless to say, she's enjoying every minute of it. The doting, that is. She must be happy because I haven't heard her say lately that she wants to go home. I haven't heard even Clothilde say that."

Stanislaus smiled and nodded, remembering how Trudi's doll gave voice to things too painful for the child herself to say. "And you? Do you want to leave?"

The deepness of her sigh surprised him. "Father Hieronymus has been so kind, but…." Her voice trailed away and she began again. "Of course I'd like to take Trudi home," there was a slight crack of emotion in her voice, "except there's nowhere I can call home anymore."

He saw her lashes try to beat back tears and took her in his arms to give her comfort.

"Even if there were a place you called home, it's still too dangerous out there for you and Trudi." He spoke gently down into her hair as he tenderly squeezed her trembling frame. "All manner of humanity is on the road now – people bombed out of their homes, maimed German soldiers, slave laborers running wild – and they're all cold and hungry and desperate. And then, of course, there's Direktor Gruber."

He realized there was another, selfish reason for not wanting her to go.

"Besides, things will work themselves out; we just need patience." He watched as she raised her head, her shining eyes meeting his own. "And then it will all be over – you can take Trudi to your sister's house and I—" he paused, "—and I can go back to Poland." He hoped she did not perceive the uncertainty in his voice.

"But you, too, must take care." She slipped from his embrace. "Gruber comes here every week."

"Every week?" Stanislaus wondered how he had failed to notice.

"Yes, the woman who comes in to help the cook told me." She looked around her to check that the garden was still deserted. "I, myself, saw Gruber arrive just last Sunday."

170

Stanislaus weighed Frieda's words carefully. If Gruber came regularly, perhaps the abbot's protection was not so secure. The Gestapo were like a dog with a bone; Gruber would never let go.

He turned to look at Frieda and saw the anxiety in her eyes. As the war became desperate for Germany, they both knew the Gestapo was becoming even more vindictive. If they discovered her husband's role in Hitler's assassination attempt—

"Frieda, promise me you'll be careful." He held her by the shoulders, bending his head to look into her eyes. "We've got to find out the times when Gruber comes, and you've got to hide."

She nodded, biting her lower lip.

He put his arm around her waist and they began to walk. "Maybe there's a way we could get you and Trudi to your sister's house."

Frieda stopped suddenly and looked at him. "I wouldn't want to go without—" She caught herself and turned her eyes away. "You, yourself, just told me how dangerous it is to be out on the road. I wouldn't be able to protect Trudi on my own."

Stanislaus sensed her meaning. If she left the monastery, she would want him to accompany her and the child. What would be the right thing for him to do? To go or to stay? The perils of the open road or the threat of Gruber? And what should he do about the Raphael? Should he tell the abbot of its existence?

"Brother Stanislaus! Brother Stanislaus!" The shout came from across the garden – Brother Helmut was moving quickly down the path. "I've been looking for you everywhere!" He panted breathlessly as he neared them. "Father Hieronymus wants to see you in his study." He struggled to regain his breath. "He says it's urgent – please come at once!"

Nuremberg.

The shop was dilapidated, long unused. Plaster hung from the walls; dust, undisturbed for months, covered the counter.

Gina looked at the captain with raised eyebrows. He answered her unasked question. "There's a door over here." He led them to a corner of the shop. "A clerk in the museum told us about it."

He pulled a large ring of keys from his pocket. "It took a lot of, shall we say, persuasion to get the city fathers to hand these over. They're the keys to all the doors."

"Doors?"

"You'll see. Come on."

Gina and Terrill followed him, descending a long concrete ramp. At twenty-yard intervals there were ten-foot-high steel doors. As the captain opened the fourth set, Terrill offered his thoughts. "Sure looks like someone has something to hide, sir."

"Yeah, that's what we thought." The keys jangled against the last set of doors, which clanged open and revealed a large chamber from which led a series of tunnels. "Right now, we're under the eleventh-century castle. Or what's left of it."

"Where do we start?" Gina looked around at the labyrinthine maze of tunnels.

"We don't."

Gina scowled at the captain's terse answer. "What?"

"We've already searched all the tunnels. There's nothing here. No works of art. Not even a bad painting of the Führer. Zip."

Terrill frowned. "Then why did the Krauts bother with all this razzmatazz, sir?"

The captain shrugged his shoulders. "Who knows? I guess they meant to put Charlemagne's crown jewels in here and then decided it was a better idea to take them and dump them in some lake. The Nazis had a lot of bright ideas. Lots of luck trying to figure any of them out."

"Something just doesn't feel right, sir." Terrill frowned and stuffed his hands deeply into his pockets, jingling the jeep keys.

"Perhaps I can interview the museum staff?" Gina's voice could not hide her disappointment.

"Sure." The captain led the way back up the ramp. "But I'll warn you now – they've all got the same story."

Gina grimaced. She had so desperately wanted to reclaim the regalia of Charlemagne. The scepter, the crown, the sword, the bejeweled gloves. She felt sick in the pit of her stomach. Now, all at the bottom of some lake.

The streets were eerily silent as Gina and Bill picked a path through the debris. They were finding their way back from the bunker without the captain, who had left to arrange an interview with a museum director for Gina.

"I don't get it," Bill said. "Why would the SS guys want to dump Charlemagne's crown jewels in some lake?"

"I don't know, Bill." Gina looked up at the gutted buildings that loomed on both sides of the street like false fronts in some horrific stage set. "But do you know what it reminds me of?"

He turned to her and shook his head.

"Do you remember what Alan said about the empty casket that had Hitler's name on it? The one we found in the Bernterode Mine next to the caskets of the German heroes?"

Terrill exhaled loudly through his teeth. "Yeah, something like if Hitler ever died, the Nazis might put him in that box and worship him as some kind of a martyr."

"Well, it's just possible that the SS officers who took the regalia away might have had a similar idea."

Terrill knit his brow. "I don't get you. What's Charlemagne got to do with Hitler?"

"Hitler calls Germany the 'Third Reich.' Ever wonder what the First Reich was, Bill?"

He smiled sheepishly. "I was never very good in geography."

"The First Reich was the Holy Roman Empire. Founded by—"

"Charlemagne?" Bill interjected.

"Yes, Charlemagne. It's possible the SS officers who took the regalia away may be planning to use them in whatever morbid cult caused them to put a coffin for Hitler in the Bernterode Mine next to the casket of Frederick the Great." She grimaced at the thought of the fabulous regalia being used in such a sordid fashion. "The story about the lake could be just a red herring."

They stopped to look at a bombed-out building that was covered with messages and photographs.

"What's that all about?" Bill asked.

Gina read some of the messages. "They seem to be communications to – or about – missing family members. This one says 'Holger, I've gone south to Wendelstein with Renate,' and it's signed 'Heide.' And the one over here," she pointed to a note under a photograph of a little boy, "is written by a mother searching for her child." Gina jumped as they heard gunfire in the distance.

"You okay?"

"It just startled me – are there still pockets of resistance here?"

Bill put his arm around her shoulder. "The Nazis, they never give up. But we're in the safe zone. And you're safe with me."

They walked in a silence punctuated by distant gunshots; Bill's right arm felt Gina tense with each shot, and he pulled her closer to him.

"There's something else that might have happened to the regalia, Bill. And I hope to God it didn't."

"What's that?"

"I think," Gina's voice trembled with foreboding, "that the SS officers could have taken the regalia away for more selfish reasons. Many of them will want to escape out of Germany after the war rather than answer for their crimes. The precious gems in the regalia, if they removed them...." Gina's voice began to break.

Terrill caught her drift. "If they pried out the jewels and melted down the gold, they could sell it off piecemeal and live the life of Riley somewhere else."

"If that happened, Bill, the SS wouldn't just be stealing valuable objects. They'd be depriving us all of a precious thousand-year-old heritage."

"I hope you're wrong. But I wouldn't put it past those creeps."

"We'll just have to wait and see what the interview turns up this afternoon. Wish me luck, Bill." She looked up at him. His arm around her shoulders made her feel secure, as though everything would be all right. "You'll keep your fingers crossed for me, won't you, Bill?"

He grinned and held up the crossed fingers of his left hand.

Errenbach Monastery.

"Ah, Brother Stanislaus! Please come in. Can I offer you some of our excellent dunkel beer?" He lifted a pitcher from the table by the window and poured the foamy, dark brown contents into two steins.

Stanislaus grasped the proffered glass, took a swallow, and sat on the chair opposite the abbot's desk.

"I must say you look every inch a monk," the abbot's face was warm and jovial, "with your habit and tonsure."

Stanislaus grimaced; he felt he looked like an old woman. "You wanted to see me, Father?"

"Ah, yes." The abbot placed his stein on his desk and sat down. "You're making a big contribution to our monastic community, keeping our books so accurately. Your arrival was indeed an answer to my prayers. The conscription of Brother Martin, our previous bookkeeper, was a great blow. I thank God that most of my brothers are too old for military service."

The abbot rose from his desk and walked to the window. "And your doctoring skills have been greatly appreciated by the brothers."

"I've had almost nothing to do." Stanislaus shrugged. "A bruise and cut here, some sniffles there – your brothers are a hardy people."

"Maybe it's the healthy supplement to their diet." The abbot pointed to his stein and laughed.

There was an awkward silence. Stanislaus wondered if it was a good time to raise the question of the Raphael but decided against it.

"Father Hieronymus, Brother Helmut said you wanted to see me on a very urgent matter. But so far we've only drunk beer and made small talk."

The Father hesitated, then spoke quickly. "Brother Stanislaus, if one of the brothers had a severe fracture of the arm, how would you treat him?"

"I'd treat for any shock first, apply antiseptic to any open wound," Stanislaus ran through the procedures, "then, when he was stable, reset the bone, preferably under anesthetic if the fracture was—" He stopped and looked at the abbot. "But I haven't heard any report of a brother with a broken arm. Is this some form of test?"

The abbot returned to his desk, his fingers toying anxiously with his crucifix. "It may be a bigger test than you think, my son." As he chose his words, the abbot studied a painting of Jesus praying in Gethsemane on the wall behind Stanislaus. "I have such a patient. He's in a barn across the lake." He shifted his eyes and looked searchingly at Stanislaus's face. "He's an American pilot. Will you go tonight to treat him, Brother Stanislaus?"

Nuremberg.

Gina and Bill took a table in a quiet area of the large tent that served as a temporary canteen. The place was almost deserted: after the frustrating tour of the underground tunnels, Gina had conducted a fruitless interview with a museum director for a couple of hours, and it was well after lunchtime. Bill was content that they had a little seclusion. Gina was obviously feeling her disappointment keenly – her eyes hardly left her plate of macaroni and cheese as she picked at the food halfheartedly.

"Perhaps Charlemagne's crown jewels are hidden somewhere else." Terrill knew it was a lost cause, but he had to break the silence. Her disappointment pained him more than he wanted to admit.

"Of course they're somewhere else!" she said sharply. "That's what the director told me at the interview. The point is where?" Her fork clattered as she tossed it on the plate in frustration. "He couldn't tell me."

"Or wouldn't?" He shrugged and turned up his palms.

Gina pushed away her barely-touched plate. "He just kept repeating that some SS officers took the relics away with the intention of dumping them into some lake. Secret orders, he said. Doesn't know where they went."

"Are you sure it's not some cock-and-bull story?" He pushed his own plate away, his appetite lost.

"What if it is?" she snapped at Terrill. "Any clever ideas?"

He saw her face redden with anger and frustration. "I'm sorry, Bill," she sighed. "I shouldn't shout at you."

He looked away as her chest began to heave; he could not bear to see the pain of her disappointment.

"You have to understand that ever since I was a young girl I've been entranced by Charlemagne. I never for one moment dreamed I'd be in a situation where the fate of his precious regalia could depend on me."

She stared down into her cold coffee. "And I think that if the relics aren't located soon, they'll never be found. So if I don't find them, no one will."

Bill sought to console her. "Don't put so much pressure on yourself, Gina. If you don't personally lay your hands on them and they aren't at the bottom of some lake, they'll come to light eventually."

She shook her head. "Not necessarily, Bill. When the Monuments Men pack up and go home, all bets are off."

"Stop blaming yourself, Gina. If the crown jewels don't turn up, it's not your fault."

"But it *will* be my fault, Bill. Because it will mean I wasn't clever enough to outwit the Nazi thieves. And I'll be blaming myself for the rest of my life."

Terrill moved his hands across the table and grasped her fingers.

She could no longer restrain her tears. "Bill, I just need a break – just one lousy, little break."

He had no words. His fingers softly caressed the back of her hand. He wanted to tell her that the regalia were unimportant, but he knew he could not. He wanted to tell her what was important, but knew he dare not.

He squeezed her hand in a vain effort to console her. God damn the lousy war.

Gestapo Headquarters, Lake Hallstatt District.

"An enjoyable lunch, Herr Direktor?"

Gruber ignored the question from Konrad, the elderly, pale-faced corporal tapping away at the typewriter on his desk, and pushed open the door to his office. He wondered how he had been stuck with an idiot for a clerk.

He hung his coat and cap on the rack and slumped in his chair, running his fingers through the messages on his desk. The usual crap. Goebbels's exhortation to total war, to root out the traitors. Gruber poured over the reports, tossed them aside, and picked up his pipe.

"Any news from Ulbrecht in Regensburg, Konrad?" Gruber shouted through the open door.

"Not yet, sir." The clerk looked up from his typewriter. "Perhaps there's some difficulty."

Of course there were difficulties for Ulbrecht, Gruber thought. Bombs, traitors. Perhaps there'd be an answer tomorrow. He stood up and walked to the window. The lake was still, the monastery's image reflected clearly in the water. Maybe he should pay another visit to Father Hieronymus and interview the Engelsing woman again. Probe a little deeper. He wasn't sure where he was headed – he just had a hunch that there was more to her story than met the eye. He could check on the painting in the crypt while he was there.

He tapped the spent contents of his pipe bowl into the ashtray. Why hadn't Ulbrecht called? His thoughts were disturbed by the clatter of the Telex. He jumped up from his desk. "Ulbrecht? Regensburg?"

The corporal took the paper from the machine. "I'm afraid not, mein Herr." His eyes flickered over the message. "Apparently an American airman has been downed in the area."

"A Yanqui airman?" Gruber leapt up from his desk. "Where?"

"A parachute was seen near Bad Mitterndorf," the corporal read from the Telex, "late yesterday evening."

"Why weren't we informed earlier?" Gruber asked angrily as he grabbed his cap and coat from the rack. "Call out the guard! And have them bring the dogs!"

Hofmann's convoy.

Hofmann shot up from the chair in his makeshift office in an abandoned house. "Of course this young man is known to me!" He spoke through clenched teeth. "Schneider, have you lost your mind?" He fixed the standartenführer with a furious glare. "You don't arrest a hero of the Third Reich!"

"He was wandering around alone," Schneider stood his ground, "and that's usually a sure sign of a deserter."

"Deserter?" Hofmann exploded. "This young man," he placed his hand on Wolfgang's shoulder, "this young man risked his life to destroy an enemy tank and kill several American soldiers." Hofmann turned to Schneider, a sneer on his face. "No doubt, that is more than your contribution to the war, Standartenführer."

Hofmann put aside his anger as he turned to Wolfgang with a smile. "Well, Scharführer Engelsing, I'm glad to see you're safely back from your Werewolf assignment. Tell me how it went."

"Sir, we were attacked." Wolfgang hesitated. "We were surrounded by an overwhelming force of Americans," he struggled to compound his lie, "who bombed us with mortars." He lowered his eyes. "The sergeant and Willi made a run for it, but were cut down. I stayed and tried to fight the Americans off, but there were too many of them. But I did pick a few of them off, I'm sure of it."

"My brave man! But how did you ever manage to survive? You must have had a lucky break."

Wolfgang thought quickly for an answer. "Jawohl, mein Herr, an unbelievable piece of luck." He stood erect as he forced himself to look the brigadeführer straight in the eye. "I was stunned by a mortar shell, sir. When I came to, the Americans had gone. Perhaps they thought I was dead." He fervently hoped the brigadeführer was finished with his questions.

Hofmann slapped Wolfgang on the back. "And then you escaped being hanged by Standartenführer Schneider!" His laugh rang around the room. "If the Reich has your luck, we'll win the war yet. Tell me, Scharführer, how—"

Wolfgang's taut muscles relaxed when a sergeant burst into the room holding a piece of paper in his hands.

"An urgent message, sir."

Nuremberg.

Terrill walked down the steps of the museum, eased his back against the wall, and lit a Lucky Strike. Gina was inside talking with some of the museum staff, and apart from a handful of MPs, the streets were almost deserted. A few Germans hurried along with furtive glances, anxious to get home before curfew. He drew deeply and blew the smoke into the crisp air. Anxious to get home. If they had a home in this God-forsaken place. Probably scuttling like rats looking for some cellar to sleep in for the night.

His mind ran over the events of the day. He felt Gina's disappointment keenly – she'd set her heart on finding the treasures only to learn the Krauts had probably dumped them in some lake. He tapped on his cigarette. Personally, he didn't give a damn for all the artwork in Europe. If the Mona Lisa itself was keeping company with the fishes, he wouldn't care. But he did care about Gina. And he wanted to go home. Away from this hellhole, where violent death waited at every corner, where boys hurled themselves at bullets that claimed their short lives. He threw his cigarette on the ground, and angrily stamped on it.

"Got a cigarette, soldier?" The heavily-accented English surprised him. The woman came down the museum steps, her shoes clattering on the flagstones as she picked her way through the rubble. She didn't look like the other German women who had often approached him, faces plastered with garish make-up, ready to sell their souls, or at least their bodies, for a pack of cigarettes.

"I'd do anything for a cigarette." She looked at him and smiled.

Hofmann's convoy.

Hofmann's eyes narrowed as he scanned the message he had just been handed. He turned to the orderly. "Have the regimental commanders report to me at once!"

"What's going on?" Schneider shouted. "I demand to know!"

Hofmann gave a grim smile. "And so you shall, Schneider. It appears," he tapped the paper he held in his hand, "that an advance party of American troops has entered Blautenberg." He turned to the map spread on top of the table. "The town of Blautenberg is here." His forefinger stabbed at the map. "An American occupation of this town bars my way to Alt Aussee. And the completion of my mission."

"And what might that be?"

"The Alpenfestung." Hofmann elected to say nothing about the art. "The final fortress. Where we can hold out until the Führer delivers the new wonder weapons."

"Defend a fortress? With two companies?" Schneider laughed.

Hofmann exploded with rage. "The Führer has promised me divisions from Italy – perhaps others from the Russian front. We will attack Blautenberg," he glanced at his watch, "in six hours. At midnight, when the Americans are asleep."

Schneider's face reddened. "I must protest! This battle group is under my control now! My orders state that I am the commander! That order comes from the Führer!"

Hofmann looked up from the map. "I'm aware of the Führer's order, Schneider. If you'll care to take a closer look, you'll see the Führer orders that you take command at eight a.m. on April 30th. In case you hadn't noticed, Standartenführer," Hofmann gave a sardonic chuckle, "that's tomorrow morning."

He turned to Wolfgang. "Scharführer Engelsing, I want you to muster your Hitler-Jugend troop. Make sure each one is armed with a Panzerfäust. There will be many Yanqui tanks waiting for you."

Wolfgang saluted and hurried to his task, anxious for a chance to prove himself, to wipe the slate clean.

"I must object in the strongest possible terms!" Schneider shouted.

"Send your objections in writing to Berlin." Hofmann turned to greet the arrival of his regimental commanders. "And while you're waiting for a reply, perhaps you'd like to join us for the battle."

Nuremberg.

"So you'd do anything for a cigarette, would you?" Terrill's voice lacked animation; he'd heard the line so many times before.

"Well, not quite anything," the woman added quickly, embarrassed by his misunderstanding. "I'm not like the others."

"Then what are you like?" Terrill regretted the almost-instinctive anger in his voice. He looked at the deep lines that framed the woman's large eyes, fixed above dark shadows on a face that had seen better years. But her shoulder-length auburn hair was still beautiful; Terrill wondered how she managed to keep it shining in a city without running water.

"I'm a clerk who works in a museum, trying to survive that swine Hitler's war." Her voice was a blend of bitterness and ennui. "My husband's dead, I have a child to raise, and yesterday we were ordered by you Americans to vacate our apartment." She spat out the words. Terrill watched as she struggled to control her temper. "Perhaps I deserve a cigarette?"

"I see. Let me get this straight – you're opposed to the Nazis."

"Yes, always." Her dark eyes flashed and her face flushed with anger.

"Yeah, well, I've heard it all before," Terrill said with a world-weariness he truly felt. "Every German I've ever met was opposed to the Nazis."

"My husband died in a concentration camp. He spoke out against Hitler and the Nazis killed him." Terrill looked into her eyes, which peered steadily into his. He trusted his old knack – he could tell by her eyes that she was telling the truth. He held out his pack of Luckies toward her.

"Danke." She took a cigarette from the proffered pack and reached up to push the hair that had fallen into her eyes back from her face.

"Well, I've got good news for you." He waved his lighter under the end of her cigarette. "Looks like the Thousand-Year Reich is going to be coming up short by about nine hundred and ninety years. Soon you'll have nothing to worry about from the Nazis."

"You're making a big mistake if you believe that." She spoke with a surprising vehemence as she exhaled the smoke. "The Nazis – they'll fight to the death."

"Yeah, well I'm telling you it's a lost cause." Terrill was beginning to get bored with the conversation.

"What are you doing in Nuremberg?" she asked, as if she owed him some conversation to pay for the cigarette but wanted to change the subject.

"I'm a sort of chauffeur."

"You're a sort of chauffeur. In the all-conquering United States Army."

"I drive a woman who's looking for art treasures that somehow got stuck to Nazi fingers."

"Well, there's plenty of that. I know from my work in the museum."

"At the moment, she's looking for something called the Charlemagne regalia."

The woman froze. "I suppose she thinks the regalia are at the bottom of a lake somewhere."

Her comment took Terrill by surprise. "That's what everyone seems to be telling her."

"But they're not. They're here in Nuremberg. And now I must go. Thanks again for the cigarette." She tossed her half-smoked cigarette down, crushed it with her heel, and began to walk away.

"How do you know the regalia are in Nuremberg?" Terrill called after her. "Please come back – there's someone I want you to talk to."

She quickened her pace. "Speak to Herr Schlossberg, the museum director. He knows." Her heels clipped on the pavement as she began to run.

Hofmann's convoy.

Wolfgang sat beside the truck, his back against the rear wheel. The rest of the troop of Hitler-Jugend milled around, their spirits high with the anticipation of battle, their nervous laughter echoing from the rock face that climbed steeply on one side of the road.

Some were engaging in horseplay and their shouts of bravado grated against his depressed spirit. How could they laugh when two of their comrades were dead and they, themselves, were about to go into battle? Ulrich, blown to hell by the American tank. And Willi. The memory of Willi lying in the bloodied pool swam before his eyes.

He fought to dislodge the image. He was supposed to be their leader, their scharführer, but he no longer believed in himself. The sun was beginning to drop behind the mountain peaks; he walked around the truck and gazed out over a cliff that fell precipitously away to a valley already in the shadows.

How could he be their leader? He had abandoned his post, lied to the brigadeführer – acts of a traitor. The old man in the square at Brettheim had been hanged for less. A traitor. Wolfgang shivered, but not from the growing cold of the evening air. Did his father's blood run in his veins? A father who wanted to assassinate the Führer?

From the corner of his eye, Wolfgang saw the brigadeführer approaching. He shot up to his feet and snapped to attention, his arm outstretched in salute.

"At ease, Scharführer." The officer returned his salute and then looked down at him. Wolfgang stared into the distance, trying to avoid the brigadeführer's eyes.

"Engelsing," his father's name on the brigadeführer's lips made him uneasy, "I'm sure I don't have to tell you that our success tonight depends much on how well your troop carries out its mission." Hofmann placed a gloved hand on Wolfgang's shoulder and fixed him with a stern but sympathetic gaze. "I'm counting on you tonight. I have complete confidence that you and your troop will succeed for the Führer and the Fatherland."

I'm counting on you tonight. I have complete confidence.... Wolfgang sensed a chance to redeem himself.

The brigadeführer smiled. "Prepare your troop, Scharführer." He gave Wolfgang a playful slap on his shoulder and withdrew his hand. "And good luck."

A farm on the far side of Lake Hallstatt. Midnight.

T he flickering light from the lantern held by Brother Helmut pierced the shadows of the barn. Stanislaus approached the injured American flyer lying on a crude bed of fresh straw. The pilot's eyes were half-closed. Congealed blood matted his dark hair and a low moan of pain came from his lips.

Stanislaus motioned for the monk to bring the light closer as he opened the medical kit hastily put together by the abbot. He found little to help treat a patient. An antiquated stethoscope, a small sharp knife, a roll of bandages, and some pieces of wood to act as a splint. And, at the bottom of the bag, a bottle of schnapps. The abbot's resources didn't extend to a proper anesthetic.

Stanislaus blinked and shook his head to rouse himself. He was exhausted. They hadn't left the monastery until after ten, and he'd had to take turns with Brother Helmut rowing across the lake in the dark.

The rattle of the barn door latch startled him. The farmer stood in the doorway, silhouetted against the pale moonlight. "Please hurry." His voice was anxious, urgent. "The Yanqui has to be moved out of here before daybreak."

"Then bring a bowl of hot water. Fast."

The farmer disappeared. Stanislaus began to run his hand gently over the pilot's arm. As he reached his lower right forearm, the American let out a scream that Stanislaus felt could be heard back at the monastery.

Stanislaus pulled the schnapps from the bag and held it up. The pilot understood and nodded as Stanislaus uncorked the spirit and pushed it toward his trembling lips.

The farmer returned and handed a towel and a bowl of hot water to Brother Helmut, who bathed the American's face, removing the dried blood. Stanislaus examined the head wound. Superficial. He looked into the flier's eyes. Dilated pupils. Perhaps a slight concussion.

Stanislaus knew there was a break in the right forearm. He had to examine it, and reached into the bag for the knife. The American saw the light shine on the blade and the fear returned to his eyes. Stanislaus offered the bottle, and the American drank greedily with his free left hand as Stanislaus began carefully to cut through the sleeve.

The American groaned as Stanislaus ran his finger over the forearm. The skin was not ruptured, thank heaven. A simple fracture of the radius, just above the wrist. He had to reset the bone quickly, to minimize the pain.

He prepared the splints and the bandage. He looked at the American. Despite the lack of language, the American understood. He took another swig and nodded.

Stanislaus beckoned Brother Helmut to bring the lamp nearer. He soaked the towel, pushed it between the American's teeth, and positioned his hands around the broken bone.

Blautenberg. Midnight.

Wolfgang paused for breath as he peered into the darkness. With his troop, he had run downhill from the edge of the forest to the outskirts of the town. The pale light of the moon caught them as they prepared their Panzerfäusts. He looked across to Feldwebel Schultz: Wolfgang's troop was under his command, as was the feldwebel's own company of one hundred men. Everything was as the brigadeführer had said it would be. The American tanks – about ten, he counted quickly – were parked in the town square, their engines switched off.

Wolfgang was stunned by the silence. Why were there were no American soldiers guarding the tanks? His breath hung in the cool air as he looked at his watch: almost midnight. The brigadeführer's orders had been clear: take out the tanks and withdraw. In ten minutes a mortar barrage would fall on the square to prevent any response by the American force.

He had ten minutes to strike and withdraw before the barrage. Wolfgang looked to his left and right and saw his troop waiting for his leadership. Now was his chance. A brief thought of Willi came into his mind and strangely gave him heart. Revenge. He caught the feldwebel's signal and waved his troop forward.

The farm.

He heard the click of the bone as it dropped into place. The American's scream died in the towel as his head fell back on the straw. Stanislaus moved quickly, positioning the splints on either side of the arm as he bound them tight with the bandage.

As he tied the ends of the sling around the pilot's neck, a man dressed in work clothes entered the barn and addressed the pilot. "Good evening." He spoke in heavily accented English. "I am here to take you to a safe house."

The man exchanged a few words in German with Brother Helmut. The monk untied a sack attached to his cord belt and handed it to the man, who again spoke to the American. "You will have certain expenses; this bag is for you, from the good brothers of the monastery."

He held out a hand to the pilot. "May I help you get up?" The pilot took the man's hand with his good arm and hauled himself to his feet.

"Now we must leave. It is not safe for you to remain here – you may have been seen in the area." Brother Helmut whispered a translation in Stanislaus's ear as the man put a hand on the pilot's shoulder and directed him out by the back door of the barn.

Stanislaus quickly rinsed the implements in the bowl of water and returned them to the medical kit while Brother Helmut tried to clean up all traces of the American's presence. They both froze when the front door of the barn banged open and the farmer's wife rushed in. "There's a car coming down the lane." Her voice was little more than a whisper.

Brother Helmut leaned forward and blew out the flame of the lantern.

Blautenberg.

Darkness enveloped Wolfgang's troop as they took their positions in the square. The menacing shapes of the American tanks were barely distinct. Where were their crews? There were no sentries, nothing.

Feldwebel Schultz tapped him on the shoulder and led his company to the other side of the square while Wolfgang signaled to his troop to take position. He selected the gray shape of one tank and raised the Panzerfäust to his shoulder.

Suddenly, a door opened in a house at the edge of the square, throwing a shaft of light onto the tanks. Wolfgang heard a shout from the doorway. A burst of submachine gunfire cut the voice off.

"Fire, Scharführer, fire!" the feldwebel shouted.

"Fire!" Wolfgang echoed the order and pulled the trigger of his Panzerfäust.

In the forest near Lake Hallstatt.

Stanislaus felt as though his lungs were bursting as he ran after Brother Helmut, weaving his way between the trees of the forest. Only the thin pencil of light of the monk's flashlight gave them any guidance through the darkness. His heart pounded against his ribs.

He knew the pursuers were not far behind. And he could hear the barking of dogs. Perhaps the American would be safe: he'd left by the back door of the barn a good ten minutes before the cars arrived.

His arms pumped harder. As he had run out of the barn towards the woods he'd heard shouts. In the headlights of one of the cars he'd seen a stout man with a bushy mustache, a man who looked like the figure Father Hieronymus had pointed out from the window. Gruber, the Gestapo man.

Only willpower drove Stanislaus on. If he and Brother Helmut were captured, their tracks would lead back to the monastery and Father Hieronymus. And eventually to Frieda.

The cry from Helmut startled him. The monk's arms grasped vainly at a tree before he slid to the ground. Stanislaus knelt beside him, the light from the flashlight revealing the pain on Helmut's face. He tried to lift the monk to his feet, but Helmut winced and fell back to his knees.

"It's my ankle. I think it's sprained." There was resignation in Brother Helmut's eyes. "You must go on, Brother Stanislaus. The lake's not far away. Perhaps I can find a hiding place."

"No, we go together." Stanislaus pulled Brother Helmut to his feet and placed the monk's arm around his shoulders.

The injured man took one step and gave a cry of pain as he again fell to the ground. "Go on, Stanislaus," Brother Helmut begged. "The rowboat is that way." He pointed through the trees. "I'll find somewhere to hide."

Stanislaus hesitated for a moment. Both heard the baying of the dogs and the shouts of the Gestapo guards.

Brother Helmut began to crawl away. "Go, Stanislaus." His voice carried through the dark of the forest. "In the name of God, go!"

Blautenberg.

Wolfgang saw his shell hit where he had aimed. Just below the turret. The explosion rang in his ears. Flames began to lick at the tank and he heard shouts from inside. The Americans had been asleep in their tanks! More explosions echoed around the square. A machine gun from the tank began to spit bullets.

"Wolfgang, Wolfgang!" Horst cried out. "I'm in trouble!" He looked across at Horst. His Panzerfäust had failed to fire. The engine of the tank roared ominously into life.

His eyes turned to the turret hatch of the tank he had hit; men began to jump out, one with his clothes on fire. Their bodies danced ghoulishly as the feldwebel's machine guns cut them down. The night air filled with noise. More tank engines started. Although half a dozen were in flames, some had escaped, their machine gun turrets spraying bullets at the Hitler-Jugend. Wolfgang saw Ernst and Manfred fall lifeless. The noise grew, punctuated by a large explosion as a tank fired a shell into the position of the feldwebel's company.

More Americans came out of the house, firing their machine guns. Smoke billowed around the square. The acrid smell of gunpowder mixed with the foul odor of burning flesh.

Wolfgang felt paralyzed, mesmerized, but the screech of tank tracks and the soul-piecing scream snapped him from his trance. The tank had run over Horst. His life and entrails had been squeezed from him. Wolfgang threw away his Panzerfäust and began to run, bullets dancing around his feet.

Then came a new, different noise. At first, a slow whistle, growing to a roar: the brigadeführer was throwing in the mortars. He had to escape. He saw the low stone wall at the edge of the square and ran for it, legs and arms pumping, lungs heaving.

Crump! The first salvo fell, the blast almost throwing him off balance. Crump! Crump! He heard screams behind him as he threw himself over the wall and huddled into a ditch.

Despite his fear, the image of Horst crushed by the tank was burnt into Wolfgang's mind. The scream, the blood. His stomach heaved and vomit dribbled from his lips.

Errenbach Monastery.

Father Hieronymus closed his eyes, silently mouthed a prayer, and crossed himself after Stanislaus told him of Brother Helmut's injury. "The Lord has laid a heavy hand on our Brother tonight. May the Heavenly Father have mercy upon him and give him strength. But he's a good man; I don't think he'll divulge anything."

Stanislaus took a seat opposite the abbot's desk and hung his head. "I felt terrible leaving him, Father. I didn't know what to do."

"There's nothing any of us can do right now, my son. Only pray, wait, and have faith. But I don't think the Lord would mind if we helped ourselves to a drink to ease our nerves. And to help us sleep." The abbot glanced at the clock as he rose to pour the schnapps. "My goodness, it's almost two a.m."

Stanislaus took the glass from the abbot. "Tell me, Father, the American isn't the first you've helped, is he?"

Father Hieronymus poured his glass of schnapps, adjusted the skirt of his robe, and sat down behind his desk. "No. There have been others. Some escaped prisoners of war, others trapped behind enemy lines like the pilot, others who were on the Gestapo's wanted list."

Stanislaus leaned forward, resting his elbows on his knees. "You're taking a big risk with the Gestapo officer always sniffing around. How do you get them out?"

The abbot sighed. "With luck, with help from our many friends, and with the grace of God. And money, of course – lots of money."

"Money?"

"To buy forged documents and new clothes. And to help compensate our friends, the owners of the safe houses, for the risks they take."

Stanislaus leaned back. "But I've seen your financial records. You have no money."

The abbot, sipping his schnapps, was slow to reply. "In the monastery's treasury, to which only I have a key, are objects of great value, articles of veneration the monastery has accumulated over the centuries. These treasures have long been deemed important to the devotion of our Lord." He took a deep breath, as if for sustenance. "But I think not. In any event, these are the source of the money that is needed to help the brave unfortunates who find themselves in danger near our abbey."

Stanislaus was surprised, but hardly shocked. "You've been selling the contents of the church treasury, Father?"

"Yes, but never the relics of the saints, of course. Today, to help the pilot, I sold a silver liturgical plate. Last week, a chalice carved of rock crystal. A month ago, an illuminated manuscript created centuries ago at this monastery in our old scriptorium."

"But who buys these things?"

Father Hieronymus smiled wryly. "That I shall tell no one, not even you, whom I trust. Let's just say I have an agent that so far has escaped Herr Direktor Gruber's poisonous tentacles." He set his glass down and studied it for a few moments. "Anyway, there you have it. I realize these treasures are the heritage of the monastery, but I ask myself: what are these dead things gathering dust in a locked room compared with the lives of men? Which would our blessed Savior choose to save?"

Stanislaus knew there was no need to answer the abbot's question. But he also knew that some objects transcend the fleeting lives of individual men to serve a larger purpose – to inspire a whole nation. The Raphael painting was such a treasure: it belonged to Poland, and its return to his homeland would be symbolic, a small but significant step toward healing a country that had been bled dry – people enslaved, cities destroyed, monuments melted down to make German bullets.

The abbot pointed to the schnapps. "May I refill your glass, Brother Stanislaus?"

Stanislaus shook his head.

Father Hieronymus drained his own. "In any event, I shall not be raiding the church treasury much longer." He smiled sadly. "Of necessity. Alas, there are very few items of value left in the treasury to sell."

Few items of value left to sell. Father Hieronymus did not appear to know of the priceless treasure hidden in his crypt. The Raphael. *The Portrait of the Young Man.* If he ever discovered the masterpiece in his abbey, he would surely sell it, as well, to fund his good works.

Stanislaus brought his hand to his lips to hide a yawn. "It's been a long day, Father. Time for me to turn in."

"Before you do, will you join me in a silent prayer for Brother Helmut and the American pilot?" Without waiting for an answer, Father Hieronymus kneeled, bowed his head, and brought his clasped hands to his chest, his lips imploring the Almighty to guide the steps of the American to safety and help Brother Helmut bear his cross.

In his own way, Stanislaus prayed for the monk and the pilot. Perhaps the airman stood a good chance of escaping to safety, but kind, sweet Brother Helmut – what was in store for him?

Guilt for not having stayed with the monk mixed with overwhelming exhaustion and began to weigh him down. His body felt leaden, but his soul was even heavier. And now, added to his worry, was another. The Raphael was not safe at the monastery.

Blautenberg.

"That's the way to beat the Yanquis!" Hofmann peered through his binoculars as the dawn light broke over the devastated town, smoke rising from the destroyed tanks. There was no sign of the Americans apart from three dozen bodies sprawled in the square.

"But surely our casualties have been high." Schneider's voice was critical.

"War, my dear Schneider," Hofmann let his binoculars fall to his chest, "is not fought in white gloves and top hats." He looked at his fellow officer with contempt. "You're about to find out that there's more to war than hanging deserters behind the lines."

Hofmann turned to his orderly. "Hauptmann, make sure we secure the town. I want machine gun ports in the houses at the far end. Have them dig in deep, to prepare for a counterattack." He breathed deeply and lowered his voice. "Have we news of our casualties?"

The orderly scanned his papers. "The full report is not yet available, Brigadeführer, but we know of thirty-three dead, including Feldwebel Schultz." Hofmann grimaced. Schultz had been a good man, a true National Socialist fighter. He recalled the time when Schultz had carried the standard during the triumphant entry into Paris.

The orderly interrupted his thoughts. "The Hitler-Jugend troop suffered badly as well, sir. Twelve dead."

"And Scharführer Engelsing?" Hofmann tried to suppress the anxiety he felt as he watched the orderly's finger run slowly down his list.

"Scharführer Engelsing is not on the list, sir. Presumed to be uninjured, sir."

"Good. Have him report to my staff car," he glanced at his watch, "in fifteen minutes." Hofmann turned his attention to a map. "And have the trucks ready to move out with the rest of the Hitler-Jugend troop and companies A and B."

"I see your Scharführer Engelsing leads a charmed life, Hofmann." There was a chuckle in Schneider's voice as he spoke.

"Sometimes, Schneider," Hofmann snapped, "heroism in the service of National Socialism brings a just reward." He looked up from the map and fixed Schneider with a stare. "And now, Schneider, the responsibility rests with you."

"Me?" Schneider struggled to grasp what Hofmann was saying.

"I will leave with my two companies in half an hour." Hofmann pulled on his gloves. "You will take command of the rest of the battle group."

Hofmann began to stride away, then turned. "It is your responsibility to defend this town against the coming American counterattack. It is imperative that you win me time to achieve my mission." He picked up his cap. "You must defend it to the last man, if necessary. The Führer will not be pleased if you fail."

As he jammed his cap on his head, Hofmann was certain he could see the blood drain out of Schneider's face.

Nuremberg.

"But how can you be so sure the woman you met yesterday was telling the truth?" Gina turned to Bill as they walked to the interview room. "She's just a clerk you ran into outside the museum. I remember her. She was running errands for the museum staff I was interviewing, but she had to leave to beat the curfew and get home to her little girl." There was a hint of anger in her voice. "She was a nobody, just someone who ran errands."

"Trust me." He opened the corridor door for her. "It's more than just a hunch. She was telling the truth. I can always tell when someone's lying by the look in their eyes. Charlemagne's treasure – it's still here somewhere in Nuremberg."

"But Herr Schlossberg has maintained again and again that the SS took the regalia away. No one knows exactly where it is. I spoke to him for hours yesterday, and that's what he says." She paused outside the door of the interview room.

"He's lying, Gina." Terrill looked at her earnestly. "I know I'm right. Grill him. And grill him hard." He pushed open the door.

Although he didn't understand a word, Bill could sense that Gina's interview with Schlossberg, the museum director, wasn't going well. The Kraut was a suave bastard. There was much shaking of his head. But Terrill knew he was lying. His eyes flicked from side to side, refusing to meet Gina's gaze. After twenty minutes, Gina sighed and stood up.

"It's no good, Bill." She shook her head. "He's sticking to his story. I'm exhausted asking the same questions over and over."

"Maybe you need to take a little break, Gina. Relax, have a cigarette. When you come back, just give it another try. I'll stay here and make sure the Herr doesn't suddenly remember another appointment."

Gina sighed. "Okay. I guess you're right; I could use a break."

As she left, Terrill locked eyes with the German and smiled.

Errenbach Monastery

"Now that I've done all my arithmetic, may I please read *Max and Moritz?*" Trudi asked the monk who was tutoring her. "I want to read the part where the naughty boys fall into the cake batter and get baked in the oven."

Hanging out the wash, Frieda smiled as she listened to her daughter's chatter. Usually, Brother Helmut helped Trudi with her schoolwork, but that morning another of the monks had the unenviable job. The day was crystalline, the air warm. Trudi and the monk were sitting on a grassy hill overlooking the lake with her doll, Clothilde, wedged in between them.

"Wouldn't you rather read from *The Lives of the Saints?*" asked the monk hopefully. "Or maybe from this book, *Bible Stories for Children?*"

Trudi knit her brow; Frieda, glancing at her, knew she was trying to think of a polite response. "No, thank you." Her pigtails swung as she picked up her doll. "Bible stories and the saints' lives make Clothilde very sleepy, and it's not her naptime yet. Besides, Brother Helmut always let's me read one of the bad boy stories from *Max and Moritz* at the end of my lessons." She flashed a winning smile at the monk who surrendered and nodded as she picked up her book. When she opened it, she cocked her head and narrowed her eyes. "Where's Brother Helmut today?"

Frieda saw the monk's face fall at Trudi's question. She took another clothespin from her mouth and secured a wet sheet to the line. She struggled briefly as a sudden gust of wind sent it flapping in her direction, almost knocking her over.

"Brother Helmut is somewhere else today. He'll be back soon." Then the monk added in a quieter voice, "May the good Lord be willing. You may begin reading, Trudi. But as you take enjoyment in the bad boys' tricks, don't forget what happens to them in the end."

"Oh, yes—they get ground up with the barley and eaten by geese!" Trudi beamed as she looked up at the monk, who shook his head in despair.

Frieda rejoiced to see her daughter so happy. All the monks loved her – Brother Helmut had called her one of God's loveliest spring flowers. The monastery had given Trudi some escape from the horrors of the previous weeks. Somewhere to call home.

Frieda laughed as she struggled to escape the flapping sheet. Once, when she apologized to Father Hieronymus for Trudi's frequent bouts of laughter in the cloister, he replied, "God welcomes the joyous cries of a young child ringing through His house."

Trudi loved accompanying the monks to pick wild strawberries and gather kindling in the forest at the foot of the mountains behind the monastery. She helped them scatter feed to the chickens and harvest freshly-laid eggs. The cook saved nuts and other treats for her, and the tailor gave her ribbons for her braids.

Trudi opened the book and ran her finger beneath the words on the page as she read in a sing-song voice:

> *So many times we hear or read*
> *Of this boy's trick, that boy's bad deed.*
> *Case in point: just take these samples:*
> *Max and Moritz, prime examples!*

Frieda flipped another sheet over the clothesline and anchored it with a pin. She and Trudi shared the tiny cell of a brother who had been conscripted, and, after only a week at the monastery, Trudi looked healthier – her hair shone, her eyes were bright, and the roses were back in her cheeks. She had fresh milk every day and plenty to eat; the monks didn't have to worry about rationing because they produced their own food. Their blessings from the abbey were many, but Frieda was content that they were earning their keep – both she and Stanislaus were so busy they rarely ever saw each other.

The abbey mouser trotted over to Trudi, arched its shining black back, and rubbed against her leg. Trudi continued reading as she stroked its loudly-purring head.

> *It's dreadful to recount the plight*
> *Of Max and Moritz's fateful night!*
> *Read and see what ills befell them,*
> *Verse and pictures will retell them.*

Her laundry basket empty, Frieda picked it up to leave. She looked around at the abbey, lake, garden, trees, sky – all so beautiful. Sometimes planes flew overhead, and often they heard bombs falling in the distance. But she felt safe at Errenbach Monastery.

She smiled as she heard Trudi's laughter.

Gestapo Headquarters, Lake Hallstatt District.

"Has there been a phone call from Ulbrecht yet?" Gruber eased his bulky frame into his chair and picked up a copy of the *Völkischer Beobachter. "HEROIC DEFENSE OF NUREMBERG!"* the headlines screamed. Gruber looked at the date of the paper. Over a week old. He tossed it aside; perhaps the Wehrmacht was still hanging onto the shrine city of the Party.

"Konrad," he shouted, "are you asleep?" Heaven knew how he had been lumbered with the dozy old fool. Sadly, there was no chance of any replacement – all the young men had been hauled off to the front.

"Sir," the old man shuffled into his office. "There have been no phone calls."

"None?"

"Well, sir, the telephone lines have been down since last night." There was a hint of sarcasm in his voice. "American bombers."

"Yanqui swine," Gruber muttered under his breath.

"But this letter came by special courier." Hans pulled an envelope from his pocket. "A motorcyclist brought it early this morning."

"You fool, Konrad!" Gruber snatched the envelope from the clerk's hands. "Why didn't you give it to me before?"

Konrad shrugged his shoulders and beat a hasty retreat from Gruber's office.

The Gestapo man's stubby fingers tore at the envelope and pulled out the letter. As he read, a broad smile spread across his face. He had been right. Engelsing. The woman at the monastery had a history. Ulbrecht in Regensburg had done his work well.

Gruber gave a chuckle of triumph. So she was the widow of one of the scum who had tried to assassinate the Führer the previous July. He got up from his desk, walked over to the window and looked out. Somewhere in the monastery across the lake was the wife of a traitor.

Father Hieronymus had lied. Gruber smiled. Of course, as a man of God, Father Hieronymus didn't lie – he just twisted the truth. It was true, as the abbot had said, that the woman's husband had died in the war. But he had died in prison, not at the front.

The Gestapo man continued to look across at the monastery. Perhaps the abbot had other secrets hidden there. He turned on his heel. Time to pay Father Hieronymus a visit. After his tête-à-tête with the good father, he could check on the Raphael.

"Konrad!"

The clerk scampered into the office. "Yes, sir. You'll be pleased to know, sir, that the telephones are working again."

"Never mind that, you old fool. Tell Georg and Rudi to prepare the boat for a visit to the monastery." He read the letter again and tossed it on his desk. Now he had the whip hand over the abbot.

And he had another trump to play. "And tell them to bring the monk we found in the forest." Gruber cackled with glee. "Yes, tell them to bring Brother Helmut."

Nuremberg.

After the door clicked shut and he could no longer hear the sound of Gina's footsteps, Terrill walked behind the desk where the German was sitting. The museum director's eyes followed him with apprehension. Suddenly, Terrill lunged forward. His left hand grabbed the German's wrist, pulling him to his feet, as his other hand reached for his groin. Terrill grabbed the man's balls and squeezed. Hard.

He silenced the German's cry of pain by slapping him across the face and squeezed again. A noise gurgled in the German's throat as Terrill tossed him roughly back into the chair and added a kick to his shin. Terrill saw the fear in his eyes as the German gasped for breath.

The director struggled with the pain for some moments before the clicking of heels and the door's swinging open announced Gina's return.

"I feel better now. It was good to stretch my—" Gina drew her brows together as she saw the tears on the German's face. "Bill, what's going on?"

"Nothing." Terrill spoke gruffly. "Just ask him again where the stuff's hidden."

"Bill, you didn't—"

"Just ask him," Terrill insisted. "Ask him."

Gina sat down and began to question the German across the desk. Terrill sensed she was getting different answers. There weren't as many '*neins,*' and the previous shaking of the German's head was replaced by a vigorous nodding. Gina's eyes widened and Terrill could sense a growing excitement in her voice as she continued her questioning and rapidly began taking notes on a pad that so far had remained blank. Finally, she stood up; her hands were shaking. A few words followed, and after a curt nod of the head the German made for the door, walking warily around Terrill.

As the door closed, Gina gave a cry of triumph and leapt into the air with joy. "He came clean! He told me where they are!" Her breast heaved with excitement. "I know where Charlemagne's regalia are hidden!"

Suddenly, she stopped and took a hard look at the sergeant. "Bill, I hope you didn't do something…," she picked her words carefully, "do something I couldn't…"

"I just had a little chat with him," he cleared his throat, "to help him jog his memory a bit."

"But, Bill, you know barely a dozen words of German."

"Sure sounds like those dozen words were enough." He smiled and winked.

Her eyes betrayed her confusion as doubts fought against her sense of triumph. Suddenly, she gave a whoop of joy as the latter prevailed. "Charlemagne's regalia! Let's go find it!" She turned to Terrill with a broad smile and laughing eyes. "Oh, Bill, I could kiss you!"

Terrill spread his arms wide. "Feel free!"

Errenbach Monastery.

"Sit down, Brother Stanislaus." Father Hieronymus got up from his desk. "We have a serious problem." The abbot's face was grave and his fingers plucked at his rosary as he strode to the window, his eyes anxiously casting over the lake. "Herr Direktor Gruber will arrive," the abbot turned and glanced at the tall-case clock in the corner, "within the hour."

Stanislaus started at the mention of Gruber's name. "How can you be sure?"

"I have a mole in Herr Direktor Gruber's office." A long finger pointed to the telephone on his desk. His eyes returned to the lake. "I shall say no more."

"It's not one of Gruber's usual visits?" Stanislaus knew he was clutching at straws.

"I doubt it. Not at this hour. Besides," the abbot sighed deeply, "he's bringing Brother Helmut with him." His cassock swung as he returned to his desk.

"God help us!" Stanislaus shot out of the chair, infected with the abbot's fear.

"Hopefully, He will. And if He will not help us, let us hope He will at least provide succor for Brother Helmut."

Stanislaus, overwhelmed by guilt, saw again Brother Helmut's eyes as he lay on the grass. "But his ankle—I didn't want to leave him."

"It's not your fault. I would have done the same, my son." Father Hieronymus fixed the Pole with a stare. "Brother Helmut is not the only problem. Gruber is coming for Frau Engelsing."

Stanislaus fought to control his fear. "For Frieda? But why, Father? "

"I think you know why. We discussed her husband when you first arrived."

"But if she wasn't prosecuted when her husband was arrested—"

The abbot raised his palm. "Times have changed. The war has become more desperate for those on the losing side."

He walked around the desk and put his arm around Stanislaus's shoulder. "But, my son, we have no time to discuss this now. Listen carefully." He led Stanislaus toward the door. "Frau Engelsing is hiding in the crypt with her little girl. Please go to her. A rowboat has been prepared for you, together with a sack of food and a case of clothing; it's all hidden under a tarpaulin in the boat. Frau Engelsing has a sister in Sulzbach – she and the child will be safe there." The abbot walked over to the window and looked at the sky. "Soon it will be dark. For the safety of the woman and her daughter, you've got to take her and the child away from the monastery soon after Gruber arrives."

Father Hieronymus placed a hand on Stanislaus's shoulder and gently pushed him toward the door.

"I'm grateful to you for returning Brother Helmut to us, Herr Direktor." Father Hieronymus led Gruber into his study. "We were wondering what had happened to him."

"I'm not here to play games, Father." He beckoned to his henchmen, who came into the room holding Brother Helmut by the arms.

"Games?" The abbot looked affronted. "I can assure you that the loss of a monk is not a game."

"Then what was he doing in the forest?" Gruber asked abruptly.

The abbot looked at the bruises on Brother Helmut's face. "Have you not already persuaded Brother Helmut to tell you?"

"He said only that he was on a mission of God," Gruber snarled.

Father Hieronymus looked at his monk and felt conscious of the sin of envy. Would he, himself, be able to resist torture, to remain true to his faith, his beliefs? "He spoke the truth, Herr Direktor. He went to comfort a man in distress—"

"Enough of this nonsense!" Gruber's shout cut the abbot short. He motioned to his officers, who pushed Brother Helmut into a chair. He pulled a document from his pocket. "You have here in the monastery a Frau Engelsing, the woman I saw last week?"

"The woman asked for, and was given, sanctuary." Father Hieronymus spoke evenly as he looked Gruber in the eye. "Surely you must respect that." He hoped that Stanislaus had acted quickly on his insistence to get her out of her hiding place in the crypt. The father looked out the window at the black night. Perhaps the Pole was already shepherding the woman and her child to the boat.

"National Socialism has no respect for sanctuary!" Gruber's response was predictable. The Gestapo direktor waved the document in front of the abbot. "Are you aware that the woman was married to a traitor?" Gruber's face reddened with rage. "One of the swine involved in the foul plot to kill our beloved Führer?"

The abbot's fingers caressed his crucifix, seeking inspiration. "I can say nothing, Herr Direktor Gruber. You are aware that a priest is forbidden to reveal a believer's confession?"

"Confession! Sanctuary!" Gruber exploded with rage. "I will not allow you to hide behind your religious nonsense!" He pushed his face closer to the abbot. "Where's the Engelsing woman?" Gruber leant forward, shouting into the abbot's face.

Father Hieronymus eased away from Gruber's foul breath. "She has already left the monastery." He hoped, prayed that he was speaking the truth.

"I don't believe you!" Gruber spat the words. The Gestapo man looked at Father Hieronymus. He knew that threats could never break the abbot's will. Not even torture would persuade him to dishonor his vows and divulge the location of the Engelsing woman.

But there was another way. Gruber signaled to his henchmen and pointed to Brother Helmut. "Tie the monk to the chair."

The crypt.

Frieda felt Trudi's body tremble as they crouched behind a sarcophagus. The pallid light of the single candle cast huge flickering shapes that moved across the wall like the shadows of demons, animating the faces of the skulls. Frieda herself was afraid, less from the gruesome gloom surrounding her, more because Gruber was in the monastery, hunting her down. She shivered, not only from the cold, but from the fear that held her in its viselike grip.

"Mutti, why are we here? I'm frightened." Trudi's wide eyes looked in horror at the bones. "Let's go back to our room."

"Soon, Liebchen." Frieda knelt down and hugged her daughter. She forced a smile. "Pretend we're playing a game. Like hide-and-seek."

"It's not a very nice game." Trudi clutched Clothilde tightly.

The scream sent new terror racing through Frieda's veins. The piercing cry of pain rang around the cloister, echoed around the vast church, and made its way down to penetrate the vaulted confines of the crypt.

"Mutti, I'm scared!" Trudi tried to hide in her mother's skirt.

Another cry rent the air. Frieda struggled to find an explanation, but none came. What was it? Trudi pushed against her mother's body as she struggled to get free. "I want to go back to our room."

"No, Trudi, we have to stay here." Frieda pulled her daughter closer. If they wandered into the cloister, Gruber could be waiting for them. Frieda suddenly started. There were footsteps in the church above. She listened carefully – perhaps she was hearing things. The footfall continued, coming down the nave, their pace hurrying.

She looked around for somewhere to hide, but knew there was no time. Her fingers reached out to snuff the candle. There was a rattle of the iron gate leading to the crypt. Frieda pulled Trudi tightly to her breast. Someone was coming down the steps.

Hofmann's convoy.

Hofmann sat back in his staff car as his driver accelerated into the fading light. His luck still held – no American fighters had threatened the skies. If one burst of bullets from a plane's machine guns hit the truck carrying the explosives, bits of the entire convoy would be scattered all over the surrounding landscape.

The Alpenfestung. He pulled a map from the glove compartment. The terrain was ideal – the mountains would make a perfect fortress. He ran his fingers over the map. If the convoy drove through the night, they could be on the tortuous climb to Alt Aussee in three or four days. Another day to store the artworks in the salt mines. And the dynamite, to be exploded if the Americans threatened to capture the art. The Führer's words rang in his head: 'The treasures must not fall into the hands of the enemy.'

Hofmann folded the map. The art would be safe once he took command of the divisions from Italy promised by Kesselring.

He allowed himself a smile for the first time that day. "Drive to the head of the convoy and stop." He lit a cigarette and drew heavily. "We'll allow the men to rest and take a meal." His eyes caught Scharführer Engelsing looking out from the back of a truck, his arm raised in salute.

"And get the Enigma machine from the truck. I have to send a message to Berlin."

The Enigma machine. Hofmann watched his driver open the case and connect the wires. It looked like a typewriter but it was an impenetrable coding machine. Unless the initial code was known, not even a mathematical genius could interpret a message sent from the magic box.

"Send this message to Berlin." He passed a note to his driver, whose fingers began to tap on the keys.

> *Arrival in designated area imminent.*
> *With expected divisions, ready to*
> *establish Alpenfestung.*

Errenbach Monastery. The crypt.

A flashlight beam preceded the feet coming down the stone steps, its light searching everywhere. Frieda cowered with her daughter. There was no escape.

"Frieda, are you there?" The voice was a whisper.

"Stanislaus! It's you!" She let go of Trudi and jumped up, scarcely able to curb her relief. "I thought Gruber was coming for us." Frieda ran into his arms. "My God, I'm so glad to see you!"

He held her briefly, then drew back at the sound of the child's voice.

"Mama, I'm frightened! There are skeletons down here!"

Frieda turned from Stanislaus and bent over her daughter to comfort her. Stanislaus shone the flashlight on them. The beam caught Trudi's pale face, her lips trembling with fear, her fingers nervously tugging at her pigtails.

"Frieda, we're still in danger." He spoke urgently. "Gruber and his thugs are still here in the monastery. We've got to leave right away – Father Hieronymus told me to take you to safety. There's a rowboat waiting for us on the shore."

"But I'm not ready. We have no—"

"There's a suitcase in the boat with clothing. And a sack of food."

Frieda hesitated; she pulled her daughter closer to her.

Trudi's sobs disturbed the quiet of the crypt. "I want to go back to our room, Mutti."

"But we're in danger, Liebchen." Frieda knelt at her daughter's side. "We must go. If we don't, we could end up like...like Max and Moritz."

Stanislaus saw the fear in the child's eyes and looked at Frieda.

"I'll explain later." Frieda picked up her daughter. "Let's go."

"Wait!" Stanislaus walked briskly over to the back of the ossuary. "There's something I need to take with me." He reached into the alcove and pulled out the wood box containing the Raphael.

"What's—" Frieda's question was deflected by Trudi's voice.

"Will Brother Helmut be coming with us?" The child's question stunned them both.

"Yes!" Stanislaus said gruffly. "He'll be joining us tomorrow." Stanislaus looked at Frieda, who lowered her eyes, acknowledging the lie. "Let's get to the boat," he began to climb the steps out of the crypt, "and pray to God that Gruber isn't already there waiting for us."

"Brother Helmut often prays to God." Trudi's voice was almost a whisper.

Another cry of pain split the air, echoing around the church as they ran down the aisle.

"Let's get going!" Stanislaus pulled open the heavy church door. "We've got to get to the boat before it's too late."

Errenbach Monastery. Later that evening.

Gruber emerged from the crypt and slumped into a pew, barely able to control his anger. The questioning of the monk had produced no results, but that disappointment was nothing compared to a new, devastating shock. The painting was gone.

Only the day before, the news of the count's death had reached him. The treasure was now his. No one else knew where the painting had been hidden. Not a single soul. Untold wealth had suddenly been within his grasp, wealth he would need to make a fresh start after the war ended. Now his treasure had disappeared. He kicked out at the pew in mindless rage.

His chest heaved as he caught the omniscient stare of the Almighty Father above the altar; he expected no help from on high. The Engelsing woman had disappeared. At the same time as the painting. His fingers rapped on the pew. Coincidence could not explain it. But what did the woman want with his painting?

His mind grappled with a situation that made no sense. A woman with a child picks up a painting and disappears. Gruber looked around the church and tried to picture the woman clutching her child, carrying the painting, struggling down the aisle. It didn't ring true.

He rose from the pew and strode towards the door, his heels pounding heavily on the stone floor. After the monk had passed out from the pain, his men had searched the monastery thoroughly and had found no trace of the woman and her child. So they must have left, either by the long road around the lake or, more likely, by a rowboat across the lake in the dark. Again it didn't add up. She had to have had help. But who? He shook his head.

There was no point in asking Father Hieronymus. The man was unbreakable, almost inhuman. How could a cleric who professed a love of God and his fellow man maintain silence while one of his flock screamed in agony? Gruber had seen a number of fools withstand torture, but no one had ever held out when forced to watch the torture of a loved one. Yet the abbot had stood by impassively. Not a word came from his lips. Gruber's pace quickened; it was exasperating.

He pulled on the huge iron handle of the church door. There were lesser mortals who would supply the information he needed. People who could tell him about the man who had helped the Engelsing woman.

"Rudi!" he shouted into the night that enveloped the church.

"Jawohl, Herr Direktor!"

"Round up all the lay staff at once. Cooks, farm workers, everyone. Bring them to the church. Now!"

He reentered the nave and slammed the door behind him. He no longer had any real interest in the Engelsing woman's crimes of the past. Tomorrow was what mattered. His tomorrow. The painting. *His* painting.

And whoever had helped the Engelsing woman steal it from him.

SHAEF Headquarters, Rheims, France.

"I don't like it." Eisenhower sifted through the reports on his desk. "The code breakers at Bletchley say they've intercepted a message." His face was drawn, heavy weary shadows dragging down his eyes as he picked up a paper from his desk.

"Apparently," he put on his rimless glasses to read the report, "apparently some Nazi general has sent a message to Berlin saying he's about to establish the Alp—" He struggled with the word.

"Alpenfestung, Ike." General Bradley eased back in his chair. "The fortress – a fortress in the Alps where the Nazis will make a last stand."

"That's a serious problem for us." The worried expression that always seemed to occupy Eisenhower's face deepened. "The war could be extended for months. At the cost of many American lives."

"It's bullshit, Ike." Patton brushed an imaginary speck of dust from his immaculately-pressed jacket. "The Krauts are finished. Done. Dead as a dodo. To use their own word – kaput!"

Eisenhower did not agree with Patton's assertion. He'd always held his subordinate's judgment in question. He did a good job as commander of the Third Army; he'd played a big part in snuffing out the German offensive in the Ardennes in December. But he was brash, big-headed, full of himself, his reputation forever tainted when he had slapped a shell-shocked soldier's face, accusing him of cowardice.

"I wish I shared your confidence, George," Eisenhower's face was impassive, "but I can't take the chance."

"Perhaps we should try a saturation bombing raid?" Bradley offered.

"In those mountains?" Eisenhower drummed his fingers on his desk. "Too risky. Too much ground to cover." He lit a cigarette and drew deeply. "I have a better idea." His eyes turned to Patton. "George, since you're so confident this Alpenfestung is a fake, I want you to turn your army south. Take the whole area."

Patton leapt to his feet and saluted. "Consider the job done, sir!"

Gestapo Headquarters, Lake Hallstatt District. Late at night.

Emil Gruber's fingers ran lightly over his moustache. At last he had a clue. The abbot may have withstood him, but the minds of ordinary people were sharpened considerably and their tongues loosened by an interview with a Gestapo Kriminal-Direktor. The picture the staff had painted was quite clear. The Engelsing woman had arrived with a man, according to a woman who worked in the kitchen. She had seen them together in the garden; she said they seemed quite cozy with each other. The man, who was dressed as a monk, kept to himself, aloof from the other brothers. He spoke German, but with a foreign accent. Pale eyes and dark, closely-cropped hair flecked with grey, a woman who came in to clean had offered. Name of Brother Stanislaus. Possibly a Pole.

In the glare of his desk lamp, Gruber looked over his notes on his desk and realized he still had little evidence. Possibly a Pole. Might be an escaped laborer. Without papers. Accompanied by a woman and child. And carrying a wooden box which held the painting. *His* painting. And why did the Pole want the painting?

For that matter, how did he even know about the painting?

Gruber's detective mind pushed the questions aside. They were irrelevant. The important question was: where? Where were the Pole, the Engelsing woman, and her brat? He needed a lead, and at the moment nothing came to mind.

They already had a day's head start and could be anywhere. He pulled out a map and scanned it. The main road ran north and southeast. North? Or south? A glimmer of an idea came to him. Perhaps the Pole wanted to head back in the direction of his homeland. To do so, he would have to go north before striking out east toward Poland.

Gruber realized he had little to go on. Even if they had gone north, the road was awash with hordes of refugees. He was trying to find a particular grain of sand on a vast beach.

He opened a drawer, pulled out the file on the Engelsing woman, and ran his finger down the first page. Lived most of her life in Munich. Surely they wouldn't head there; the city was in ruins and already in the hands of the Americans. When he flipped it over to the next page his eyes widened. The woman had been born in Sulzbach. Twenty-five miles north. What's more, she had a sister living there.

His hand reached for the telephone.

The road to Sulzbach.

G estapo officer Georg Essler looked at the unending line of refugees and gave a weary sigh. Gruber had finally gone mad. The war as good as over, the country blasted to hell, and what did the Kriminal-Direktor order him to do? Check the papers of all people heading northeast on the Sulzbach road. He stood by his car and watched the sullen mass of humanity, angry, scared, impatient, jostling to get closer so they could be on their way. The task was impossible. He and Rudi had been checking identity papers since just after dawn. They'd come up with two deserters, German soldiers heading north to surrender to the Americans before they were captured by the Russians; but they weren't looking for deserters and couldn't handle them anyway. Apart from them, all they'd found was some dumb escaped laborer.

But not the one Gruber was looking for. That one was supposed to be tall, with dark hair. Possibly a Pole. Accompanied by a German woman and her small daughter. And carrying a wooden box. He groaned – it was a lost cause; they may even have passed by before the roadblock was set up. And what was the point, anyway? He called over to Rudi. "Let's give this another couple of hours."

His colleague looked up in surprise as he handed an elderly woman's passbook back to her and motioned her forward. "Have new orders arrived?"

"No, but so far we're just pissing in the wind." He looked at his watch. "If we don't find what we're looking for by noon, let's leave."

"But our orders were to—"

"Rudi, Rudi, when are you going to start using your brain for something besides a hat rack? In case you hadn't heard, the Americans will be here soon. Are you going to be standing over there checking papers when their tanks roll through?"

"But that's a treasonable offense, we took an oath—"

"The Third Reich is as good as dead, my friend. I advise you to start fending for yourself. Me, I'm getting the hell out of here." He looked at his watch again. "Still, I'd rather play safe and wait until Gruber goes to lunch."

Hofmann's convoy.

Hofmann urged his driver on as the convoy began to climb into the mountains toward Bad Aussee, where the only road to Alt Aussee branched off to the north. His eyes anxiously scanned the skies and he was relieved to find them unsullied by any prowling enemy aircraft. The last thing he needed was an air attack. What he did need was time. Time to get to Alt Aussee before the Americans. Time to meet the divisions promised by the Führer to establish the Alpenfestung.

He lit a cigarette and blew the smoke through the open windows as he pondered his plans. He doubted Schneider would be able to hold off the Americans for long. He'd seen several Yanqui counterattacks: they blasted their opponents with blistering artillery fire for hours until all resistance was annihilated. Then they moved in with tanks.

His fingers drummed anxiously on the dashboard. He needed another three or four days to get to Alt Aussee. He glanced in the rearview mirror of his staff car. For the moment, he had only ten trucks. Two with the Führer's treasure, one with the dynamite to destroy it all, should it be necessary, and the others carrying the two companies and the remnants of the Hitler-Jugend troop. And Scharführer Engelsing. Wolfgang. So like his son, Kurt, at his age. Kurt, who—

"Sir, we have a problem." His driver's voice snapped him from his reverie.

The road to Sulzbach.

The lumbering horde on the road north troubled Stanislaus. He stayed close to Frieda, afraid of losing her and Trudi in the milling throng. He looked around at the crowd slowly trudging along the road. Everyone was trying to escape, seeking to find some refuge. Germans bombed out of their homes pulled handcarts piled high with belongings they felt unable to abandon. Wounded soldiers, helped by others, shuffled along, trying to get home. Broken-down trucks littered the roadside. And everywhere was the smell, the smell of sweating horses and despairing humanity.

Stanislaus felt no pity for the refugees. For years they had oppressed his nation, stood idly by while he and thousands of slaves had labored for them. Now they were like him, running from danger and death.

He was tired and frustrated. The cord binding the painting to his back cut into the flesh of his shoulders and the screams at the monastery still rang in his ears. Someone had endured torture for their sake. He shuddered. Someone had suffered great pain to make their escape possible. Father Hieronymus? He knew the cries of pain also weighed heavily on Frieda's mind, but by tacit agreement they did not speak of it – their own survival required their full attention.

In this mob, they would never reach Frieda's sister's home. His eyes turned to meet those of Frieda, who gave him a wan smile. In this miserable mass of desperate human beings, only she commanded his respect. Perhaps more than respect. She had helped him when he had not expected help. Although he wanted to return to Poland, he could not set Frieda and Trudi adrift in this seething sea of humanity.

The progress of the mob had slowed to a virtual standstill in the last hour. Arguments were breaking out as people tried to push their way forward.

"What's causing the delay?" Frieda asked.

Stanislaus tried to see over the heads of the crowd. "I'm not sure; could be an accident, maybe a spot-check by a Gestapo unit." Motioning Frieda to stop by the side of the road, he set the bag containing their food on the ground.

"We've got to find another route, Frieda." He wiped the sweat from his brow. "I don't like whatever is causing this jam-up. Besides, we'll soon need to find shelter for Trudi." He looked around and pointed to a path leading up a hill by the side of the road.

Frieda nodded, picked up the suitcase containing their clothes, and clutched Trudi's hand. They turned toward the path. The tide of lost humanity swept slowly past them, unchecked, like waves washing by pebbles on a beach.

Hofmann's convoy.

Hofmann's jaw slackened in horror at the scene he saw through the windshield. About three hundred men in all types of uniform – Wehrmacht, Luftwaffe – stood in the road blocking his progress. Haggard, unshaven faces stared at the car with sullen anger. They seemed to have discarded all weapons and, with them, their identity, organization, and pride.

His teeth clenched as he tried to deny a despair that enveloped him. Had it come to this? The might of the Third Reich reduced to this aimless, shambling mass that shuffled along the road? With the despair came a violent rage that squeezed the air from his lungs.

He leapt down from his car and grabbed a soldier by the lapels of his tunic. "What do you think you're doing, you idiot?"

"We're going to surrender." The voice was slurred.

"Surrender? *Surrender?"* Hofmann reached to release his pistol holder.

"I wouldn't do that, Brigadeführer."

Hofmann froze as he felt a rifle prod into his back. He turned his head slowly to see a corporal looking at him boldly.

"You do know that what you're doing is treason, don't you, Corporal?"

"And what you were about to do is murder, Brigadeführer."

Hofmann slowly removed his hand from his holster and weighed his options. He could call out to his men. They would quickly annihilate the rabble, but he could see from the look in the corporal's eyes that he would exact revenge before he fell. Hofmann would lose not only his life but his mission. The promise to his Führer would not be kept.

"What are your intentions, Corporal?" He watched the corporal's eyes carefully.

"They're quite simple. All these men, me included, we've have had enough." The corporal did not lower his rifle. "In case you hadn't noticed, Brigadeführer, the war is over. Every man here wants to surrender."

"So you said."

"Yes, but to the Americans. Anything would be better than falling into the hands of the Russians." He spat on the ground.

Hofmann struggled to turn a bad situation to his advantage. If he let them go, it was possible that they might run into the not-so-tender mercies of Schneider, who lived to shoot traitors. On the other hand if, as he expected, Schneider had failed to repel the counterattack, the rabble would instead run into the Americans.

The Americans. That was the answer. Their advance would be delayed if they had to deal with hundreds of German soldiers wishing to surrender. He would be given extra time to get to Alt Aussee and complete his mission.

"Very well, Corporal. Just clear the road ahead and let my troops through."

"I'm afraid it's not as simple as that, Brigadeführer."

Twenty miles south of Sulzbach.

The wooden hut sat a hundred feet below the brow of a steep hill; it looked deserted, but Stanislaus approached with care. The door was open, hanging from the rusted hinges, and no smoke came from the squat chimney on the steeply-pitched roof.

Stanislaus's breathing was labored. The climb up the hill with the painting strapped to his back and the bag of food in his arms had taken a toll, but more than these weighed him down. His heart as well was heavy. He had begun to doubt that he could get Frieda and her child to the safety of her sister's house, much less that he could make good on the promise he had made to himself to return the masterpiece to its rightful place in his homeland.

He turned toward Frieda, who was struggling up the path with Trudi, their coats billowing about them in the wind. Beyond, in the far distance at the bottom of the hill, the human tide still surged forward in the fading light, like ants but without purpose, going nowhere. He signaled for her to stay back.

"Be careful!" Frieda called out as he neared the hut.

He went in, took a quick look around, and satisfied himself that the place was empty. As he stepped out to beckon them to join him, the first needles of a cold rain fell on his face.

Stanislaus's eyes adjusted to the darkness of the interior of the hut, which was small and smelled of mildew. He pulled out a flashlight and directed it around the single room; the beam picked out a scarred wooden table, a low bench, and a chair with a broken leg. In a corner lay the clue to the hut's purpose: large, round cheese wheels. From his cow-milking days, he knew that, in the summer, some Bavarian dairy farmers had their cows taken up to high pastures to feed on the mountain grasses and alpine flowers that produced a sweeter-tasting cheese.

The walls had been darkened by the soot of wood fires that raged in the hearth the farmer had used to heat the milk and separate out the rennet. On the table, some moldy bread, a crumpled cigarette packet, and an empty tin can suggested that others had occupied the hut since the cowherd had vacated it the previous fall. The single room was divided by a blanket that hung on a rope between the walls; beyond the blanket was a small narrow cot.

"Mutti, it's not nice here. I don't want to stay – let's go back to Brother Helmut."

The child's shrill voice slashed through the silence and tore at Stanislaus's frayed nerves. He glowered at Frieda, who cast him a look beseeching tolerance. A sudden remorse filled his heart along with a sweet sadness for the woman to whose burdens he was loath to add; he resolved to be pleasant to the child for her sake.

Frieda clutched her daughter against her body. "Don't worry, Liebchen, we'll soon be at Aunt Erika's home. Won't that be nice?" She squeezed her daughter and rocked her from side to side, as much to console herself as Trudi. Across the room she saw Stanislaus begin to fix the flashlight to the rope that held the blanket. She knew how much she and Trudi owed him, how they needed his protection and how far afield they were taking him from the place he wanted to go. She was pained that her daughter was adding to his stress.

To her surprise, when he finished tying up the flashlight, he turned and smiled at the girl. "Trudi, how would you like something to eat?"

The girl's eyes lit up. "Oh, yes, Herr Konec," she clapped her hands, "may I please have some apple strudel?"

Frieda winced, but Stanislaus made his way to the knapsack that lay in the half shadows by the door of the cottage; he dug into the bag. "Let's see what we have. Ah, here's some pumpernickel bread. And some delicious Tilsiter cheese."

Trudi slipped from her mother's arms and squatted on the bench with Clothilde. "I don't like Tilsiter cheese. Even Brother Helmut knows that."

Frieda's heart fell as she looked at Stanislaus. She knew how hard he was trying, but he seemed unperturbed as he continued to root around in the food bag. His hand emerged with something wrapped in waxed paper. "Look, Trudi, I've found the apple strudel!"

Pigtails bouncing, the child jumped from the bench and ran to Stanislaus, who unwrapped the waxed paper and held the treat out to her.

Her face fell as she looked at what he held in his hand. "That's not apple strudel! That's only dried apple slices! Brother Helmut knows I don't like dried apples!"

Stanislaus looked at the pile of dried apple and frowned. "Oh, dear. I guess Brother Helmut forgot to pack the pastry, the raisins, the nuts, the cinnamon, and the powdered sugar. Perhaps they would have made this strudel taste a lot better."

He looked up and winked at the child. After a while her pout became a smile, which turned into a giggle. When he held out the dried apples and she took a piece, he began to laugh with her and Frieda joined in.

For a few precious moments, despite all the hardships they had endured, they all laughed.

Hofmann's convoy.

"What is it you want?" Hofmann tried to curb the anger he felt toward the coward with the rifle.

"Your trucks," the corporal, his expression fixed, replied in a voice without emotion.

"The trucks?" Hofmann shouted. "Don't you understand I'm on a mission for—" He stopped suddenly as he realized that the corporal and the other wretches no longer cared about any mission. Or even the Führer. They cared only for their own worthless skins.

"Those trucks contain two companies of Waffen-SS, armed to the teeth." He fixed the corporal with a stare. "And if you kill me, they will annihilate you and your friends within a minute."

Hofmann heard others in the group mutter as they grasped his argument. "And what if you did have the trucks? Are you going to drive them on the open road? Trucks with German markings? The American fighter bombers would cut you to ribbons!"

Others began to crowd around the corporal, shouting at him, waving their arms.

"Very well, Brigadeführer, I will make a deal with you."

Hofmann struggled to control his fury. The Third Reich had come to this – a corporal making a deal with a brigadeführer. Only his promise to the Führer stopped him from attacking the blackguard for the sheer satisfaction, even if it cost him his life.

"You will stay here with your staff car and driver while your trucks pass through." The corporal held his rifle steady, aimed at Hofmann's chest. "You will be allowed to join them after ten minutes." The others shouted their approval of this ploy. "Just to make sure you don't pull a fast one."

"But I'm a brigadeführer in the Waffen-SS!" The veins in Hofmann's temples throbbed. "Don't you trust my word?"

"We have learned to trust no one, mein Herr." There was contempt in the corporal's voice. "Particularly SS officers."

Hofmann clenched his jaw, fighting back his rage. "Very well. I shall give the orders to the truck drivers." He turned on his heel.

"And I shall come with you." The corporal gave a world-weary smile.

Hofmann did not speak as he strode towards the trucks. The corporal was nothing, a nobody. But he would make a pact with the devil to achieve his mission.

Errenbach Monastery.

For most of the day, Father Hieronymus had knelt on the priedieu before the crucifix in the corner of his cell, refusing food and drink.

216

Tears welled in his eyes, blurring the figure of Christ on the cross; his vision was unsure, as, indeed, for the first time in his life, was his faith. His fingers brushed away his tears and he looked up at the Savior's face. The lone candle helped dispel the darkness, but not the shadow of his doubt. He felt empty, devoid of soul. The wooden rosary beads slipped quickly through his fingers, but his prayers brought no solace. His body shook with a mortal pain, a pain that clenched his heart.

He had been in the presence of an abomination of evil. The physical manifestation of the evil had departed: Gruber and his henchmen had gone; Brother Helmut was now in the infirmary. With an ache in his heart, the abbot wished that Brother Stanislaus could be there to help the monk with his broken fingers.

Father Hieronymus prayed fervently for Brother Helmut. The monk was a true man of God, a paragon of Christian virtue. The abbot's body was again wracked with sobs. Brother Helmut's screams of agony would not leave his ears.

And he, a man of God for many years and Brother Helmut's spiritual father, had said nothing. Gruber's henchmen had pulled all of Brother Helmut's fingers from their joints. Father Hieronymus clutched at the cross that hung around his neck. Just a few words would have spared Brother Helmut pain. Yet he had said nothing. He recalled Gruber's odious sneer and looked up at the sweet visage of Christ, trying to obliterate the face of the devil incarnate.

Why had the Lord given him such a choice – to spare Brother Helmut or to help Frau Engelsing and her child escape? Whose life was more important? He had thought there was another choice: the choice between good and evil. To resist evil, to defy Gruber.

But the pain would not leave his heart. Why did God allow such evil to happen? He threw himself prostrate before the crucifix. His plaintive cry filled his tiny cell.

"My God, my God, why hast Thou forsaken me?"

Nuremberg.

Gina strode briskly along the tunnels that had brought such disappointment the previous day. Now she felt a warm glow of anticipation:

at last, Charlemagne's regalia. She gave Bill a smile of triumph. From ahead, the sounds of pneumatic drills biting into stone reverberated along the tunnel.

"I gotta hand it to you, Lieutenant," the captain walking at her side shouted above the din. "If you hadn't given us this new information, we'd never have found this hiding place. We're eighty feel below street level."

"Let's just hope my information was correct." A nagging doubt crept into Gina's mind: what if the museum director had lied?

The noise ceased suddenly as the party approached the end of the tunnel. Two soldiers, stripped to the waist, laid down the drills, their torsos glistening with sweat. A huge hole had been punched in the false wall. Gina stepped forward, her hand sweeping through the cloud of dust that hung in the air. She tried to control her excitement as she walked toward the newly-made entrance.

"Lieutenant, you'll need this." The captain reached out with a flashlight. "And please watch your step."

"I'll take it, sir." Terrill grabbed the flashlight and made his way across the rubble. He gave Gina a reassuring look. "Just wanna make sure everything's hunky-dory." He shone the light ahead as he stepped over the broken bricks into the chamber. His eyes scanned the beam for trip wires, booby traps. You could never be sure with the Krauts.

"Okay," he beckoned Gina forward, "it's all clear."

"Can you see anything?" Gina ducked as she stepped through the hole.

Terrill let the flashlight wander over the chamber. "I'm afraid the place looks pretty empty."

Gina's heart fell.

"Wait, there are some containers in the corner." Terrill swung the light. "Looks like they're made out of copper."

She took the flashlight from him and moved forward, directing the beam to the tops of the containers. "Bill, I can see labels!" She bent down to read them. Suddenly, she shot up. "My God, Bill – we've done it! We've found Charlemagne's regalia!" Her finger flicked the flashlight switch to the off position.

In the half-light of the lamps outside the chamber Terrill could make out her smile. He reached out to cup her face in his hands and felt her lips searching for his.

The hut.

Stanislaus cursed under his breath. He had used most of his matches, but his efforts to light a fire had failed; the dry straw had taken flame, but the wood of the broken chair had proved too damp. He shivered. High on the hill, the cabin offered little protection to the nighttime chill. He had tried to fix the door but it hung from the hinges, allowing a cold draft into the building.

"Trudi's sound asleep at last." Frieda emerged into the weak light from the other side of the blanket that served as a partition. "When she went to bed, her teeth were chattering, but putting our coats over her did the trick." She looked down at Stanislaus, who was busy moving the remaining straw into a corner of the hut. "I'm sorry she keeps going on about the monastery and Brother Helmut," she sighed, "but it was a very happy time for her." Frieda fought to hold back tears. "She's been through so much, and she's only a child."

"I completely understand Trudi's point of view." The clouds of Stanislaus's breath hung in the air. "I wish we were back at the monastery, as well." His fingers sifted through the straw and plucked out a few pieces that were hard or sharp.

"What do you think we should do tomorrow?" Frieda rubbed her upper arms vigorously, trying to force some warmth into her goose-bumped flesh.

"Well, first of all, we should get an early start. With any kind of luck maybe it'll be clear tomorrow." His hands piled up the straw into mounds to serve as bedding. "We need to find a back road the others don't use. And then we'll try to get you and Trudi to your sister's house."

"And you, Stanislaus? What will you do?" Frieda blew into her cupped hands.

He frowned. "I'll do what I've always said I would do. I'll try to go home." He looked at the box. *And I'll try to take that treasure back with me,* he thought. "Anyway, let's try to get some sleep now."

He discreetly turned his back and fiddled with the flashlight as she settled herself on the bed of straw, tugging on her dress, which had ridden up above her knees as she lay down. The room went black as he switched off the flashlight. "We need to save the batteries."

He lay down beside her in the dark, his head resting against the box.

"Stanislaus?" Frieda's voice was hushed.

"Yes?"

"I'll always be grateful for what you've done for Trudi and me."

"We helped each other, Frieda."

The straw offered scant comfort from the cold earthen floor. He closed his eyes, praying for sleep that wouldn't come. Scenes of the day replayed endlessly in his mind. The world outside had become a place without rules, a society in shreds. That morning, they had seen a fight break out between two men over a handful of old, wrinkled potatoes that had fallen off the back of a cart, and one of the men hit the other in the face with a rock.

Stanislaus bit his lip as he remembered. He worried that he, too, was losing his humanity – he had wanted to stop and help the injured man, but like the others, he had fixed his eyes forward in a stare and continued walking, stumbling, falling into the bottomless abyss of war as if nothing had happened. He shivered, dreading what the morrow would bring.

There was a rustling in the hay next to him. "Are you all right, Frieda?" he whispered.

"Oh, Stanislaus, I'm freezing. I can't stop shivering!"

"Come here, Frieda – perhaps I can warm you."

As she rolled over and touched him, his arms enfolded her in a loose embrace. The position was awkward and uncomfortable, and he tried to ignore the softness of her skin, the sweet scent of her hair. Suddenly, his lips found hers and pressed, softly at first, then harder. Her arms pulled him closer and he felt her hips move against him.

The urgency of her body overwhelmed him.

The hut.

F rieda awoke slowly, reluctant to leave her sleep and her dreams. She smiled as the memory of the previous evening slowly forced its way into her consciousness.

The warm glow of the image faded as the cold fingers of a new day slid over her body. She turned on the straw, seeking the warmth of Stanislaus, but he was not there. She sat up, pulling her jacket around her to ward off the cold. Her eyes found him standing by the half-open door. Her smile vanished as she saw his frown. Her first thought was that he regretted what had happened between them the night before.

"Is something wrong, Stanislaus?" She clambered to her feet.

"The bag of food," he looked at her desperately, "it's gone." His eyes darted anxiously to the corner where they had slept; the box was still there. "Your suitcase has also disappeared."

Frieda's hand flew up to her mouth as she inhaled sharply. "But how?" Frieda ran across to Stanislaus.

"I don't know." He put his arms around her. "They were probably stolen by one of the refugees." He leaned forward and whispered in her ear. "We can't go far without food."

Frieda felt stabs of conflicting emotions. She felt violated that someone had been in the hut, on that night of all nights, but she knew the disappearance of the food was worse. And her suitcase; in her mind she ran over what was inside: clothing for both her and Trudi, a few keepsakes—

"Stanislaus! My passbook was in the suitcase!"

He pulled her tighter to him and rocked her in his arms. There were no words of comfort he could speak to help assuage what had befallen them; the only comfort he could offer was the warmth of his body.

"Are we going to Aunt Erika's today?" The heads of Trudi and Clothilde peeped out from behind the curtain.

"Very soon, Liebchen." Frieda quickly broke from Stanislaus's embrace. *Very soon.* It stung her that lying to her child had now become almost an automatic reflex.

"Good morning, Trudi!" Stanislaus called out with a cheer he did not feel as he walked over to the child.

"Good morning, Herr Konec."

"Trudi, we need your help." He forced a smile as he squatted down before her. "Do you know anything about berries?"

"Do you mean strawberries, Herr Konec?"

"Yes, strawberries. The kind that grow wild in the forest in the spring."

"Oh, yes, Herr Konec, I know all about wild strawberries. I picked them with Brother Helmut in the forest by the monastery." She nodded twice to emphasize her achievement.

"Then you must be an expert on strawberries. Trudi, do you think if we went out to look for some, you might be able to help us find them?"

"Oh, yes, Herr Konec! Brother Helmut said Clothilde and I were the best strawberry pickers he ever knew." There was a childish pride in Trudi's eyes.

He stood and fetched two of the buckets the cowherd used for milking and handed the smaller one to Trudi. "Here, we can use these. Shall we go out and see who can collect the most?"

"I'll win! I'll win!" Trudi picked up the bucket, grabbed her mother's hand, and made for the door.

"Just a moment." Stanislaus grasped the cords tied to the painting and slung it over his shoulder. "Better not leave this behind."

Nuremberg.

"I gotta tell you, Gina, it does my heart good to see you looking so happy again." A merry smile played across Bill's face as he navigated the jeep through the rubble of the city. "You're like a puppy with two tails."

Her infectious laugh charmed him. The war would soon be over, the war that had always brought unceasing coldness, a chill that had frozen his heart and spirit. But now, with Gina, he felt a warmth wash over him. There was only one good thing about the war: it had brought them together – they never would have met in peacetime.

"Bill, I'm so happy!" Gina could barely contain her excitement. "I never dreamed I'd ever even be in the same room as Charlemagne's regalia, let alone that I'd be the one to find them. We did it, Bill, we did it!"

"Yeah, it's amazing what a little heart-to-heart chat can do."

As she caught his eye she smiled and shook her head; she didn't care to know the details of Bill's confrontation with the museum director. "I can't wait to tell my dad all about it when I go home."

"Go home." Bill's sigh was audible. "What sweet, sweet words those are." He glanced to his left. "But maybe not for them." He nodded toward the side of the road where people were heading out of the ruined city, shuffling along with heads bowed, some pushing wheelbarrows with all their worldly goods.

Gina gasped. "Oh, Bill! Look at that woman!" She pointed to the right side of the road. "What's happened to her?"

Terrill flinched as his eyes took in the pathetic sight. The woman wore a threadbare coat and her skirt was torn. But his attention was drawn inexorably to her head: she had been shorn of her hair. She resembled nothing so much as the pictures of concentration camp victims he hoped never to see in the flesh. Around her neck she wore a sign.

"What does it say?" His voice was angry. "Gina, tell me what it says!" He slowed the jeep.

"What?" Gina was still stunned by the chilling apparition.

"The sign around her neck – what does it say?"

Gina peered through the windshield and translated. "It says *This traitor has been punished,*" her eyes scanned the words at the bottom of the sign, *"for fraternizing with the enemy."* She looked away, closing her eyes tightly, trying to erase the image. "It's horrible, Bill, horrible. How could anyone do that to another human being?"

Terrill was about to hit the gas pedal to get Gina away from the nightmare, but saw something that made him pause. The woman's eyes. He had seen those eyes before. His stomach clenched. He remembered her hair, her auburn hair, the hair that was now just a few unsightly tufts protruding at odd angles from her scalp. She was the woman who had given him the lead on the regalia. The woman who had begged a cigarette. He had been the enemy with whom she had fraternized. Someone had seen them. Just a goddamn cigarette. Just one lousy little cigarette, damn it all to hell.

"I don't think the war will ever be over, Gina." Terrill began to ease the jeep down the street. "There's still plenty of Nazi bastards around to keep it alive."

"Bill, shouldn't we stop and see if we can help her?"

"And invite more punishment for her?" Terrill looked at the woman once more in the mirror. But for that poor creature the treasures of Charlemagne would never have been found.

He looked at Gina but said nothing.

On the hill outside the hut.

Stanislaus put down the buckets as they crested the brow of the hill above the cottage. "Let's rest here a moment," he said. The weather had cleared but the grass was still wet, so they sat on the edge of a large rocky outcrop.

Stanislaus looked out at the beautiful panorama before them. The hill ran down steeply to a fast-flowing stream, beyond which was a green plain. In the far distance rose the cloud-capped Bavarian Alps. The sweeping expanse of mountains magnified the world and buoyed his spirits; in a world filled with misery, at least some places remained untrammeled by the war.

He took her hand. Frieda smiled.

"I hope we come through it all, Stanislaus." She looked over at Trudi. The girl sat close by, adorning Clothilde's yarn hair with purple clover blossoms she had picked.

"Stanislaus, thank you for being so kind to my little girl. You made a desperate situation into a game – that's better than trying to hide the truth from her." She sighed. "Which is what I seem always to do."

Stanislaus turned his gaze to the far-off mountains. "When I practiced medicine, I had several seriously-ill young patients. I learned then that in a crisis half the battle is keeping the child's spirits up. Besides, she's your daughter." He squeezed Frieda's hand and smiled at her. "I really like Trudi – she has your eyes."

He stood, picking up the box. "But we'd better get going." He took a closer look at the stream in the valley below. The water flowed steeply down the side of a mountain in almost a cascade, then flattened out before descending into fast-moving rapids that swirled around exposed boulders. In the flat part of the stream, stepping stones for fording the stream had been moved into place. Beyond the river he could see a road; he was astonished to see that it was deserted.

Frieda had seen it, too. "Do you think—"

"Will there be strawberries down there, Mutti?"

"I hope so, Trudi." And if not, there will always be nettles, she thought, remembering her mother's recipe for nettle soup, a dish she had learned to make during the privations of the last war.

"Then let's get down there quickly, Mutti, before the cow eats all the berries up."

Stanislaus stopped and peered in the direction of the child's finger. A cow, half-hidden by the foliage. How had he missed the animal?

He adjusted the box on his back and picked up the pails. "Cows mean fresh milk." He grinned at Frieda. "I'm an expert in that – my second career was in milking."

His laughter hid his underlying fear. Tiny wild strawberries, even with milk, wouldn't sustain them for long. He had to find real food.

Hofmann's convoy.

Hofmann was frustrated. Throughout the day the convoy had been halted, hiding in an orchard away from the road. Soon after daybreak he had seen American jabos prowling in the clear morning sky and knew the convoy could make no progress until nightfall. He looked up, urging the sun on towards its night's rest behind the mountain peaks. He glanced at his watch. It would be another hour before the convoy could set out for Bad Aussee.

The orchard was quiet. Most of his men were gathered around the field kitchen, eating supper before they resumed their trek. Time to prepare for the journey through the night ahead. He turned toward his staff car but stopped as he saw the scharführer.

225

The lad was sitting at the foot of an apple tree. He remembered a day when Kurt had sat with his back against a tree, just as Engelsing was now doing, but with his arm around the shoulders of his sweetheart. It was the day of some family celebration – a birthday party – and he remembered wondering if Kurt would marry the girl and have children with her.

There would be no more family parties; he would have no grandchildren. He gazed up into the still-blue sky and saw a crow fly overhead. Kurt was dead. His life given for the Führer. And what lay ahead for Scharführer Engelsing? Or, for that matter, for himself?

He thrust the thoughts aside as he climbed into his car. As he reached for his maps, he heard the shout of his orderly, who was running though the apple trees.

The orderly stopped and saluted, trying to catch his breath; his face was ashen. "Sir, sir…"

Hofmann looked at him sharply. "Out with it, man. What is it?"

"Sir, the Führer is dead."

The hut.

W hen he awoke shortly after dawn, Stanislaus felt unrested; several times during the night his sleep had been disturbed by Trudi's cries. His own stomach growled with intense hunger pangs. He reached for Frieda, but his arm found only air and straw.

He rolled over, tried to adjust to the faint light, and anxiously scanned the empty room. She was not there. He rushed to the door and was relieved to see her emerge with Trudi from behind the cottage.

Frieda's arm was wrapped around the child, whose head hung low. "Her stomach's upset." Frieda pressed her lips together and frowned with concern. "She's not well."

Stanislaus scooped the girl up in his arms. "Come, little one." Frieda followed as he took the child into the cottage, pushed aside the blanket, and laid her on the cot. "Rest a while."

"Herr Konec, I don't think I can help collect berries today." Trudi took the doll he held out to her. "And Clothilde wants to go back to Brother Helmut."

Stanislaus smiled and mopped the perspiration from the child's brow with his handkerchief.

Frieda sat on the edge of the cot and brushed the stray hairs off the child's forehead. "Try to get some sleep, Liebchen."

"When I wake up, will you tell me a Max and Moritz story, Mutti?"

"Yes, Liebchen, I will."

"I want to hear the one where the bad boys steal Widow Tibbet's roast chickens by going on her roof and pulling them off the stove with a fishing pole."

"Of course, Liebchen. Now get some rest. You've got to get well."

"Mutti?"

"Yes?"

"I'm not hungry now, but when I get better can we have some roast chicken?"

227

Frieda frowned. "No, dearest, I don't think we'll be eating roast chicken any time soon."

"I didn't think so. And we won't be going home soon, either, will we, Mutti?"

The question broke Frieda's heart. "No, Trudi."

"I didn't think so." She closed her eyes. "I think I'd like to go to sleep now."

Frieda spread the coats over her daughter and kissed her forehead. When she stood up and pulled aside the blanket, she found Stanislaus pacing the floor. "What's wrong?" she asked.

He stopped and looked at her with a rueful expression. "I blame myself for Trudi's condition."

"But surely she's only suffering from an upset stomach?"

"More likely the milk. I shouldn't have given her unpasteurized milk." He was angry with himself.

"Don't blame yourself, Stanislaus." She was pained to see him so upset.

"I'm a doctor, remember? I should have known better." He sighed and turned toward her. "Anyway, what's important now is that she gets lots of fluids. I'll make a fire – we need to boil everything we give her."

He picked up kindling wood and placed it in the hearth. As he wiped the residue off his hands, he looked at her and, despite his exasperation, the warmth in her eyes brought a smile to his lips. "Are you all right, Frieda?"

"There's nothing wrong with me that a nice roast chicken wouldn't put right!"

They both laughed nervously as he pulled her to him, but his smile quickly vanished. "We really do need food. Real food. Without it, we'll never reach your sister's house."

"I know that, Stanislaus, but where can we get real food?"

"I have an idea. The cow we found belongs to a farmer. Chances are he has other things on his farm besides the cow."

Hofmann's convoy.

The news had struck Hofmann dumb with speechless horror. The Führer was dead. The man who had led Germany to great glories was no more. He felt hollow and raw.

When he had assembled the men and told them, he thought he had heard a collective groan of despair; some of the younger ones, particularly Scharführer Engelsing and his Hitlerjugend platoon, had struggled and failed to hold back their tears.

He circled the treasure truck and felt in his pocket for the keys to the locks. Goebbels, too, was dead. Of all the leaders, Goebbels had been the only one fit to replace the beloved leader. Hofmann undid the lock and freed the bolts that held the tailgate. Goering, that fat bastard, had sat in his Karinhall mansion, addled by drugs while the Luftwaffe he controlled fell to pieces. And the greasy Himmler had proved such an abysmal army commander that the Führer had been forced to remove him.

Hofmann climbed into the truck, his flashlight illuminating the contents. He wondered what those vain hangers-on were doing now that the Führer was gone. He could not see any of them leading Germany in a last-ditch struggle for survival. The beam ran across crates containing the count's art, destined to join the Führer's collection in the salt mine. The Führer's art collection – what good was it to him now?

He knew what Goering, Himmler, and the others would be doing. Abandoning Germany. Trying to save their own miserable skins. As the beam fell upon a small box, he recalled a speech made by Rudolf Hess in '34 on the night a million party members took the oath of allegiance to the Führer. *'Mein Führer,'* he had shouted, *'Adolf Hitler is Germany and Germany is Adolf Hitler.'*

He picked up the small box. How true were Hess's words, even though Hess, himself, had flouted them and fled to England. And now Hitler was dead. And so was Germany – Hofmann's Germany was dead.

He absentmindedly read the words on the box he held in his hands. *Book of Hours. 14th Century. Bruges.* From the moment he had heard of the Führer's death, Hofmann knew there was little chance of establishing an Alpenfestung. Without the Führer, the promised divisions would melt like the Alpine snow in spring. But he would push on. Perhaps a miracle would happen. He doubted it, but he would keep his soldier's oath to the Führer.

And if the miracle didn't happen? Hofmann tossed the little box back on the pile of crates as though it were nothing more than an empty cigarette package. He knew what he had to do.

Gestapo Headquarters, Lake Hallstatt District.

Gruber looked angrily at the telephone. It had rung once that morning with bad news: Hitler was dead. Everything was now in chaos. But what was that to him? He was still in the same fix and desperate to hear other news, but the damn telephone did not ring.

He had heard nothing at all from the men he'd sent to cover the road to Sulzbach. No news of the Engelsing woman and her accomplice, not to mention his painting. Almost forty-eight hours without a word. His fist thumped on his desk in frustration. There was no sign of the two men, and he knew the reason why. They had fled. Deserted. With the Americans approaching, his men had disappeared to save their own skins.

Seething, he rose, hooked his thumbs through his belt loops, and began to pace the room. Hunting the two men down and hanging them for treason was no longer an option. He had only Konrad, his dumb clerk, and a couple of other men who would also probably disappear if he turned his back. He stopped pacing long enough to reach for the pipe on his desk. He tamped down the tobacco and lit it.

Gruber could hardly blame them. Hitler was dead and Nazi Germany was collapsing. Their world would soon be no more, fallen into an abyss of defeat and destruction. He took several deep slow puffs on his pipe. He knew he should be looking to save himself. Like the others, he should be arranging to jettison his Gestapo trappings and find a new identity.

But his insurance policy had disappeared. The painting. With the art treasure, he could have hidden away until the storm had passed. Now it seemed beyond his reach – he would never find it. Somewhere, the wife of a traitor was wandering around with a foreign accomplice who had a fortune in a box.

But there was one last hope. He sat back down and blew a smoke ring; he was feeling more optimistic. The Engelsing woman's sister in Sulzbach. If he knew where she lived, he could set a trap. He made some notes on a pad. He didn't have her sister's address and he didn't know her last name, but his Gestapo contacts in the Sulzbach area would have ways of tracking her down.

He looked up from his jotted notes and remembered the brief interrogation of the Engelsing woman at Errenbach Monastery. How innocent she had looked sitting in the abbot's office, how angelic was her little girl. He ground his teeth and snapped his pencil in two as he thought about the woman he hated.

Hofmann's convoy.

Hofmann's mind was still in turmoil as he jumped down from the truck and secured the lock. The Führer was dead, the Alpenfestung probably no more than a pipe dream. He walked past the trucks of the convoy. A few men were stretching their legs, saluting him as he passed. Most were dozing in the trucks. He looked up at the clear blue sky, happy hunting grounds for the American planes. There could be no progress; he dare not move on the road until dusk.

The despairing looks on the faces of his men brought home an unwelcome truth: with the death of the Führer they had lost what little hope remained. To maintain their morale through the challenging days ahead would be difficult.

He strode towards his staff car, which nestled in the shade of an apple tree in full bloom. His thoughts turned to his son, Kurt, who had fallen for the Reich in the skies somewhere over Hamburg. Had almost a year passed? His heart still ached for his boy.

Better days came to his mind. Before the war, before the Führer came to power to rescue Germany. Times had been hard. He had eked out a living doing whatever he could. Sometimes the music lessons his mother had insisted upon since he was five came in handy and he was able to earn a few marks playing the organ in churches – once, even in the Cologne Cathedral. Kurt always sat with his mother in the pew closest to the organ loft, and the young boy's face always glowed with pride as he heard his father fill the apse with the joyous music of Bach and Buxtehude.

Hofmann savored the sweet memory for a few moments before it turned to sour longing for what could not be. When Kurt died, well-meaning friends told him that good remembrances would one day crowd out the pain. He now knew that would never happen.

As he approached his car, his eyes caught the spire of a church in a small town, about half a mile down the road. The tower boasted a clock. Almost two. Six hours before dusk, before the convoy could set out.

The impulse seized him. But he would need help.

"Scharführer Engelsing!" His shout rang out. Within moments, the Hitlerjugend leader had leapt from his truck, running to him before coming to attention and saluting.

"Scharführer, I have another special mission for you!" He saw the mixture of fear and obedience on the young man's face. "Don't worry," he smiled and gave a low chuckle, "this time there are no American tanks to battle."

He opened the door to his staff car and lifted his arm to direct the scharführer inside before leaping up after him.

"Hans, take us to that church."

"But, sir—" The corporal stifled his objection and reached for the gear shift.

"It's all right, Hans – the American fighter planes don't seem to be interested today."

The hut.

Stanislaus and Frieda sat on a wooden bench outside the cottage. The sky was beginning to cloud over but the sun was trying to force a way through.

"At last Trudi seems to be sleeping comfortably." Frieda sighed her relief. "Thank you for treating us to such delicious food." She took another bite of the chicken leg in her hand, closing her eyes as she savored it.

He grinned. "When I was practicing medicine in Warsaw, I never dreamed that one day I'd be stealing chickens. And I almost lost the poor bird. When I carried it across the stream, I slipped on the stepping stones."

"Thank God you're safe." Frieda looked earnestly into his eyes. "Stanislaus, I know I've said it before, but I just don't know what Trudi and I would ever have done without you."

"We all have to eat," he said modestly. "Anyway, I'm glad I got the fire going again so we could roast the bird." He picked at the chicken breast. "But I think we need to come up with a new food source – the farmer I borrowed the chicken from might have his shotgun cocked next time." He pulled off the wishbone to save for Trudi. "Besides, I didn't like leaving you and Trudi alone."

"I have to admit I was a little nervous when you left, but we were all right." She nibbled the last bit of meat off the chicken leg and tossed the bone down the hill.

"I didn't like leaving that thing behind, either." He nodded at the box, visible through the open door.

"You mean the painting?" Frieda asked. "The one you brought with you from the monastery?"

Hofmann's convoy.

The streets of the town were deserted, apart from a small boy whose large eyes followed Hofmann as he sprinted up the steps leading to the church door. Perhaps the people had abandoned themselves to their fate as the Americans approached. At least there were no white sheets, the awful signs of surrender.

Wolfgang struggled to keep pace with the brigadeführer. What kind of mission did his leader have in mind? In a church? But he welcomed a new adventure, something to offer escape from the thoughts that had plagued his mind ever since he had heard the news. The Führer was dead. What would happen to Germany now? And what about him? What would happen to him?

Hofmann flung open the door. The church was large with soaring walls encrusted with Baroque ornamentation; a wide aisle led to the gilded altar, above which was a painting of the Nativity. White marble cherubs guarded the Holy Family; in the cornices above them were marble saints with swirling garments who had looked down sternly upon congregations spanning centuries. Hofmann saw the pipes high on the west wall and his eyes searched for the stairs leading to the organ loft. He spotted the opening between two columns and ran towards it, his boots thudding on the marble floor, then rattling on the wooden steps as he climbed.

Wolfgang clattered up the steps behind the brigadeführer. Without the Führer, there was little hope for Germany. They paused at a landing.

His treacherous father's wish had at last been fulfilled. His face flushed, more with shame than with physical effort. Germany had no leader.

At the top of the steps, Hofmann opened a door and found the organ. He looked around and found the lever to the bellows mechanism tucked away in a little passage by the side of the keyboard. "Scharführer Engelsing, I want you to operate this lever." He demonstrated by lifting the rectangular wooden beam before pushing it down. "Maintain an even rhythm while I play."

Wolfgang looked at the officer with wide eyes. Germany was struggling for life, yet his commanding officer wanted to play the organ? The reflex that had been drilled into him since he had joined the Hitler-Jugend thrust the thought aside. The reaction to obey. He reached for the lever.

Hofmann settled himself on the bench, his feet testing the pedals, his hands clenching and unclenching to seek the warmth they needed.

He would play for Kurt one last time.

The hut.

Frieda had caught Stanislaus off guard with her question and he removed his arm from her shoulders. They had never discussed the contents of the box before; he had thought it better if she didn't know what was inside. "How did you know it's a painting?"

"I saw the marking, *Raphael, Portrait of a Young Man,* on the side you place against your back when we're on the road. Did Father Hieronymus ask you—"

"Father Hieronymus never knew it was in his crypt. The painting was stolen from my country and hidden there."

"How did you know?"

"It's a long story. It doesn't matter."

"And now you're—"

"Trying to get it back to Poland. When I discovered it was at Errenbach Monastery, I didn't know what to do. I would have entrusted it to Father Hieronymus, but there were reasons I couldn't." He leaned forward, clasping his hands and resting his forearms on his thighs.

"Oh, Stanislaus, it's such a risky undertaking," she placed her hand over his interlocked fingers, "to carry a priceless masterpiece on the open road right now."

"Perhaps. Anyway, enough of that. At the moment, our main concern is getting Trudi well." His eyes warmed to her again. "I know how precious an only child is. My son was an only child, too."

Frieda pulled her hand back. "Trudi's not an only child."

"You have another? You never mentioned that to me."

Frieda's eyes flashed. "And you never mentioned the painting."

"But what happened…?" As he saw her anguish, he was sorry he had begun to ask the question.

Frieda took a deep breath. "What happened to my other child? My son, Wolfgang, is fighting somewhere in the Hitler-Jugend. Perhaps he's dead by now. But he's been dead to me for a long time – the Nazis killed the boy I loved." She covered her eyes with her palms and her shoulders began to shudder.

He put his arm around her and she rested her head against his chest. "I didn't know. Frieda, I'm sorry."

She wiped her eyes with the flat of her hands. "Don't be. In a way you were right when you said Trudi is my only child." A single tear raced down one cheek. "The monsters got hold of my son and filled his young mind with hatred and changed him into an unthinking automaton."

Cradling her in his arms, Stanislaus gently rocked her until he no longer felt her body shake with sobs. For a long time they sat on the bench locked in embrace, speaking to each other only through the language of their touch.

The church.

The nave rang with the stark opening theme of Bach's Passacaglia in C minor spiraling down to the lower registers. As the majesty of the music flowed from his feet on the pedals, Hofmann realized the somber tones matched his mood. Hitler was dead. Germany was finished, spiraling slowly into a final Armageddon.

The music found an echo in Wolfgang's mind as he worked the lever. It sounded like music his parents had once taken him to hear with his baby sister at the Frauenkirche in Munich. A good life, before he had learned that his father was a traitor. He pushed at the beam, trying to stem the tears in his eyes. Why had his father betrayed him?

Against the simple bass theme repeated by his feet, Hofmann's fingers began to dance in musical variations. The war would soon end, but he had one last mission to fulfill. Had it been only two and a half weeks ago that he had been closeted with the Führer, who had ordered him to destroy his treasures before letting them fall into the hands of the enemy? The variations that played against the relentless, unchanging bass became richer, more complex; to him they seemed like the voices of men arguing with a destiny that could not be altered.

The pomp of the music reminded Wolfgang of the raised arms, raised voices, raised spirits of the Party Rally in Nuremberg when he had paraded with his troop before the Führer. How he had felt the Führer's power like an electric bolt when the great leader had looked at him, how from that moment his life had been transformed.

As the fugue began, Hofmann thought about his orders. The Führer would not shrink from destroying beauty when a higher principle was involved. When the RAF bombed the lovely city of Lübeck, hadn't the Führer retaliated with the bombing of England's most beautiful cities – Bath, York, Canterbury? Hofmann remembered Paris and wished he had been there the preceding August. He would have ensured that the only brightness coming from the City of Light was from the flames of its destruction, a Führer order the retreating coward Choltitz had failed to carry out.

Wolfgang had more than taken an oath of allegiance to the Führer, he had worshipped him. And now the Führer was gone. The sun in the sky had been snuffed out; he felt alone in a dark world, bereft, abandoned. Tears streaked his cheeks as he pushed down hard on the lever.

Hofmann's fingers began to tire as he played the convulsive counterpoint. He once again saw Kurt's smile. Had Kurt died so the enemy could acquire and enjoy the possessions of the Reich? As the music slowed, his hand briefly left the keyboard to brush tears from his eyes.

Wolfgang pushed the lever down as the music swelled. In his parents' Munich apartment, his mother had played little tinkling, feminine compositions on the piano; the brigadeführer's playing was different – masculine, powerful, masterful. At that moment, Wolfgang knew that all the loyalty he had had for the Führer was now vested in Brigadeführer Hofmann. Wolfgang would fight for him, obey him.

Hofmann pulled out another stop as his fingers flew furiously over the keys in the accelerating tempo. The Führer's order was clear. The variations in the upper register became more insistent, but the bass thundered on. It must be done. The sustained last chord boomed out and echoed around the church. The treasures must be destroyed.

US Third Army Base.

"Wow, Gina, get a load of this!" Bill put his coffee down and held up an Extra edition of *The Stars and Stripes.*

Gina gasped as she read the headlines. "Hitler's dead? So that's what the buzz I heard outside was all about."

"Yep, he's dead all right." He grinned. "Maybe you can ship that coffin we saw in the mine at Bernterode to Berlin."

"This is no time for humor." She held her hand out for the paper. "Can I see that?"

As Gina pulled *The Stars and Stripes* from Bill's hand and began reading, Terrill realized she was right. It wasn't a time for humor. Roosevelt died last month. Hitler died three days ago. And his buddy, Kolevsky, blown to hell? No mention of him in *The Stars and Stripes.*

US Third Army Base.

G ina slammed her tray down on the canteen table.

"What's got you all het up?" The sausage on Terrill's fork paused on its way to his mouth.

"I'm fed up, Bill. We're making no progress. Absolutely no progress. There's so much to be done, and all we do is sit here and wait." Gina sat down; as she began sipping at her coffee, she made a face. "God, this stuff's awful. When are we going to get some decent java?"

"What do you mean," Terrill mumbled as he chewed on his sausage, "what do you mean no progress, Gina?" He swallowed and wiped his lips. "The Kraut's are finished, the war should be over in another few weeks, and right now Hitler's being poked in the butt by a devil with a pitchfork." He took a swig from his mug. "Now, that's what I call real progress."

"But our men haven't yet taken Alt Aussee." She nervously tore her roll into small bits.

"And?"

"Bill, do you know what the Nazis have hidden down in that salt mine?" Gina's words were delivered with excitement mixed with frustration. "Thousands of masterpieces; works by all the great masters – Vermeer, Michelangelo, van Eyck, Rubens…"

Terrill sighed loudly as he pushed his plate away. "Gina, I hate to be the one to break the news to you, but for our guys at the front, art is the last thing on their mind."

"But the priceless works of art—"

"The priceless works of art might as well be Mickey Mouse comic books to those guys." He wadded up his paper napkin and tossed it onto his plate. "Right now, they wouldn't give a plugged nickel for all the Michelangelos in the world." He leaned forward and looked at her coldly. "But I'll tell you what they'd give five million dollars for, if they had it." His eyes caught hers for a moment before she glanced away. "A ticket on a boat back to the good old USA." His hand reached out and rested on hers. "To their homes. To their wives. To their girlfriends."

Gina was flustered as she pulled her hand back and picked up her mug. She felt her face flush as she realized how selfish she must have sounded. She knew the lives of men were important, but so was the art, and every day it sat in a salt mine was another day the works were at risk. A heavy silence hung between them and seemed to separate them.

Bill looked into her eyes – so brown, he thought, like melted Hershey Kisses – but she shifted her gaze to her coffee cup, her long lashes hiding her eyes from him. He wondered if he'd been too hard on her. He knew how important all the art stuff was to her. He'd begun to understand why, but he still wasn't sure.

Gina took a sip of her coffee and looked up at him, a self-conscious smile playing on her lips. "You know, Bill – this coffee's not so bad after all," she said softly.

Bill realized Gina felt chastened. He hadn't meant to lecture her, he just had said what he felt. He needed to change the subject. "Say, Gina, when you're done with your grub, how about you and me getting in some more target practice?" He smiled at her. "You know, you're getting to be a real good shot."

Gestapo Headquarters, Lake Hallstatt District.

Gruber scanned through the files, tossing most of them into the blazing stove in the corner of his office.

His search for the Engelsing woman had come to a grinding halt. The Gestapo office covering the Sulzbach area wasn't able to track down her sister, because there was no longer an office there – his contacts had suddenly decided to take up residence elsewhere. He'd finally heard from his brother, who reluctantly had agreed to let him stay with him and his shrew of a wife for awhile; but that was scant consolation.

He added his Gestapo passbook and Nazi Party membership card to the fire. He would need a new identity; at the very least, he had to lose his present one. The Americans would probably seek out Gestapo officers and he was sure they wouldn't bother much with the niceties of the law.

He watched in morbid fascination as the edges of his membership card turned brown and curled. Inexorably, the card began melting toward its center, toward the photograph of him. Tongues of fire leapt up and began eating his picture, swallowing his face. Just as Germany had been devoured by war.

He groaned in desperation. How long he would have to stay with his brother, with whom he had never got on particularly well, he didn't know. His hand reached for the poker and stirred the stove, encouraging the fire. Unlike other Gestapo officials, who had been lucky enough to have had rich Jews in their regions, he had little money. The painting, the treasure that had been virtually snatched from his hands, would have made all the difference. He kicked the stove in futile rage. With the painting, he would have been be made for life; without it, he faced a life of uncertainty and fear.

The door of his office creaked on its hinges; he looked up to see the unwelcome figure of Konrad, his clerk, walk in. Konrad was an idiot. Otherwise, like everyone else, he would have already run for cover.

"Well, what is it, Konrad?" There was an angry impatience in Gruber's voice. "Can't you see that I'm busy?"

"I'm sorry, Herr Direktor," Konrad gave a sheepish look, "but it's about the thief who was picked up this morning."

"Thief?" Gruber exploded. "The Führer is dead, the world is falling to pieces, and you want to waste my time talking to me about some common thief?"

Konrad ignored the jibes. "I was asked to pass on to you these items that were found on his person." He placed a large, sealed envelope on Gruber's desk. "I was told that you might find them interesting."

On the road to Bad Aussee.

"If Colonel Philpott were here right now, I'd give him a big kiss on both of his fat cheeks!" Gina's mood had gone from mud gray to rainbow-colored when Philpott had passed on her new orders from the regional commissioner late that morning. American troops were expected to capture Bad Aussee within the next few days, and the regional commissioner wanted Gina to get as close as possible to the front line so she'd be in a position to move up the mountain to the Alt Aussee salt mine.

"Just think, Bill – soon we'll have our hands on all the art." A breeze came in over the windshield, sending strands of her dark brown hair dancing across her face.

Bill frowned as he navigated another hairpin turn. "Now, hold your horses, Gina. Far be it from me to rain on your parade, but we're not going anywhere near the front line. Too risky."

"Bill, it's sweet of you to be so thoughtful." She gave his knee a playful pat. "I'm touched by your concern, really I am; but I'm not afraid to get as close as we can."

"Maybe you're not afraid, but I am." He reached under his seat. "Look, Wonder Woman, make sure you carry this." He pressed an M1911 pistol into her hand.

Gina took the weapon reluctantly. "Bill, why do you think I need a gun?"

"Because war is a dangerous place to be." He dropped the shift a gear as the jeep met a hill. "And it's always possible that I may not be—"

"Don't say it, Bill, don't say it." Suddenly, Gina felt afraid.

"It's not just the Germans." Bill scowled as he spoke. "The whole place is full of refugees – Hungarians, Italians, Poles. They've all got a score to settle," he spat out the words, "and they don't care who they settle it with." He glanced across at her to make sure she understood his words.

"I'm certain—look out, Bill!"

Terrill saw the lamb in the middle of the road a moment too late. Instinctively, he pulled on the wheel and slammed on the brake. The rear end of the jeep slewed into the ditch at the side of the road.

Stanislaus wandered along the deserted road, his spirit almost broken. They had made short work of the small, scrawny chicken he had stolen the day before and his search for food had begun anew. That morning, he had found another dairy farm, but the farmer had refused his pleas, driving him off his land with a pitchfork.

He was disconsolate. His hunger shrieked in his stomach, and he knew that Frieda and Trudi were suffering the same distress. He had to help them, he thought, as his feet shuffled aimlessly down the hill. His plan to return to Poland was now just a forlorn hope; day-to-day survival would be hard enough. Besides, his place now was with Frieda and her daughter. The Raphael portrait was, at that moment, worthless. You couldn't eat a painting.

Stanislaus came to the sharp bend at the bottom of the hill. He decided to try the next farm. If he had no luck, he'd return to the hut and try to take Frieda and Trudi back to the monastery, although Trudi's weakened state would make such a journey difficult.

As he turned the corner, he saw them. An American soldier and a woman in uniform standing by a jeep with its rear wheels in a ditch by the side of the road.

Stanislaus was about to turn and retrace his steps when the soldier saw him and pulled out a rifle from the jeep. There was no option. He walked towards the jeep, holding his hands in the air.

Terrill leveled his rifle at the stranger, motioning him forward. The stranger shuffled hesitantly towards the jeep with his hands up. Terrill could see the unkempt man was not armed, but he was tall and looked strong, and Terrill decided to take no chances. He took an aggressive step forward; the man stopped, his hands still held high above his head.

"Do you think this guy's a German?" Terrill called to Gina, who was watching the confrontation anxiously. "Say something to him in German."

"Sind Sie deutsch?"

"Nein. Ich bin kein Deutscher. Ich bin polnisch."

Terrill listened uncomprehendingly at the exchange that followed. "What's he saying?" he said without taking his eyes from the man. "Who the hell is this guy?"

"He says he's a Pole. An escaped slave laborer. He's looking for food for his wife and child. I think he's harmless."

Terrill still held his rifle steady. "Maybe, Gina. But if he's an escaped slave laborer, what's he doing with a wife and child in Germany?"

"I don't know, Bill. Who knows what goes on in this war?" There was exasperation in her voice. "But don't you see? He can help get the jeep back on the road."

Gestapo Headquarters, Lake Hallstatt District.

Gruber picked up the sealed envelope. Written on the front was a simple description. *Items found in the possession of Josef Flaschberger, arrested May 4, charged with theft.* He ripped open the envelope, wondering why he was wasting his time on such a trivial matter.

He tipped the contents onto his desk, his hand swatting at a coin that rolled loose. His fingers sifted through the items, taking care to avoid the sharp knife in their midst. A tool of the thief's trade, no doubt.

There was little of interest. A few Reichsmarks, some Reichspfennigs. Clearly the crook had not been very successful, although the lady's watch was clearly stolen, as were the three gold rings and the jeweled pendant that had once graced some woman's neck.

A waste of time. His world was crashing down about his ears and now he was being asked to spend his time looking at a petty criminal's meager haul. A lifetime of police routine made him pick up the thief's passbook to check the crook's details.

As he opened it, his hand began to shake. "Konrad! Konrad!" he shouted through the open door.

The clerk appeared in the doorway. "Jawohl, mein Herr."

"Where is this man?"

"What man, mein Herr?"

"The man, dummkopf, who was found with these articles." Gruber pointed at the watch and the rings.

"Mein Herr, the man was arrested by Officer Schmidt—"

"I don't want a report, idiot! I want to know where the man is!"

He's in the jail across the road, sir. Do you want me to type out the charge sheet?"

"No, you fool!" Gruber's face reddened with impatient rage. "Have the man brought to me immediately! And prepare the car. Fill the tank with the last of the gasoline."

"I'm afraid there's none left, sir."

Gruber brought his fist down on the desk in exasperation. "Then commandeer some from whatever sources you can find!"

"Right away, sir." Though faced with a difficult task, the clerk was glad for the opportunity to get away.

Gruber opened the passbook again. He would ask the thief where he had stolen the document. The right answer could lead him to the painting. He looked down at the identity photograph in the passbook. The face of the Engelsing woman stared back at him.

Kaltenbach. A field kitchen.

"Fräulein, I'm deeply grateful to you. My wife and child are starving."

Gina thought she could see tears brim in the Pole's eyes when she told him they could get him some food at the field kitchen at Kaltenbach. "There's no need to thank me."

"But what, may I ask, is an American woman doing in such an advanced position?" The Pole's question caught Gina off-guard.

"I don't think you'd understand." Gina reached into her pocket and pulled out a Hershey bar. "I'm working to recover art treasures the Nazis have stolen."

"Art treasures?" The Pole's eyes were fixed on the chocolate in Gina's fingers.

"Valuable paintings, sculptures, and the like. We want to get them back in the hands of the real owners." Gina saw the look in the man's eyes and handed him the chocolate bar.

The Pole broke off two-thirds of the bar, carefully wrapped the paper around it, and placed it in his pocket before devouring the rest. As the delicious taste covered his tongue, Stanislaus closed his eyes and thought about the painting back in the hut.

"Tell him to stay in the jeep, Gina." Terrill turned off the ignition and jumped down in front of the field kitchen.

Gina passed on the order to Stanislaus and joined Terrill by the hood of the jeep. "Bill, something strange has come up." She knit her brow.

"Strange, Gina? Look, I'll just go get this guy some food from the canteen and we'll send him on his merry way. It's the least we can do – we'd never have made it this far if he hadn't helped us with the jeep."

"It's not that, Bill." Gina's voice had a puzzled tone. "This man claims he's got a valuable painting. A Raphael masterpiece – *The Portrait of a Young Man.* You remember, Bill, I told you about that painting."

"Yeah," Terrill racked his brain as he pulled out a pack of Luckies from his breast pocket. "Say, isn't that the painting that was stolen from that Nazi big shot?" As he held out the pack to Gina, Bill grinned at his ability to retrieve an obscure nugget of information concerning fine art.

"The Nazi big shot was Hans Frank, Hitler's Governor-General of Poland." She took a cigarette and edged it to his proffered lighter. "And there's a bit more we know. The painting was mentioned in Count von Schellendorf's notebook, the one we found when he died. It was the only work that did not have the Alt Aussee label on it."

"Did you ask this guy about any of that?"

"Yes."

"What did he say?"

"He just looked at me blankly."

"Doesn't make much sense, does it? What would a guy like that," Terrill arched his thumb in the direction of the Pole, "be doing with a painting stolen from a Nazi big shot and written down in some rich guy's notebook?"

"That's the whole point exactly." Gina drew heavily on her cigarette.

Terrill narrowed his eyes as he thought. "Did he offer any explanation on how he got it?"

"His story is unbelievable. He says he heard about the theft when he was a slave laborer. Knew the painting was hidden in some monastery. Says he found it in the monastery's crypt a week ago. Thinks maybe I should take charge of it. Can you believe all that?"

Terrill shrugged his shoulders and stared at the ground as he considered the tale. "No one could make up a story like that, Gina. I can usually tell when a guy's trying to pull the wool over my eyes." He held his cigarette between his index finger and thumb and inhaled deeply. "Probably one of the few advantages of growing up in Hell's Kitchen – you either develop a gut feel for who's lying to you, or you live to regret it." He tossed his cigarette on the ground and stamped on it. "Personally, I'd believe him."

"But if he is telling the truth, then what do we do?"

"Why not just take him back and have a look at the painting?"

Gina looked at her watch. "We're running late as it is, and I have my orders from the regional commissioner." Gina couldn't hide the frustration in her voice. "We've got to get moving. I've got all the records to prepare for the classifications when we reach the art hidden in the mines. Alan's replacement is due to arrive later and I need to get everything ready for him. We've got to account for all the works stolen by Hitler as well as those stolen by the count and listed in the notebook we found. I've got a mountain of work."

"Gina," Terrill reached forward and grasped her arms, "it's your call." He looked into her eyes. "I'll do whatever you ask."

Gina smiled, grateful for his support. "We can't go back – we have to go on. One painting, however valuable, against a whole cache of treasures is no contest."

She began to head for the jeep, then stopped. "Say, I know what I can do – I'll ask him to bring the painting back here on Tuesday. He could meet us over there, in front of that chapel." She pointed to a small octagonal building, the apex of its pointed roof topped by a cross. "Perhaps we'll be able to get away from Alt Aussee by then."

"In this war, 'perhaps' is a big word." Terrill strode away from the jeep. "But in the meantime, I'll get this guy some food." He gave Gina a smile. "He's pretty skinny and he sure deserves it."

Bad Aussee.

The Americans would soon arrive.

Hofmann stood on the outskirts of Bad Aussee looking up at the mountain road that led to Alt Aussee and, beyond the village, to the mine. He could do little to stop them. Clouds shrouded the peaks, the sun peeking through at a quiet countryside that belied the convulsions of a once-proud nation in its death throes. His mind struggled with a certainty he once had thought impossible: there would be no Alpenfestung, no phoenix of National Socialism rising from Germany's ashes. The war was lost.

Hofmann tried to control the rage that seethed within him, a useless fury of impotence. From a fearsome battle group, he had been reduced to a motley collection of fifty soldiers and a dozen or so Hitler Jugend. Probably they all had reached the same conclusion long ago: Germany was defeated.

Memories began to flood his mind, a time when everything had been so different. Poland conquered within a month. The proud entry into Paris. Standing at the outskirts of Moscow, the towers of the Kremlin tantalizing on the distant horizon.

The memories gave him but a brief respite from his rage. All that vaunted power had been reduced to a convoy of five trucks. He had commanded divisions; legions of tanks had awaited his orders. Now five trucks. He looked at them, awaiting the ascent to Alt Aussee after dark; besides his paltry force, they carried the art and the explosives. He thought of the irony: at the end of the war, all he had were some of the finest artistic treasures in Europe and the means to destroy them.

He lit a cigarette and drew deeply as unwelcome memories stole into his mind. *I know the sorrow this message brings you* the first telegram had read. Kurt was dead. Sorrow – it had driven his wife, Magda, to the brink of insanity after Kurt was killed. He recalled how she looked on his brief compassionate leave – her face gaunt with grief, her once-sparkling eyes dulled by pain. Magda had never been strong and had taken to her bed, her heart broken by the death of their only child.

He had received the second telegram in Poland while fighting a futile rear-guard action. The message had been brief. Magda, too, was dead. She had refused to go to the shelter during an American air raid. The bomb had destroyed everything that was left in his private life.

Now all he loved had been lost. His son. His wife. The Führer. And soon the war, the war that had given his life meaning. He took a long drag on his cigarette and exhaled slowly, watching the smoke swirl in the air. And what of himself? He, too, was lost. What lay ahead for him? Ignominious surrender? Being ordered around by some pimply-faced American in a prisoner of war camp? Shot like a dog on some trumped-up charge?

He angrily tossed away the cigarette butt. And if he should survive the camp, what sort of life would he have then? A clerk in a factory? A teller in a bank? A pitiful existence.

The rumble of artillery fire in the distance brought him back sharply to the present. The Americans were on their way. The Americans who had robbed him of everything important in his life. The order – destroy the art before it falls into the hands of the enemy – brought the Führer's words into his mind: *Revenge shall be our battle cry.* The Americans had robbed him of his family, and with his last breath, if necessary, he would make them pay.

Suddenly, he felt invigorated, his spirits refreshed. *Revenge shall be our battle cry.* He had one last mission. He would carry out the Führer's final order.

Bad Aussee. US Army encampment.

Gina toyed with the scrambled powdered eggs that occupied one of the compartments of her mess tray; it was not yet dawn, and the mess tent was almost deserted. She had hardly slept the night before thinking about what lay before her. All the information they'd received pointed to the most massive repository of stolen Nazi art treasures. Michelangelo's *Bruges Madonna.* Jan van Eyck's *Adoration of the Lamb.* Vermeer's *Astronomer.* And thousands more. She was going to help rescue the world's greatest assemblage of stolen art, a collection unmatched even by those of the Paris Louvre or the Leningrad Hermitage.

She blanched at the saltiness of the eggs and tossed her fork onto the mess tray. Despite the immense trove that lay ahead, her thoughts kept turning to the Pole she and Bill had met on the road. And the Raphael portrait he claimed he had.

The "divine Raphael" they called the master, and his art was the culmination of the High Renaissance. Even in his own time he was so beloved that, when he died on his thirty-seventh birthday, all of Rome filed past as his body lay in state. His Madonnas were second to none and his Vatican frescoes as magnificent as those in the Sistine Chapel, but with his portraits he attained the pinnacle of his genius. She had once seen a print of his *Portrait of a Young Man* and she remembered wondering if the unknown subject might be the handsome Raphael, himself.

But how could an escaped slave laborer in tatters wandering the back roads of Austria have possession of a Raphael masterwork? The Pole's story didn't add up. She absentmindedly twisted a lock of hair around her finger. Yet the Pole had seemed so knowledgeable. He was well-spoken – his German was as good as hers – and he knew the painting had been in the Czartoryski collection. She was certain he'd seen the work in Krakow because he had described it in some detail. If he didn't have the painting, why would he lie and say he did?

The painting had somehow disappeared from the hands of the former Nazi Governor-General of occupied Poland. Had the Pole been the thief, and was he now having second thoughts about having stolen it? She cut a corner off her slice of Spam and chewed without tasting it. Raphael's *Portrait of a Young Man* was also one of the works listed in Count von Schellendorf's notebook, the notebook he appeared to have been reading when he died. What possible connection could the Pole have with Count von Schellendorf? She blew through her teeth in exasperation – it was all such a muddle.

She should have asked Bill to turn the jeep around immediately, to go back with the Pole to collect the masterpiece he claimed to have, but her orders were to get to Alt Aussee as soon as possible. Perhaps the Pole would keep his promise and bring the painting to the chapel in Kaltenbach. She'd be able to deal with it then, after she'd completed her initial investigations of the trove at Alt Aussee and after Donovan's replacement arrived to take over.

She pushed away her mess tray and blotted her lips with a paper napkin that seemed to dissolve upon contact. Bill had said he believed the Pole's story. The whole thing seemed like a long shot to Gina, but for the moment she'd put her trust in Bill's instincts and hope to retrieve the Raphael masterpiece later. After what she expected to find at Alt Aussee, the Raphael would be the icing on the cake.

"Gina! Gina!" She looked up to see Bill racing in, a wild smile on his face. "Good news, Gina! They expect Alt Aussee to be taken early tomorrow!"

Above Alt Aussee. The mine.

"Move it! Move it!" Hofmann urged on his men as the crates passed along a conga line of troops. The entry to the mine was across a large court-yard; there, trolleys awaited the crates to take them along tracks running horizontally, straight back into the inner reaches of the mine. The artworks that Hofmann had safely transported through the perils of war would now join the rest of the Führer's immense collection inside the mine.

Time. He had so little time. Hofmann looked at his watch: just past noon. They'd driven through the night to make the tortuous ascent from

Bad Aussee to Alt Aussee, then on to the mine, another mile high into the mountains.

Hofmann knew the Americans were not far behind. He had left a company at Bad Aussee to thwart the enemy advance. When the unloading was finished, he would send the rest of the men and the Hitler-Jugend back down to the town of Alt Aussee to help in its defense. A delaying action, no more.

He knew he was sacrificing men to buy him time. Only he and Scharführer Engelsing would remain, and both would be hidden when the Americans arrived. The enemy would believe they had captured an empty mine. Then, for them, would come an unpleasant surprise.

The hut.

"I don't know how to advise you, Stanislaus."

Frieda sat next to him on the bench before the hearth, warming herself against the chill of the spring day. He had told her about meeting the American woman on the road, and she could see he was struggling to make a decision. She knew how much returning the painting to his country meant to him, but that course of action would take him away from her and Trudi – a terrifying thought.

"If it were up to me, Stanislaus," she hoped he would not detect her own self-interest, "I'd trust the Americans with the painting. They'll be able to protect it much better than you could."

She looked over at Trudi, who was sitting up in her bed, Clothilde on her lap. "And if you're very, very good, Clothilde," she overheard Trudi saying, "I just might give you a bit of my Spam. Spam is wonderful. Spam is the most delicious food I've ever tasted."

Frieda smiled to see her daughter improving and turned back to Stanislaus. "The Americans were kind to you. I don't know what we would have done without the food they gave you. Trudi's feeling much better – she's even acquired a taste for American canned meat."

Stanislaus arched his back and yawned, his bent arms rising high in the air. "You're right, Frieda." He lowered his arms and took her hand. "I've got to learn to trust people again. You'll have to bear with me – I spent five years trusting no one. No one at all." He gave her hand a squeeze. "Until I met you, that is."

Frieda blushed. "I'd like to think there's still some goodness left in the world. That brave American woman – if what she says is true, she's risking her life to save the art." She thought of Hans and his passion for beautiful things. "And I would like to believe that somewhere in the world there's still a reverence for beauty."

Stanislaus considered her words. "You're probably right, Frieda. But I don't have to go to Kaltenbach to meet the woman until Tuesday, so I still have a couple of days to think about it."

Gestapo Headquarters, Lake Hallstatt District.

Gruber sat at his desk sucking on an empty pipe. On top of everything else he had had to endure, he was out of tobacco.

At first, things had gone very well. As he expected, the prisoner had sung like a bird. Thank God he wasn't another Father Hieronymus; a thinly-veiled threat of a firing squad had quickly loosened the thief's tongue. A cottage. High on the hill. Path leading up from the road. The thief had seen the woman leave the road, accompanied by a child and a man. It all tied together. Like all opportunists, the thief had waited for his moment: he had stolen their bags while they were asleep in the cottage.

In one bag was food, which he'd eaten; in the other were clothes for a woman and a child, which he had sold, and a little money. And a passbook. But only one. The man with the Engelsing woman probably had no identity papers. Everything matched up with the information he'd obtained from the monastery staff.

And then came the clincher. The thief was certain he'd seen the man carrying a wooden box strapped to his back up to the cottage. The painting. Gruber felt his pulse quicken. If he could get the painting—

But his plan had hit a snag. Gruber couldn't follow up on his lead with an empty fuel tank, and his clerk, Konrad, had been out searching for gasoline all morning without luck.

The painting had been within his grasp. He knew where it was. Or at least where it had been. The Engelsing woman, her accomplice, and the brat might very well have moved on by now. Taking *his* property with them.

There was a rap on his door. He could tell from its timidity that it was the ineffectual Konrad. "Come in, and it had better be good news!" he shouted.

"Begging your pardon, sir," Konrad opened the door and spoke from the threshold without entering, "but there's no gasoline anywhere to be found. I checked everywhere." He ran down a list of businesses and private citizens who claimed not to have any of the fuel for which Gruber would have given his left arm.

Gruber could have kicked himself for letting Georg and Rudi take the one Gestapo car that had an almost-full tank of gasoline when they had set out to check passbooks on the road to Sulzbach. That was the last he had seen either of the men or the car with the gas.

"What about the ambulance?" Gruber asked. "Have things got so bad that even the ambulance has no fuel?"

"I didn't check with them, sir. I thought they would want to hold onto their gasoline for an emerg—"

"This *is* an emergency, dummkopf! I need that gasoline for important Gestapo business! Now go!"

"Very good, sir," Konrad murmured, quietly closing the door.

Gruber pulled Frieda's passbook out of his desk drawer. He glowered at her photograph. *I'll find you, Engelsing. And my painting.*

Alt Aussee. The mine superintendent's office.

"Herr Superintendent," Hofmann hovered over the diminutive man in the white work clothes, "I want you to place the explosives here, here," his finger stabbed at the plan of the salt works on the superintendent's desk, "and here," his finger pointed to areas deep within the mine.

"But mein Herr," the superintendent's white cap spun in his fingers, "such an explosion will destroy the mine, and with it the livelihood of families who have worked the salt for generations." His eyes dared to meet the brigadeführer's for a moment before darting away. "It will also destroy all the contents, both the objects that have been brought there over the past months as well as those your men placed there this morning."

"Do not question my orders!" Hofmann's shout caused the superintendent to flinch. "Just do as I tell you! And make sure that all the explosives are linked to a firing device situated here." His finger indicated a position about fifty meters inside the entrance to the mine, hidden away from the eyes of any American soldier who entered.

The superintendent nodded obediently and hastened from the office, anxious to escape the presence of the SS officer.

Hofmann smiled, but there was disquiet in his smile. His plan was taking shape, but time was against him. He looked at his watch. Four o'clock. The Americans would probably take Alt Aussee early the next day. And then they would come storming up the mountain to the mine.

He studied the map of the mine again. He needed to talk to Scharführer Engelsing: all the pieces of his plan had to be in place before the Americans arrived.

Hofmann found Engelsing seated on an empty box by the entrance to the mine, his feet up on his knapsack, face resting on his hands, eyes staring vacantly at the brick wall.

"Tired, Scharführer?"

Hofmann's question snapped the young man from his thoughts; he leapt to his feet and saluted. "No, sir. I'm ready for your orders." His body was rigid, his back arched, his eyes fixed at a distant point ahead.

"At ease, Scharführer." Hofmann picked up an empty crate and sat down as he patted the top of the box upon which Wolfgang had sat. Wolfgang felt uneasy as he sat down.

"What were you thinking about, Wolfgang?" Hofmann looked down at the knapsack. "Going back home?"

"Oh, no, sir," Wolfgang stammered, surprised at the brigadeführer's using his given name. "I was thinking about what's going to happen to us. But I was wondering—"

"What do you think about the war, Wolfgang?" Hofmann looked down at the knapsack. "Going back home?"

"I don't know, sir." Wolfgang found his commanding officer's familiarity disturbing. "We have lost so many men." And boys. Wolfgang closed his eyes as he thought of Horst, his guts squeezed out of him by an American tank. "And now the Führer is dead."

Hofmann stood, removed his cap, and ran his fingers through his hair. "Wolfgang, the war is lost." He saw the startled look in the young man's eyes. "But we still have one last duty to complete for the Führer." He placed his hand on Wolfgang's shoulder.

"And you will play a vital role in carrying out that duty."

The road toward Alt Aussee.

"Bill, just look out there – isn't it beautiful?" Gina gasped as she gazed out over a valley that plunged below them and, beyond, at snow-capped mountains that soared above. "It's so wonderful to be in a part of Europe that's escaped the war. After all the ruined cities we've seen, how lovely to see all those pretty towns." She turned to him and smiled. "You know, that last town we went through looked like a stage set for *Hansel and Gretel.* Complete with the gingerbread."

"Right." Bill found a lower gear as the road to Alt Aussee became steeper. "And while you were admiring all the pretty little houses, I was making sure there weren't any crazed teen-aged boys aiming rifles at us from upstairs windows."

"Relax, Bill. You worry too much. We're in what used to be Austria now. Those red and white flags we saw flying from houses show Austrians are glad to be rid of the Nazis."

Bill honked his horn as he approached a blind curve, although there was little likelihood anyone else was on the road. "You know, Gina, in all my time over here I've never run into anyone who ever said that they supported Hitler. Kind of makes you wonder how the guy ever managed to come to power."

Gina glanced down from the jeep, appreciating the spring wildflowers growing by the side of the road.

"Perhaps that's not a good idea on this road." Terrill twisted the wheel as he negotiated another hairpin turn. "We're not exactly driving down Fifth Avenue at the moment." On his side, a yard from the edge of the road, the cliff fell away precipitously. One false move on his part and the jeep would plunge a thousand feet down the side of the mountain.

"I'm sorry, Bill." She pulled at a wisp of hair the wind had blown across her face, "but I'm so excited. All that art just sitting in the Alt

Aussee salt mine – Bill, here's my chance to use what I know to make a difference on something important to the world."

Terrill pulled on the wheel again as they continued to zigzag their way toward the summit. He longed to share her excitement but couldn't; he wanted to be back home walking down the streets of New York, where the fear of a Nazi ambush did not await him around every corner. The road began winding through a pine forest so dense the filtered sunlight was like scattered golden coins upon the forest floor.

He couldn't share in her excitement, yet he marveled at her joy, her smile, her sense of purpose. Goddamn it, against all of his instincts, he had fallen in love.

Alt Aussee. Late evening.

Hofmann looked across at Wolfgang, asleep in the corner of the mine superintendent's office, the shaded lantern throwing pale yellow light on his huddled form. He lay on his side, his head resting on an arm and his knees drawn up. Wolfgang's jacket was lying in a heap on the floor and Hofmann picked it up and gently spread it over the young man's chest and shoulders.

He, too, was tired, but he could not allow sleep to claim him yet. The coming day would decide if his promise to the Führer could be fulfilled. He rubbed his eyes as he sat down in the superintendent's desk chair. In the morning, the Americans would arrive. And he would destroy all the Führer's treasures.

His mind ran again over his plan. The explosives were all in place, and he hoped the troops he had sent back down to the town of Alt Aussee to offer a last defense would buy him time. But he knew their efforts, however valiant, would not delay the Americans long.

He reached for the coffee pot resting on the stove. Only he remained. Just he and Scharführer Engelsing. He poured a cup and grimaced at the acrid taste. Engelsing wouldn't fail him; he was a brave young man, like his dead son, Kurt.

His finger ran distractedly around the rim of the coffee mug. Engelsing knew much of his plan, but not all. The scharführer knew how they were to destroy the art, but how they were to get away from the Americans, he, himself, was not sure. His hand rested on the white uniforms on the desk into which they would change at dawn. In truth, he doubted they would get away; not after the welcoming party he had planned for the Americans.

As he downed the rest of his coffee, he mulled over the details of the plan one last time. The detonator was hidden some fifty meters inside the tunnel. He and the scharführer would lie concealed with their weapons in the superintendent's hut, allowing the Americans to enter the mine. Then, when the moment was right, he would provide a distraction, giving Engelsing the opportunity to sprint into the mine and activate the detonator.

Hofmann set the coffee mug down and allowed himself a smile as his eyelids began to droop. Not only would the Führer's collection be blown to pieces, but so would hundreds of Americans.

He would have kept his promise to the Führer. And to himself.

On the road to Sulzbach.

G ruber fumed. He had wanted to set out the day before, but Konrad had not found enough gasoline until after nightfall. Now, his progress was slow. He hissed at the riffraff clogging the road and honked at them to get out of his way. His destination was about five miles away, he estimated, and time was of the essence. But so was precision. He pulled over to consult his notes and the hand-drawn map.

He breathed deeply, trying to contain his emotions. The odds were still against him. He had lost much time. And he had come alone. No one else could be trusted. And he was not sure the man and the Engelsing woman would still be there. With the delay and with their food gone, perhaps they had moved on.

But it was his only chance. He folded up his notes and put them in his pocket. He picked up the pistol, checked the magazine, and snapped it shut. His only chance.

Outskirts of Alt Aussee.

"Hold it! Hold it there!" An MP jumped in front of the jeep and raised his arm. Terrill brought the jeep to a halt and glanced past the MP at the small town of Alt Aussee. Quiet, almost undisturbed by war. High mountains looming on all sides, a sparkling lake in the background.

"What's going on, Bill? Why the holdup?" Gina's voice betrayed her impatience to push on to the mine.

A lieutenant bent over to address her. "Excuse me, ma'am. Road's closed."

"I'm with the Monuments, Fine Arts and Archives task force. It's essential that we head up to the mine as soon as possible so we can investigate a cache of stolen art hidden there."

"Sorry, ma'am. No non-combatant troops are allowed past this point. We're not sure the mine's been cleared of German troops." The lieutenant stood up. "Some of our boys are up there now checking it out."

The lieutenant stepped back as columns of surrendering German soldiers began to march by on both sides of the road, their hands on their caps above sullen faces.

Bill turned to Gina. "Looks to me like maybe we got it all wrapped up here." His glance turned to meet the sad eyes of a young man who'd had the bad luck to play for the wrong team. "Although—"

"I think they're being overly cautious. Drive on, Bill," Gina shouted, "drive on!"

Bill looked skeptical but suppressed his doubts as he quickly put the jeep into gear and stepped on the gas. With the defeated German troops hiding them from the lieutenant's view, they slipped up the road toward the mine.

The hut.

Stanislaus was delighted to see the smile return to Frieda's face. Trudi was much improved, thanks to the food he had obtained from the Americans. She was up and about and had resumed her heart-to-heart conversations with her doll.

"I heard her tell Clothilde how nice you are." Frieda beamed as she tilted her head at her daughter, who sat in front of the hearth rearranging the bows on her doll's yarn braids. "She told her doll that if she was very, very good, next time you'd bring back some Spam for her." Frieda laughed as her hand reached out to touch Stanislaus's. "I think it's her way of showing she's grateful."

Stanislaus felt a swell of pride as he looked at the child.

"Clothilde's warm now." Trudi spoke to no one in particular, clutching the doll to her. "But she still wants to go back to be with Brother Helmut."

Frieda stole an anxious look at Stanislaus, but he said nothing. He was deep in thought, still turning over in his mind the decision he had to make. He glanced down at the wooden box that housed the painting. Did he trust the American woman's promise to return the treasure to his homeland? Should he deliver it into her hands the following day or should he carry on alone?

He looked at Frieda and realized he had no option. He couldn't desert her, he couldn't leave her to return to a land he might no longer recognize as home. Home now was wherever Frieda was.

She glanced up and saw him looking at her. "What are you thinking about?" she asked.

"You, actually."

"A good thought, I hope?"

He reached over to fondle her fingers. "A very good thought."

He smiled and glanced at the hearth. "But right now I think I need to bring in some more firewood; those logs burn quickly."

As he rose, Frieda looked at him, her heart swelling. Stealing a side-long glance at Trudi, who was still engrossed with her doll, she stood and gave Stanislaus a brief embrace. "I love you," she whispered, her lips brushing his cheek.

Stanislaus stepped outside. The day was beautiful, with clouds casting fast-moving shadows on the forested hills across the valley. He took a deep breath of the crisp mountain air. He had made his decision. He would take the painting to the American woman and then he would return to the monastery with Frieda and Trudi.

Suddenly, a movement at the bottom of the hill caught his eye. A man was leaving the road and beginning to climb the hill. Even at a quarter mile distance, Stanislaus recognized the short, squat figure lumbering towards him. Gruber.

The salt mine.

Hofmann dropped to his knees and peered through the bottom edge of the window as the first American soldiers approached. A lieutenant led the troop of about twenty men, all crouching low and holding their rifles, ready to fire at the first sign of danger.

As he watched the Americans, his hands reached for the MP 35 sub-machine gun lying on the floor. A precautionary move. He had no intention of firing; he wanted to lure the enemy into his trap.

"Brigadeführer—"

Hofmann raised his index finger to his lips to silence Wolfgang. He knew American tactics well. Without any provocation they would pound a fusillade of bullets toward any noise.

He saw Engelsing look down shamefaced, his cheeks red. A quick glance through the window allayed his fears; the Americans had not heard Engelsing's whisper and continued their careful, nervous approach. He reached out and ruffled the young man's hair, then gave him an encouraging wink. The scharführer's lips arced in a small smile.

Hofmann was pleased – the first part of his plan was working. The Americans were being lured into the mine. Soon they would be destroyed, along with the Führer's art.

Engelsing looked strange in the white uniform of a salt mine worker. The shabby clothes hung uneasily on his sparse frame. A smile crossed Hofmann's face; perhaps he looked even more ridiculous in his white overalls, a cloth cap on his head.

His eyes returned to the courtyard in front of the entrance to the mine. The area was deserted. All the mineworkers had fled as soon as the explosives had been positioned. His attention was riveted on the officer, who edged his way cautiously into the courtyard.

Hofmann felt the tension clutch at his stomach. The American officer paused for a moment, then shouted and called his men forward. The soldiers rushed into the entrance to the mine, their wild shouts echoing from the mountains.

On the hill.

Sweat came from Gruber's brow; he fought for his breath as he struggled with the gradient. Desperation drove him on. The thief's information was correct. He had seen the man, the accomplice, standing outside the cottage. Gruber forced his bulk up the hill. The painting. His passport to survival. His hand reached for the pistol in his pocket.

"We've got to get out of here!" Stanislaus rushed inside. "Gruber's coming up the hill!" he shouted, picking up the box and threading his arms through the cords to strap it to his back, then reaching for Trudi.

"Gruber? But how—"

"Heaven knows." He picked up the child and made for the door. "Come on, let's get going!"

"Clothilde doesn't want to go," Trudi began to kick and squirm, "doesn't want to go!"

"Tell Clothilde we're going to go see Brother Helmut," he was surprised by how quickly the lie quieted the child, "but we've got to be fast about it."

Frieda stopped to collect some food.

"Leave it, Frieda!" Stanislaus snapped, grabbing her hand and pulling her to the door.

As they emerged into the light, Stanislaus shielded his eyes from the sun. Gruber was halfway up the hill, still over a hundred yards away.

"Get up to the top!" He urged Frieda on, knowing that Gruber's bulk would slow him down. "We can still escape by going down the other side of the hill and crossing the stream."

The zing of a bullet through the air made Frieda stop. "Oh, dear God!"

"Keep going!" Stanislaus shouted. "If we stop, we're finished!"

Alt Aussee Salt Mine.

Terrill felt uneasy, his lips drawn tight, his eyes fixed on the road ahead. "I'm not sure we should be doing this, Gina." Terrill pulled on the wheel of the jeep as the vehicle navigated a tortuous bend on the road from the town of Alt Aussee to the mine. "Our men might not have cleared the site yet."

"You worry too much, Bill." There was excitement in Gina's voice. "Besides, if there was still any German resistance up ahead, we'd have heard gunfire by now."

"It's my job to worry for you." Bill stepped down a gear to cope with the incline. "Besides, in case you hadn't realized," he stole a glance at her, "I care a lot for you."

Gina threw him a smile. "I know, Bill, but it's important to get to the mine as quickly as possible." Her hands were clenched, her knuckles white with anxiety. "You've seen how all German authority is breaking down. Only last week, Goering's private train, carrying most of his art collection, was looted by a marauding mob. It's vitally important to ensure the site is secured as soon as possible."

She raked her fingers through her hair nervously. "Do you have any idea what's hidden in that mine? Thousands of masterpieces. Can you imagine what would happen if civilians, drunken German soldiers, escaped slave workers found their way in there? Theft, pillage," she raised her voice, "perhaps wanton destruction of some of the greatest artworks in the world."

Terrill could hear in her voice the fire of her passion for art.

"On top of that, Bill, there's another threat. Once the war is over – which may be in a matter of weeks or even days – this territory becomes part of the Russian zone."

"Are you kiddin' me?" Bill scowled. "Hey, that's not fair. After all, it was our guys who fought to capture this area!"

"You're absolutely right, but that's what was agreed with Stalin. Anyway, we've got to move fast. If the art is still here when the Russians arrive, God only knows what will happen to it."

Terrill nodded. He could see the urgency of getting to the art, and his respect and admiration for Gina were growing. Many men would jump at the chance to get away from the front. Not her. Dedication – dedication to works of art. He couldn't help but admire her spunk.

But he wanted to keep her safe. Hell, he wanted to keep himself safe, to survive the war. Maybe after the war they could—

His thoughts were hurried from his mind by the sight of the man wearing white overalls shuffling along at the side of the road. He looked like a civilian, but Terrill couldn't take any chances – not after what he'd seen. The image of a mere boy came to his mind, a boy running toward him, seeking to kill him.

He slammed on the brakes, switched off the ignition, and reached for his rifle.

On the hill.

Gruber's shot was wild, born of desperation. At such a long range, he had little chance, but he had to try to slow them down. He cursed and resumed the arduous climb. He'd seen them as they'd hurried from the cottage. Even at a distance, he'd recognized the Engelsing woman. The man was carrying the child. And strapped to his back was a wooden box. The painting.

The thought of the treasure made him redouble his efforts as he struggled up the hill. He gasped for breath and his legs screamed for rest, but he forced his way up the steep incline. He could no longer see them – they were climbing behind the cottage. He had to hope that, with his burdens of the child and the box, the man was also tiring. Gruber pushed his reluctant legs forward. The painting. Without it, he had no future; with it, the world was his. He reached the cottage and leaned against a wall, his chest heaving. The painting. Nothing else in the world mattered.

Stanislaus glanced back as they reached the brow of the hill. His arm ached with Trudi's weight, but he urged Frieda on. "Get over the top of the hill." He struggled for breath. "We'll be out of his line of fire."

"When will Clothilde get to see Brother Helmut?" The child's eyes ran over the hill falling away from them.

"When we cross the stream." Stanislaus looked down at the watercourse running through the valley below. Swollen by snowmelt, the stream was even deeper than when he had crossed it just days before. The water lapped at the stepping stones, which provided the only way to get across. Soon after the shallows of the stones the water deepened, the flow gaining strength as the banks narrowed. A hundred yards below the stepping stones, the watercourse angrily churned against rocks, tossing foam into the air before descending into rapids.

Stanislaus knew he was taking a risk. One slip on the stepping stones could mean disaster.

"Come on, let's go!" He picked up Trudi and set out down the hill. Gruber was not far behind, and he had already announced his intentions. They had to risk the stepping stones. There was no other option.

Alt Aussee Salt Mine.

"Nein! Nein!" The German shrank back, his arms held high as Terrill pushed the muzzle of his rifle into his belly. Words, incomprehensible to the American, flew from the German's mouth.

"What's he saying, Gina?" Terrill's finger tightened on the trigger. "What's he saying?"

"Wer sind Sie?" She asked the German to identify himself. As the man spoke, his hands were in motion and he pointed to himself. "Ease off, Bill!" Gina shouted. "He says he's the superintendent of the mine." She smiled her relief. "He says he controls the production of salt."

Her smile disappeared as the German continued speaking. Terrill watched the German's eyes, which were large with apprehension, and knew something was wrong.

"What's up, Gina?"

"He claims there's an SS general hiding somewhere in the mine. The general's armed." Gina's face paled. "Explosives have been placed…" she spoke haltingly as she translated, "throughout the mine."

Terrill was alarmed at the look of horror on Gina's face.

"He says the general intends to destroy all the art."

Terrill waved the man away and leapt back into the jeep. "We're leaving. There's no way I'm exposing you to this kind of danger." He reached out to turn the ignition key.

"No, Bill! No!" Gina grabbed his hand, pulling it away from the key. "It's more important than ever that we push on." Terrill was startled by the vehemence in her voice. She was grasping his wrist with a strength that hurt.

"But some demented Nazi is planning to blow up the mine!" The anger in his voice surprised him. "You could easily be killed!"

"We have to go on, Bill! We have to try to save the art!"

Terrill withered before her eyes that were filled with a mixture of desperation and pleading.

"Bill, perhaps we can warn our soldiers, get them to find the German general before it's too late."

"I tell you it's too risky!" he shouted. "I'm responsible for your safety!"

"And I'm responsible for this mission. We do *not* go back!" Her face was stern. "That's an order, Sergeant Terrill." She tapped on the lieutenant's insignia on her shoulder. "Do you understand me, Sergeant?"

"Yes, ma'am!" Terrill gave a formal salute. He struggled to contain his rage as he jumped down from the jeep. "But you stay here with the jeep while I go forward and try to warn our guys about the explosives."

He checked his rifle, making sure the ammunition magazine was full. "I'll call you when it's safe."

He looked along the road. A wall about four feet high ran about two hundred yards up the hill to the entrance of a courtyard. A GI lounged by the gatepost smoking a cigarette as if the war were already over.

"Hurry! Get a move on!" Her shrill voice urged him on.

"Where's your pistol?"

"Right here." Gina pulled out the gun from under her seat.

"Don't hesitate to use it. Shoot anything that moves that isn't wearing an American uniform." He held her in his eyes; he didn't want to leave her alone.

"I'll be all right. For God's sake, go and warn our men!"

By the stepping stones.

Frieda looked anxiously behind as they reached the fast-moving stream at the bottom of the hill. There was no sign of Gruber, but she knew he would soon appear.

She was uneasy about their escape across the stream. There were about a dozen stepping stones leading to the opposite bank of the stream, which had been fed by the recent rain. The water was fast moving, sometimes washing over the stones. Below the stepping stones, the stream's bed seemed to drop sharply, and Frieda could see tall underwater grasses undulating in the current. She looked downstream: after a hundred yards or so, the watercourse narrowed, the water churning before meeting the rocks leading to the rapids below.

"Stanislaus, I'm—"

"No time." He cut her short, as he unstrapped the painting from his shoulder. "Here, hold onto this." He handed her the box. "I'll carry Trudi across, then come back for you." He took the child in his arms and stepped onto the first stone.

"I'm frightened," Trudi whimpered, clutching her doll tightly.

Gruber saw them as he reached the top of the hill. He paused, wiping the sweat from his brow, his lungs gasping for breath. The man had stopped and was talking to the Engelsing woman.

As he began his descent, he saw the man give the wooden box to the woman before picking up the child and moving onto the stepping stones. Perhaps he had a chance after all. The woman had the painting. His painting. If he could get to the bottom before the woman crossed…. He felt for the gun in his pocket as he hurried down the hill.

Stanislaus hoped his forced smile would give Trudi courage. "Every step we take is one step closer to Brother Helmut." He moved onto the second and third stones; the water lapped at his feet, soaking his shoes.

He placed his foot carefully on the fourth stone, the roar of the rapids ringing in his ears. Almost halfway. He cursed as his foot slid on moss on the fifth stone, causing him to lose his balance for a moment. He felt Trudi's arms and legs tighten about him as they teetered on the slippery stone.

Suddenly, the child screamed. "Clothilde! Clothilde! She's in the water!" Trudi wriggled in his arms; Stanislaus fought to hold his footing. "Clothilde!" Trudi squirmed in his arms again, tipping his balance; Stanislaus's arms flailed as they fell into the water.

"Trudi!" Frieda screamed as she saw her daughter floundering in the water. Instinctively, she ran out onto the stepping stones, the box still in her hands. She saw Stanislaus surface, spluttering. "Stanislaus! Stanislaus!" she shouted frantically. "Get Trudi!"

She began to step to the next stone but her foot slipped on the wet surface. As she fell, the box flew through the air and landed in the water.

Alt Aussee Salt Mine.

Hofmann peered cautiously through the corner of the window of the superintendent's hut. He was thankful that the Americans were careless, almost irresponsible. Most of the troop had entered the mine. There were only three soldiers in the courtyard in front of the entrance to the mine: two were sitting on boxes, the other was leaning against the gate, smoking.

"See how foolish the Americans are, Scharführer," he whispered, beckoning Wolfgang to the window. "We couldn't ask for a better situation."

He picked up his submachine gun and checked the magazine. "You remember my orders?"

"*Jawohl,* Brigadeführer." Wolfgang answered boldly, trying to conceal his anxiety. "When you open fire, I'm to run into the mine. The detonator is fifty meters from the entrance, hidden behind a canvas sack. I'm to activate the power and depress the plunger." He placed his hands together in front of his body and pushed down, just as he had been shown. "Then I'm to run back to meet you so we can escape."

"Excellent." Hofmann patted the young man on the shoulder. He hadn't told Engelsing that escape would be a miracle. He felt a pang of regret for the youth. He was truly fond of him, but war was war and he had seen so many others die. No matter. The art would be blown to hell, along with the Americans. The Führer's order would be fulfilled.

"And your Luger pistol?" His smile was unwavering. "The pistol I awarded you for your bravery?"

"Here, sir." He tapped the pocket of the baggy trousers he was wearing.

"Don't hesitate to use it if anyone threatens your mission. And remember, Engelsing, whatever happens, you must accomplish your mission." Another glance through the window.

Terrill edged his way along the wall, crouching for protection. He stopped and slowly raised his head above the wall. The only sound came from the whir of a distant airplane. Where was the danger? To his left, a hut. No sign of any movement. Perhaps the mine superintendent had been telling a pack of lies. Perhaps he wasn't even the mine superintendent.

He ducked back beneath the wall and looked down the road. Gina sat in the jeep, some fifty yards away. His eyes turned to look up the road. About a hundred yards along the wall, the gate that opened onto the courtyard. The GI guard was still leaning against the gatepost.

Terrill decided to get closer before calling out. He didn't want to get shot up by a trigger-happy dogface.

Suddenly there was a burst of automatic gunfire. The guard at the gate began to dance, his arms and legs thrown out at curious angles. The dance lasted for a few seconds before the soldier's body fell to the earth.

Hofmann saw the American fall. His second burst of fire caught the guards at the entrance to the mine. As their bodies sprawled on the ground, he called out, "Now, Scharführer, now!" He stood aside as the young man appeared in the doorway. "I'll cover you from here. Fire the detonator and get back fast!"

The stream.

Gruber swore. Fate was against him. The painting was in the water, drifting downstream. The woman was hanging onto a stepping stone, the man making his way toward the struggling child. But the Gestapo man's eyes turned to the box, bobbing in the water. He watched aghast as the current pulled his painting toward the rapids. At last a stroke of luck – the box snagged on an overhanging branch of a tree at the edge of the stream. He changed direction, running for the tree. He would deal with the others after he recovered the treasure.

Stanislaus spluttered as he came to the surface, gasping for breath as the cold water seized his body. He saw Frieda, her hands grasping at a stepping stone. He looked downstream and saw the box caught by a branch. And Gruber. The Gestapo man would get the painting.

"Trudi!" Frieda screamed. "Where's Trudi?"

Stanislaus turned quickly in the water, looking downstream. There was no sign of the girl. He took a deep breath and plunged back below the surface.

Alt Aussee Salt Mine.

Terrill's sniper's instincts took control. He slowly raised his head a few inches above the wall. Identify the source of fire. Eliminate the threat. If the gunman saw Gina and the jeep—

He saw the man. A few yards to the right of the hut, changing the magazine of his submachine gun. Although he was dressed like a mine worker, Terrill smelled a rat. Mine workers didn't carry guns. The man was fully exposed, without cover. Terrill's eyes scanned the courtyard. A young man was running across it toward the mine entrance. No threat.

In an instant, his eyes returned to the man. He was walking to the other side of the hut, looking down the road. Christ, he'd see Gina. Terrill's hands swiftly brought up his rifle, resting on the wall. The man was raising his submachine gun, pointing the muzzle down the road, aiming at the jeep.

Terrill's eyes narrowed as he looked down the rifle sights. A body shot might not stop the man from firing at Gina. He needed a head shot. His finger caressed the trigger.

Hofmann looked through the sights of his machine gun. What on earth was a woman doing sitting in a jeep outside the mine? He glanced quickly over his shoulder at Engelsing, running towards the mine entrance. He turned back to look at the woman. He could take no chances. His finger began to squeeze the trigger.

The pain erupted in his brain. He fell to his knees, the gun spiraling from his hands. He grasped a final image. Kurt.

Wolfgang was halfway to the entrance, his hands pumping as he ran, when he heard the shot echo from the mountains. A single shot, unlike the bursts of the brigadeführer's machine gun. He heard a cry, stopped, and turned. His leader had fallen to the ground, his body twitching with the same death throes he had seen when Willi had been shot.

He hesitated, his hand reaching for the pistol in his pocket. The brigadeführer's order rang in his ears. *Whatever happens, you must accomplish your mission.* He ran toward the mine, his eyes stinging from the tears that blurred his vision.

The stream.

Gruber paused at the base of the tree leaning out into the water. The painting was caught in the twigs at the end of a branch, some twelve feet into the stream. The current pulled at the box, but it was snagged tight. The painting was as good as his. Crawling on his stomach, he edged his way forward on the branch toward the snared box.

Stanislaus cast about frantically as he reached the bottom. The water was clear but he couldn't see Trudi. He pulled himself along the reeds waving in the current. His head began to feel light as his lungs begged for oxygen. He was about to return to the surface when he saw the child. Her legs were caught in the reeds. He plowed his way forward, driving his body toward her.

Gruber felt the branch sag under his weight. He stopped to make sure the box hadn't been disturbed. He edged forward again, his hand reaching for the treasure. His treasure. He reached out carefully, his fingers seeking purchase on the box. Almost there.

Alt Aussee Salt Mine.

Terrill jumped over the wall. The man was dead, but he pumped three more rounds into the body. He turned; the teenager he had seen earlier was almost at the mine entrance. His eyes caught the glint of the sun on the pistol in the youth's hand.

Terrill began to run after the boy, then stopped, raised his rifle and fired. The bullet kicked into the ground. He had to take a more deliberate shot. He dropped to one knee, took careful aim, and pulled the trigger. Nothing. He cursed. The rifle had jammed. The young man disappeared into the mine.

The stream.

Stanislaus's fingers clawed frantically at the reeds wrapped around Trudi's ankle. The reeds would not yield. He grabbed the child and pulled. He knew he could soon lose consciousness, but he tugged with the last vestige of strength within him. Suddenly, the child came loose. Stanislaus pulled her to him as he raced to the surface.

Gruber's arm was stretched to its full limit. The water was tugging at the box, but his fingers grasped its corner. His hat fell from his head and ran away on the water but he ignored it. Just a little more purchase and he'd be able to lift the box out of the stream. Then he'd deal with the Engelsing woman and her accomplice.

Gruber grunted as he pulled himself along the branch with his free hand. He had it! His right hand began to pull the box from the water. The painting was his!

Crack! His eyes widened with horror at the sound of splitting wood. The branch broke and pitched him into the fast-flowing water.

Alt Aussee Salt Mine.

Wolfgang was afraid. The darkness of the mine enveloped him; a few bulbs gave a little light but failed to penetrate the gloom. He paused to catch his breath. The detonator was on his right, fifty meters ahead, but he couldn't see it. Hidden under a canvas sack, the brigadeführer had said.

Tears streaming down his face, he edged his way forward, holding his pistol high. His father was a traitor. The Führer was gone. The war was lost. And now his leader was dead. He had nothing left to live for save one thing: the completion of his mission.

His eyes at last fell upon the hidden detonator. About thirty meters ahead.

One of the American soldiers who had entered the mine was coming back from the mine's interior.

"What the hell is going—"

Wolfgang aimed his pistol and fired.

The stream.

Stanislaus gasped as he broke the surface, his lungs greedily sucking the air. His free hand held onto a stepping stone as he heaved Trudi's inert body onto its surface.

"My baby! My baby!" Frieda screamed as she scrambled between the stones, her hands reaching for her child.

"Turn her over," Stanislaus shouted as he pulled himself onto the rock. "Turn her over! On her stomach, head to the side."

"Oh, my God!" Frieda struggled; Trudi's clothes were heavy, sodden with water.

"Here, let me do it." Stanislaus turned the child on her stomach and knelt over her, one knee positioned on either side of her. He placed his flattened hands on her back and began pumping with an even but desperate rhythm.

"Stanislaus, she's gone!" Frieda wailed, tears mingling with rivulets of water that dripped from her hair. "Her face is blue. Oh, my baby, my baby!"

Gruber held onto the box as the current pulled him towards the gorge, his feet kicking hard. Perhaps he could get to the bank. But the water tugged remorselessly, spinning him and the box around like a top. He struggled desperately, but his waterlogged clothes and shoes were pulling him under.

He heard the roar of the water, growing stronger every moment. The turbulence lifted him briefly and then crashed his head down against a rock. The box sprang loose from his grip, tumbling down the torrential cascade, followed by Gruber's lifeless body.

Alt Aussee Salt Mine.

Terrill heard the shot as he reached the entrance. His fingers frantically freed the jammed magazine; quickly he clicked a replacement in place as he edged forward, his back against the wall.

There was little light. A few bulbs barely penetrated the gloom and he began to sweat as the monster that lurked deep in his mind began to surface. Mr. Shapiro's coal cellar. His eyes narrowed, seeking the comfort of the meager light struggling to dispel the darkness.

Suddenly, he saw the boy in the shadows, about thirty yards ahead on his right. He looked like he was pulling at some kind of fabric in a recess in the wall. The pistol was tucked into his belt. Just beyond the boy a GI was lying on the floor, clutching at his blood-stained uniform and gurgling. A desperate cry came from his throat.

The boy turned to the noise, pulled his pistol from his belt and shot the soldier in the head. A wild rage seized Terrill. Everything he hated about Germany and the Nazis crystallized into the form of the evil, blond-haired bastard. He dropped to one knee and took aim.

The lights went out. He was back in Mr. Shapiro's coal cellar again. The monster was free.

The stream.

Stanislaus brushed water from his eyes and quickly resumed his rhythmical pressing of Trudi's back. He cursed himself for having taken so long to find the child at the bottom. He saw Frieda kneeling by her daughter's head, her face contorted in fear and anguish.

"My baby, my baby," Frieda's lips quivered, "she's gone."

"Wait, look!" Stanislaus spoke quickly as water trickled from Trudi's lips. He redoubled his efforts, pumping frantically. There was more water, then suddenly the child heaved and gagged, groaning as she spat out the water. Stanislaus's fingers could feel the child's lungs fill with air. But he continued pressing until he could recognize a regular rise and fall.

Frieda took out a handkerchief and gently wiped Trudi's face and lips. The tears that ran down Frieda's cheek were of happiness and relief.

"Gruber!" Stanislaus shouted as he turned his head. "Where's Gruber?" Fear returned to their eyes as they both looked downstream. But they saw nothing except the churning water and the spray that hung over the gorge.

Trudi coughed and spluttered but recovered quickly, color returning to her face as she began to breathe deeply.

Frieda clasped her precious girl to her, raining kisses on her face. She turned to look at Stanislaus, a weary look of joy spreading over her cold, bedraggled face. "Thank you, Stanislaus." She freed a hand to grasp his. "Thank you."

Stanislaus smiled but said nothing. Perhaps, he thought, he should follow Father Hieronymus's example and thank God.

Alt Aussee Salt Mine.

Terrill didn't know how long the lights were out. An eternity. He thrashed about, his fingers clawing at the earthen floor of the mine, just as they had scratched at the door of Mr. Shapiro's coal cellar. The monster grabbed him, torturing him in the darkness of his cell.

When the light returned it found him in a fetal position, his body drenched in sweat, his rifle cast aside. His hands shook as he struggled to shake off his demons. He struggled to his knees, his eyes fighting to focus in the light.

The boy had pulled the burlap away. Still shaking, Terrill recognized what had been hidden. A detonator. The superintendant had been right. When the plunger was pressed, all of the soldiers and Gina's art deep inside the mine would be blown to hell.

He scrambled across the floor, his hands reaching for his rifle. The boy had heard the noise and leveled his pistol.

The shot echoed around the chamber.

Terrill saw the startled look on the boy's face as he fell to his knees, the pistol spinning from his hand. The boy began to crawl back to the detonator, his hands reaching for the plunger.

Another shot. The boy's hands flailed at the plunger for a moment before thudding to the floor.

Terrill turned his head to look behind him. Gina's face was ashen. The pistol fell from her fingers, clattering on the ground.

SHAEF Headquarters, Rheims, France.

G eneral Eisenhower rubbed his eyes and glanced at his watch; in a couple of hours it would be dawn. In the last few days, he and his staff had slept little as they tracked the collapse of the Wehrmacht, watching, waiting as the Germans surrendered to local Allied forces. He reached for his pen and a sheet of paper.

A few hours earlier, General Alfred Jodl, chief of staff for the German High Command, had signed the Acts of Military Surrender. Eisenhower had declined to attend, preferring not to honor with his presence the representative of a regime whose offenses against humanity were so odious; his recent tours of the concentration camps were still fresh in his mind. After Jodl had signed the papers, the German general was brought to his office. Dispensing with any niceties, Eisenhower had stood behind his desk and had made it clear that Jodl would be held personally accountable for any violation of the surrender terms.

With millions dead and Europe savaged, there was little cause for jubilation, but Eisenhower had arranged for a bottle of champagne to be brought in for his staff to mark the occasion. No doubt they would savor the joy and triumph. Eisenhower sighed. For him there was only relief and gratitude.

He tapped the desk with his pen as he struggled to find the right words to send to the Combined Chiefs of Staff, words to mark a momentous event, words that might resound down through history. But he was exhausted. The Supreme Commander pulled the paper in front of him and wrote, simply:

The mission of this Allied Force was fulfilled at 02.41, local time, May 7th, 1945.

Kaltenbach. *The meeting point by the chapel.*

Terrill leaned against the front of the jeep and looked at his watch. The sun was beginning to dip in the sky. "Looks like the Polish guy ain't gonna show, Gina."

"I'm sure he understood he was to meet us here." She looked up at the octagonal walls of the chapel, trying to hide her disappointment. "Just a few more minutes, Bill."

Terrill nodded. He could sense her conflicting emotions. Her harrowing experience in the mine had tarnished the elation of having saved the treasures. And hearing that the Germans had surrendered. In the mine, he had seen a part of her he had not witnessed before. Now this letdown. Her eyes looked tired and she bit her lip nervously.

"What do you think happened, Bill?"

"Who knows?" He offered her a cigarette and noticed her hand shook as she leaned forward towards the flame of his lighter. "War forces people to go where they don't want to go, to make and break promises."

"But he said he had a Raphael, Bill." She peered down the road, looking for any sign to restore her fading hopes. *"Portrait of a Young Man.* One of the greatest works of art by one of the greatest masters of all time. "

"Well, it looks like the Young Man had an appointment somewhere else." He flicked his cigarette away. "But, hey, at least you gotta be happy with the haul you found in the salt mine. If it hadn't been for you keeping up with target practice, all that art would now be just a pile of cinders."

She turned to face him, her deep brown eyes beginning to glisten. "I wasn't even thinking of the art when I pulled the trigger, Bill. There was something more important I wanted to save."

He shoved his hands in his pockets and looked down at the ground as he kicked at a stone in the road.

"You, Bill." He raised his head and she looked into his eyes. "And now the war's over. But still I can't shake this awful feeling of sadness that's weighing me down." Her lower lip began to tremble. "I saw the look in his eyes, Bill. He was just a kid, and he looked so scared. Why would he do it, Bill? Why would a boy want to blow up all the art?"

Bill sighed and looked up at the sky. "That German guy we stopped on the hill outside the mine, he said some general wanted to blow it up. I guess that kid must have been just following orders." He reached up, pulled a blossom off an apple tree, and plucked off its petals distractedly. "I think there was a lot of just following orders that made this war a hell-hole. In the beginning, the crazy Kraut who led the parade talked big and millions fell into line behind him. To just follow orders." He turned and, looking earnestly into her eyes, spoke softly. "What you did was right, Gina."

"And what you did that day the snipers attacked the truck, that was right, too. But being right didn't stop you from grieving. That boy was somebody's child. Somewhere there's a mother who's waiting for a son who will never come home from the war. Because of me." She angrily flung the cigarette down and brought the tips of her fingers to the corners of her eyes to brush away tears.

"Not because of you, Gina. Because of all the lousy things that happened here before you ever even got here." Terrill swung around abruptly to stare down the road. A skein of returning geese flew overhead, their calls momentarily drowning out the noise of distant army vehicles. "I sure wish that Polish guy had shown up with the painting, Gina. Maybe that would have cheered you up."

"It's a huge disappointment, Bill. I could kick myself right now for not having followed up with him the day we met him on the road. I can't believe I let the *Portrait of a Young Man* slip through my fingers."

"Well, maybe the Young Man is somewhere else, but at least I'm still here." He turned to look at her sheepishly. "I haven't thanked you yet for saving my life."

Gina's smile was warm. "Then I guess that makes us even, Bill." She reached out to take his hand. "If it hadn't been for you, I'd have been shot that day the Nazis ambushed us."

He squeezed her hand and tilted his head toward the jeep. "What are you going to do, now that the war's over?" They began to walk back to the jeep.

"Are you joking, Bill?" Her eyes began to sparkle again and her face regained its animation. "I've got months of work left for me here. I have to get back to Alt Aussee – all that art has to be identified, catalogued, examined to see if it requires restoration, shipped to a collecting point. Then we have to determine each piece's provenance, and—" She smiled. "Sorry, Bill. Got carried away again. What about you? Will you be going home to New York?"

"Maybe you haven't heard, Gina," he took her arm to help her into the jeep, "but there's a place on the map called Japan." He sighed. "Most of our guys over here know they'll be headed for the Pacific."

"No, not you, Bill." She remained standing by the side of the jeep.

"But—"

"My report to the regional commissioner will insist," there was a mischievous glint in her eyes, "that you are an indispensable member of my team. You'll be staying here with me."

"But, Gina—"

"That's an order, Sergeant Terrill." She giggled as she touched the insignia on her shoulder. "An order. Do you understand?"

"Yes, ma'am!" Terrill saluted before taking her in his arms.

Errenbach Monastery.

"Praise be to God!" Father Hieronymus threw his hands in the air as he greeted Frieda and Stanislaus. "To see such happy, smiling faces!" He grasped the hand of Stanislaus and shook it vigorously before embracing Frieda and then bending down to lift Trudi high above his head. "And how are you, my little alpine flower?"

"Where's Brother Helmut?"

The laughter of Stanislaus and Frieda was so infectious the abbot joined in, although he wasn't sure what the joke was about. "He should be here soon." Father Hieronymus lowered the child to the floor, his warm smile never leaving his face. "But first, we have something else in which to rejoice."

Stanislaus and Frieda stared at him blankly.

"You haven't heard? They announced it on the radio this morning. The war is over! Thanks be to God!"

There were cheers of celebration, but Stanislaus could sense that Frieda's joy was tempered by an apprehension of what still lay ahead for her and Trudi. The war might be over, but it would be a long time before things returned to normal. Everywhere was still chaos. Gangs of escaped slave laborers still roamed the countryside. Pockets of rabid Nazis would still fight on. Even if Father Hieronymus allowed Frieda and Trudi to remain a while at the monastery – as surely he would – the future offered little to a German woman facing the world alone with her child.

"Brother Helmut!" Trudi's excited cry broke into his thoughts.

Stanislaus looked to the doorway framing the monk's slight body. Stanislaus's eyes, begging forgiveness for leaving him in the forest, briefly caught Brother Helmut's. "I'm sorry—"

"There's no need." The monk smiled and shook his head to dismiss his protest, then turned his attention to the child tugging at his cassock. "And what have we here?" He bent down and gave Trudi a warm smile, his bandaged hands hidden deep within the pockets of his cassock.

Stanislaus could tell by the stiff way the monk held his arms that his hands pained him greatly. So Brother Helmut was their unsung benefactor, the hero who had suffered torture so that they might escape the clutches of Gruber.

"Max and Moritz!" Trudi jumped and clapped her hands. "Oh, please, please may we read some Max and Moritz, Brother Helmut?"

The monk looked at Father Hieronymus, who nodded and tilted his head toward a corner of the room. "Perhaps you would like to help Brother Helmut by turning the pages, Frau Engelsing?"

Frieda withdrew to the corner, where she sat alongside the monk as he read to her daughter.

"I'm certain you'd want to know, Stanislaus," Father Hieronymus pulled up on the skirt of his cassock as he sat down at his desk, "that the American flyer you and Brother Helmut treated escaped safely." The abbot motioned to Stanislaus to take a seat.

Stanislaus sat down and smiled, remembering the abbot's role in saving the pilot, how he had traded dusty monastery artifacts for a human life.

"And what of you, Stanislaus," the abbot lowered his voice, "I presume you'll be going back to Poland now?"

Stanislaus cast his eyes down and shook his head. "No. Not now that the Russians have taken over my country." He glanced over at Frieda; she was smiling and looking his way and he beckoned to her to join him.

"I want to stay here. In Germany. Everything I love is here." He stood up and put his arm around her.

"So now you know what happens to naughty children!" They all glanced over at Brother Helmut, who was moving his head solemnly from side to side at the frowning child.

Trudi looked down at her storybook to study a scary illustration. *"I* will never become a gingerbread cookie." She put the book in Brother Helmut's lap and ran across the room to throw her arms around Stanislaus's waist. "I'm not naughty, am I Herr Konec?"

Stanislaus laughed and put his free arm around the child.

Father Hieronymus looked at the happy family, for family they were. He had despaired of ever seeing them again after they left the monastery, but he had prayed hard for them. His eyes turned toward Brother Helmut sitting in the corner with a beatific smile on his face, his ailing hands out of sight.

"Is everything all right, Father?" asked Frieda.

"Right? Oh yes, everything's more than all right," he answered. "I was just thinking."

Father Hieronymus looked at Brother Helmut again and remembered the day he had almost lost his faith. "Yes, I was just thinking. Sometimes, when God answers our prayers, He does so in His own good time."

Author's Afterword

Although *Look Long into the Abyss* is a work of fiction, the general historical background does reflect actual conditions in Hitler's odious Third Reich as it collapsed in 1945. German citizens and soldiers were executed for 'cowardice.' Thousands of concentration camp victims were herded on the open roads, many to their deaths. Some of the twelve million forced laborers, enslaved from Nazi-occupied countries, escaped and ran amok. Hitler Youth, having endured brainwashing since childhood, fought with savage ferocity.

And stolen artworks abounded. To protect cultural treasures in war areas, Roosevelt established the Roberts Commission, which recommended the appointment of specific art experts to the staffs of military commanders. Known as Monuments, Fine Arts and Archives Officers – or 'Monuments Men' – they risked their lives and applied their ingenuity and expertise to rescue much of Europe's cultural heritage stolen by the Nazis. In my novel, the locations of caches of looted art and other artifacts are factual, although the characters are fictional.

At the mine in Merkers, to which Eisenhower, Bradley and Patton paid a visit in April, 1945, hundreds of millions of dollars in gold bullion and currency were discovered along with art treasures and valuables stolen by the SS.

In addition to artworks, caskets containing the bodies of Frederick the Great, King Frederick William, and Hindenburg – along with an empty coffin bearing Hitler's name – were found at Bernterode behind a five-foot-thick brick wall in a mine used as a munitions dump.

As described in my novel, the Charlemagne regalia were walled up within a sealed-off room inside a maze of tunnels extending deep beneath the castle and streets of Nuremberg, with one entrance through a secret door within a shop on a side street. The Nazis, hoping to retain the regalia as symbols of future resistance, did spread the story that the SS had thrown the relics into a lake. A Monuments Man, Lieutenant Walter Horn, convinced a city official to reveal the treasures' actual whereabouts.

Even as bombs rained down on Berlin and the Russians entered the city, Hitler still gazed at the model in his bunker of the art museum complex he had hoped to build in Linz, Austria. The ill-gotten art to be displayed was stored in the salt mine at Alt Aussee, Austria, in which the local party leader, convinced that Hitler's scorched-earth decrees called for the destruction of the art and the mine, had placed bombs. Largely through the actions of the salt workers, who removed the bombs and blasted the entrances to the mine shut, the treasures were saved.

And Raphael's *Portrait of a Young Gentleman?* Hans Frank, Hitler's Governor-General of Poland, did steal treasures from the Czartoryski collection in Krakow, including works by Leonardo, Rembrandt, and Raphael. After he fled with the paintings and was arrested at his home in Bavaria, the Leonardo and the Rembrandt were recovered, but the Raphael had vanished. To this day, there has been no trace of the masterpiece.

LaVergne, TN USA
15 September 2010
197156LV00003B/54/P